PENGUIN BOOKS

1335

DON'T GO NEAR THE WATER

WILLIAM BRINKLEY

DON'T GO
NEAR THE WATER

BY

William Brinkley

PENGUIN BOOKS

Penguin Books Ltd, Harmondsworth, Middlesex
AUSTRALIA: Penguin Books Pty Ltd, 762 Whitehorse Road,
Mitcham, Victoria

—

First published by Random House 1956
Published in Great Britain by Jonathan Cape 1957
Published in Penguin Books 1959

Made and printed in Great Britain
by Richard Clay & Company, Ltd
Bungay, Suffolk

Contents

One: Don't give up the ship

In peacetime Lieutenant-Commander Clinton T. Nash had been in charge of a Merrill Lynch, Pierce, Fenner, and Beane office in the Midwest. Not long after Pearl Harbour he had been commissioned directly from his brokerage office without the corrupting effect of any intervening naval training. Except for a correspondence course in *Navy Regulations* this naval virginity had been chastely preserved down to his present duty on the island of Tulura in the western Pacific, where he was executive officer of the Public Relations Section of the giant ComFleets command. Nevertheless the exec's office and desk, behind which he now sat waiting for the exact moment to call in the officers waiting outside for the regular morning conference, were nautical enough to do credit to the captain of a heavy cruiser.

On the desk, wedged between book-ends fashioned in the shape of miniature anchors, sat a small but comprehensive library of naval literature, including Bowditch's *American Practical Navigator*; *Naval Leadership*; *Watch Officer's Guide*; *Navy Regulations*; *Modern Seamanship*; *Naval Customs*; *Traditions and Usages*; and *How to Abandon Ship*. Although the exec did not smoke, the desk thoughtfully held a brass ashtray, for the use of visitors, sawn off from a five-inch shell-case which he had procured from the U.S.S. *Wisconsin* when she had visited Tulura. Alongside it was another sawn-off shell-case of three-inch calibre, for paper-clips. Facing the exec was a desk photograph of the U.S.S. *Yorktown*, a vessel which he had never seen but whose likeness was very attractive, being in full colour. In the right top drawer of the desk was a pair of 7×50 binoculars, and in the right bottom, deeper drawer a sextant which the exec had requisitioned from the Fleet Supply officer. The binoculars he took with him, slung around his neck, on trips to the beach. The sextant was an instrument of great mystery to the exec, who knew only that it was used somehow in navigation, but he was hoping to master it with the aid of Bowditch.

Arrayed along the walls were a barometer, a ship's bell clock, and a framed 'Golden Dragon' diploma which proved that the exec had been aboard ship when he voyaged across the international date-line en route from San Francisco to Tulura. From a hook hung his hat, with the gold braid turned a sea-going seaweed green from prolonged soaking, in the basin of his BOQ room, in Morton's salt water. Watching him from that wall which the exec faced from his chair, and set just at eye level from the sitting position, was a varnished, yard-long legend which the exec had had a Seabee carpenter's mate carve out of wood: 'Don't Give Up The Ship!' Beneath it hung another non-nautical expression, also carved from wood: 'Think Big!' One other non-nautical item decorated the wall – a framed Merrill Lynch citation with a gold seal, which had been presented to the exec for having led all company brokers in his state, in the year 1941, in the sale of securities.

The executive officer was a man of medium height, lean, almost scarecrow-built, except for a small pot belly which was grafted on to his midriff like a Dutch oven. He had a head of classically spherical shape, and it was totally hairless. The combination of this configuration and aridity, together with the nicely polished surface, was responsible for the name by which he was known, not to his face – 'Marblehead'. To compensate for the absence of growth on his head, the exec had grown a moustache to fill the space between his nose and his upper lip, but this only accentuated the general bareness, like a tuft of grass in the desert. But his legs, emerging from the British khaki shorts, which he had procured, these being more smartly cut than the U.S. counterpart, from His Majesty's Public Relations liaison officer on Tulura, more than made up for the upper baldness. They were extremely hairy, a black, curly growth, abundant to the point of luxuriance. With his gleaming head, and wearing shorts, he had, in the words of the correspondent Jerry Wakeley, 'more skin showing than any man in the Pacific'.

Coming to his feet, the exec ranged around his office, giving it a final check for shipshapeness. He walked over to the barometer, and noting a small spot on its glistening face, took out his handkerchief, wet it slightly, and rubbed the spot away. Continuing smartly around the room, he gazed a moment, expressionlessly, at the Merrill Lynch citation – then a suggestion of a smile traced his lips. Moving on, he adjusted slightly the 'Don't Give Up The Ship!' legend. Then he stood for a solemn moment looking at the 'Think Big!' injunction below it. Circling back to his desk, he sat down. Suddenly an expression of irritation crossed his face. He grabbed up his phone.

'Brownell,' he shouted, 'why isn't my three-inch shell full of paper-clips?'

Almost immediately the door opened and a young lieutenant (junior grade) hurried in with a small box in his hand. 'Sorry, Commander,' he said apologetically. While the exec watched stonily, the jg emptied the box of paper-clips into the shell. He hurried back out and the exec was alone again.

He picked up the one piece of paper on his desk – a Navy dispatch – and read it again. His eyes moved meditatively to the twin sayings on the wall and closed for a moment. Then he placed the dispatch carefully back on the desk.

The exec noticed that he still had a few minutes left. He took out his Bowditch, and opening it to the section on the sextant, started reading studiously: 'When a ray of light undergoes two reflections in the same plane with two plane mirrors the angle between its first and its last direction is equal to twice the inclination of the reflecting surfaces ...'

'Ding-ding! ... Ding-ding!'

Glancing up at the ship's bell, the exec closed the book with a sigh of relief. He picked up his phone and spoke to his assistant, Lieutenant (jg) Calvert Brownell, in the outer office.

'Four bells, Calvert,' he said briskly. To the exec it made sense for a Navy officer to use Navy language. 'Let them in.'

Flowing into the room, the Public Relations officers took seats in front of the exec's desk, arranging themselves rank-wise, with the lieutenant-commanders in the first row of chairs, backed successively by the lieutenants, the lieutenants junior grade, and, in the last row, the ensigns. The exec, calling the conference briskly to order, listened to the regular reports of the department heads – the number of correspondents and visitors who had arrived since yesterday morning's conference, the Press conferences, interviews, and round-the-island trips arranged for today, a vigorous complaint by a CBS correspondent that NBC was being shown favouritism on radio transmission time, a demand by a correspondent named Gordon Ripwell that he be given a corner room in the BOQ, and like matters. Usually the exec handled each problem as it arose, but this morning he cut off each with a curt declaration, 'What say we navigate that one to-morrow?' The department heads, sensing that their executive officer had something special on his mind, speeded up their reports and soon had them over.

'Routine department head reports received,' the exec said crisply. 'Now, stand by for something important.'

Collie-like the exec lifted and scratched his bare, hairy leg. Replacing his foot on the floor, he moved his swivel chair circumferentially several times in a way he had before announcing something big.

'Sailors!' he said. 'We received a dispatch from Washington this morning. It seems that a really large name is on his way out here!'

This was nothing much. Public Relations Headquarters was always overstocked in large-name visitors.

The exec leaned forward, pulled the huge *Navy Regulations* from between the miniature-anchor book-ends and with both hands banged it on the desk. The sound crashed deafeningly through the room and the two shell-case trays jumped.

'Tarzan,' he said, 'is on his way here!'

'Tarzan!' The name came echoing out of the chief of the radio section, Lieutenant-Commander Arnold Gladney.

'Tarzan!' cried the chief of the photographic section, Lieutenant-Commander Wayne Hereford. The two lieutenant-commanders were as alike as two plump and happy little pigs from the same litter and were known as the 'Echo Twins'. It usually took any newly arrived officer a couple of months to be able to distinguish one from the other.

'Roger,' the exec said, relaxing back in his chair. 'Tarzan. That is to say, Edgar Rice Burroughs, the creator and author of Tarzan – and therefore the same as Tarzan for our purposes – has left the mainland for Tulura. He's coming out as a correspondent.'

'A correspondent?' said Lieutenant-Commander Gladney. 'Who for?'

'What difference does that make?' the exec said impatiently.

'I think the whole idea is four O!' Lieutenant-Commander Gladney said suddenly.

'I think the idea sparkles!' said Lieutenant-Commander Hereford.

The exec selected a paper-clip from the three-inch shell. Cocking his arm, he let go at a metal wastebasket eight feet away. The paper-clip hit home with a sharp ping. A pleased look crossed the exec's face.

'Tarzan is so world-wide famous,' he said, 'that the idea immediately impels me Navy public-relations-wise. But the dispatch just arrived this morning' – he tapped the piece of paper on his desk – 'and what with one thing and another I haven't been able to give the matter its merited thought. So I'd like to throw the conference open to a top-of-the-head discussion on this entire matter. Tarzan! There's something enormous there or my name isn't Joe Blow. Okay, Sailors, who'll fire a torpedo?'

No one fired one for a moment. Then Ensign Christopher Tyson III, a Correspondents' Aide, spoke up from the back row. Tyson, a handsome youngster with a pouty, almost insolent face, looked as if he should still be in prep school, though actually he had obtained his degree from Princeton the day before he entered the Navy. His poutiness came from the fact that being so young and such a junior ensign he got all the odd jobs nobody else wanted.

'What's Burroughs – or Tarzan – going to cover out here, Commander?'

'Cover?' the exec said blankly. He aimed another paper-clip for the wastebasket. It was a near miss, and the exec frowned slightly. 'Why I don't know, Tyson. Nothing especially, I guess. But, you know, the name is associated with islands …'

'I haven't read him in quite a while,' Tyson said. 'But let's see. Tarzan, as I recall, operated in Africa.'

'Anyhow he's associated with the jungle, native life, that sort of thing,' Lieutenant-Commander Nash said impatiently. 'Heaven knows there's enough jungle on these islands. Jungle …' he repeated, his eyes blooming wide with an air of discovery. 'That's probably why the Navy is shipping Tarzan – that is, Burroughs – out here. All this jungle in the Pacific. He's got millions of readers. Any time he mentions the Navy, there's a ballast tank full of high-octane publicity.'

'I don't see where Edgar Rice Burroughs's mentioning the Navy in a Tarzan comic strip is going to help the Navy,' Tyson said. Tyson was one of those combat-itchy, eager-beaver types of which there were a couple at Public Relations Headquarters, and had even requested duty on a ship. Maybe he figured this querulous attitude was one way to get it. 'To me …'

'Belay that attitude!' the exec shouted, banging *Navy Regulations* on his desk. 'You rarely see anything where real Public Relations is concerned, Tyson! I don't expect much out of an ensign, especially a young and inexperienced ensign, but I hate negativeness as the mortal enemy of Naval Public Relations. Anyone with a drop of IQ,' the exec said, eyeing the ensign intently, 'ought to see the fantastic possibilities in this!'

The exec brusquely flung a fresh paper-clip. 'Let's think big!' he said. 'It just might be one of those great ideas. If it isn't, what have we lost? I for one will be glad to have Tarzan aboard!'

'I will too,' said Lieutenant-Commander Gladney.

'So will I,' said Lieutenant-Commander Hereford.

'Why, a million dollars wouldn't purchase your way into a Tarzan comic strip!' the exec exclaimed. 'And here the Navy has a chance to get in for free! With a name like Tarzan, and with an oceanful of Tarzan-like jungle around us – if that isn't a natural my name just isn't Joe Blow and we might as well close up shop right now and go to sea! Now, let's do a little creative thinking.'

Opening the bottom right drawer of his desk, the exec carefully removed his sextant. He sat back deep in his chair, cocked his feet on the desk, and, hoisting the sextant, began to squint through its telescope at various objects in the room.

'Tarzan ... Tarzan ...' The exec, while sighting through the sextant at the ceiling, began to sort of chant the name: 'Tarzan ... The jungle ... native life. Okay, Sailors, what do you say we lay down a bombardment that'll rattle their teeth back in Little Falls, Michigan?'

This was the exec's birthplace and, in these conferences, a kind of mythical guinea-pig for any public-relations idea.

'Commander!' Lieutenant-Commander Gladney said. 'I just got a flash. How about putting Burroughs on an LST and having him do a beaching on an island? Maybe this next operation, hunh? Burroughs is connected with the islands, anyhow with the jungle, which in the public mind is associated with islands. An LST is the Navy way of coming to islands. Get it!'

The exec looked a moment from his sextant to the radio section chief. 'I'm afraid that won't do, Arnold. Burroughs is too important a person to put on an LST in a combat operation. It'd have to be a cruiser at least.'

'Well, that's out, then,' the radio chief said sadly. 'You can't beach a cruiser on an island.'

Raising his sextant again, the exec peered with absorbed concentration through it. 'All right, Sailors,' he said. 'Steady as you go. Keep it coming.'

'Commander!' said Lieutenant-Commander Hereford. 'I'm getting one now! Maybe we could get Burroughs to do a series of strips of just Tarzan going along on an LST operation. Burroughs wouldn't have to make an operation himself to do that. We could fill him in – or bring some LST officer up from Muranu to fill him in on the technical junk.'

The photographic officer sat forward excitedly on the edge of his chair.

'Burroughs wouldn't have to go anywhere but Tulura,' he took off. 'Just have Tarzan make the operation in the strip. Show Tarzan with the crew, a few breeze sessions – Tarzan and the crew arguing whether it's tougher to fight a crocodile bare-handed or land on a beach full of Japs – naturally, the Japs'll be tougher. Tarzan watching the whole business of the LST going on the operation, seeing this through Tarzan's eyes, the whole welter of the war through the eyes of Tarzan. If Tarzan says it's tough, the American people'll know it's tough, they'll take Tarzan's word for it, quicker'n they will Com-Fleets' even – no disrespect intended,' the photo chief added hastily. 'Throw in a couple of air raids and a submarine attack, and when D-day at last comes, have Tarzan hitch-hike along in an assault-wave LCVP to the beach. He steps out of the LCVP and starts to strangle a Jap, only the Jap slips it and gets Tarzan down and is about to let him have it – that'll show what a formidable enemy we're up against, anybody who could get Tarzan down – when a Marine and the boat coxswain rush up out of the LCVP and give the Jap the business, saving Tarzan's life,' the photo chief said breathlessly, 'and making him – and the millions of Tarzan's admirers – for ever grateful to the Navy.'

'That works in my original LST idea!' Lieutenant-Commander Gladney cut in. 'And don't forget the famous Tarzan yell as he reaches for the Jap.'

'You just have Tarzan step out of the LCVP,' Lieutenant-Commander Hereford cut back in, 'grab for the Jap's throat ...'

'Belay it!' The exec halted it, bringing his sextant down. 'I've heard worse ideas – Wayne, Arnold. But it has one fatal fault – we can't tell Burroughs what to write in a comic strip. There's nothing correspondents resent more than being told what to write.'

'You could tell him it's just an idea, Clinton,' the photo officer said disappointedly. 'They don't necessarily resent ideas, provided you're real tactful about it.'

The exec reflected a moment, then shook his head decisively. 'No, I'm afraid that's out. Definitely out. You just can't tell a correspondent what to write. They're very sensitive about that. It's all right to use Burroughs, but he mustn't know it. Get the difference? Well, let's get on with Burroughs from there. I've got a feeling we're beginning to target in ...'

The exec resumed his sextant squintings and, simultaneously, his chanting.

'Tarzan ... Something tells me there's *something*, if I can just think of it. It's too great a natural to miss – Tarzan ... islands, jungle life, natives ... By Jupiter!'

The exec started from his chair, holding to the sextant. Laying the sextant down, he plucked the big Bowditch from his desk library and banged it, in an ear-piercing noise, on the desk. '*Natives,*' he shouted. 'By Jupiter, Sailors, I've got it, I've got it!'

The exec's eyes glared into the 'Think Big!' injunction on the wall dead ahead.

'Why don't we take Burroughs down to some atoll-like island,' he said, 'and photograph him with a bunch of these natives like they have in Tarzan? ... Get it? He's gathering material for his strip?'

'Say!' said the photo chief, who saw a way to keep a four-man camera crew busy for a couple of weeks.

'But where does the Navy angle come in?' the radio chief asked.

'Navy angle!' the exec exclaimed. 'Jumping Jupiter, man, where's your IQ?' He picked up his sextant and started jamming it into the air like a cheer leader. 'Navy men standing with the natives! Navy ships in the background in the harbour! Natives leaning against a Navy Quonset or a Navy LST! Navy angles unlimited! Movies and stills. And, Arnold ...!'

'Yes, Clinton,' the radio officer said meekly.

'You might as well lay on a broadcast. Have these natives jabber a little over some national network. Then the interpreter can interpret how happy they are under Navy administration.'

'I'll see if I can sell any of the boys on it,' Lieutenant-Commander Gladney said. 'Personally it sounds like a four O natural.'

'I think NBC might be better than CBS,' the exec said. 'The natives could chorus the NBC signature. Bongo, bongo, *bongo*! Heh, heh.'

'Pretty funny, Commander.' The radio chief laughed appreciatively. 'But we've got to be careful not to show partiality, Commander,' he cautioned. 'Give NBC an exclusive and CBS screams like you were throttling their maternal grandmother. And vice versa.'

The exec bunched his lips. 'That's a point. All right then, belay the exclusive. We'll throw it open to all the networks!'

The exec sat back limply in his chair, and lifted and scratched his hairy leg happily. His face and head were shining.

'Well! That's a load off!' He laughed briefly and placed his sextant carefully back in the drawer. 'I was beginning to get worried there, fear we wouldn't think of something. Burroughs is too much of a natural out here to pass up, I was sure of that. Well!' The exec looked across at Lieutenant-Commander Hereford. 'You really think my idea will ride, Wayne?'

'Commander, it's *picturable*,' the photo chief said. 'One of the big four that're sure-fire always picture-wise – babes, children, dogs, natives.'

'Arnold?'

'Sound-wise,' the radio chief said, 'it's four O. Natives jabbering away – considering that people don't understand a word they say, it's a baffling thing why they always eat it up,' he said reflectively. 'But they do. You take *Trader Horn*, for example …'

'Now,' the exec said, cutting off this disquisition on basic public-relations principles, 'we've got one more extremely important item to settle on this Tarzan thing. Who,' he said, 'is to command it?'

The exec scratched the heavy underside of his leg and continued: 'It's a big job! We need an officer to follow through, take charge of the project, script it, unify it, lay on still-picture, motion-picture, and radio crews, arrange transmission lines, pick the atoll on which to go on location, line up the natives, conduct the briefing sessions, requisition the necessary Navy props – ships, sailors, and the like – take Burroughs down there. In a word, run the whole show – co-ordinating everything with me, of course.'

'What officer have we,' the exec posed the question again, 'who is brilliant and experienced enough to do all this?'

The exec's eyes flashed like a chicken-hawk's across the rows of officers and came to roost on an officer in the third row.

'There's just one man – I mean officer – for this job,' the exec said decisively. 'Ross!'

Lieutenant (jg) Ross Pendleton smiled condescendingly. He was a figure with Hollywood-leading-man looks and black wavy hair, who before the war had been a radio-network producer of the famous day-time serial 'For the Love of Elaine'. Now he was one of several 'radio correspondents liaison officers', which involved him about two hours a day, making arrangements for radio correspondents on Tulura to transmit their reports back to the States. Except for these two hours Pendleton devoted his entire time to two interests: women and a prospectus for a post-war radio show for Ivory Flakes. Pendleton frequently mentioned that his experience entitled him to at least a lieutenant-commandership – and in fact the exec treated him with a respect out of all proportion to his rank, since Ross sometimes subtly called attention to his pre-Navy salary. 'I used to make forty thousand a year,' he would say.

'Ross,' the exec said, 'is the only officer I know who could really do a job on this. Provided it really sends him. Does it, Ross?'

Lieutenant (jg) Pendleton let the silence gather around him a moment, while he reflected on the pleasantness of running around the islands for a while and ordering things up.

'Clinton, I've been sitting here thinking,' he said with easy condescension. 'Trying to visualize the thing in sound and on film. The basic idea is okay, but frankly I think inexperienced direction could foul it up beyond recognition.'

'That's precisely why I was thinking of you, Ross,' the exec said.

'I'm pretty busy,' Pendleton continued, 'but if I left detailed written instructions, maybe Gladney here' – he glanced condescendingly at his immediate chief – 'could take over for a while.'

'I'm always ready to pitch in,' Lieutenant-Commander Gladney said humbly, 'wherever I might be needed.'

'Then I'd be willing to undertake it,' Pendleton said, 'but only on one condition – that I be given a one hundred per cent free hand.'

'Oh, of course you'd have to have a free hand!' the exec said.

'I can't dope out the proper artistic conception,' Pendleton said, 'I can't even operate with a lot of rank-heavy would-be producers, who never got nearer a *show*' – he bore down on the word – 'than a dollar-fifty tour of Radio City, leaning over my shoulder and telling me how to put one of these things together.'

'Oh, of course, Ross!' the exec said. 'I know enough about these things to realize you've got to let your director go in order to dope up a proper artistic conception.'

'With that clear understanding, Clinton,' Pendleton said smoothly, 'I'll undertake it.'

'Roger!' the exec exclaimed. 'Full speed ahead, Ross! Heh, heh.' The exec laid the way for a joke. 'Money is no item – as we used to say at Merrill Lynch when it was the customer's. A joke, of course,' he added, lest anyone think slanderously of his peace-time employers. 'Now, Sailors, everyone is to give Ross everything he asks for and to let him alone. Is that clear? I aim for us to come up with something really fleet-size on this one, a real production. Something that'll make every Little Falls in America realize that it's the Navy that's winning the war.' The exec stared dead ahead of him at the sign, and intoned it aloud. 'Think Big!'

For the scene of the Burroughs operation Lieutenant (jg) Pendleton, after inspection jaunts to several islands, selected an atoll, about thirty miles away in the Tuluran Chain, named Gug-Gug as being less civilized than Tulura itself. One morning about a week after Pendleton had flown there, Lieutenant-Commander Nash sent for Ensign Max Siegel, one of the Correspondents' Aides.

Ensign Max Siegel was virtually the only officer at Public Relations Headquarters with sea duty in his past. He was happy enough to be on Tulura after being on a destroyer, especially since he had not asked for the duty. His name had been plucked from the mammoth files of the Bureau of Personnel in Washington, by one of the Navy's IBM machines – out of some unfathomable error, Max felt sure, since he had never had a day's journalistic training or experience, though actually he felt that a tour in the reservations department of a travel agency would have been better preparation for his present duty.

Among Ensign Siegel's duties was the conducting of visitors on orientation tours of the island, and Correspondents' Aides were also called Sightseeing Officers. The job meant that you got to know every inch of the island, though Max would probably have got to know it in any case. He had an inquisitive mind and was the sort of guy who would explore thoroughly any new area, people, or experience he happened to be set down in. Max had a kind of tongue-in-cheek attitude about his job. In escorting correspondents, congressmen, and other visitors on tours around the island, he played to the hilt his role of Sightseeing Officer. He had boned up intensively on the history of the island and, it was suspected, invented a lot more.

'On your left, gentlemen,' Max's lion-deep voice would boom from his post at the wheel of his jeep, 'you have the ruins of Palan, levelled by the six-inch gunfire of United States Navy cruisers –' Max had learned to get in nice plugs for the Navy like that, especially with appropriations-powered congressmen. 'On your right, gentlemen, just out to sea beyond the promontory there, is where the seeds of the present Pacific conflict were, in a sense, born 424 years ago.' Ensign Siegel would halt the jeep. 'In those exact waters the lone ship of another Navy man possibly some of you have heard of – Ferdinand Magellan – was set upon by a fleet from Japan. Magellan, outnumbered some three to one, was on the point of being sunk, when a small but gallant flotilla of Tulurans in war-canoes stroked rapidly to his aid. Swarming heedlessly up the sides of the Jap vessels, the Tulurans captured them bodily, winning the day in the famous Battle of Palan Point. To this day the Tulurans have been fiercely pro-Navy and anti-Japanese.'

Lieutenant Morey Griffin, who was Ensign Siegel's room-mate, made it a point once to look up the 'Battle of Palan Point' in the *Encyclopaedia Britannica* in the Fleet Library and in the many volumes on Pacific and naval history in the Public Relations Historical Section, but could find no mention of such an engagement. But none of Ensign Siegel's awed charges ever challenged him. And after all, Max did know a lot about the island. He had studied languages at Harvard and spoke Spanish fluently. He picked up languages the way some people pick up hotel towels or match-covers for souvenirs, and about as easily. He hadn't been two months on the island before he was speaking a remarkably able Tuluran, a language with a lot of Spanish in it. Max further impressed his customers by stopping in a village and jabbering in their own language with the natives.

Just to look at Ensign Siegel destroyed your faith in evolution. He had a great sense of humour and used to remind the other officers that he possessed what the rest of them lacked, a claim to real naval distinction. There was no doubt, he said, that he was the ugliest man in the Navy. He was a huge blockbuster of a man, 225 pounds and six feet four inches, with pendulous arms and a body as hairy as something swinging in an African tree. His face was as coarse-featured as a chunk of blasted rock. He had a boondock of coarse, rusty hair that grew in all directions and looked like nails left out in the rain. Uniform-wise Max wore whatever was handy and more than once was asked to leave the officers' club for wearing a grey uniform shirt with khaki pants.

But Max Siegel, afflicted with a monstrous body, had a beautiful soul. Or perhaps the word should be heart, for Max once told Morey Griffin he was a 'dissenting freethinker', though you could never be sure when Max meant things like that and when he didn't, or sometimes, even quite what he meant. He was one of the gentlest men you could have known. Griffin once took a ride with him when he went on a busman's holiday to a Tuluran village. They'd no sooner pulled into the village than hordes of brown youngsters were surrounding the jeep, piling affectionately all over Siegel, like little squirrels, and yelling, 'Mahx! Mahx!' Max Siegel did a lot for the Tulurans. Sometimes he seemed to be less a Public Relations officer for the Navy than for the Tulurans. He probably figured that the Navy had enough Public Relations officers anyhow and that the Tulurans really needed some public relationing. Max always furnished the visiting congressmen with a good pitch on the Tulurans. Before taking a congressman to view Palan's remains, he would have found out beforehand his exact shade of politics. Then he would lead him in to see the makeshift town hall. If it was a New Dealing congressman, he would see a picture of F. D. R. above the speaker's platform in the auditorium. This picture of the incumbent was regularly there anyhow. But if it was a Republican congressman, there would be alongside it a picture of Herbert Hoover. Max sent off to the States and got this photograph. Since it had been so long and the Tulurans had poor memories regarding the details of American politics, they didn't know or had forgotten who Hoover was, but being a placid people they were pleased to have his picture and thought him handsome. It always made a good impression on Republican congressmen to walk into the hall and see

Herbert Hoover looking down at them. Max figured it wouldn't hurt when the time came to take up Tulura affairs in the House Appropriations Committee. After a while Max went so far as to get a picture for the hall, for the benefit of Southern congressmen, of Robert E. Lee.

Max was a tremendous baiter, and congressmen gave him a great field to exercise this talent. He knew just how far to go and usually went there. Before taking a party of congressmen on a tour of the villages, he gave the Tulurans a build-up by reading excerpts from a guidebook issued to all U.S. military personnel and adding comments of his own. ' "The Tulurans," ' he would read to the assembled congressmen, ' "are well aware of European standards of conduct and politeness and will expect American officers, in particular, to be courteous, especially in dealing with priests, women, and the aged." ' Then Max would add on his own, 'If they expect an American officer to be polite, you can imagine what they expect of congressmen. Don't forget that to these people, who don't know any better, you men are fairly important.' Max had a way of rattling these things off and being on to something else so quickly that by the time a congressman got to thinking about what he had said it was too late. ' "Some of the islanders who retain elements of their native religion," ' he would continue, skip-reading from the guidebook, ' "consider spoiling of the ground, even by spitting on it, extremely irreverent." However you were brought up,' Max would add, 'kindly use your handkerchief here.' He would continue reading, ' "Sexual approaches to a married woman have always been taboo, and are not tolerated by the natives," ' and add, 'Civilized customs haven't fully reached here yet.'

Ensign Siegel liked his job. He liked the Tulurans, a gentle people. He considered his billet an accident, the duty astonishing, and the correspondents, congressmen, and other visitors he dealt with, fascinating specimens.

Summoned that morning as he was about to take off for Palan to supervise the hanging of Herbert Hoover's picture in preparation for the impending visit of an old-guard Republican congressman from Ohio, Ensign Siegel went on up to the exec's office. He walked in and stood at ease before the exec's desk.

'Have a seat, boy,' the exec said. 'Well, how's the world treating you?'

The exec always tried to put his officers at ease with a bit of small talk before getting on to the business at hand.

'No complaints, Commander,' Ensign Siegel said.

'I should think not. This duty here, it's not like being on one of those destroyers, is it?' the exec remarked. 'They jump up and down quite a bit, I hear.'

'More so than Tulura, anyhow,' Siegel said.

'Heh, heh,' the exec said. 'Max, you do have a delightful sense of humour. And a sense of humour is one of the best pieces of equipment a man can have in life,' the exec said philosophically. 'You know, this place is a little like a destroyer – it jumps up and down here sometimes, too, doesn't it? Heh, heh.'

Ensign Siegel laid on a resonant chuckle from his organ-sized chest. 'Well! You have quite a sense of humour yourself, Commander.'

'I've been told I have,' the exec said frankly. 'Sometimes, though, I feel I had more at Merrill Lynch than here. So much responsibility in my present position!'

'Nothing deadens a sense of humour like responsibility,' Ensign Siegel said agreeably.

'You have no idea,' the exec said. 'Of course,' he added, to correct any possible misimpression, 'you realize I had a great deal of responsibility at Merrill Lynch, too?'

'I should think so!' Ensign Siegel exclaimed. Siegel himself had done a short term in the brokerage business – his uncle's firm in New York. But he carefully kept this fact from the exec in order to avoid prolonged discussions of stocks and bonds. 'I can't imagine anything more responsible than taking people's money away from them, to invest in things like stocks and bonds, uncertain at best.'

'Well, stocks are the foundation of the American economy, don't forget,' the exec said in slight reproval. 'And everyone ought to own a piece of the American economy; I used to hammer it into my customers. Occasionally I'd even buy some stock myself. You know, actually,' the exec said reflectively, 'the two jobs are more similar than meets the eye. At Merrill Lynch I was trying to pry money out of people. Here I'm trying to pry Navy stories out of the correspondents. Both involve overcoming a natural human sense of resistance, and that has always appealed to me as a challenge. However,' the exec said with sudden briskness, 'I didn't send for you to talk about that, did I?'

The exec scratched both his bare legs simultaneously, using both hands, then, cocking the happily scratched legs on his desk, sat back deeply in his chair.

'Siegel,' he said, fixing the ensign in the eye. 'I've got good news for you. You're going to be part of it.'

'Part of what, sir?' Ensign Siegel said.

'Of the Burroughs do!' the exec said enthusiastically. 'You're going to get to be Pendleton's assistant.'

'Oh,' Ensign Siegel said, unstirred.

'I just got an operational dispatch from Pendleton in the field,' the exec said, staccato-like. 'He's laying it on full-steam! All the Navy props are set up! The LST is beached on the island! Still picture, motion picture, and sound crews are ready to roll! But Pendleton has got himself slightly caught in a bight. That's Navy for having difficulty.'

The exec used Navy language to such a degree that frequently his terms stumped even sea-going officers. However, in doubtful cases he thoughtfully defined what he was talking about.

'I'm sorry to hear that,' Ensign Siegel said.

'Well, it doesn't amount to much,' the exec said. 'It's only a little non-co-operation on the part of the natives. I don't suppose they know a great deal about public relations, do they? Anyhow, Pendleton could use an assistant, a sort of interpreter, who could get the idea across to these backward folk. You're the only officer I know around here who speaks that jabber. They're Tulurans down at Gug-Gug too. So you're going into action, Max! What do you say!'

'What precisely is the nature of the non-co-operation, Commander?' Ensign Siegel said.

'Pendleton didn't send any of those details,' the exec said. 'I imagine he's too busy. Probably knocking himself out. He's such a worker. So I read it that it doesn't amount to much. Probably just the language barrier. This Burroughs thing has such fantastic possibilities, Max! We don't want to miss a trick. It's got to be right! It's too much of a natural to be anything but right. So look alive now! Get yourself some orders out, tell the travel department I said to give you a Priority One flight ticket and shove off for Gug-Gug!'

Within the hour Ensign Siegel was headed for Gug-Gugina PBY, to do what he had not the vaguest idea. In early afternoon he was climbing up the gangplank of the repair ship *Aphrodite*, which was anchored off the island and which Pendleton and his technical crews were using as an hotel while cranking up the Burroughs operation.

'Permission to come aboard!' he said, saluting the officer of the deck. 'Ensign Siegel reporting for temporary duty, sir. In connexion with the Edgar Rice Burroughs matter.'

'Jesus Christ, another one?' the officer of the deck, taking the salute, said.

'Where can I find Lieutenant (jg) Pendleton, sir?' Ensign Siegel inquired respectfully.

'Your chances are about eighty-five to one,' the officer of the deck said, 'that you'll find Mr Pendleton in his sack.'

Ensign Siegel followed a seamen second messenger down a passage-way to a forward stateroom. He stepped inside. In the total darkness the sound of snoring came from somewhere a few feet away from him. He found a light-switch and clicked it. Pendleton was sprawled out in the lower bunk in his shorts and T-shirt, his mouth open, yet oddly managing to smile – a blatantly lecherous smile. Siegel watched and listened to him a few moments, then walked over and shook him awake.

'Sorry to do this,' Ensign Siegel said. 'I hear on all sides, including yours, how you've been knocking yourself out.'

'Oh, hello, Max,' Pendleton said.

The radio liaison officer rubbed his eyes sleepily, then very slowly pulled himself up until he was sitting on the edge of his bunk.

'You know, Max,' he said, 'a ship really has a strange effect on me. It just makes me sleepy all over. I guess it's the rhythmic move-ment.'

'Especially when they're at anchor,' Ensign Siegel said.

'I was dreaming about a nurse I know on Tulura and hope to know better,' Pendleton said happily. 'Ensign Alice Thomas. There we were, the ensign and me … I wish you'd waited five minutes, son. Anyhow, welcome aboard.'

'That's what the officer of the deck said,' Ensign Siegel said.

'A little churlish on this ship,' Pendleton said. 'One of those vessels where the Public Relations word hasn't fully penetrated yet. You wouldn't believe it, but I had a little trouble getting two small boats assigned to us.'

'Two!' Siegel said. 'Why the hell do you need two?'

'Lots of trips to make to that island,' Pendleton said. 'And I've got a crew of nineteen men here and I don't know how many tons of camera and radio gear. Actually, we could use three boats, but I was trying to take the *Aphrodite*'s needs into consideration.'

'I'm sure the captain must be eternally grateful to you for that,' Siegel said. 'Well,' he sighed, 'here I am. Nash tells me you've completely fouled things up, and sent me down to straighten them out.'

Pendleton grinned self-confidently. 'You don't need to worry about Clinton and me, son. He eats it right out of my hand.'

'Why the hell am I here?' Ensign Siegel said bluntly.

Lieutenant (jg) Pendleton propped himself up in his bunk against two pillows. 'Hand me a cigarette, will you, Max, old boy?'

He lighted up and slowly blew out a long stream of smoke. 'Get this picture,' he said. 'I've got the LST standing by. Sound crew ready to record. Motion-picture and still crews ready to shoot. Everything all ready to roll. And then guess what happens?'

'For Christ's sake!' Siegel said impatiently. 'What is it? What the hell is the trouble?'

'The trouble?' Pendleton said. 'Why, the trouble, my boy, is that the natives won't act like natives.'

Pendleton inhaled deeply and slowly blew out three perfect smoke-rings.

'Mainly,' the jg went on, 'it's the costume problem. Why, they wear pants and shorts over there just like anybody else! And this old goat who's sort of their chief or mayor seemed to actually resent it when I suggested they put on breech-cloths for the filming.'

'Breech-cloths!' Siegel exclaimed. 'Why do you have to have breech-cloths?'

'Siegel, don't you have any picture sense at all? It doesn't say "native" unless they're in breech-cloths. Goddamn it, I tried everything!' Pendleton said. 'I pleaded with them. I shouted at them. I even hinted, without saying so of course, that we might move them off their goddamn island if they didn't pop to. The jokers still didn't budge.'

'I can see your general line of approach, Ross,' Siegel said. 'What do you have in mind next? Lining them up on the beach, moving in a cruiser, and spraying them with six-inch guns?'

'By God, I feel like it!' Pendleton said. 'The whole operation is in a dead stall!' Pendleton smoothed his wavy black hair back and sighed wearily. 'Considering what I have to do, I ought to be at least a lieutenant-commander.'

'Considering what you've done,' Ensign Siegel said, 'you ought to be a seaman second.'

'Siegel,' Pendleton said crisply, 'suppose you just leave the production of this show to me. You've never produced a *show*, I don't believe, have you?' he said contemptuously.

'Christ no!' Ensign Siegel said. He stuck his legs out in front of him. 'So this is the "minor difficulty" you dispatched Nash about.'

'Oh, I didn't want to get Marblehead stirred up,' Pendleton said blithely. 'I figured if you could trot over there and babble some Tuluran with them, it would fix the whole thing up.'

'Pretty simple, eh, Ross?' Siegel said easily. 'Now that you've laid the groundwork so well. Christ, they'll probably shoot any Navy officer on sight!'

Pendleton grinned. 'Oh, I'm not worried about that, Max.'

'You wouldn't be,' Siegel said.

'Listen son, all I want is a little co-operation. Wearing breech-cloths – that isn't much to ask. After all, we did liberate them from the Japs.'

'Ross,' Siegel said, 'has it ever occurred to you that these people aren't bit players or movie extras? This isn't a Radio City production.'

'Oh, the hell it isn't!' Pendleton said. 'This is just Radio City in uniform. Listen, Max, what say we don't get philosophical about this? What say to that, son? And what say you just buzz on over there and spray a little of your Tuluran over them? That's all it'll take. Do you want me to go with you?'

'Christ, no!' Siegel said. 'I'd like at least a fighting chance to come back alive.'

Pendleton smiled happily. 'Just in case you don't, Max, I'll personally recommend you for the posthumous Public Relations Silver Star, with crossed typewriters. Turn out the lights when you leave,' Pendleton said, sliding down into his sack. 'Ensign Thomas calls me.'

At exactly 1400 a small boat, obtained from an increasingly churlish officer of the deck, took off from the *Aphrodite* for the island with Ensign Siegel aboard. In about twenty minutes the boat docked at a small landing which fronted on to the collection of houses that made up the only village on the tiny island. Most of the houses were of the thatched-roof kind, but two or three were wooden-frame dwellings. Sitting in the middle of the village was the best structure of all. This structure was automatically identified by the ensign as the seat of the island government, such as the government might be. He made his way there and into the office of the island leader or mayor.

The mayor, a thoroughly dignified man of about sixty-five, wearing a clean white shirt, and trousers which were not so clean but were trousers, changed expression when he sighted Ensign Siegel. The arrangement of his features reflected his most recent experience with a U.S. naval officer. It altered slightly, but no more, when Ensign Siegel started speaking Tuluran. For a full half-hour Siegel talked with the mayor on various irrelevant subjects, such as fish and crops, speaking in a courteous manner. The mayor, under this influence, warmed up slightly more. Then Ensign Siegel launched carefully and very slowly into a take-out on the subject of public relations. The mayor obviously knew nothing about it, but after a while he began to get fascinated. The ensign discoursed on this subject for about an hour. Then the mayor sent for a few of the island's other leading Tulurans. The assembled Tulurans listened to Ensign Siegel give his pitch again. By then it was time for dinner and the meeting recessed, the Mayor taking the ensign back to eat with him. The boat coxswain also joined the dinner-party.

After dinner the Tulurans gathered again in the island hall and listened to Ensign Siegel for another couple of hours. At this point one of the Tulurans left and was back presently carrying a jug of palm toddy, which is a strong beverage, being made of fermented coconut sap. The jug passed back and forth, Ensign Siegel stopping his talk only to take his turn. With the circling of the palm-toddy jug, the questions began to come on more heavily. After a while, as the discussion continued, some of the Tulurans began to get quite high and happy. Ensign Siegel began to get a little high also. Under the hospitable custom the jug was passing back and forth from Siegel to one of the Tulurans, back to Siegel, then to another Tuluran, and so on, which meant that Ensign Siegel was drinking exactly the quantity of palm toddy the combined Tulurans were drinking. Ensign Siegel was an extremely difficult man to get drunk – he had a sponge stomach, Lieutenant Morey Griffin used to say – but under this custom even Siegel began to weave a little in his chair and some of his Tuluran words had more or less syllables in them than they should have had.

Soon several of the Tulurans started giggling. They giggled because of the palm toddy and because of Ensign Siegel, who struck them as an extraordinary naval officer. Also they had never seen a visitor who had been able to stay on his feet so long under their drinking custom. But mainly they giggled because of the idea that was being presented to them. More and more it came to strike them as quite funny. By midnight the whole house was shaking with laughter over it and Ensign Siegel could barely get any Tuluran syllables out. Soon after that, with the jug emptied, all the Tulurans, laughing and singing, escorted the ensign back to his small boat. Ensign Siegel woke up the boat coxswain and climbed in. As the boat shoved off he stood aft holding himself against the gunnel with one hand and flapping the other towards the Tulurans. The Tulurans all waved back, shouting happy, obscene remarks having to do with men's clothing.

It was 0100 when Siegel, exhausted and swaying a little, climbed up the gang-plank of the *Aphrodite*. Uncertainly, he saluted the officer of the deck, who reprimanded him severely for keeping the boat so long. From the O.O.D., Siegel marched across the deck and rocked down the passage-way to Lieutenant (jg) Pendleton's stateroom. The radio liaison lieutenant junior grade was lying in his bunk snoring loudly. His being asleep somehow had the effect of making Siegel seize him violently, in both of his big hairy hands, and shake him awake.

'General Quarters, Commander Pendleton!' Ensign Siegel roared. 'The Japs are attacking! Fifty Zeros overhead! Five battleships moving in! Get up! Get up or, Yankee sailor, you die! You may anyhow before I'm through with you!'

Pendleton came to almost epileptically, and flinging himself out of the sack, grabbed for the helmet on one hook and the kapok life-jacket on the other.

'Secure from General Quarters!' Ensign Siegel suddenly roared.

'Zeros heading back to Tokyo! Jap battleships routed! Sit down, you son of a bitch!'

'What the hell …' the startled Pendleton said, letting his legs drop him to a sitting position on his bunk.

'Listen to me, Pendleton,' Siegel said, lurching against the bulkhead, then collapsing in a chair. 'After what I've been through this afternoon and tonight and this morning you're lucky I didn't slice your throat in your sleep. God damn it, Pendleton! Do you realize you practically started a revolution over there?'

'Is that so?' Pendleton yawned heavily. 'Listen, Max, never mind the philosophy. Just give me a report, eh, old man?'

'They're going to do it!' Ensign Siegel shouted. 'That's the report! They're going to do it! They'll wear the jock-straps!'

Suddenly Ensign Siegel's voice plummeted from a shout to a quiet matter-of-factness, almost a whisper.

'Only thing, Buster,' he said, 'is that you'll have to furnish them. There isn't a jock-strap on the whole island. That's your problem, Buster. I'm going back to Tulura.'

'Why, that's no problem at all,' Lieutenant (jg) Pendleton said blithely. 'Aren't we on a repair ship, which has facilities for anything? We'll simply get the ship's sailmaker to make up an order of a couple of dozen breech-cloths.'

The Public Relations officers sat in the air-conditioned projection-room of one of the auxiliary Public Relations buildings. They were waiting, with considerable anticipation, for the première of the filming of the Burroughs visit to Gug-Gug to begin. Presently the lights went out, there was a hush, and a title flashed on the screen: 'Tarzan Visits Pacific Navy.'

Soon Lieutenant (jg) Pendleton's satiny voice could be heard emerging from the sound-track, telling, as pictures began to come on the screen, of the achievements of Navy men in the Pacific and then working into a climactic line of how one day recently an important visitor came to see these Navy men, who took him to see some of the esoteric-type settings he had made famous in his writings. The camera faded to Burroughs arriving aboard the LST. There were long shots of Gug-Gug set in the blue ocean – beautiful shots, for Public Relations had some highly talented photographer's mates, of the LST with Burroughs aboard approaching the island, then, framed by the doors of the opened bow-ramp, of a group of natives standing on the shore in welcoming fashion. Presently, with the LST beached, the camera moved in to show a setting of the bow-ramp with Burroughs in the centre of it and clustered around him a number of Navy men and the natives. The camera moved over the various faces and, in the case of the natives, expertly over their bodies, showing them all clothed in new, magnificently tailored breech-cloths. This went on for a while; then some of the Navy men were saying things into the microphone; then Burroughs, smiling fondly at the natives, was saying things. Then, as the camera trained on the natives, there came out some Tuluran dialogue, half smothered in giggles, which made Siegel, who had been about to fall asleep in one of the back rows, start up in his chair. The lights came on.

'Bravo!' the exec yelled from the first row, clapping enthusiastically. 'Bravo! Brav-o!'

Waiting for the applause, mainly his own, to die down, the exec then spoke.

'Tremendous!' he exclaimed enthusiastically. 'Mr Tarzan himself smack in the middle of a beached LST! What a natural! What a plug for the Navy! Probably cost you over a million dollars to buy that kind of publicity – not that any amount of money would buy it – and we got it for absolutely not one cent! The looks of those natives! Why, they almost seemed to giggle, I'll swear! They just loved it, didn't they? How innocent and childlike they are! And that talk of theirs! How authentic! How charming! Well done, Ross! My personal commendation!'

Nobody in the States ever used the film, of course. It was just as well, Ensign Siegel thought. There were probably very few Tuluran linguists among American movie audiences, but it was just possible there could be one, and one would have been enough. The Tuluran dialogue on the sound-track was charming all right. The mayor of Gug-Gug and the welcoming committee of prominent islanders had been discussing with the highest enjoyment their brand-new breech-cloths. Translated, it would have fried the ears off a four-hashmark boatswain's mate.

MELORA I: *The Passionate Sailors of Mendoza*

'The Tulurans' – Ensign Max Siegel intoned passages, occasionally amended by himself, he had memorized from ComFleets Bulletin 232–44 – 'Guide to the Western Pacific' – classification 'Restricted' – as he escorted the two congressmen down the dirt-road street of the village – 'are rightfully proud of their heritage that dates back to the time of Magellan's discovery of the island in 1521. It was in 1557 that Admiral Jaime Ruiz de Mendoza landed by orders of Charles I and proclaimed Spanish sovereignty. Today's Tulurans are the result of the marriages between the native women and the Spaniards, starting with the passionate sailors of Mendoza. The modern Tulurans are usually short, slender, and lithe, light brown in colour, with round heads ...'

'When the hell are we going to get over to that Seabee battalion you said had all those men from New Jersey?' Representative George Janson (R., N.J.) broke in bluntly.

'I believe you said there were a number of men from North Carolina there, too, young man?' Representative Arthur Smithfield (D., N.C.) asked in a courteous Southern accent.

'It's a strange thing,' Ensign Siegel said, 'how most of the men in that Seabee battalion come from New Jersey and North Carolina. Both of your states, gentlemen, must have unusual numbers of construction men.'

'What are we waiting for then?' Representative Janson said impatiently. 'It's very interesting that these people here have round heads – what other kind of heads the hell are there anyhow? – but what I want, Ensign, is to drop in on some of my boys.'

'Presently, gentlemen, presently,' Ensign Siegel intoned. Siegel was well aware of the interest of visiting congressmen in seeing as many men from their states as possible, who might have numerous voting relatives at home. Siegel himself did as much as anyone to provide men from specific congressional districts – however, he intended to get the Tulurans in first. He continued: 'We all must remember that the Tulurans, as more or less wards of the United States Government, look upon you congressmen as the Great White Fathers. You know, of course, that the U.S. has had possession of Tulura since the Treaty of Amsterdam in 1899. A few minutes more in the village here, gentlemen, and we're off to see those concentrations of constituents.'

Breathing a little heavily, the two congressmen continued down the road on either side of Ensign Siegel. They were a pretty striking sight in the Tuluran village. The representative from North Carolina, a square-framed man with a mop of iron-grey hair, was wearing a white Palm Beach suit, a blue bow tie with white polka dots, a wide-brimmed yellowish Panama hat, and white shoes. The representative from New Jersey, a tall, cadaverous man, was wearing a visored Navy officer's hat without the insignia, a red sport shirt, printed with green palm trees, which he had picked up in Honolulu, and Navy khaki shorts from which his stilt-like legs protruded in a milky whiteness which suggested they had not seen the sun since he was a child. He was wearing short black silk socks and perforated brown-and-white shoes.

The village was named Tanalolo. It was Ensign Siegel's 'exhibition village', where he regularly brought visitors as part of the well-balanced orientation tour of the island he had worked out. Siegel had picked the village as a nice contrast to naval installations. Remote, it had kept its untarnished Tuluran atmosphere.

'Most of the natives live in rectangular wooden houses with thatched roofs,' Siegel began to intone again from portions of the guidebook he had committed to memory. 'Observe examples to your left, gentlemen.'

'Very interesting, young man,' Representative Smithfield said politely.

'Fascinating,' Representative Janson said shortly, removing his Navy hat and mopping his brow with a big white handkerchief.

'Notice how the hibiscus, primroses, orchids, prickly pears, mountain roses, sweet acacias, and frangipani brighten the landscape.' Ensign Siegel picked up on a memorized passage, indicating examples with a wave of his hand. 'The mangrove, mulberry, palm, corkwood, bay cedar, and screw pine trees are found in abundance on Tulura, which, unlike many flat atolls and islands of the Pacific, abounds with scenic spots from its 1227-foot mountain tops to its silken sand beaches. One plant, the swordgrass, is to be especially guarded against, for it can give a very nasty cut. You might watch those legs there, Congressman Janson. There is a lively business in palmetto and aggay plant weaving and the manufacture of bags and fancy articles from land snail-shells.'

'Snail-shells!' exclaimed Representative Janson temperishly.

'Cooking is not done in the house but in a separate building,' Ensign Siegel continued, 'in case you're wondering what those small structures next to the main houses are. To the old diet of breadfruit, taro, yams, coconuts, and fish, the Spanish added the Mexican tortilla, tapioca, sweet potatoes and the flesh of chickens, pigs, cattle, goats, and deer. In addition to these, the Tulurans eat mangoes, papayas, musk-melons, pumpkins, cucumbers, maize, lima beans, onions, wild figs, bananas, guavas, peppers, pandanus, egg-plant, peanuts, tropical chestnuts, pomegranates, edible perch, eels, and the coconut crab. I can lay on for you gentlemen this evening one of the customary five-hour Tuluran banquets.'

'My God, no!' Representative Janson said.

'We would certainly enjoy such an interesting occasion,' Representative Smithfield said graciously, 'and it's very thoughtful of you, young man, to offer it. Unfortunately, I believe we're having dinner with the admiral this evening. Isn't that right, George?'

'We're certainly going to do something besides eat wild figs and eels, I can tell you that for sure,' Representative Janson said tersely.

'The missionaries' – Ensign Siegel changed to a new subject – 'did not try to put the native women in Mother Hubbards but they decidedly changed the native costume, which today is Spanish-style clothing for both men and women. In the good old days the Tuluran men wore nothing, except for the occasional breech-cloth. The women wore short skirts of woven fibres with the upper part of the body bare ...'

'The Republicans have traditionally been opposed to change,' said Representative Janson in a burst of congressional humour.

'I believe if my esteemed friend, the gentleman from New Jersey, will check up on his history,' Representative Smithfield said wittily, 'he will discover that the missionaries who wrought these regrettable fashion changes got their foot in during a Republican administration.'

'My distinguished colleague, the gentleman from North Carolina,' Representative Janson said, 'has reminded me of an interesting fact, which is that virtually all of our country's expansion occurred during Republican administrations ...'

'The Tulurans have simple forms of amusement,' Ensign Siegel gently interrupted this oratory. 'Most any occasion becomes the cause of celebrating with songs, jokes, gallons of palm toddy, and games. The original games included contests of speed and strength in the water, spear-throwing, wrestling, and foot-racing. Under the Spanish, card games, cockfights, and tossing coins at the raised end of a corncob largely replaced the native games, but in recent years, under the American accession, base-ball and volley-ball and other active sports have become popular. The Tulurans are a musical people. The "Aluna Song" is typically Tuluran. It is spontaneous, following the pattern of the round, challenging the wit of the singers. It continues for hours.'

'Like some other things I know,' said Representative Janson, sighing.

Detecting a certain restlessness in his escortees, Ensign Siegel halted the party in the middle of the road.

'And now, gentlemen,' he said, 'I have a very special treat for you.'

Siegel led the congressmen over to a house, where on the porch steps sat an old man with bright eyes. As the party approached, the old man got up respectfully. His eyes rested first on Representative Janson, with his brilliant-hued shirt and his white crane-like legs, then upon Representative Smithfield, in his Palm Beach suit and polka-dot tie, with the curious gaze he might devote to two strange species of jungle birds stalking into his yard from the boondocks.

'Good morning, Mr Seguro,' Ensign Siegel said in Tuluran to the old man.

'En-sine!' The old man spoke back happily, and clasped Siegel around the shoulders.

'Mr Seguro,' Siegel said in English for the benefit of the congressmen, 'I want you to meet two of the most leading Americans. Congressman Janson of the third congressional district of New Jersey! Congressman Smithfield of the fifth congressional district of North Carolina!'

The old man, with an uncomprehending grin, took the hands which the congressmen proffered.

'What's going on now?' Representative Janson said.

'The congressman,' Siegel translated in Tuluran, 'says you have the finest-looking village he's seen since he left the great state of New Jersey, Mr Seguro.'

The old man grinned more broadly.

'Well, time's a-wastin', Ensign,' Representative Janson said. 'What say we kick on over to those Seabees – right about now, huh?'

'The congressman,' Siegel translated in Tuluran, 'asks me to compliment you on your charming home.'

The old man's grin widened to clear across his face.

'They certainly seem to be a happy and friendly people,' Representative Smithfield noted favourably.

'And now, Mr Seguro ...' Ensign Siegel prompted.

'Oh, yes, sorry, sorry, En-sine ...'

Mr Seguro disappeared hurriedly inside his home and was back in seconds carrying an earthenware jug and a couple of Dixie cups from the supply Siegel had given him for these occasions. The old man wordlessly handed each congressman a cup, and still saying nothing, twice tilted the jug, which gurgled generously.

'Drink up, men!' Ensign Siegel commanded in resonant tones, and the congressmen reflexively tilted their Dixie cups.

Representative Janson immediately started coughing and choking. Ensign Siegel reached over and started enthusiastically pounding the congressman on the back.

'What in the name of God is this?' Representative Janson sputtered, getting his breath back. 'Aviation gasoline?'

'Palm toddy,' said Siegel mildly. 'An indigenous beverage prepared from fermented coconut sap.'

Representative Smithfield, who had swallowed his with no difficulty, looked pleasantly surprised.

'Well, I declare!' he said. 'Tastes a good deal like North Carolina white mule.'

'The natives like their liquor,' Siegel intoned. 'Other intoxicating drinks are prepared from corn, rice, or shredded coconut. I'm sure your host, Mr Seguro here, would be happy to offer you samples of these, if you're interested ...'

'My God, no!' said Representative Janson.

'I'm doing all right with this, thank you, young man, but I will,' Representative Smithfield said, holding out his Dixie cup, 'take a little sweetening.'

The Tuluran happily gave Representative Smithfield's cup a generous refill.

Representative Janson took a few more cautious sips from his Dixie cup of palm toddy. He set the cup down on the porch, shook hands with the old man, and turned to Siegel.

'Now, Ensign,' he said firmly, 'we've done all the honours here, so let's get back to the jeep now and drive straight over to that Seabee battalion ...'

Abruptly the congressman stopped, looking at something over Mr Seguro's shoulder. He was sighting so intently, almost like a pointer at the first scent of a quail, that Ensign Siegel and Representative Smithfield turned instinctively to follow the line of his gaze.

A girl was coming down the road towards them. The mouths of the three Americans fell open.

The girl, who appeared to be about twenty years old, was wearing a white blouse with puffed sleeves and a blue-print skirt that held her body like a wrapper for some exquisitely formed fruit. She was a flawless palomino tan; her black hair fell half-way down her back. The movements of her body, which was slim yet rounded, were lithe and effortlessly graceful. Her features, Ensign Siegel could see as she drew upon them, were finely made, with lips slightly full. She was startlingly beautiful.

Then the girl had stopped, obviously just to chat a moment with the old man.

'Melora!' Siegel heard Mr Seguro greet the girl happily in Tuluran. 'Good morning!' Siegel was surprised to see the old man lift his hat as he spoke, a remarkable gesture of respect from an older Tuluran to such a young one. 'How is your father?'

'He's very well, thank you, Mr Seguro,' Siegel heard the girl say. 'How are Maria and Pedro?'

The old man and the girl were standing slightly apart in a conversational cluster. As they continued to exchange pleasantries in Tuluran, the two congressmen, who Siegel could see quite clearly were almost overcome, presently formed another conversational cluster.

'Christ, what a build!' Representative Janson said.

'What lovely hair!' Representative Smithfield said.

'God, that mouth!' Representative Janson said.

'What an incredible skin!' Representative Smithfield said. 'And those eyes!'

'God, those legs of hers!' said Representative Janson. He turned interrogatively towards Siegel. 'Who is this, Ensign – Miss Pacific?'

'I never saw her before,' Ensign Siegel said in truthful awe, and wondered pretty frankly why the hell not.

'Perhaps, Ensign,' Representative Janson said, 'we could fix it up with the young lady this evening to enjoy one of those Tuluran dinners you were talking so interestingly about.'

'Yes, indeed,' said Representative Smithfield; 'it would give us a chance to see some of the real Tuluran life.'

'I believe you gentlemen said you were having dinner with the admiral,' Ensign Siegel said factually.

'We made a mistake about that,' Representative Janson said. 'Our dinner with the admiral is tomorrow night. Isn't that right, Arthur?'

'Yes, I was mixed up on that,' Representative Smithfield said. 'You lose all sense of time out here in the Pacific.'

'Yes, we're entirely free this evening,' Representative Janson said. 'And you've made this whole Tuluran picture seem so interesting, Ensign, from your interesting descriptions – I might add, I don't think I've ever heard a better presentation, and I intend to tell your commanding officer the same thing – that I have an appetite to see more of it and in particular to have one of those five-hour banquets.'

'As you mentioned, I believe, young man,' Representative Smithfield said, 'these people are sort of wards of our government, and the congressman here and myself do have a special responsibility towards them.'

'So go right ahead and tell the young lady we're free,' Representative Janson said eagerly.

Ensign Siegel suddenly felt a passionate desire to get his congressmen the hell out of there.

'Gentlemen,' he said, 'important as I think the Tulurans are, I don't feel you should neglect your own constituents …'

'Maybe she has a sister,' Representative Janson said.

'You take the sister,' Representative Smithfield said.

'Now, over at that Seabee battalion,' Ensign Siegel continued urgently. 'I was just over there yesterday, and I myself, who wasn't even looking for them, ran into at least a dozen men from the third

New Jersey congressional district and an approximately equal number from the fifth North Carolina congressional district ...'

'The hell I'll take the sister!' Representative Janson said.

'All right, we'll flip for the sister,' Representative Smithfield said.

'The hell we will!' Representative Janson said. 'I saw her first.'

'Gentlemen,' said Siegel, 'Seabees can be pretty sensitive people, and if these men from New Jersey and North Carolina, who have put off trips to the beaches and things like that, don't get their visit, I wouldn't be surprised if they wrote a few letters home to their voting relatives ...'

'Now, Ensign' – Representative Janson turned to Siegel – 'if you'll go ahead and make a date with this girl – and, ah, you might ask if she has a sister for Arthur here.'

Ensign Siegel, a little frantic, suddenly remembered a memorized passage which had been entitled, in the guidebook, 'An Ounce of Prevention'.

' "Many of the women, especially the younger ones, may look attractive," ' he began to intone, ' "but it should be remembered that gonorrhoea is widespread among the natives, and chancroid and yaws are prevalent. Skin diseases, eczema, boils, contagious impetigo, parasitic diseases, and streptococcus infection are prevalent among the natives. Poliomyelitis and cerebro-spinal meningitis have occurred in epidemic proportions. Leprosy is present." '

Looking at the immaculate, exquisite girl, glowing with health, who stood about a yard from him, Representative Janson said, 'Ensign, I'll take my chances.'

' "The father and brothers of an unmarried Tuluran girl will not look kindly upon the American who trifles with her," ' Ensign Siegel's voice rose ominously, quoting. ' "Tuluran girls are rigorously chaperoned. A Tuluran girl never goes anywhere except with at least three members of her family with her" ...'

'I'm sure that if you explain the circumstances,' Representative Janson cut in firmly, 'namely, that we're members of the United States Congress on a fact-gathering tour, you can arrange it. Now, Ensign, go ahead and ask her,' he said commandingly.

With a sudden idea, and turning towards the old man and the girl, Ensign Siegel made as if he were waiting for an opening in their conversation. He appeared to be listening intently to their talk. Then

Siegel turned back to the congressmen. A disappointed expression filled his face.

'Gentlemen,' he said slowly. 'I was just about to ask her. Then – I can hear her talking now ...'

Ensign Siegel, pausing, inclined his head towards the conversation between the old man and the girl. He turned back again to the congressmen.

'Her husband and three children,' Ensign Siegel said. 'She's talking about her husband and her three children.'

'A husband!' exclaimed Representative Janson.

'Three children!' exclaimed Representative Smithfield. 'She couldn't have ...'

'I'm sorry, gentlemen,' Ensign Siegel said gravely, 'but that's the way it is.' He quoted sternly: ' "Tulurans, having been under regular Navy Administration for forty-six years, will expect Americans to be kindly, earnest, and well-mannered people with strong moral principles." '

'Married!' Representative Janson said miserably.

'Three children!' Representative Smithfield said incredulously. 'I'd never believe it.'

'Actually, I have four – and very sweet children they are,' a softly modulated voice said in impeccable English.

The three heads of Representative Janson, Representative Smithfield, and Ensign Siegel snapped around like jerked puppets. They stared in horrified disbelief at the source of the remark, which was the girl. Ensign Siegel, looking at the girl, saw some of his quoted guidebook words flash across his mind like the huge illuminated words on the Times Building news ticker – CHANCROID ... YAWS ... GONOR-RHOEA. An enormous flood of embarrassment engulfed him.

A great speechlessness that seemed as if it could never be broken seized the three Americans.

'Madame,' Ensign Siegel finally managed to mumble, and saw a smile in the girl's eyes at the word, 'I am Ensign Siegel of the United States Navy.'

Instantly he realized how ridiculous this sounded.

'I gathered you were in the United States Navy.' The girl's eyes were amused as she looked up at Siegel where he towered hugely above her. 'How do you do?' she said politely.

'How do you do?' Ensign Siegel heard himself echo. Then he said in weak, stuttering tones, 'This is Representative Janson of the United States Congress and Representative Smithfield of the United States Congress!'

'How do you do?' the girl said with flawless manners.

'How do, ma'am?' Representative Smithfield said, jerkily removing his Panama hat.

'Pleased to meet you!' Representative Janson stuttered, removing his Navy hat. In his confusion he dropped the hat. He stooped and scooped it up fumblingly. 'It's a real pleasure to meet you!'

The honours in etiquette were all on the side of the girl, who was the only one at ease. The congressmen hurried into the behaviour they would have put on on finding out suddenly that she was the daughter of their most influential constituent.

'We're honoured to have two members of Congress visit Tana-lolo,' the girl said in that flawless English. 'What states do you represent?'

'New Jersey,' said Representative Janson meekly.

'North Carolina,' said Representative Smithfield contritely.

The girl smiled pleasantly. 'Both sides of the Mason–Dixon line,' she said. 'This *is* an honour.'

'Thank you, indeed,' Representative Janson said respectfully.

'The honour is all ours,' Representative Smithfield said gallantly.

The girl turned easily to Ensign Siegel, who wished he could find some place to go into the ground. 'So you speak Tuluran,' she said with polite interest. 'An unusual accomplishment for a Navy officer.'

'I get around the villages,' Siegel heard himself explaining. This sounded stupid in his ears, so he added, 'I like languages.' That, he felt instantly, was no improvement. He had a completely frustrating sensation of being unable to be anything but stupid in the presence of this girl.

But before he could think of anything further to say, she turned back to the congressmen.

'I'm sorry to have to leave this pleasant conversation,' she said, 'but you know how it is when you have four children. You two look as if you're parents yourselves,' she said in tones of sweet inquiry.

'I have three,' Representative Janson said shamefacedly.

'I have five,' Representative Smithfield admitted, avoiding her eyes.

The girl turned back to Siegel. 'I'm sorry I didn't have my children – all four of them – along for you to meet,' she said, her eyes mischievous. 'They are such sweet children.'

'I'm sure they must be a constant source of amusement to you,' Ensign Siegel said impassively.

'I have enjoyed them very much,' she said.

After a quick goodbye in Tuluran to the old man, she was gone. The two congressmen and Ensign Siegel watched in silence as she walked lithely down the road.

'Whew!' Representative Smithfield sighed.

'Where the hell did she come from?' Representative Janson said, mopping his brow. 'Smith College?'

Ensign Siegel turned to the congressmen. ' "Light thunderstorms occur throughout the year," ' he said loudly, from a guidebook memory passage, ' "especially during the summer. The season of the most serious storms, typhoons, and typhoon-type tropical disturbances is from August to December, November being called by the natives *Humalong*, 'remain-in-the-village time'. At least one damaging storm hits Tulura each year." '

Ensign Siegel picked up the palm-toddy jug from the porch and took a solid slug of it straight from the jug. 'Gentlemen, remain-in-the-village time is over. Let's get cracking over to that Seabee battalion.'

As he shovelled the gentlemen from North Carolina and New Jersey back into the jeep, Ensign Siegel was making rapid mental plans for a solo cruise back to Tanalolo, at flank speed.

Two: The Education of Admiral Boatwright

IN all history there has been perhaps no human project so staggeringly complex as the planning of the average assault operation of the Pacific campaign of World War II. Consider: Hundreds of thousands of units of humanity, jeeps, Quonset huts, ammunition, chocolate bars, drums of gasoline, cans of peaches, C-rations, tubes of toothpaste, pairs of socks, and underwear, travelling thousands of different routes from origin to final destination, and item, quantity, and route all of necessity determined months ahead – each must needs come ashore at its specific time, on its specific spot on a tiny atoll set in the great ocean wastes. The co-ordination, sense of detail, and fore-sight required to bring this off called for a wizardry little short of sublime.

This job belonged to Vice-Admiral D. D. Boatwright. He was the brains of the Pacific War. It was his genius which largely planned the great island assaults, synchronized a million men and thousand of millions of dollars' worth of material to the right spot at the right minute. The Navy had furnished Admiral Boatwright its finest edu-cation and it found in him a veritable naval Clauzewitz. The Navy had taught Admiral Boatwright just about everything, except one thing.

Before Pearl Harbour, reporters seldom came around the Navy, and those who did were treated as identified enemy agents dedicated to filching its innermost secrets. Even for a considerable time after Pearl Harbour an admiral might go along for months, having to do nothing but fight the war, and never encounter a reporter. But by the beginning of 1945 the Navy's attitude had undergone a wondrous change. The Navy, abruptly falling madly in love with the power of the Press, had opened the floodgates, and reporters were descending like schools of happy barnacles on the Pacific Fleet. While earlier only the wire services and largest newspapers had sent out correspondents, now they came from score upon score of publications and organiza-tions never before represented in a theatre of war. War correspon-dents came from newspapers all over the States, from remote radio stations, from trade magazines, from fraternal publications, true-confession magazines, even from comic magazines. They made for Tulura, where his planning wizardry had brought Admiral Boat-wright to one of history's critical moments and roles. It brought him also into the one situation for which none of his training had prepared him: intercourse with the Press.

In the great Pacific spaces, logistics was the inherent problem and Admiral Boatwright's theme song. His favourite opening word to any sentence was 'Logistically'. After a while the word was picked up by correspondents and officers, who would be having a drink at the officers' club and observe, 'Logistically, this is one hell of a fine rum sour', or be discussing another inherent problem in the Pacific and remark, 'Logistically, I could do with a piece of tail'. Admiral Boatwright was a logistics fiend. He hated to see manpower or material diverted to any use but winning the war – the basis, no doubt, for his despising the entire Public Relations lash-up, which he considered as essential to the winning of the war as a guinea-hen under glass.

'Logistically,' Admiral Boatwright used to tell his chief, Com-Fleets, 'I recognize the need for something of everything in war, where you're dealing with a civilian Navy, though I must say we seem to be consuming a criminal amount of ship space for Coca-Cola. I never realized before that a wartime Navy floats mainly on Coca-Cola. But I fail to see why we need so *many* correspondents. What do they all find to write about? The communiqué gives all the essential facts. You take this compendium.'

Admiral Boatwright would produce a stapled sheaf of eight legal-size, single-spaced pages listing the correspondents attached to Com-Fleets. He lifted it as though it displaced as much tonnage as the U.S.S. *New Jersey*.

'Here's a correspondent for the Fort Worth *Star-Telegram* and another correspondent for the Dallas *Morning News*. Now, those two cities are thirty-two miles apart. Why couldn't they go together and have *one* correspondent write for both?'

His chief smiled patiently. 'Boats, you may be a bear at the craft of logistics; but you don't know the first thing about the craft of journalism. Each paper wants to be able to say it has its *own* correspondent covering the Pacific.'

'Then their saying it is an outrageous luxury for the Navy to indulge. The Navy manpower tied down in that disgracefully overstaffed Public Relations bureaucracy over there! And the space they take up! Three big buildings!' Admiral Boatwright said, livid. 'As much as Plans, Operations, Intelligence, Communications, and Logistics combined!'

He pulled from his pocket a fat roster of ComFleets Public Relations personnel.

'I've been in the Navy forty years now, and until I arrived on Tulura I had never even heard of the billets they've got over there. Listen to this –' And the admiral began to read from the roster:

'Media Officer, Magazine Liaison Officer, Radio Correspondents Liaison Officer – there are seven of those, Recording Officer, Research and Historical Officer, Public Relations *War* Plans Officer, Public Relations *Operations* Officer, Public Relations Engineering Officer, Radio Photo Officer, Photo Supply Officer, Fleet Motion-picture Officer, Fleet Still-picture Officer, Motion-picture Training Officer, Motion-picture Planning Officer, Correspondents' Aides ... Sweet Jesus!' Admiral Boatwright exclaimed in rage. 'What's the Navy coming to?'

Admiral Boatwright shook the roster. 'And what is the purpose of these hordes over there? Their sole purpose and duty is to pet and pamper the correspondents. The correspondents who themselves with their expendable curiosity take up the valuable time of Navy men who *are* in the Navy. The last one of those Public Relations oddballs ought to be out on a ship – most of them chipping paint. And nine-tenths of the correspondents ought to be in uniform.'

'Sh-sh,' ComFleets said. 'What you just said is heresy. Boats, you just don't correctly estimate the great weight of American public opinion. The correspondents determine what the public thinks about us. What the public thinks about us determines our appropriations. Our appropriations determine the size of the Navy.'

ComFleets sighed. 'They ought to have taught us more about all this at Annapolis in addition to navigation. Maybe it wasn't true so much when we were midshipmen. Long time back, wasn't it? But to-day there aren't too many things more important to running a Navy than public relations. I'm not sure I like it. But then,' he said wistfully, 'there have been a lot of things in my life I haven't liked – but have learned to live with.'

'I'll never like it,' Admiral Boatwright said roughly.

'Hell, Boats, we'll just have to glamorize you for the Press. Make a character out of you. Why don't you grow a beard? Or start wearing your fly open?'

That was the trouble with Admiral Boatwright, really. He knew how to launch thousands of ships and hundreds of thousands of men to beat into submission the enemy's great island fortresses. He took the most complex logistical problems in the annals of warfare and wrenched from them victory after victory. He was a genius, really. But he had about as much glamour as a stuffed barn-owl. He just wasn't a character. Reporters at heart resent the absence of glamour, since that absence threatens their livelihood. Being resented, Admiral Boatwright was in turn resentful.

When asked for interviews, Admiral Boatwright consented only after a direct order from his chief and then only during the hour of five to six a.m. This was when he took his jungle constitutional, followed at ten paces by an armed Marine – this over his objections. He figured if he had to give an interview he would give it when he couldn't do anything else anyhow. The first correspondent who accepted these terms had to go to bed for a week with a heart condition. Clad in Marine fatigues and clodhoppers, and with his barrel chest utterly unwinded, Admiral Boatwright set a fierce pace on his walks, singling out the roughest terrain and thickest underbrush to plough through. 'Did you ever try to take notes while galloping through a couple of miles of boondocks?' the correspondent asked a friend from his bed. 'The son of a bitch almost killed me – intentionally, I think.'

After that journalist's experience, the requests for interviews with Admiral Boatwright suddenly vanished. The admiral still had to give an occasional Press conference. It was painful to watch him; watch the reporters snipe, bait, paw, and gnaw him. One correspondent in particular, Gordon Ripwell, hated Boatwright's guts.

'Admiral – back in 1943 Bull Halsey informed us – I was present when he said it – that the Navy would have the Japs licked by Christmas,' Ripwell would begin. Rip never just asked a question. He gave a prologue, made a speech which frequently included passages on naval strategy for the benefit of the naval officer giving the Press conference, then asked a question. Someone once remarked that when Ripwell attended a Press conference it was difficult to tell who was being interviewed – Ripwell or the naval officer who was supposedly giving the conference.

'That was in 1943,' Ripwell would say, 'that Halsey had the war over by Christmas, and here we sit – the present year is 1945, Admiral. Meantime we have had assaults on Tarawa, which took 3,286 casualties. On Tulura here, which took 2,896. On Saipan – a D-day I and others present there won't be soon forgetting – which took 17,166. Iwo Jima, which took 22,906 American casualties ...' Ripwell would cite the losses in a tone that suggested that Admiral Boatwright was personally responsible for the murder or maiming of these men.

Admiral Boatwright's face by this time would be flushing a pomegranate purple. 'I was wondering, Admiral, if there's to be more and more of this, or if you visualize upcoming Okinawa as the last island assault before we take on the Japanese home islands.'

The question was a trap, the important word being 'island'. What Ripwell really wanted to know was not whether Okinawa was the last island assault, but whether the next strike was going to be at the China mainland or directly at Japan. Admiral Boatwright saw this, of course, and he was not the man to fall into a trap where naval matters were concerned. The trouble was, he could barely restrain himself from saying it was a trap. He should have laughed the question off. Instead his blood pressure would go rocketing.

'The Navy never expected the war to be concluded in 1943,' he would snap.

'Well, sir,' Ripwell would say blandly, 'I was only quoting a famous Navy admiral.'

'Quoting one of the best, I might add ...'

'Admiral,' Rip would say with elaborate patience, 'let us not get into a discussion on the batting averages of the various and numerous admirals. To get back to my question, about Okinawa being the last island before the mainland of Japan ...'

'I would say that's top secret information,' Admiral Boatwright bit out.

It was a serious tactical mistake for Admiral Boatwright to say that. He would never make such a tactical mistake in a naval problem, but he made bloopers with the Press.

Ripwell laughed smugly. 'Ex-*cuse* me, Admiral. I wouldn't want to pry loose any of the Navy's secrets.'

It was all Admiral Boatwright could do to keep from blurting out 'The hell you wouldn't!' as Ripwell smirked over another excuse for a phrase he consistently summoned in his dispatches, 'Close-mouthed Navy sources refused ...'

In a moment Ripwell would be back pot-shotting at the admiral.

'In the Second Battle of the Philippine Sea, in which some of us here participated, the tiny Seventh Fleet was supporting the landing which the Third Fleet was to protect from attack by sea.' (Ripwell talking, not the admiral.) 'Those supposedly stupid little Japanese sailed a decoy fleet from Japan down towards Luzon for the purpose of sucking the Third Fleet up north – which they did. Meantime the main Jap fleet, which had been routed four days after the landings by typical Navy fly-boy exaggeration, and another Jap force converged on the helpless Seventh and sank two carriers, three destroyers, and a hundred planes – all because the Third Fleet was chasing ducks up north. A look at the waters around Okinawa' – Ripwell, while the admiral inwardly boiled, would step forward to the admiral's map at the front of the room and pick up the admiral's pointer – 'reveals the possibility of another such foul-up by your Navy ...'

Glamour, a minimum of glamour, would have protected Admiral Boatwright from all this. Wearing a baseball cap, like Mitscher, or making wild but thrilling predictions, like Halsey, would have saved him from it. Admiral Boatwright was far too much the sane strategist to indulge in wild predictions. As for baseball caps, he would have looked as foolish in one as Herbert Hoover.

But something had to be done to make Admiral Boatwright glamorous, make a character out of him. He was a genius, and if he was a son of a bitch to the correspondents, he was just about the most vital American son of a bitch in the Pacific. No matter. If this kept up, the Press would destroy him. Normally it was a job for Public Relations. There were plenty of people in the shop who could have glamorized the admiral into a naval MacArthur if only he'd put himself in their hands. The hitch was that if any Public Relations officer had so propositioned Admiral Boatwright, he would have been blasted out of his office so hard and high he wouldn't have descended until he landed on the Japanese home islands via the China mainland.

Admiral Boatwright got glamour anyhow. Not consciously, for if he'd known he was getting glamour he would have fiercely stopped the whole operation. Glamour crept up and seized him by the scruff of the neck, or pants, and by that time there was nothing he could do about it.

The operation itself was really very simple.

It was at his chief's insistence that an armed Marine accompanied Admiral Boatwright on his jungle forays. There were still a few Japs rustling around the boondocks, and ComFleets did not care to have his ace planner picked off, though it was beginning to appear that if the Japs didn't, the Press would. Admiral Boatwright bitterly resented the bodyguard. It was a sordid waste of manpower, in his book, to have one fighting man engaged at doing nothing but protecting another man.

Once a month Admiral Boatwright jeeped quickly around the island – a sort of inspection of his ship. One day he was passing through a native village when a small boy coming out of nowhere darted in front of the jeep. The driver slammed on the brakes, inches short of the youngster and almost hurtling Admiral Boatwright through the windshield. The admiral stepped on out anyhow and satisfied himself that the child was unharmed, just scared a little. As he was bending solicitously over the lad, Admiral Boatwright heard him mutter something in Tuluran. Almost simultaneously he felt something seize the seat of his pants.

Admiral Boatwright straightened up in disbelief and looked down – squarely into the upturned eyes of a nondescript mutt of a dog which none the less appeared capable of staring even a vice-admiral down if necessary. The odd thing, though, was that the dog was not biting his flesh. Yet he was holding him very immovably by the seat of his trousers. It was the technique used by a fine retriever which grasps the duck firmly without harming the duck-meat. The dog held him fast until the boy, apparently satisfied that the big admiral wasn't going to harm any little Tuluran boys, said something else in Tuluran. Whereupon the dog let go the admiral's seat.

'Well, I'll be damned!' Admiral Boatwright said. He was fascinated. 'That is some trick. Your dog, sonny?'

The boy, while using Tuluran to the dog, used English for the Navy.

'Yes, sir, Captain.'

'Admiral!' The boatswain's-mate driver ,who was long since out of the jeep, violently barked a correction. 'He's a vice-admiral!'

'Never mind, Jenkins,' Admiral Boatwright said.

The admiral regarded the dog admiringly.

'Never seen a manoeuvre like that. Damned if that isn't something!'

At this point a grown Tuluran with a very broad smile approached and identified himself as the boy's father.

'Some dog your boy has,' the admiral chatted.

The man grinned amiably and waited.

'Just what did you say to make him, ah …' The admiral indicated his own stern.

'Say "*Rudi busso!*"' the little Tuluran said.

'In English,' the boy's father said, 'means "Seize pants!"'

The dog, hearing the words, made for the admiral again. The boy quickly spoke two more words: '*Argo busso!*'

'Means "Release pants!"' the father said.

'Well, I'll be damned,' the admiral said. '"*Rudi busso!*" "*Argo busso!*" That is some dog!'

'Dog named for old Navy man and discoverer of our island,' the grown Tuluran said. 'Magellan!'

'A very interesting name,' the admiral said agreeably.

'Smart watchdog,' the grown Tuluran said succinctly.

At the word 'watchdog' Admiral Boatwright got a canny look in his eye, which meant he was overtaken by an idea. It was not greed for the dog. He would never have thought of lifting a boy's dog in peace-time. But this was war, and no time for luxuries.

'Wouldn't want to sell that dog, would you, sonny?'

The little Tuluran hesitated. He may have been overwhelmed by the admiral's stars.

'Would like to have dog, Admiral?' the big Tuluran answered for him. 'Yours.'

The Tulurans are a wonderfully tractable people and nowhere more so than in doing favours for the Navy, which has been long with them.

'That's very kind of you,' Admiral Boatwright said. 'But I couldn't take him from the boy.'

'Horseshit,' the man said gently. The admiral looked startled, but the man seemed to consider it only a mild expletive. The Navy has been long with the Tulurans. 'For U.S. Navy, which has given us back our island, one dog is little enough.'

It was a pretty speech, and the admiral wavered.

'Besides,' the man said, 'the boy has other dog. Have not, Mario?' the father said more loudly to the boy.

This sounded suspicious indeed. But the boy said in a small voice, 'Yes, I have another one. Please take him. I would be happy for him to join U.S. Navy.'

'Take him!' the boy's father said fervently. 'Admiral, we want you to have dog!'

'But are you sure ...' the admiral began.

'Oh, yes,' the man shouted. 'We proud you take dog. We proud!'

Before long Admiral Boatwright was forced into a position where he could not have refused the dog. At least he later ordered his conscience to tell him that. Really, they wanted him to have the dog. They were proud such a high-ranking Navy officer should want him. Once he saw his master talking with the man in uniform, the dog proved tractable enough himself, submitting gladly to Admiral Boatwright's head-scratchings. Admiral Boatwright understood dogs much better than reporters. Back home in Virginia he had a fine Irish setter and he knew just how to scratch a dog's head the way any dog likes it – just behind the ears. Still the admiral hesitated, a little uneasy at the idea of taking a boy's dog.

'Him horseshit good watchdog,' the man said. 'Dog caught sixteen Japs in occupation.'

'Is that so?' Admiral Boatwright was much interested.

'Hates Japs!' the man affirmed. 'Can smell Jap mile off! When smells Jap, comes right up, and pulls at *your* pants.'

That did it.

When the admiral drove out of the village he was accompanied by a dog in the back seat of the jeep. He was happy to be fifty dollars poorer. He had insisted, over genuine protests, on leaving twenty-five dollars with the boy and a like amount with the man.

'If that isn't the damndest thing this dog does, Jenkins,' the admiral remarked every few minutes to his boatswain's-mate driver as they drove along. Then he would turn and look as if unable to believe the dog was there. The dog was indeed sitting quite erect in the middle of the back seat, bearing the stoic look of a man just inducted into the Navy. The admiral repeated, to himself, '*Rudi busso!*' and '*Argo busso!*' until he was sure he had thoroughly memorized the commands.

The next day Admiral Boatwright held a private demonstration for his chief in ComFleets' office. At the command '*Rudi busso*', Magellan instantly seized ComFleets' pants. Admiral Boatwright briefed his chief on the dog's Jap-smelling history and finally persuaded him that the dog was as ideal protection as he could possibly have. Even a Marine, he pointed out, couldn't smell Japs. The Marine, cursing all dogs, was sent back to troops. Admiral Boatwright was happy to have that man-power problem off his conscience.

Every morning between five and six the dog would trail the admiral as he crashed through the boondocks on his constitutional.

It was a fine arrangement for three weeks; then the dog disappeared.

It happened as Admiral Boatwright emerged from a section of unusually thick underbrush into the clear and became aware that the dog was no longer with him. He waited a moment, thinking the dog had held back to do some exploring. When he didn't show, the admiral retraced his steps. He searched for two hours, shouting, 'Oh, Magellan!' at intervals. It was the only time anyone had ever known Admiral Boatwright to be late for work. At Headquarters the first thing he did was to send a platoon of Marines over the route he had gone that morning. The Marine platoon, whose previous experience had been limited to H-hour assaults on Tarawa, Saipan, and Iwo Jima, failed to turn up a trace of the dog. Admiral Boatwright promptly had a notice mimeographed and distributed by the hundreds all over the island. It began: 'Fm: ComFleets. To: All Hands on Tulura. Subject: Dog, Missing. One dog belonging to D. D. Boatwright, Vice-Admiral, USN, has disappeared. Name: Magellan. Colour: Reddish-brown and curly. Size: Knee-high. Large ears, long tail. Breed: Indefinite' – and went on to direct anyone getting a scent of his whereabouts to report same to the admiral.

A week later a Seabee carpenter's mate showed up at Admiral Boatwright's office. He had seen a dog answering the description in a native village. That same evening Admiral Boatwright drove over for a look. He took with him the Seabee and also Ensign Max Siegel, who joined the entourage after Boatwright sent a crisp word to the Public Relations Section.

'In case you've got one officer, among your legions over there, who can speak any Tuluran,' the admiral's note went, 'send him over. Have important mission in Tuluran village this evening.'

Though most Tulurans on Tulura spoke at least some American, Admiral Boatwright logistically wanted a Tuluran-speaking officer along in case the dealings over the dog should get complicated.

Lieutenant-Commander Nash was enormously gratified to be able to reply in the affirmative to the admiral's note. Before sending Siegel to the admiral he briefed him carefully in manners.

'I have no idea what the admiral wants you for – probably something to do with Navy–Tuluran relations,' the exec said, 'but I want you to be extremely careful every word you say, Siegel, you hear me? Admiral Boatwright is one of the greatest crosses we in Public Relations have to bear. He's utterly unpublic-relations-minded. One of those old-fashioned naval types, fast disappearing, thank the Lord, who thinks a Navy is merely a collection of ships.'

'A remarkably provincial attitude,' Ensign Siegel said soberly.

'Isn't it?' the exec said. 'Now, for heaven's sake don't say anything to ruffle him. Try to be a credit to Public Relations.'

'I'll do my best, Commander,' Ensign Siegel said.

'You'd better,' the exec warned. 'And if you see an opening, get in a word on how important we are here. Something that will impress him.'

'I'm sure that would,' Ensign Siegel said gravely.

A couple of hours before dusk the party of four took off for the village where the dog Magellan had allegedly been sighted, the admiral riding in the front of the jeep with the boatswain's-mate driver, Siegel, who had now been briefed on the mission, and the Seabee in back. As they drove along, Siegel reflected how anywhere in the Navy but here it would be unheard of that an ensign should have any dealings with an admiral, or even get within twenty feet of one. It was a measure of his rapid adjustment to the Tulura scheme of things that he felt no self-consciousness whatsoever about jeeping along with three stars. Indeed, Siegel found himself charmed from the first word by the admiral.

'You're one of those Public Relations oddballs, aren't you?' was the first word.

'Yes, sir,' Siegel said.

'What a collection of freaks!' the admiral said.

'Yes, sir,' Ensign Siegel said.

'They've got everything but the bearded lady!' the admiral said.

'I think there may even be one of those, sir,' Siegel said. 'She represents a chain of Texas newspapers.'

'My God!' the admiral said. 'Is there one newspaper in Texas which doesn't have somebody out here?'

'The Navy has been able to dig up one, I think, sir,' Siegel said. 'A paper in Whitesboro, Texas. But I think the Whitesboro *County Clarion* man is due out here next week.'

'My God!' the admiral said. 'Sometimes I get the damndest feeling. It's that we're fighting the war not to lick the Japs but to provide fodder for those multitudes of typewriter mechanics over there. What an outrageous logistic waste that booby-hatch is!'

The admiral, turning in his seat, looked hard at Ensign Siegel. 'I don't see how any self-respecting naval officer can stay there,' he said.

'Yes, sir,' Ensign Siegel said.

'But of course I hardly consider a Public Relations officer a naval officer at all. I consider him a freak,' the admiral said frankly, looking at Siegel.

'Yes, sir,' Ensign Siegel said.

'Oddballs and freaks,' the admiral repeated.

Abruptly the admiral turned almost entirely around in his seat and leaned over the back of it, facing the ensign. A crafty look came over his face.

'Just between you and me,' he said, 'I've got a plan cooked up. Next island we invade I'm going to put all the correspondents on one ship and all those Public Relations legions over there on another. Then I'm going to issue secret orders to the skipper that will steer the two ships into Tokyo Bay, where the Japs will capture them both and be obliged to take care of all the correspondents and Public Relations oddballs and freaks for the rest of the war. It'll drive the Japs nuts, free our hands to fight the war, and get the war over a year earlier. How about that, son?'

The admiral spoke with such minute and eager craftiness that Ensign Siegel could scarcely be sure whether he was joking or not. Siegel was almost sorry when presently, following the Seabee's directions, they were driving into a Tuluran village. The admiral directed his driver to pull up.

'Same village all right,' the admiral estimated the situation. 'Looks like you did it, lad,' he said to the Seabee. 'If this means I get that dog of mine back,' he said possessively, 'it'll be another Seabee "first" as far as I'm concerned. Now,' he said to the Seabee, 'I think you and Jenkins better just wait here. We don't want to frighten them by too many forces. Son,' he said to Siegel, 'you come along with me.'

The admiral and Siegel climbed out, and with the admiral setting a brisk pace, started walking down the dirt-road main street of the village. It was one of the few villages on the island Siegel hadn't been in before. He spoke greetings in Tuluran to the family clusters sitting on the steps of the thatched houses in the approaching dusk. Surprised, they returned the greetings in friendly manner.

Towards the end of the street Admiral Boatwright, who had been sighting keenly along it all the while, spoke quietly to Siegel.

'Ah,' he said, 'there the boy is.'

The boy was sitting on the step of a hut chewing on a piece of palm-heart and looking happy. As Admiral Boatwright approached and the boy recognized him, his happiness changed to alarm.

'*Rudi busso!*' the boy suddenly shouted.

Out of nowhere Admiral Boatwright felt a familiar grasp on the rear of his pants. He turned and looked down. The dog looked up and caught the admiral's eyes. He looked sheepish, like a man caught AWOL. But he didn't let go.

'Well, so he came back,' said the admiral. 'Isn't that a remarkable feat, son?' he said to Siegel.

'I've never seen anything quite like it,' Siegel said, watching with fascination the dog holding securely to the admiral's pants.

Suddenly a grown Tuluran came running out of the hut and Admiral Boatwright recognized the boy's father.

'Admiral!' The grown Tuluran was almost overcome by the vision of a personal visit to his hut by a U.S. Navy admiral.

'Sorry, Admiral, sir ... the dog, he come back. He miss the boy.' The grown Tuluran waited, then added, 'And the boy miss him ...'

'But your boy's other dog ...' the Admiral said.

The man bowed his head. 'No other dog, Admiral. We were try-ing ... But you take dog. You take dog back. Please!'

'I wouldn't think of it. You should never have let me take him.'

'I guess dog prefer civilian life,' the man said, and lest he be mis-understood, hastily added, 'No reflection on horseshit U.S. Navy!'

'Aren't they a gentle, accommodating people, son?' the admiral said to Siegel.

'They like being friends, sir,' Ensign Siegel said.

The admiral cleared his throat. 'It was my fault,' he said to the father. 'I should never have taken the dog.'

'Not Admiral's fault, Admiral, sir,' said the man, who had grown up surrounded by the Navy. 'Admirals, they don't make faults.'

Admiral Boatwright's lips were creased by a sad smile.

'Admirals make faults, too,' he said. 'Lad,' Admiral Boatwright addressed the little Tuluran, 'if you'll have your friend release me, I'll be going.'

In his excitement over the visit of a U.S. Navy admiral to his hut the father had not noticed that his son's dog was still holding the admiral fast.

'Mario!' he said in some alarm. 'Tell dog let go Admiral's pants.'

'Magellan stay?' the boy said uncertainly.

Admiral Boatwright smiled gently. 'Yes, sonny, Magellan stay.'

'You sure, Captain,' the boy said uncertainly.

'Mario,' the grown Tuluran corrected, 'the Admiral's an admiral!'

'Never mind the rank,' Admiral Boatwright, who was now really anxious to be gone, said, 'just get me loose, son.' He directed Siegel: 'Tell them I really would be – well, unhappy now with the dog.'

Siegel explained the admiral's position in Tuluran to the boy's father, who, enormously pleased to hear a U.S. naval officer speak his language, promptly began to launch into all sorts of conversational matters, having nothing to do with the dog.

'Son,' the admiral cut in crisply after a few minutes, 'how's for cutting the jabber and getting me loose?'

Ensign Siegel, equally engrossed in talking with the grown Tuluran, came out of it suddenly to realize the dog was still in possession of the admiral. Quickly he spoke to the boy in Tuluran, explaining very specifically that the dog was his to keep.

'*Argo busso!*' the boy at last said, and the admiral was free again. The dog whimpered a little and rubbed against the boy's leg. Admiral Boatwright hitched up his pants, which were somewhat drooping now. He patted the little Tuluran on the head. He shook hands with the grown Tuluran, who tried to give back the fifty dollars, which the admiral declined. Then the admiral reached down and for a moment scratched the dog behind the ears. Quickly he turned and walked down the village street, trailed by Siegel, got into his jeep, and drove off.

Next day the Marine, happily snatched from impending glory on Okinawa, had back his old job of walking ten paces behind Admiral Boatwright through the boondocks.

That was all there was to the dog incident, a very trivial thing.

Admiral Boatwright, immersed in planning the Okinawa assault, promptly forgot the whole matter.

Indeed, no one would ever have known about it had not a correspondent for one of the popular slick magazines needed a sale. For months he had been trying to peddle to his editors a piece on Admiral D. D. Boatwright, the great master logistician. The unfeeling bastards in New York, with no notion in their big, fat Madison Avenue foxholes of just what it meant to be the great logistician of the Pacific, probably not knowing what the word meant, and no appreciation of the fact that this man was going to be famous in history, or would be if they just ran a piece on him and paid the correspondent $1,000 for it, kept firing back: 'Subject completely lacking in human interest.'

The correspondent had worked damn hard on the piece and besides he needed a sale pretty badly just then. A dog! By God, a dog had human interest, if a vice-admiral didn't. He decided to track down what was behind the mimeographed notice Boatwright had composed when the dog was lost. He wanted some answers to certain questions in his mind, such as 'Where did the admiral get the dog in the first place?' A Tuluran boy! he discovered. By God, there was human interest for you. A dog! A boy! And a vice-admiral of the U.S. Navy. Even the bastards in New York would have to admit that was a gold-mine of human interest.

The bastards did, and soon the correspondent's entirely fresh treatment of his Boatwright piece, bursting with human or at least dog interest, was on the stands in the United States. About the time the article was out, the wire services and newspaper correspondents also picked up the incident and filed stories.

When the clippings arrived from stateside, Captain Jarvis, the head of the Public Relations Section, shuddered through them and packed the whole batch over to ComFleets. He would not have dared send them to Admiral Boatwright, and it was with some fear and trembling that he sent them to ComFleets.

ComFleets couldn't have been more pleased. With mounting pleasure he read and reread the clippings. Then he sent for Admiral Boatwright. His friend took a seat across the desk, where ComFleets looked at him steadily for several moments. Sombrely he fingered the clippings.

'We have here some newspaper clippings from the States,' he said sternly, 'concerning a recent operation on Tulura.'

'What are those typewriter mechanics up to now?' Admiral Boatwright said.

'Now and then,' said ComFleets, 'the thought crosses my mind that you are not wholeheartedly public-relations-minded.'

Admiral Boatwright, who had known ComFleets since they were midshipmen together at Annapolis, grunted.

'While I had wind of some parts of this operation,' said ComFleets soberly, 'I regret that you didn't see fit to cut me in all the way.'

'What's that?' Admiral Boatwright said, frowning. 'You know I fill you in on everything.'

'This logistics operation involved,' said ComFleets, holding up a clipping, 'the return of a dog.'

The eyebrows of Admiral Boatwright arched a suspicious fraction of an inch.

'There appear to be approximately as many versions of this as there are clippings,' ComFleets said, studying one intently, 'but I presume they all have in mind the same operation. At least they're all about the same admiral.'

ComFleets commenced going through the clippings, picking out sentences at random and reading them off as matter-of-factly as ships' tonnage reports. 'According to the Chicago *Daily News*: "If a popularity contest were held today by the Tuluran children, the prize would be won hands down by a tough old vice-admiral of the U.S. Navy – D. D. Boatwright."

'The Los Angeles *Times* reports: "The admiral had become very attached to the dog when news reached him that the little Tuluran boy from whom he had bought him was wasting away from grief at his loss. Unhesitatingly the admiral rushed the dog to the boy's bedside, where there took place a joyous scene of reunion."

'According to the Atlanta *Constitution*: "One reliable Navy source revealed today that the admiral is planning to adopt the Tuluran boy. 'That way,' said the source, 'he could have both the boy and the dog.'"

'The New Orleans *Times Picayune* feels: "The incident proved that a man can be simultaneously a vice-admiral and a human being."

'And the *American Magazine*: "Up and down Tulura this bluff, crusty Clausewitz of the Pacific is now known affectionately as –"'

ComFleets raised his eyes from the clipping, and looking quietly at his old friend, said in reverential tones, ' "Bow-wow Boatwright!" '

At the phrase, Admiral Boatwright, who had sat stunned and disbelieving during the recital, leaped forward and seized the clippings. As he swept through them the disbelief was chased away by a purple fury.

' "The *human* admiral"! "Child wasting away from grief"! "Going to adopt the child"! ' His mouth seized on the phrases as he riffled through the clippings and flung them to the floor. ' "An admiral secretly nuts about Tuluran boys – and dogs." '

ComFleets grabbed up a couple of clippings and began reciting phrases himself. ' "Dog-loving admiral" … "mad about dogs" – it sounds as if you were the founder and guiding spirit of the SPCA. "Admiral takes time off from busy war" – oh, my, "busy war" – "to return dog to Tuluran child." Wow! Bow-wow!'

And ComFleets collapsed into his chair in helpless laughter.

'Slop!' Admiral Boatwright let out an infuriated bellow. 'This is the mushiest pack of slop, fabrications, distortions, exaggerations, and outright lies in the history of the American Navy! I'll confine them to their quarters! I'll break them! I'll courtmartial them! I'll ship the last one of them back to the States …'

ComFleets pulled himself up in his chair and wiped the tears from his eyes.

'Boats, can't you see? You're famous. A hundred and fifty million Americans suddenly know all about you. Not anything about your Navy career, naturally. But they know you're daffy about dogs and kids. Just like you were *human*!'

Admiral Boatwright dropped into his chair. His teeth ground audibly against each other. His white-knuckled fists seized the clippings one by one and wadded them.

'They're trying to make a fool of me. These goddamn correspondents have it in for me.'

'Fool?' ComFleets exclaimed. 'They've made a hero out of you! More so than if you'd sunk the entire Jap fleet with a single PT boat! Boats, you're in! You've got glamour! You're a character! You're the *human* admiral.'

Suddenly Admiral Boatwright's fingers, which were squeezed around a clipping, relaxed; the clipping fell gently to the floor. His taut frame unloosened until it rested back in the chair. His face coloured down from deep purple to its normal ruddiness and he rubbed his hand across it. He gave a mirthless laugh.

'So that's the way it's done, is it? That – I mean, translating it quickly, that's how you get the kind of Navy you want. My sweet Jesus!'

ComFleets studied his friend carefully for several seconds. Then his own features slowly lighted up in triumph.

'Boats,' he said, 'you have just discovered the greatest logistics secret of your career.'

A couple of nights later the officers' club was startled to see Admiral Boatwright walk in, amiably greet several correspondents standing at the bar, order a drink, and spend a tactical quarter-hour, no longer, chatting with them.

Three days after that Admiral Boatwright dropped over to the correspondents' room in the Public Relations building, sat down a few minutes, and breezed about nothing with some of the reporters.

Not until his next Press conference soon thereafter, however, did the correspondents believe it.

'Bow-wow,' a correspondent asked the admiral, 'what is your estimate of the length of time it will require to take Okinawa?'

No one laughed. It was the first time Admiral Boatwright had been addressed as anything but Admiral. A death-quietness held the room, and a terrible tension as the correspondents waited.

Admiral Boatwright fixed his questioner in the eye a moment, then quietly replied, 'That's a good question, Jack. I would say ...'

It was the first time Admiral Boatwright had ever addressed a correspondent by his first name. From being a complete unknown to the U.S. public, Bow-wow Boatwright thereafter steadily remained one of the most widely – and favourably – publicized admirals in the Pacific Ocean. Logistically, everyone agreed, it was a very fortunate thing, for the Navy really needed Vice-Admiral Boatwright.

MELORA 2: *Never Mind the Frangipani*

'Who is she?' Ensign Siegel said.

It was the first day, so snowed had Siegel been with VIPs, that he had been able to get back to the village of Tanalolo since taking Congressmen Janson and Smithfield there a week ago.

'Who is who?' Mr Seguro said. 'Just a moment.'

The old man disappeared inside the house and was back presently with an unopened jug of palm toddy. He uncorked it and passed the jug to Siegel.

'Try this,' he said.

Ensign Siegel took a swig.

'I think this is the best I've had,' he said, passing the jug back to the old man.

'Old stock,' the old man explained, taking some himself. 'We made it two months ago.'

'Who was that girl we were talking to last week?' Ensign Siegel said.

'Last week?' Mr Seguro said.

'Last week when I brought the two congressmen here,' Ensign Siegel said.

'The two congressmen?' the old man said.

'Yes, that girl we were talking to right here,' Ensign Siegel said, a little impatiently.

'That girl you were talking to?' the old man said. 'What girl were you talking to?'

'That's what I want to know,' Ensign Siegel said impatiently. He turned to the old man. 'Now, Mr Seguro,' he said very slowly. 'Last week I brought two congressmen over here. One of them was wearing a white suit and the other a red shirt with green palm trees on it. While we were talking right here in front of this porch a girl came along. Now' – Siegel breathed hard – 'my question, Mr Seguro, is, *who* was that girl?'

'You mean those men in the costumes?' the old man said. 'They very important men in Yew-nited States?'

'Yes,' Ensign Siegel said shortly. 'Congressmen are pretty important people.'

'They all wear costumes like that?' the old man said.

'Sometimes,' Ensign Siegel said, trying to hold his temper. 'Now who was she, Mr Seguro?'

'Who's that?' the old man said.

'The girl, for heaven's sake!' Ensign Siegel burst out. 'That girl who came down the road.'

'The girl that came down the road?' the old man said. 'Which girl would that have been, En-sine?'

'There weren't six or seven of them, Mr Seguro. Give me some of that palm toddy,' Ensign Siegel said, his lips taut.

Siegel drank off three long gurgles.

'Now, Mr Seguro,' he said, 'who was that girl that came down the road while you and I and the congressmen were standing right here talking and then she stopped and you and the girl talked and then the congressmen and I talked to her.'

'Oh-h-h,' the old man said, his eyes lighting up in comprehension. 'Why didn't you say so? Why, you must mean Melora.'

Ensign Siegel took a deep breath. 'Now, *who* is Melora?'

'Who is she?' the old man said. 'Why, she's a Tuluran girl.'

Ensign Siegel's hands clenched. He clasped them restrictively on his lap.

'I gathered that,' he said very softly, with great effort. 'I didn't think she came from Australia.'

'Well, you're wrong about that,' the old man said reprovingly. 'Australia is exactly where she came from.'

Ensign Siegel's eyes glared at the old man.

'My, what a lovely day,' the old man said, sighing contentedly. 'The frangipani are in bloom.'

'Never mind the frangipani,' Ensign Siegel said curtly, finding it very difficult to remember that he had always been attracted by the Tuluran refusal to be hurried. 'Now, what's this thing about Australia?'

'Just that you were completely wrong about Melora not coming from Australia,' the old man said righteously.

'All right, I was wrong, Mr Seguro,' Siegel made his confession. 'I didn't mean to contradict you.'

'You see, I know the facts,' the old man said pontifically, 'and you don't.'

'That's certainly the truth,' Ensign Siegel said, sighing heavily.

They drank for three or four minutes without saying a word.

'Those frangipani certainly are lovely,' Ensign Siegel said finally.

'Frangipani?' the old man said. 'I thought you wanted to know about Melora.'

Ensign Siegel felt unable to speak. He took a slug of palm toddy.

Suddenly the old man began to rattle off information. 'Melora was in Australia about a month ago on her way back to Tulura. She had been away from Tulura for about four years and we were all very happy to see her back. She had been in Europe,' the old man stated matter-of-factly, 'for four years.'

'Europe!' Siegel exclaimed.

'Europe is over beyond China,' the old man explained to the ensign.

'What in the world was she doing in Europe?' Siegel asked.

'Why, she was going to school, of course,' the old man said, a little disgusted at the stupidity of the question. 'Madrid – that's in Spain,' the old man said, educationally.

'How'd she happen to get to go to school there?' Siegel said.

'Get to go to school there?' the old man said disgustedly. 'Why, she couldn't go any place else. She's an Alba. All the Albas go to school in Spain.'

'Who are the Albas?' Siegel asked.

The old man looked incredulously at the ensign. 'You mean you don't know who the Albas are?'

'Well, I haven't been here very long, Mr Seguro,' Siegel said apologetically.

The old man shook his head. 'Just the same, you should have heard of the Albas. They're the most important family on Tulura. Any time anybody's in trouble they go to the Albas and the Albas take care of it. Yes, sir! They trace their ancestry to Admiral Ruiz de Mendoza.'

'Oh, I've heard of him,' Ensign Siegel said.

'What a lovely day,' Mr Seguro said. 'The sweet acacia should be out any day now.'

'Now, about Melora,' Ensign Siegel said, hurriedly bringing the old man back to the subject. '… Uh, where does she live?'

'Two miles out in the country,' the old man said. He eyed the ensign critically. 'What do you want to know that for?'

'Why, I just thought I might call on her,' Ensign Siegel said.

'I wouldn't waste my time if I were you,' the old man said. 'They wouldn't let you in the door. They're an old family and very particular.'

'But I am an officer of the United States Navy,' Ensign Siegel said.

'Doesn't mean a thing,' the old man dismissed this. 'Her people are the highest type of family. She was educated in Europe, remember.'

'Yes, I remember that,' Ensign Siegel said.

For a few moments they sat there. Finally Ensign Siegel said, 'Mr Seguro, I really would like to see her again.'

The old man turned and looked at the ensign. Then, suddenly, because he liked Siegel, he seemed to be seeking a way, in spite of what he obviously considered the monstrous obstacles.

'You weren't educated in Europe, were you?' he tried.

'No, I'm afraid not,' Ensign Siegel admitted. 'But I did go to a pretty well-known American school. Harvard.'

'Hair-vard?' the old man said. 'Never heard of it,' he said, as if he were an authority on the better schools.

'Maybe you could ask the Albas if they have,' Ensign Siegel suggested.

'Doubt if they have.' The old man dashed this idea. 'I once heard Mr Alba say Americans are very nice people but there's not a chance in the world of being educated there. You learn Tuluran at Hairvard?' The old man sought a way out.

'No, they don't teach it there,' Ensign Siegel said. 'I learned it right here.'

'Must not be much of a school if they don't teach Tuluran,' the old man said.

The ensign and the Tuluran had some more palm toddy, and sat thoughtfully. Finally the old man sighed and shook his head hopelessly.

'No, I'm afraid there's nothing we can do. Mr Alba would be very angry with me if I introduced you to Melora.' The old man sighed again. 'Ah, that Melora,' he said. 'She is such a smart girl. So much up here,' the old man said, tapping his head. 'She does so much for our children. She wants them all to be very smart. She wants them to learn everything.'

'Your children?' Ensign Siegel said quizzically. 'Why is she so interested in the children?'

'Why is she so interested?' Mr Seguro said, in astonishment at such a stupid question. 'What's so strange about the school-teacher being interested in children? I don't know how it is in the Yew-nited States, but out here our school-teachers are very interested in the chil ...'

'School-teacher!' Ensign Siegel shouted. 'You mean all the time we've been sitting here she's been just a block down the road?' he said, almost beside himself.

'Where else would a school-teacher be, but in the school,' Mr Seguro said logically. 'I don't know how it is in Yew-nited States, but here ...'

'Goodbye, Mr Seguro!' Ensign Siegel was half-way down the step. 'Thanks for the palm toddy!' he shouted back over his shoulder as he headed down the road towards the schoolhouse.

Three: Thinking Big

ENSIGN MAX SIEGEL and Lieutenant Morey Griffin shared a room on the second floor of BOQ (Bachelor Officers' Quarters) 4, not that there was an MOQ (Married Officers' Quarters) within 3,000 miles. Both Siegel and Griffin had experienced sea duty, Siegel on destroyers and Griffin on a minesweeper, making them almost the only two officers at Public Relations Headquarters who had ventured offshore. They got along well, even though aside from their seafaring past they had almost nothing in common.

Ensign Siegel was one of the most relaxed men you could have found in the war. Nearly everyone in the Public Relations Section liked the duty, naturally; but there were three or four itchy young officers who were always trying to get sea duty. None of them had ever heard a shot fired in anger. That was the difference, of course. Max had participated in five combat operations, and in the last one his destroyer had been torpedoed from under him – a combat record which in the Public Relations Section on Tulura was unique.

As a Correspondents' Aide, Max had one of the few full-time jobs in Public Relations. His job meant going out to the airfield to meet a new correspondent, seeing that the correspondent got a room in the correspondents' BOQ, got fresh sheets and towels, got a mess card, a ship's service card, a liquor card, sets of khaki shorts and short-sleeved shirts, field shoes, sun-helmet, and sun-glasses, making sure he took his sick-bay shots, taking him on an orientation tour of the island's naval installations and Tuluran villages, arranging travel orders for off the island, setting up interviews with admirals and Navy heroes, getting his typewriter fixed if it broke down – in general, ministering to all the correspondent's needs and requirements. It meant similar things for other civilian visitors to ComFleets Headquarters – parties of congressmen, editors, and publishers, business wheels, labour chieftains, and others who regularly dropped in to check up on the war.

Each of these parties was accorded the VIP treatment, which appropriately varied, however, according to rank. Ordinary congressmen, for example, were met by, in addition to a Correspondents' Aide, a captain and a station wagon and given corner rooms in the VIP BOQ, while a congressman who happened to be a member of the Naval Affairs Committee was met by flag rank and a Buick and put up in the guest-room in the cottage of ComFleets. When Tulura was alerted that the chairman of the Senate Naval Affairs Committee was en route, the preparations took on the aspects of those for the Second Coming, and indeed the code word for this visitor was 'God'. 'ETA for God is 1400', a report might go, or a planning conference might raise the point of who should be invited to the cocktail party the admiral was throwing for God.

Max was not a man to be overawed by senators and representatives. Before a tour he would pull his jeep up in front of the VIP BOQ, stride inside, and bellow down the corridor: 'All members of Congress! Front and centre!' Congressmen's faces, startled and angry at this cavalier method of addressing the nation's law-makers, would pop out of doors. Then Max would erase the expressions and have the congressmen bursting from their rooms by booming: 'Pictures!' As they clustered voraciously around him, he would pull the 11 × 14 blow-ups one by one from a large envelope and pass them out. 'You, Congressman Jones, astride a submarine! You, Congressman Brown, morale-building our boys at the Fleet Hospital! You, Congressman Smith, giving Admiral Boatwright the word on naval strategy!' The congressmen would be so carried away by the pictures, which made the best kind of campaign material back home, that they wouldn't be paying too much attention to Max's comments as he distributed the pictures. 'Of course, this service means a new shipment of film will be needed. Another ship tied up on non-essentials! But nothing's too good for our constituents. Right, men? Gentlemen! The admiral is waiting to mesmerize you! Let us not hold up the war by too lengthy narcissistic looking at pictures!'

Before they knew what had hit them, Max would have the congressmen in a jeep and buzzing up the hill to a briefing by the admiral, getting them in a good mood on the way by telling them some joke, such as the one about the two admirals asking each other what was the most embarrassing moment in their life. Or if he felt he'd gone rather far and they were starting off on a trip around the island, he'd dial their minds to other matters by issuing steel helmets to all the congressmen with the word, spoken in the tones of someone reading off a casualty list: 'Gentlemen, I don't want unduly to alarm you, but we'll be driving through a boondocks area where several dangerous Japs have been flushed lately. Only last week three men were killed and their bodies mutilated in an ambush on the road we'll be taking.' Tulura was safer than Park Avenue on a Sunday afternoon, but Max was able to communicate to the congressmen on a sight-seeing tour the feeling that they were practically in a forward Marine platoon.

'That vicarious sense of fear is good for them,' Max used to say. 'They take home at least a little of what it is to be scared by a Jap in the bushes.'

The main thing the congressmen wanted to see, however, was neither the bushes nor the war efforts nor the admirals nor the Tulurans. What they wanted to see was represented in one congressman's standard opening line on visiting a new installation: 'Is anybody here from West Virginia?' Most of all they wanted to see men from their own states or districts, voting age or not – an eighteen-year-old might have fifty registered relatives at home and might drop a line mentioning how Congressman White had dropped in to see him. The Seabees were notoriously the most versatile organization in the war and they proved it nowhere better than here. Tented on a hill about four miles from Headquarters was a Seabee battalion which Max made a regular stop for any visiting congressman. Max would have found out long ahead of time, from a copy of the Congressional Directory he had sent off for, which district in which state the congressman represented. He had also sent off for those W.P.A. state guidebooks which describe in such detail the population, industry, history, and the like of all the towns and villages in a state.

A few days before the congressman arrived, Max would jeep over to the Seabee battalion. He would appoint a half-dozen men to be residents of various towns in the congressman's district and hand out to the men scripts excerpted from the guidebook, setting forth pertinent facts about their respective towns. The day before the congressman's visit, Max would return and hold a dress rehearsal, quizzing each man on facts about his assigned home town and even suggesting regional accents. If it was a senator, he would have a dozen men lined up. Congressmen and senators were overwhelmed to find this goldmine of voters from their districts or states and, thanks to Max Siegel, came away from their visit to Tulura with a very warm feeling. One Seabee, a shipfitter second class, had a record of having been from fourteen states and nineteen congressional districts. It was no idle boast, that famous Seabee motto: 'Can do!'

Max Siegel was very popular with both officers and enlisted men, as anyone who can make people laugh is likely to be popular. If the enlisted men genuinely disliked to stand with him the all-night Public Relations watch that rotated once a month among the junior officers, it wasn't that they didn't like being with Max, who was always vastly entertaining, besides having absolutely no sense of caste. What they hated was having to wake him in the morning. The Junior O.O.D. came on at 2000 and turned in at midnight on a cot in the Media Section downstairs. The enlisted man on watch stayed awake to summon him in case of an air raid or a correspondent wanting something, and to awaken him anyhow at 0700. Max was a dangerous man to awaken, his huge body smashing about and rumbling threateningly when anyone tried it. It always took at least ten minutes to do it, and the contortions on his face, Max being an almost spectacularly ugly man, were a chilling sight in the eerie dawn and the empty building; besides which the enlisted man had to be very agile to avoid a bruised arm or bloodied nose. It was somewhat like entering a cage and shaking awake a sleeping gorilla, though the instant he got really awake Max was as friendly as a beagle pup.

One night a month Max Siegel drank two bottles of whisky and one of burgundy. Once a month the officers drew their take-home liquor rations, consisting of the two bottles of whisky – choice of Four Roses or Paul Jones – and their choice of a bottle of either burgundy or sherry. This was in addition to the drinks at the officers' club, where all month long you could have all you wanted at the bar, at five cents a drink. Most of the officers spread their three bottles over the thirty days for room-drinking. But Max Siegel would start drinking in his room about seven o'clock on the night of ration day and by early in the morning would have drained the three-fifths. He showed almost no effects from the first bottle, which he would have finished by around ten o'clock. Even the second bottle of Four Roses or Paul Jones would produce little noticeable change in him. He would kill that one by midnight. Not until he started on the burgundy, which he always chose instead of sherry, would he begin to get looped. Sometimes, when the liquor and burgundy were all gone, he would top the evening off with a few shots of palm toddy. Max's room would be open to all comers that night and a large number of officers would drop by, to gaze in awe at Max's drinking and to listen to Max hold forth on subjects ranging from the symbolic meaning of the Stock Exchange, based on his six months in his uncle's brokerage firm before going in the Navy, to the emotional complexion of the Tulurans, to the future of Public Relations in the military services. He foresaw the day when there would be one Public Relations officer for each combat man in the Navy, and the fleet commanded by the president of the Associated Press, with a six-star rank of Admiral-Admiral, who would decide on operations solely on the basis of their news value, with transmission ships occupied by nothing but correspondents, with no operational dispatches being permitted until the fleet was wiped out to provide a good news item.

Siegel considered his Navy work fascinating, if unusual from a naval point of view. The job of Correspondents' Aide got on some officers' nerves, having to serve as everything from bellhop to nursemaid for a crew of individualistic, often highly temperamental civilians. Some of the Public Relations officers actually came to hate all correspondents with that bitter, unreasoning hatred which the civilian recently put in uniform can have for the un-uniformed civilian who begins to make demands on him and who sometimes even makes ugly allusions that if he were put on a ship he would run it aground in five minutes. The job never got on Max's nerves. He considered the correspondents interesting specimens.

Lieutenant Morey Griffin had been a rewrite man on a San Francisco newspaper before the war. In contrast to Siegel, he was the idlest man on Tulura, which is saying plenty. He worked in the Media Section, which meant his job was to get out Press releases and scare up naval heroes for the correspondents to interview. But there were so many other officers in the same section doing these things, that the available Press release and hero material was greatly out-numbered by the Public Relations officers available to handle it. Morey felt no inclination to compete for the work, and so he led a life almost totally devoid of labour of any kind. Every morning he got out of bed at eight forty-five, just in time to get to the chow-hall, a couple of hundred yards away, at eight fifty-five, five minutes be-fore the hall closed admissions for breakfast. Once in, an officer could take as long as he liked. Finishing his breakfast at about ten o'clock, Griffin then returned to his BOQ room, shaved and showered leisurely, then walked up the hill to the Public Relations Head-quarters – hitching a jeep ride, if he could, for the distance of about three city blocks. Stopping in the correspondents' room, he gathered up the latest newspapers from the States, which the Public Relations Section subscribed to by the dozen, and either read them there or car-ried a batch through the swinging door to the adjoining Media room and read them at his desk. This easily filled his time until noon.

At twelve Morey rose from his desk and with some of the other officers wandered on down to the chow-hall. Sometimes he stopped by his BOQ room first and mixed a pre-lunch cocktail from his monthly rations – the officers' bar did not open until five o'clock, a time schedule Morey was constantly complaining about. Finishing chow between one and one-thirty, he returned to his room, took off his clothes, and sacked out until about three-thirty. Then he dressed and dropped by the Fleet Library and checked out his daily mystery, went back up to his office, and read or breezed with the correspon-dents for another hour. At four-thirty he returned to his room, took another shower, and promptly at five o'clock appeared at the bar, where he was always the first officer in.

Even on Tulura, Ensign Siegel was amazed at this perfection of idleness.

'Of course no one here puts in a full day's work,' Siegel occasion-ally mentioned to his room-mate. 'But it's pretty remarkable, Griffin, how an officer of the Navy can get by – at least in time of war – with doing nothing. I mean absolutely *nothing*.'

'Well, they've got plenty of help up there without me,' Griffin said. 'I'm sacking out for the duration. If they need me, they can come wake me up.'

Morey did have one remaining wartime ambition, which was to get assigned to Sydney, Australia, as United States Navy Public Relations liaison officer to His Majesty's Royal Navy. No such billet even existed at present.

'Why, we're practically snubbing our chief ally – the British people,' Morey often pointed out. 'I mean, the British having a liaison officer here and us not having the common decency to reciprocate. Why, it's practically a slap in the face. The Badger, I might say, agreed a hundred per cent with me when I pointed out the situation to him the other day. That's off the record. The Badger can't be put in a position of criticizing British–American relations.'

The Badger was Lieutenant-Commander O. S. B. Badgett, RNVR, His Majesty's Public Relations liaison officer to ComFleets Headquarters on Tulura. He was named for one of those magnificent beards that only members of His Majesty's Navy seemed capable of raising.

'Non-reciprocation is a hell of a way to treat your allies,' Griffin said.

'But it's an entirely different situation,' Ensign Siegel once pointed out to Griffin. 'We got a lot of British correspondents gassing in and out of here for the Badger to worry about. There are practically no American correspondents with the British fleet.'

'That's a mere technicality,' Morey Griffin said. 'It's the *principle* of the thing.'

Morey Griffin's concern about British–American relations had really originated one night in the officers' club, when he and Siegel were standing at the bar. Over the rum sours Morey was volleying off a barrage of gripes, of which he always had a plentiful store despite the resort-like nature of his life. The subjects that night were Morey's favourite ones – what a jerk Lieutenant-Commander 'Marblehead' Nash was and how life without a woman was twisting his personality, probably incurably.

'Somehow,' Griffin said, 'I can't believe that that crossbreed between a stock-ticker and a naval dictionary exists; anyhow, that he's in that job. Even the Navy personnel system couldn't make a mistake like that. It's sort of like you picked up the papers, and read that one of the Jukes boys had been made president of U.S. Steel.'

'We really have it rough, don't we, Griffin?' Siegel said. 'Especially you.'

'Long as I'm here, Chaplain,' Griffin said, 'I might as well spit it out. I jes' don't think I can stand it one night longer unless I gets meself a piece of tail. Every night I clobber my pillow and cry myself to sleep. Tail! Ten years of my life for one small tender piece of tail!'

Whoever coined the remark, 'You never think about anything but sex', must have been talking to Morey Griffin. One wall of Griffin's and Siegel's BOQ room was almost covered with marks indicating the days since Griffin had last had sex. A fresh mark went up each day with a hashmark for each fifth day. Morey Griffin could be amusing, but that night Siegel was a little tired from having met four different parties of visitors at the airfield while Griffin was sacking out. He wanted to forget about Nash, and talking about women, he felt right then, wasn't going to genie them up like Aladdin's lamp or something. So he was glad when they were joined by a couple of strangers. They were both ensigns, were very blond and handsome, looked about seventeen years old – and of course wore wings.

After a round the fly-boys mentioned that they were fresh from a stop-over at Sydney, Australia.

'As a Texas boy,' one said in a drawl that made this identification redundant, 'ah've always held that the most beautiful women on earth were to be seen on the streets of Dal-las. But then ah hadn't seen Sydney!'

Griffin's eyes took on a hungry look which invited the pilot to tell more.

'But what makes it really rugged, friend, is that in Sydney there's a *man* shortage.'

'I can't believe such a condition exists anywhere,' Morey said. 'But go on, young fellow.'

'Fact!' the Texan said. 'A really critical *man* shortage. Y'see, practically every Aussie man who can *do* it is off fightin' the war, and ah'm tellin' you, it's really *pitiful* about those women. Thousands of gorgeous, luscious, sexy Aussie women! Man, they corner you in bars, cut in on other dames at dances, drag you off the streets. They've gone plumb crazy!'

Griffin gulped down his drink and ordered another round, plunking down twenty cents to pay for the four drinks. His hand was trembling as he lifted his fresh rum sour.

'Go on, son,' he said grimly.

The pilot looked Griffin in the eye. 'You know what they need in Sydney?'

'I can guess,' Griffin croaked, 'but you tell me, son. I like the sound of your voice.'

'Studs.' The pilot set his glass down hard on the bar. 'They need a few hundred good *studs* – preferably from the U-nited States Navy. It's like the song says.' The pilot's young tenor rose in 'The Battle Hymn of the Republic', the music, that is, of the great Civil War hymn, though with different words:

> *A rapid trip to Sydney is a very urgent need,*
> *You can't deprive the Navy of its ancient right to breed,*
> *So send us down to Sydney and we'll sow the merry seed*
> *While the Air Force wins the war …*

'Yikes!' the pilot said in joyous memory. He raised high his rum sour. 'Friends, ah give you the women of Sydney! The wild women, man-hungry women of Sydney!'

'I don't think I'm going to be able to sleep tonight,' Griffin said mournfully, feebly raising his own glass. 'For today I'm going to put two marks on my wall.'

Not long after that Griffin began to be seen a great deal in the Badger's company. He even took up handball, the Badger's favourite game, although Griffin detested any form of exercise. Soon, every afternoon, Griffin could be seen out on the handball courts, which adjoined the tennis-courts, slapping the ball around with the Badger.

'It's obvious,' Griffin once confided to Siegel, 'that if they do send anyone to Sydney they'll have to consult the Badger.'

'Well, I never thought I'd see you playing handball,' Siegel said. 'It means you're actually doing something for thirty minutes a day.'

Otherwise Griffin's idleness remained unchanged, except that he now had a reason for it. 'I'm saving my strength for Sydney,' he explained to Siegel.

'You are getting pretty old, I guess,' Siegel said. Griffin, at thirty-five, ranked Siegel in age by ten years. 'I guess a man of your age does need to hoard his energies for being United States boudoir liaison officer in Sydney.'

All in all, Ensign Max Siegel and Lieutenant Morey Griffin hardly seemed two officers likely to get court-martialled. It all began at one of the daily conferences of Public Relations officers.

'It isn't the admirals that the people back in Little Falls, Michigan, give a toot about,' Lieutenant-Commander Nash said. 'Not the captains, the commanders, lieutenant-commanders! Not even – except a little so – the lieutenants, the lieutenants junior grade, and the ensigns! You know who it is the American people are dying to hear about?'

'Who's that?' asked Lieutenant-Commander Wayne Hereford.

'The enlisted man!' the exec burst forth. 'The little guy who used to play left guard on the high-school eleven, or jerk sodas down at the corner drug-store. The civilian in uniform! Joe Blow of Kokomo!'

The exec swivelled furiously in his chair, then bringing it to a stop, leaned intently forward.

'What we need, Sailors, is a department consecrated to one vision – telling the people at home, mainly the small papers, the bi-weeklies, the weeklies, the little dailies, about their sons, husbands, and fathers, manning the ships and the bases. A Home Town News Department! A Joe Blow Department!'

'What an exciting idea!' Hereford said. 'But tell me, Commander – who's going to give us the raw material for stories about enlisted men? There are so many of them!'

'A good question!' the exec said. 'But I've thought of it. I propose that we instigate an entirely new duty aboard each naval vessel – a Home Town News or Joe Blow officer. This officer will feed news about the Joe Blows on his respective ship into us here. We'll process it! Then we'll forward it back to the respective home-town paper in the States!'

'You mean that there'd be an additional officer put aboard each ship just to write up news items about the crew?' a voice spoke slowly from the second row. It was Lieutenant Morey Griffin. 'I don't know about other ships, but there isn't room for another officer on a minesweeper. No place for him to sleep, Commander.'

'I've thought of all that!' said Nash, with a little irritation. Selecting a paper-clip from his three-inch-shell tray, he aimed it for the wastebasket. It missed. 'No, we wouldn't put any more officers aboard. Simply, we would do this: We would direct the commanding officer of each ship to designate one officer in his complement to be the Home Town News officer in addition to his other duties. The gunnery officer, the navigation officer, or whatever officer he pleased. We'd leave that part of it up to the skipper – since he knows his own officers' qualifications best.'

'On a minesweeper,' said Griffin, 'those guys are pretty busy with their regular duties of running the ship. I don't know how they'd take to having to dig out and write up news items about the crew when they were off watch.'

'Nonsense,' said Commander Nash, aiming another paper-clip for the wastebasket – it hit. 'I was out on a ship once – the *General John F. Kay* was her name – voyaging from San Francisco to Tulura,' he said, glancing attestingly at his 'Golden Dragon' diploma on the wall. 'Most of the officers spend most of their time lolling around the wardroom drinking coffee. They have lots of time.'

'Anyhow,' said Griffin, 'I doubt if most of them know a news item from a hole in the ground.'

'I'm glad to hear you making these objections, Griffin,' Nash said evenly. He picked up a pencil and began to tap it ominously on his head, the bald sounding-board bouncing a staccato, Morse-code-like noise around the room. It was a noise the officers knew as a sign the exec's level of irritation had begun to take a strain. 'The devil's advocate, eh, Griffin? I realize naturally that you don't have many professional journalists aboard ship. One thing I thought of was to fetch the officers the commanding officers appointed as additional-duty Joe Blow officers into Tulura – or even to the States – for a special intensive course in journalism.'

'That would make the job popular anyhow,' said Griffin. 'For a tour of duty at a journalism school in Frisco, the captain would probably appoint himself to the job ...'

The exec, yanking *Navy Regulations* from his desk library, banged it on his desk, the deafening impact effectively cutting Griffin off.

'Belay that negative attitude, Griffin!' he thundered. 'Must you always take advantage of the fact that I try not to run too taut a ship here? Now, let's watch it, or I will start getting taut. I realized that taking an officer off each ship for this journalism course might leave some ships short-officered, even if temporarily. So I killed that idea at birth. What we'll do is to mimeograph up forms and ship them out to the ships. We'll leave spaces for Name! Rate! Home Town! Age!

Colour of Hair and Eyes! – so we can work in a little description, a little colour for the sake of realistic writing – Hobby! and the like, and then a big space for "New Items" about the man. All the Joe Blow officer'll have to do will be to fill in the spaces. You don't need any journalistic experience just to fill in spaces. We'll do the rest. Simple, isn't it?'

'It sure is,' Griffin said.

'I think the idea sparkles,' said Lieutenant-Commander Hereford.

'I think the idea is four O, Commander,' said Lieutenant-Commander Arnold Gladney. 'To me it's anachronistic that though there are more enlisted men than officers out here – except, of course, in such highly specialized duties as us here in Public Relations – there is vastly more news coming out of the Pacific about officers than enlisted men. That's a real mathematical anachronism,' he said, puzzled. 'Though I see why,' he added brightly. 'Civilian correspondents are interested mostly in names – officers, naturally.'

'Naturally,' said Nash. 'Civilian correspondents have to be concerned about the big picture. That means officers. After all, officers think up and give the commands which make the big picture. This new department would be consecrated to the little picture. The little picture,' he repeated with a small glow, pleased with the phrase. 'Now let's look alive!'

The exec leaned down and opened the right bottom drawer of his desk. Carefully he removed his sextant. Sitting back deep in his chair, he cocked his feet on the desk, and raising the sextant, commenced to aim it around the room.

'Sailors,' he said while peering through it, 'I've thrown out the idea to you. All we need now is someone to head up the Joe Blow Department. As a general principle, let me say it must be one of our finest, most energetic officers. Volunteers?'

. No one spoke up. This absence of volunteers arose from the fact, obvious to every officer in the room, that being in charge of the Joe Blow Department would be an onerous job, requiring lots of detail work. It was obvious that it might require six or eight hours' work a day, and no officer cared to let himself in for this.

'I get it,' the exec said presently. 'No one wants to blow his own horn, eh?' He rested his sextant on his lap. 'Well, that's understandable – even commendable. Modesty is the hallmark of a good officer.

76

However, look at it this way. It's going to be one of our most creative departments. Therefore we need a really competent officer for this one. What a challenge! His beat: the Navy's fathomless enlisted-men corps! His mission: to saturate ships and home front with morale by throwing the footlights into the faces of these presently unknown, unsung heroes! I'd love to have the job myself if I didn't have to be exec. Your own command – and, Jupiter, what a command! Probably end up as one of our biggest departments.'

With absorbed concentration the exec examined the ceiling through his sextant for several moments. Still no volunteers spoke up. Then, lowering the sextant, he ranged his eyes over the batteries of officers, starting with the lieutenant-commanders in the first row.

'Two and a half stripes,' he said, 'are just a shade too much rank for even this important a job.'

The exec's eyes moved on to the second row and came to rest on Lieutenant Woodrow Wilson Shoemaker, chief of the Historical Section, a job which consumed perhaps three hours of his day.

'Woodrow cannot, I'm afraid,' the exec said, looking intently at Shoemaker, 'be spared from his present duties. For one thing, I doubt if there's another man – officer, that is – among us who has the proper grounding in history necessary to do a proper job of C.O.'ing the Historical Section. No, Woodrow, you needn't volunteer.'

Shoemaker, who had never opened his mouth or moved a muscle, released an inner sigh. The exec's eyes moved to the next row and rested on Lieutenant (jg) Ross Pendleton, who put in about two hours a day on his Navy job.

'Ross,' the exec said with his usual respect for the former radio producer, 'unless you have some special interest in the job yourself – well, to be forthright about it, I'd really hate to think of trying to handle the radio correspondents without you.'

Pendleton laughed with easy condescension. 'Clinton, this thing just isn't on my level. I wasn't manager of a radio station in Emporia, Kansas.'

The exec, resting back in his chair, gazed thoughtfully at the 'Don't Give Up The Ship!' legend dead ahead of him on the wall.

'You know, Ross,' he said, 'what you just said about Emporia, Kansas, gives me an idea. The officer who heads up this department ought to be a sort of a Joe Blow himself. Doesn't that make sense?

Someone preferably from the great middle belt of America. Someone who was born, bred, and if possible schooled in the guts of America – the Midwest. Now we're getting somewhere. Siegel' – the exec's eyes suddenly slipped to the last row of officers – 'what about you?'

'I was bred, I believe, in the Midwest,' Ensign Siegel said. 'But my folks moved on and I was born in Boston and I went to Harvard.'

'I despise the very idea,' the exec said, puckering his lips distastefully, 'of putting a Harvardite with a blind spot about the guts of the country bossing a grass-roots show like this. That goes for any Ivy Leaguer.'

'In that case I'm eliminated,' said Ensign Christopher Tyson III, who was the best tennis-player on Tulura. 'Princeton.'

'I wouldn't consider you, anyhow,' the exec said, eyeing Tyson contemptuously. 'You're far too young and inexperienced – as your handling of the correspondent Gordon Ripwell testifies. Besides that,' the exec added, 'we're getting so much rank around here we need a junior ensign just for the odd jobs.'

'Christ knows Ripwell has plenty of those,' Tyson said.

'That remark is precisely what I mean about your immaturity,' the exec snapped.

The exec tried a few other officers and eliminated them all for reasons having to do either with geographical origin or, as with Shoemaker and Pendleton, with the importance of their present duties. He sat back grimly in his chair.

'We're really hitting bilge-bottom,' he said. 'Jupiter, how short-handed we are here! If Washington could sit in on this conference – Jupiter! they'd take some sort of action. Namely, they'd ship out fagairtrans those fifteen additional officers and thirty-five yeomen I've requested. Well!' he said, expelling breath.

Arcing his swivel chair, the exec's eyes, which seemed glued like marbles on to his face, roamed the rows of lieutenants, lieutenants junior grade, and ensigns.

'One way or another all of you are unsuitable. Except ...'

Suddenly chair and eyes stopped.

'Lieutenant Griffin!' the exec said with abrupt enthusiasm. 'Now someone tell me why I didn't think of Griffin! You know what we'd often do at Merrill Lynch?' the exec said suddenly.

'What was that, sir?' Griffin inquired respectfully.

'Often we would give a job to the very man who opposed it. Like you have this.'

'That's a very interesting policy, sir,' Griffin said. 'What was the philosophy behind it?'

'No philosophy!' the exec said. 'We just did it.'

'Sir,' said Griffin, 'may I respectfully suggest that I didn't "oppose" it. I deliberately, trying to be helpful, devil-advocated it, as you say ...'

'Griffin,' the exec interrupted menacingly, 'what do you say we just have a look at your doss-ee-ay?'

Hoisting his sextant again, the exec began to sight through it at the top of the door, while Lieutenant Morey Griffin moved uneasily in his chair.

'For one thing,' the exec said, his eyes ranging from the sextant to Griffin, 'you're a pretty average Joe Blow sort.'

'It's nice of you to say that, sir, and the job is a challenge all right,' Griffin said nervously as Nash resumed his sextant gazings. 'The only thing, I did serve on a ship once, and I don't know how detached I could be about writing up news items on the men at sea. My actual experience, that is to say, limits the sense of imagination which this job, as you so rightly observed, demands.'

'That sounds pretty confusing to me,' Nash said suspiciously. 'Incidentally, Griffin,' he added testily, 'do you have to keep throwing your sea duty up to us? Just remember, sea duty isn't everything the way the Navy is today. Today's Navy more and more has honourable duty ashore as well as afloat – witness us here. I know plenty of officers who rank you,' he said meaningfully, looking at Griffin over his sextant, 'who haven't been near a ship.'

'So do I,' Griffin said soberly. 'Sorry, Commander. I didn't mean it in a boastful way at all. Quite the contrary. What I meant is that sea duty is not only not everything in the Navy today but can actually be a serious handicap to a man. But besides that,' he went on hurriedly, 'I'm not, unfortunately, from the Midwest. I'm from San Francisco. The only time I was ever out of California was to cross the country to go to midshipmen's school in New York. And that was in an airplane. The crossing, I mean. Frankly,' Griffin summed up, 'I'd love to have the job, but I'm honestly forced to say that I don't feel quite qualified.'

'California is not in the guts of America, I'll admit,' Nash said. 'But – did you ever go to a university, Griffin?'

'U.C.L.A.,' said Griffin proudly.

'That's in your favour,' said Nash, lowering his sextant and eyeing Griffin critically. 'A cross-section, mass-production, assembly-line school.'

'Sir,' said Griffin, who was getting alarmed at this snowballing threat to his leisure, 'someone has just occurred to me. I don't know why any of us hasn't thought of him before. I should have thought of him before myself, but it took your recent remarks in some manner to put him in my mind. Sir, might I dispassionately offer a candidate to head up this critical department?'

Abruptly, Lieutenant Griffin had come to his feet. His voice sang loudly through the room to where even the exec, laying his sextant down, listened attentively, as if captured by the conviction in Griffin's tones.

'Commander!' Griffin said, 'I give you an officer who – a point magnificently in his favour for a job like this – is probably too modest, the hallmark of a good officer as our exec has said, to suggest himself. An officer who has never been to sea. An officer who is small-town through and through. A good man – that is, officer – an honest officer, a selfless officer. An officer who,' Griffin said, his voice coming to the climax of someone making a nominating speech at the Republican National Convention, 'hails from Iowa, which is as Midwestern as corn on the cob and Carl Sandburg. Sir, I respectfully offer you and suggest that the ideal candidate for Home Town News or Joe Blow officer is: Lieutenant Noah Pratt!'

The officers, swept up by Griffin's speech, turned, to the last officer, to look at an apple-cheeked little man with very straight and very black hair parted so severely in the middle as to look like the centre stripe for a black macadam road. With all these eyes on him, Noah smiled gently. Nash sat back in his chair and gazed steadily at Noah, a man of meek and retiring nature who worked in the Media Section. Noah blushed.

'You know, I entirely overlooked Noah,' the exec said slowly, looking at Pratt. 'But the only reason,' he explained it, apparently so Pratt wouldn't feel hurt, 'was that sometimes I just don't usually realize Noah is even there, he's so inconspicuous. Inconspicuous! By

Jupiter! I believe you may actually have something, Griffin. Brief us a little on your background, Noah,' the exec said, anchoring himself deep in his chair again and hoisting the sextant back to his eye.

'Well, sir,' Noah said diffidently. You had to listen carefully to hear Noah's tenor voice. 'I was born, grew up, and have lived all of my life in Cartertown, Iowa, which has a population of 8,000. Father and I are the proprietors and operators of Pratt and Son, a department store serving a city and farm market of 25,000 with everything from women's lingerie to power-mowers. I did depart Cartertown for four years to study business administration at the University of Iowa – though Father wasn't very keen on that, being a self-made man. But then I came right back to Pratt and Son, where I stayed until I volunteered for a commission in the Navy – and where I shall return when the war is concluded.'

'Whenever that is,' said Griffin.

Nash looked irritably from his sextant at Griffin. 'Mind your rudder, Griffin,' he snapped.

'Not bad, Noah,' the exec said genially, gazing through the sextant at his ship's bell. 'You had, I gather, some executive responsibility in the department store?'

'Yes, sir!' Noah said proudly. 'I am the "Son" of the store's name. I did all the buying – with Father's approval of the orders, of course – and under his supervision directed the store's personnel.' Noah smiled shyly. 'As a matter of fact, this is a coincidence, for only last week I received a letter from Father that he plans to officially retire when I reach forty, two years from now, making me President of Pratt and Son. Though, of course, as he mentioned,' Noah added honestly, 'he expects, as chairman of the board, to keep an eye on the store as long as he's alive, and continue to do all the hiring. But I'll be President.'

The exec lowered his sextant and carefully replaced it in the drawer. A decisive look came across his face.

'You know, Sailors, I see it all now. It is an advantage, now that I give the matter its merited thought,' he intoned, 'to have a man in charge of this who is so inconspicuous that you don't realize he's even there, a man who just fades into the landscape. That's what Joe Blow is, anyhow. Unsung! Unrecognized! Almost invisible. Like you, come to think about it, Noah.'

The exec pulled himself erect in his chair. 'Noah, it's a real responsibility I'm putting on you – considering that you've never had a naval command – but I'm going to take the chance. I'm giving you a try – a try, you understand,' the exec said threateningly, 'in command of our newest and one of our most vital divisions, the Home Town News Department, which I hereby commission. Noah, from now on you are Lieutenant Joe Blow!'

Noah looked stunned.

'Commander,' he said humbly, 'all I can say is: I'll give it everything I've got.'

'Let's hope that's enough,' the exec said briskly.

He sat forward intently, his elbows on the desk, his chin resting in his clasped hands, his eyes looking dead ahead into the 'Think Big!' legend on the wall. 'Sailors,' he said, 'I have a feeling that somehow this has been one of our most fruitful sessions. Only heaven knows what will come of it. Conference dismissed!'

Lieutenant-Commander Nash promptly got off a dispatch directing all commanding officers of all ships to designate additional-duty Home Town News officers from their present complements. Then Lieutenant Noah Pratt and the yeoman he was given got up a Joe Blow form, under Nash's supervision, with spaces for police-blotter-type information about the subject enlisted man, followed by a big space for 'News Item', and sent the forms out to the ships. Then they sat back and waited for the avalanche of answers which would furnish Noah the material with which to start swamping home-town newspapers all over the States. Several weeks passed without an avalanche. Only a few forms trickled back to Tulura for Noah and his yeoman to write stories from and dispatch to stateside home-town newspapers. Probably the Home Town News officer on the ship, not fully appreciating, from his narrow vantage point, the importance of the programme, got busy with his main duties of helping run the ship and just didn't get around to filling out the Joe Blow forms. Nash spent a lot of time trying to figure a way to prime the flow. One day at a conference he came up with it.

'It's a pure case of laziness on the part of these officers on the ships,' he said angrily, 'and of downright stupidity – not realizing that in this Public Relations Age a navy is something bigger than merely running ships. But let's don't let *their* laziness and *their* stupidity put *us* off course. We can do the whole thing right from here! Why don't we procure rosters of personnel from all the ships? Then every time the ship does something – shells a beach or carries a load of troops to Guam – all the Home Town News officers aboard has to do is fire us a brief dispatch saying so. If the lazy meathead can't even do that, most times we won't even need to wait for a dispatch – we'll just pluck the item out of operational dispatches.'

The exec leaned forward excitedly.

'Do you begin to get it? We get up a story on the event with some blank spaces in it, mimeograph it off, then simply fill in the man's name from the ship's roster, like "Blank Blank of Blank was aboard the U.S.S. *Missouri* recently when that ship's sixteen-inchers disabled Yokohama", and fire it back to the guy's home-town paper. Visualize it! The *Missouri* alone has 2,700 men aboard. Any time she did anything, just anything at all, men would automatically mean 2,700 stories in papers all over the States!'

The exec paused for breath.

'Think of it! The thousands of ships we have! The hundreds of thousands of men – Navy men! – on them! The millions of stories that would be gushing from them to us! From us to the thousands of tank-town papers in the U.S. We'd swamp them under! Why, this thing might be to naval public relations what the invention of the machine-gun was to land warfare!'

'Commander,' said Lieutenant-Commander Gladney eagerly, 'we can't miss. It's the most water-tight conception I ever heard of. Why, it's like sailing the Fifth Fleet, all guns blazing, into every city room in America! These tens of thousands of stories! Why, it'll sink them, Commander!'

'Commander,' said Lieutenant-Commander Hereford enthusiastically, 'these possibilities stagger the imagination!'

'Not mine, Wayne,' the exec said crisply.

The exec got off a dispatch to all ships, directing them to forward ships' rosters and home-towns fagairtrans to Tulura. That did it. Hundreds of big fat bundles were soon hitting Public Relations Headquarters. Administrative-wise it was a revolution. From a small compartment of the Media Section with a desk in one corner and his single yeoman, Noah's department blossomed into a separate section, filling the entire middle portion of the first floor and employing eleven men. A loft of space was required to store the ship's rosters alone.

Noah got much less meek and retiring after that, and found himself working feverishly to keep out from under. A single action of the *Missouri*, as Nash said, meant 2,700 stories. Noah himself wrote the basic story in each case and his men filled in the thousands of blanks. The story would lead off with a bombardment, for example, and the fact that the local Joe Blow took part in it. The second paragraph would relate how happy Blow was aboard ship, and the third and fourth would detail why – the soda fountain aboard, the library, and so on. Four or five more paragraphs would be taken up with the history of the ship. A stencil of the story would be cut, the form run off on a mimeograph machine, each form filled in with a man's name from the ship, 2,700 letters addressed and mailed to home-town papers.

'The Home Town News Department this week,' Noah was soon able to announce proudly – and loudly, his voice enlarging in direct ratio to his job – at the daily conference, 'dispatched 28,125 stories to newspapers in forty-eight states and Puerto Rico.'

'Tremendous!' the exec exclaimed. 'Noah, I can't help pointing out – and in front of your co-shipmates, notice – what a seaworthy job you're doing with those ships' rosters. Thinking big! That's what I like to see. We're perfecting a new journalistic technique that may be revolutionary. After all, this is the age of mass production, and we may be really the first to apply it to news stories. Even an Associated Press story has some individuality to it. It's Joe Blow of Kokomo people want to hear about! Let us never forget that!'

'I can't speak for the other officers,' Noah said loudly, 'but in our department, sir, we never forget it. Guess what our goal is? A hundred thousand stories a week from Tulura deluging the home front!'

'Why stop at a hundred thousand, Pratt?' the exec said reprovingly.

'I mean just our immediate goal, Commander,' Lieutenant Pratt apologized. 'After that, who knows? Commander! Now that I've given Home Town News' report … do you mind if I scoot out? We're really snowed. Suh-nowed,' he repeated.

The centre portion of the first floor soon resembled the mail-order section of Sears Roebuck at the summit of the Christmas shopping season. Before long, eighteen typewriters and four mimeograph machines were blazing away, filing cabinets with ships' rosters were stacked to the overhead, and three chief petty officers, eighteen yeomen, six seamen first class, and four seamen second class, plus additional mail help that had to be employed in the Post Office, manned the operation. As the ships' rosters poured in and Navy vessels flung about the Pacific doing their Joe Blow-newsworthy chores – it didn't take much to make a good Joe Blow item, as Nash pointed out – the Home Town News Department was forced to go on a three-watch, twenty-four-hour basis. Noah really drove himself, working self and crew like a pack of beavers building the Grand Coulee dam. He pushed the weekly total of Home Town News stories up to a steady 50,000, and still going, and passing in the corridors outside his office you could hear his voice loudly giving commands to his crew. 'McCloskey! Bring me the *New Jersey*'s roster!' ... 'Chief! I want this batch of stories on the night plane to Pearl without fail!' ... 'Hogate! See if you can move that mimeograph a little faster!' and a shrill, frenzied laugh. 'You're holding up the war! Faster, man! Faster!'

It got pretty noticeable, Noah working sixteen hours a day and the rest of the Public Relations officers devoting no more than a half to two or three hours to their professional naval duties.

'Have you noticed how Lieutenant Blow never even drops in here any more?' Lieutenant Griffin observed one night at the bar. 'It's unnatural for a man to work that hard. On Tulura, anyhow.'

'Jealous because you didn't get the job?' asked Lieutenant (jg) Pendleton. 'Now that it's turned into a real wheel job and Noah's bossing more men than some ships have in their crews.'

'Didn't get the job!' Griffin exclaimed testily. 'Hell, I refused it. You think I, with my extensive big-city newspaper experience, want to do filler copy for a bunch of tank-town sheets?'

'You know,' Pendleton said, 'lately Noah's been so busy he's been having chow sent to his office.'

'Chow sent to his office!' Griffin looked unbelieving and outraged. 'You know, if it was anybody else I'd say they were bucking for a Legion of Merit. But Noah ... He's probably got a very depressing IQ, but, I swear, I think he's the one guy out here with a pure heart. Not after something all the time, I mean, like Pendleton here, for example, with his Radio City background.'

'I know,' Pendleton said. 'It's too bad all of us can't be as selfless as Noah. How're your plans for getting that frig-off liaison job at Sydney coming along, Morey?'

'For Christ's sake,' Griffin said, looking over his shoulder. 'Don't talk about that out loud. It's at a delicate stage, like the diplomatic discussions before the signing of a four-power pact. Sh-h. Here comes Nash.'

The exec was a picture of the model tropical officer as he came in. He was wearing his British khaki shorts, which with the ankle sock afforded two great hairy expanses of leg. His lieutenant-commander oak leaves gleamed brightly on the collar of his short-sleeved shirt. His head was almost swallowed by a Frank Buck helmet bearing the huge Navy officer's shield – though this was a Navy-issue item on Tulura, the exec was the only officer at Headquarters who had had the nerve to wear one. He was twirling a native-made officer's swagger stick of the type which had recently gone on sale at ship's service.

Striding up, the exec halted, removed his Frank Buck hat, and rapped his swagger stick smartly on the bar.

'Rum sour, Leatherneck!' The exec looked briskly around him. 'Well! I don't see Noah here, I don't, I don't. That boy really puts us all to shame!'

'It's not that we aren't willing, Commander,' Griffin said defensively.

'I do seem to remember,' Nash said, and tapped his swagger stick ominously on the bar, 'that you had a chance to be Lieutenant Joe Blow, Morey. I seem to remember that you turned it down.'

Morey shifted his elbow uneasily on the bar. 'Only because I wanted to see the best man get the job, Commander. The best man for the job, that is.'

'Oh, of course, the best man for the job,' Nash said with a chuckle that had just a tiny edge to it. He looked around meaningfully at the other officers.

'Commander, we do a job all right,' Morey said. 'Myself, I never quite get through with it all in the Media Section. Sometimes it's true that the specialized nature of our work doesn't require all of us to put in a full twelve hours a day every day. You take Ross here. Now the best radio liaison officer in the world couldn't put in more than forty-five minutes a day here on Tulura. But you've got to have a liaison officer, to keep the radio correspondents happy. I can't imagine what the radio correspondents would be like without a liaison officer. Probably even more hasty-tempered than they are anyway, if that's possible. Of course, I suppose Ross could pitch in a hand somewhere else in his free time. We can always use more help in Media.'

'It's really thoughtful of you, Morey,' said Lieutenant (jg) Pendleton, flaming up, 'how you look outside yourself for examples. The exec knows about my work – which is far too technical for you to understand – and I dare say doesn't need any reports on it from a fifty-dollar-a-week newspaper hack. Do you, Clinton?'

'Sixty dollars a week,' Griffin corrected the radio programme officer.

'Now, Sailors, I didn't mean to stir anything up. You know that I'm against "made" work. I often reproach myself for not running a taut enough ship here. I'm not a sundowner – Navy for martinet,' the exec explained. 'Indeed I've always been the genial sort. I guess my years at Merrill Lynch taught me that you can't persuade people to put their money into watered stock without you're genial about it, heh, heh. A joke,' the exec added, lest his company's fine name be reproached.

The exec rapped Griffin playfully and painfully on the shoulder with his swagger stick.

'Yes, siree,' he continued. 'I'm against "manufactured" labour. But sometimes if a man keeps a weather eye open, an idle hand – not that we have much of that, except for the one or two usual goof-offs in any big organization – can find work to do. If nothing else, he can always think! Why, I thought of the Joe Blow Department idea itself when I wasn't doing anything else. Well, I'm having chow with the captain tonight,' he said, glancing at his watch. 'Now don't you boys think I was mentioning Noah as a comparison to anyone's detriment. All the same, an executive officer can't help but be impressed by the lad's devotion to his work. Up there right now chewing a fried Spam sandwich and slashing through that sea of rosters while we stow away rum sours!'

The exec plunked down a nickel for his drink. He paused a moment, then pulled out a quarter and plunked it down on the counter. 'Leatherneck! Set up a round for everybody!' he said with a sweep of his hand. 'Night, men!' and, sticking his Frank Buck hat on his head and twirling his swagger stick, he was gone.

Ross turned viciously on Griffin. 'Why do you have to bring me up! I do twice the work you do.'

'I guess you do at that,' Griffin said glumly. 'Sometimes you put in a full two hours a day.'

Morey sloshed his rum sour. 'God damn!' he said emphatically. 'We've got to do something about Lieutenant Blow. The little beaver is derailing the gravy train. I think,' he said thoughtfully, rubbing his chin, 'I'll mosey up to his shop after chow, just to see what the atmosphere is like. I might pick up some ideas. Like the exec said, an idle hand can always think. Want to come along, Max?'

Ensign Siegel, who had been standing observantly at the bar during all this, belched.

'Listen, Griffin,' he told the lieutenant, 'don't get a fry on. Don't let Nash make you feel insecure. Yeh, I'll come. Noah ought to rev down, for his own health. That whole Joe Blow Department ought to rev down or the war'll never get over. All the ships, supplies, manpower tied up in sending this junk back to home-town papers! Who gives a continental what Joe Blow does! All this coddling treatment for Joe Blows! First thing you know, Griffin, we'll have enlisted men calling officers by their first names.'

'Meantime,' said Griffin, looking steadily at Siegel, 'let's see if we can at least avoid the catastrophe of ensigns calling full lieutenants by their last. Off your ass and let's go, Siegel.'

After chow, Griffin and Siegel, instead of going up to Noah's Home Town News Office, first came back to the bar and stayed until it closed. By the time they did make it up to Home Town News it was well after midnight, Noah had retired to his room to snatch a few hours' sleep, and a chief petty officer was supervising the comparatively small 0001–0800 watch – four yeomen sitting at typewriters filling in the blank spaces from the ship's roster of the U.S.S. *Jackson*, an AKA, in an account of how the vessel had recently sailed a shipment of ten-in-one rations from the west coast to Pelelieu.

'In the vast Pacific spaces,' one paragraph of the story went, 'the cargo-ship *Jackson*'s job is as crucial to final triumph over Japan as the planes of the U.S.S. *Yorktown* – the Navy carrier on which *The Fight-*

ing Lady was filmed – bombing to rubble the cities of Nippon. Supplies are a vital part of the war – supplies are the *Jackson's* job. Blank space of blank space is in the crew of the *Jackson*, a fighting ship even when she is carrying ten-in-one rations.'

'A very stirring account,' Griffin said, looking over a typing yeoman's shoulder. 'Ought to get the Pulitzer. Well, Chief, we're just on the town.'

'Make yourself right at home, sir,' the chief said genially. 'Just please observe the no-smoking sign in our Ammo room, heh, heh,' the chief made a joke and laughed at it, giving a grand sweep of his arm towards a great battery of metal filing-cases stacked to the overhead. 'Names! I never knew even the phone directory had so many names.'

With a flourish the chief pulled open one of the deep drawers. With both hands he lifted out one bulging folder and handed it to Griffin. 'The ship's roster of the U.S.S. *New Jersey*. 2,718 names! 2,718 stories any time the *New Jersey* does anything – even gets under way, if you've got a right bright Joe Blow officer aboard.'

'Used to know a man on the *New Jersey*,' Griffin mused. 'Wonder if he's still aboard.' He whisked through the large sheaf. 'Yup! Lieutenant Junior Grade Jonathan Rogers. Say, I know a man on a command ship – the *Mount Erskine*. Got her?'

The chief stepped swiftly down the line of filing-cabinets. 'Now this here is our M drawer – one of our M drawers.' He pulled open the drawer, extracted the roster of the *Mount Erskine*, and handed it to Griffin.

'Mortimer Jorgenson, his name is,' Griffin said, and started flicking excitedly to the J's. 'God damn, here he is. *Lieutenant* Jorgenson! Two promotions since I saw him in midshipmen's school. And the stupid jerk almost busted out! We used to call him Mortimer Snerd. Say, this is fun! You won't be offended if we check up on some of our contemporaries and old arse-hole buddies, Chief?'

'Help yourself, sir! You don't mind if I get back to the *Jackson*? Mr Pratt expects us to have it aboard the 0645 plane to the States – we've got space reserved for 200 pounds of Home Town News stories. Here, use this desk.'

For an hour or so Griffin and Siegel thumbed through the ships' rosters checking on their friends from midshipmen's school. 'Albritton – he's first lieutenant now on the *James D. Foster*,' Siegel would say. 'Old Wainwright,' he would exclaim over a folder, '– "Wacky Wainwright" we used to call him – he's exec on his minesweeper! God damn! This is fun!'

Once, thumbing through the ship's roster of an APA named the *Ankletooth*, Siegel abruptly laughed. 'Here's a great naval name for you. "Farragut Jones, Boatswain's Mate Second Class." Imagine parents named Jones who would stick a poor defenceless baby with the name Farragut.'

Lieutenant Griffin looked up from an aircraft-carrier roster. 'Just foresighted. He ended up in the Navy, didn't he?'

'He probably had to, with a name like Farragut Jones,' Siegel said.

'Farragut Jones.' Griffin, still feeling some of the effects of the hours at the bar, suddenly doubled up with laughter. 'Farragut Jones!' he repeated. He started laughing until the tears came.

Siegel looked disgustedly at the lieutenant. 'Griffin, you've had it. Rock-happy.'

'Farragut Jones!' Griffin repeated, roaring hysterically, so that the typing yeomen looked up, momentarily, baffled.

'The perfect Joe Blow,' Siegel said. 'The Navy would have him on a poster or something if the Public Relations brass ever got hold of him.'

'He's from Appleton, Nebraska ...' Griffin said, taking the *Ankletooth*'s roster from Siegel. 'Say ...' He looked curiously over at Max. 'What did you say? The perfect Joe Blow?' He rubbed his chin. 'You know, he is at that. With a name like that. A boatswain's mate. From a jerkwater town in Nebraska ...' Griffin rubbed his chin a little longer. 'You know, Siegel, I think you've got something for a change. Why, this man is a gold mine! I think I'll try my hand,' Griffin said abruptly. 'Been one helluva long time.'

Seating himself at one of the several vacant typewriters, he tickled his fingers over the keys without depressing them. Then he stuck in a sheet of paper and after gazing a moment into space batted out a date-line:

WITH THE U.S.S. ANKLETOOTH AT SEA

He gazed off another moment, then wrote:

Despite the handicap of being a Boatswain's Mate Second Class, Farragut Jones of Appleton, Neb., has established himself as one of the most popular men aboard this battling U.S. Navy ship. The writer says 'despite this handicap' because a boatswain's mate has to boss the deck crew in some uncommonly distasteful jobs, such as chipping paint, scrubbing down decks, and cleaning heads. A head is Navy for bathroom. But so relentlessly has Boatswain's Mate Jones instilled his men with the philosophy that even paint-chipping, deck-scrubbing, and head-cleaning is a part of winning the war that *Ankletooth* is one of the smartest, tautest vessels in the entire Pacific Fleet. And as one of Farragut's two naval namesakes, John Paul Jones, once observed: 'A taut ship is a happy ship.'

When he had finished writing the item and pulled it out of the Remington and read it, Griffin liked it so much that he decided it would be a shame to throw it away. So while Siegel read it over, he looked up the Appleton paper in the Home Town News Section's copy of Ayer's newspaper directory. Then he got an envelope and addressed it to the Appleton *Weekly Courier*.

Siegel picked up a pencil, changed one word – 'philosophy' to 'notion' – and gave the copy back to Griffin, who folded it, stuck it in the envelope, and licked the flap. Then, as the two officers started out, Griffin held the envelope delicately between his thumb and middle finger and dropped it in a huge bin labelled 'Outgoing Mail' that was filled with several hundred other envelopes addressed to newspapers all over the States.

'Guess that ought to answer Marblehead's libel that Lieutenant Morey Griffin is caulking off,' said Griffin.

During the next few weeks Griffin and Siegel, with Griffin doing the writing, fed a steady stream of Farragut Jones stories to the Appleton *Weekly Courier*.

WITH THE U.S. ANKLETOOTH AT SEA – Boatswain's Mate Second Class Farragut Jones of Appleton, Neb., played a critical role recently when this battling U.S. naval vessel delivered a batch of United States Marines – the land arm of the Navy – to duty on Guam. By 'critical role' the writer means that Farragut was in charge of the deck force which had to keep the ship in apple-pie, shipshape condition – no easy task with a pack of sea-going bellhops, as the untidy Marines are known humorously to Navy men, aboard. Farragut is well in the tradition of one of his two famous naval namesakes, David Farragut, who once observed, 'Damn the Torpedoes! Full Speed Ahead!'

Griffin and Siegel procured a copy of the history of the *Ankletooth* from Lieutenant Shoemaker and interlarded authentic details of the ship's shape and history in the stories of Farragut Jones.

WITH THE U.S.S. ANKLETOOTH AT SEA – As a member of the crew of the U.S.S. *Ankletooth*, a battling, 12,450-ton vessel measuring 455 feet overall and equipped with two Babcock and Wilcox boilers, now commencing her third relentless year of hustling troops and cargo around the Pacific, Boatswain's Mate Second Class Farragut Jones of Appleton, Neb., is one of the most decorated APA men in the entire Pacific Fleet. Namewise and otherwise, Farragut is almost the perfect prototype of the unknown, unsung Navy men who are sweating the United States to victory in the Pacific. By 'unsung' the writer means that most untutored civilians think only the men who fire the guns and shoot the torpedoes win the war. Not true. Farragut never fires a gun, never shoots a torpedo. But without the APAs and men like Farragut manning them, there could scarcely be a war. Even with the APAs, Farragut Jones knows it's a long war, that, as one of his ancestral name-sakes, John Paul Jones, said, 'We have only just begun to fight.' But fervently hopes that before too many more years in the Pacific he will be able to raise the joyous shout of the other one: 'We have met the enemy and they are ours!'

Griffin and Siegel must have got off a score of Farragut Jones stories when the word was passed one day that all officers were to assemble for a special conference. The exec held up a bundle of clippings.

'Something mysterious is going on,' he said slowly. 'It appears that unauthorized persons are horning in on Naval Public Relations.'

Sombrely the exec passed the clippings from the Appleton *Weekly Courier* around. As he scanned through them, Griffin felt a pride of authorship that the *Courier*'s editor had changed scarcely a word in his stories.

'Where did they come from, Commander?' he asked.

'Navy Department!' exclaimed Nash.

'You mean Washington?' Griffin said incredulously.

'That's where the Navy Department was located the last time I heard,' Nash said irritably. 'The editor of the Appleton paper has written to the Navy Department with the most ignorant suggestion I ever heard of.'

The exec whipped a letter off his desk and read:

In view of the notable record, accumulated by one of Appleton's own, Boatswain's Mate Second Class Farragut Jones – 'one of the Navy's most decorated enlisted men' – and in view of his name, epitomizing the Navy, I respectfully suggest that the Navy give earnest consideration to returning Farragut to the United States for a hero's welcome in the town where he grew up. As a symbol of the Navy's enlisted man, the Navy might then elect to take Farragut on a tour of the war plants where naval items are produced. This would provide the workers with a look at the type of man using the items they turn out, and hearing about the effectiveness of those items first-hand from Farragut would give them a thrilling dose of morale. This is up to the Navy – understand, I'm not, as a country editor, trying to tell you admirals how to run the Navy. Myself I never have even seen a body of water bigger than Groundhog Creek. It may be that Farragut cannot be spared from what would appear to be the heroic job he is doing. My sole concern is that, should the project of returning Farragut briefly to the States be accepted, we here in Appleton have at our hero first.

The exec threw the letter down on his desk. 'This hicktown meathead editor wrote this garbage to SecNav, who passed it on to Navy Department Public Relations, which has forwarded the letter to us asking for more details about Farragut Jones. Imagine how this makes us look to Washington! Not even knowing about these stories! Not even ever having heard of Farragut Jones!'

The exec looked steadily at the 'Don't Give Up The Ship!' legend, then suddenly spun in his chair. '*Ankletooth*'s Joe Blow officer must be sending stories directly to the States! Violation of security regulations – in wartime a general court-martial offence punishable by up to and including death. Going over our head! Not going through the chain of command! Who does he think he is! Probably just an ensign, too. Also, there is obviously something fishy going on here – at the least the *Ankletooth*'s Joe Blow officer is guilty of gross exaggeration. Navy's "most decorated enlisted man" indeed! Why, an APA couldn't have the most decorated enlisted man! They never do a damn thing but ferry troops around.'

'Doesn't it say "most decorated *APA* enlisted man"?' asked Griffin.

Nash looked sharply at Griffin, then examined a clipping.

'Why, so it does. How did you know?'

'I just read the clipping,' said Griffin.

'Anyhow, that doesn't change the point. That sounds like a ruse. How would *Ankletooth*'s Joe Blow officer know that anyway?' Nash said in a burst of irritation. 'And him only an ensign!'

'Maybe he checked around with the other APAs,' Griffin said. 'Even an ensign could do that.' He looked at another clipping. 'Not a bad piece of copy, incidentally.'

'I don't care if Ernie Poyle wrote it!' Nash said, inflamed. 'It's put us in a very embarrassing position. Public Relations going on without us knowing about it!'

'But wasn't that the whole idea of the Joe Blow Department?' Griffin said. 'To get more Navy enlisted-men stories? This batch of clippings ... well, I'd say, sir, that we've hit the jackpot.'

'Jackpot or not, it's supposed to go through us!' Nash shouted. 'You can't have every Tom, Dick, and Harry taking Naval Public Relations into his own hands! Why, we might have chaos! I'm getting off a dispatch to *Ankletooth*'s commanding officer, ordering a full explanation! But before I do I just wanted to double check.'

The exec leaned forward and looked fiercely around the circle of officers. 'Anyone here know anything about this?' He whirled on the chief of the Home Town News Section. 'Noah, you sure you don't know anything about Farragut Jones?'

'Never heard of the individual,' Noah said, his voice almost inaudible for the first time in a long time. 'Like I checked and told you, sir, it sure didn't go through our shop.'

Griffin started to say something, but looking at Siegel's impassive eyes he let his lips fall together wordlessly.

'All right, Sailors,' the exec said grimly, dismissing the conference. 'I'll get off that dispatch. We'll get to the bottom of this, or my name isn't Lieutenant-Commander Joe Blow of Kokomo.'

As soon as they were outside and Griffin could get Siegel aside, he grabbed him by the collar. 'Jesus Christ, man! Whoever thought that hicktown editor would do something like this? The son of a bitch should have been grateful to get some decent copy for a change to fill his lousy hick sheet.'

'He's grateful all right,' said Siegel. 'He just wants more of it.'

'Listen, Max,' Griffin said nervously. 'This is serious. What we gonna do?'

'Lieutenant,' said Siegel, 'I don't know.'

94

'I don't want to get anyone on the *Ankletooth* in trouble,' Griffin said magnanimously.

'Why, I wouldn't worry about that, Lieutenant,' Siegel said. 'All the *Ankletooth* will do is send back an answer they don't know anything about it. They aren't going to get in any trouble, Lieutenant.'

'Listen, Siegel,' Griffin said. 'Don't give me that Lieutenant business. You're in this, too, you know.'

'Now, Lieutenant,' Siegel said calmly, 'this is no time for you to start alienating me. You're going to need what friends you've got left.'

'I'm sorry, Max,' said Griffin. 'I'm a little rattled. Just call me Morey. What we gonna do?'

'I guess we better go in and see Marblehead, huh?'

'I guess so,' Griffin said miserably. 'I guess we better go in before he sends that dispatch out. It might go a little easier to tell him voluntarily than to be found out later involuntarily.'

'Don't give up the ship, I always say,' said Siegel, 'and you better, too.'

The two officers turned and went back upstairs and knocked at the commander's door.

'Come in!' They heard an irritated voice, and opened the door. The exec was pecking away furiously at his typewriter.

'Commander,' Griffin said, 'could we see you a moment?'

'Can't you see I'm trying to get off this urgent dispatch to the *Ankletooth* about this Farragut Jones!' Nash said, irritated. 'Wait outside for fifteen minutes, will you?'

'Commander,' said Griffin quietly, 'this concerns the Farragut Jones matter.'

Slowly Nash looked up at Griffin. He said nothing for a few moments. Then: 'All right, spit.'

'Commander,' Griffin began, and immediately had to clear his throat, 'I'm afraid we – Siegel and I, that is – had a certain finger in the Farragut Jones series.'

Nash's eyes swelled, then returned to a cold, cold size.

'You see,' Griffin went on in the engulfing silence, 'Siegel here and I had an idea for getting the Navy some more publicity – that being what we're here for – and one night when we were up in the Joe Blow Section, pitching in, we came across this man with the perfect

Navy name.' Griffin laughed hollowly. ' "Farragut Jones." You'll have to admit that's a pretty good Navy name. Won't you, Commander?'

The exec, listening with fingers pursed to lips, did not move an eyelash.

'As Siegel here said,' Griffin went on, ' "That's just about the perfect Navy name. If the Navy knew about it they'd probably do a special public relations campaign just on this man alone." That's about what you said. Isn't it, Max?'

'Something like that, Lieutenant,' Siegel said. 'You may not have quoted me word for word exactly – it's been a long time and a man can't always remember a direct quote word for word – but that's about it, certainly the guts of what I said. Guts,' he repeated, looking at Griffin.

'So there we were,' Griffin said, clearing his throat. His eyes rested unhappily on the wooden 'Don't Give Up The Ship!' legend on the wall. Then the other legend below it gave up an idea. 'We were just trying, like the sign there says, to "Think Big". So we sat down and wrote these stories about Farragut Jones. Actually, the idea wasn't bad. Was it, Commander?'

The exec did not speak or move for a full minute, but he never took his eyes off Griffin. Then he pulled the *Ankletooth* dispatch out of his typewriter, crumpled it slowly, and tossed it in his wastebasket, where it hit the empty metal with an ominous crackle. The exec sat up high in his chair and spread his fingers on his desk. Suddenly both hands shot forward, pulled out the huge copy of *Navy Regulations*, and banged it once on the desk, in a terrible noise. The sawn-off five-inch-shell ashtray jumped a full inch and crashed back on the desk.

'I should not be surprised to see both of you young men cashiered! Dishonourably discharged. Or worse. Meantime, consider yourselves confined to quarters pending the court-martial.'

'Confined to quarters!' Griffin exclaimed. 'What are we going to eat!'

'You can eat bread and water as far as I'm concerned!' the exec shouted. 'Now, *git*!'

'But, Commander,' Griffin whined, 'we were just trying to do what you said, not be an idle hand all the time but think up ideas ...'

'Belay it, I say!' the exec suddenly shouted. 'Go to your quarters, both of you! Or shall I call the shore patrol! Sabotaging my vital Joe Blow programme of making every American Navy-conscious, that's what you've tried to do! Sabotage in time of war! You'll be lucky to escape with a bad-conduct discharge instead of ten to twenty years in Portsmouth. Shove off! Both of you!'

Griffin filed miserably out, followed by Siegel, who appeared exceedingly calm.

'Great God!' Griffin exclaimed when they were outside the exec's office. 'A court-martial! Great God, Max! Confined to our room! What are we going to do about eating – and drinking!'

'At least the first part of that will be taken care of when we get to Portsmouth,' Ensign Siegel said reassuringly.

'Great God, Max!' Griffin exclaimed. 'Don't joke about this! This is serious, man! Why, that son of a bitch is capable of doing it, you know! That Joe Blow project's really his pet!'

'Well, it was not a bad piece of copy, incidentally,' Siegel said.

'Max, you're in this, too, don't forget that!' Griffin exclaimed. 'You ought to know that by now!'

'Yes, I know it,' Siegel said slowly, and suddenly a smile of contentment enveloped his face.

Lieutenant Griffin, astonished and outraged, glared at his ensign-room-mate.

'What the hell are you grinning about?' he shouted furiously. 'A court-martial! Confined to our room! And you stand there grinning like a water-buffalo in a mud bath!'

'More coffee, Lieutenant?'

'Thank you, Ensign, I don't mind if I do.'

The morning sun of the islands filtered into a room in one of the BOQs and across the forms of two officers propped up comfortably in their beds against three pillows each. They had just finished a hearty breakfast in bed of sunnyside eggs, bacon, toast, and orange marmalade and were now enjoying their third pot of coffee, for which they had dispatched the steward's mate to the mess-hall.

'You know, Max,' Lieutenant Griffin said, 'it's strange how I failed fully to see the possibilities of confinement yesterday. Room service!'

Siegel's first act had been to send word to the mess-hall that, considering as how he and Lieutenant Griffin were confined to their room, they would be obliged to have their meals in.

'What other choice did they have?' Ensign Siegel said. 'After all, you can't let a U.S. naval officer starve.'

After breakfast Ensign Siegel and Lieutenant Griffin prepared a list of a dozen books and sent Henry, the BOQ steward's mate, to the Fleet Library to check them out. The two officers stayed in bed all morning reading, propped against their three pillows each. The requisitioning of these pillows from general stores had been Siegel's second act upon confinement.

'Here's a passage from *Henry V* that's always been a favourite of mine,' Ensign Siegel said, and read aloud a few lines.

'This is one of the best twists Ellery Queen has come up with yet,' Lieutenant Griffin said a little later from his book. 'Listen to this one.'

The reading of the two officers was interrupted at noon by the arrival of lunch on trays. They ate a hearty lunch and afterwards spent an enjoyable couple of hours playing gin rummy. Siegel, who liked chess a great deal and had tried many times, unsuccessfully, to find someone on Tulura who played, attempted to teach the game to Griffin, but after an hour or so, Griffin gave up. 'Max,' he said, 'it's just too much like work.'

By mid-afternoon they found themselves hungry again, and even Siegel hesitated to send to the mess-hall for between-meal snacks. However, a thought of Griffin's solved this problem.

'Isn't Lieutenant Junior Grade Marconi Pendleton away to one of the islands on one of his radio missions?' he said.

'Why, I believe that's true,' Ensign Siegel said. 'What do you have in mind?'

'I don't know if you're familiar with those interesting shipments Mrs Pendleton dispatches her husband weekly from the home front?' Lieutenant Griffin inquired.

'Yes, indeed,' Ensign Siegel said. 'What a devoted woman Mrs Pendleton must be.'

'Almost as devoted,' Lieutenant Griffin said, 'as the many Navy nurses on Tulura who think they're going to be Mrs Pendleton, not knowing that the position is already taken. You know, I think I'll just step down to Pendleton's room. I don't suppose cruising two doors down the passage-way would be a serious violation of our confinement?'

Ensign Siegel reflected a moment. 'I hardly see how it could get us in any worse than we are,' he said. 'In any case I can mount a lookout for Nash.'

Lieutenant Griffin returned from the short trip with his arms full of tinned delicacies. They made a delightful tea-time snack.

The evening Ensign Siegel and Lieutenant Griffin devoted to drinking numerous shakers of rum sours which Henry fetched from the officers' bar, which was hardly a stone's throw away from the BOQ.

By the third day the two officers were growing quite plump, rested, relaxed, and well read.

'Isn't it commendable how the service improves every day?' Ensign Siegel said over breakfast in bed that morning. 'Four pieces of bacon! It was a happy thought, sending for that extra shaker of rum sours for the steward's mate.'

By the fifth day of confinement, largely owing to the lavish passing out of rum sours to the various steward's mates, the two officers found themselves receiving the pampering to which a guest at the Greenbrier hotel is accustomed. They were served delicate omelets and golden griddle cakes for breakfast – items which never showed their faces in the mess-hall – and thick steaks cooked to order for dinner; their bed-linen was changed daily and their beds made every time they got out of them.

'There's only one thing softer than working on Tulura,' said Lieutenant Griffin, by now almost overcome with euphoria, 'and that's not working on Tulura.'

Ensign Siegel and Lieutenant Griffin would have been quite surprised to know that Lieutenant-Commander Nash had completely forgotten about them. The reason was that among the swelling ranks of Public Relations officers the absence of a mere two was entirely unnoticeable, especially since hardly an officer there did a job specific enough to be missed if he should vanish into the atmosphere. Presumably the pair of them might have had breakfast in bed for the duration had not Admiral Boatwright had a rare moment of leisure. From the pile of copies of all dispatches that routinely went to his office, he happened to glance at a dispatch from Washington to Public Relations. Nash got a call from the admiral's aide to come over on the double, the admiral wanted to see him.

Grabbing up his Frank Buck helmet, the exec sped on over to the building next door, where Admiral Boatwright's aide ushered him immediately into the admiral's office. There he found the admiral and Captain Jarvis, the titular chief of Public Relations, huddled over some newspaper clippings. Jarvis was a regular Navy officer who before being assigned recently to his present billet had commanded a cruiser.

Nash stood at attention in the middle of the vast room with his Frank Buck helmet in his hand. The admiral gave a disgusted look at the helmet but apparently he had something more important on his mind right now.

'Nash!' he thundered. 'I've got you here about this Farragut Jones matter!'

'Farragut Jones?' Nash said, uncomprehending. 'Oh, Farragut Jones!' he said again, starting to tremble, and suddenly remembering why he hadn't seen Griffin and Siegel around in the last few days. 'Farragut Jones!' he said a third time.

'You got the name straight now?' the admiral said crisply.

'Farragut Jones!' Nash said for the fourth time, uncontrollably. 'Sir, you'll be happy to hear I've got the two officers who are respon ...'

'Sit down, Nash, for God's sake sit down!' Boatwright roared. Nash lowered himself into a chair. 'I got to reading some of this junk that goes back and forth between your office and Washington and something caught my eye. Farragut Jones, Boatswain's Mate Second Class!' the admiral boomed.

'Aye, aye, sir.' Nash's voice shook.

'Aye, aye, what?' Admiral Boatwright boomed. 'Boatswain's Mate Farragut Jones! Do you realize, Nash,' the admiral's voice rose thunderously, 'that John Paul Jones was the founder of the United States Navy and that David Farragut was its first admiral? Boatswain's Mate Farragut Jones! What a name for a Navy man! Probably from an old Navy family – what with two naval namesakes – David Farragut and John Paul Jones,' he repeated, with a look at Nash, as if to make sure he got it.

'I should imagine he was born with the last name of Jones, sir,' Nash said. 'But you're right about the Farragut part. Anyone who names his son Farragut must have the good judgement to prefer the Navy to the Air Force. No other reason for naming him Farragut. Otherwise they would have named him something like Billy Mitchell Jones – or Charles Lindbergh Jones.'

Admiral Boatwright looked up at Nash for a long moment, then returned to the clippings, which were the Griffin-written stories on Farragut Jones which had appeared in the Appleton *Weekly Courier*.

'Sir,' Nash began, 'you'll be happy to know I've got to the bottom of ...'

'I hate to say it,' Boatwright interrupted, 'since I've always thought all Public Relations people a bunch of either freaks or oddballs. But any outfit which can reach down into the millions of men in the war-time Navy and pull out a boatswain's mate second class by the name of Farragut Jones ... That's initiative! That's imagination!'

'But Admiral, sir ...' said Nash.

'I asked Jarvis here to bring me the whole file on Jones, and I've just been telling him that I think the Farragut Jones idea is excellent,' said Admiral Boatwright.

'And I told the admiral,' Jarvis said, 'that I didn't rightly know whose idea it was. It started before my present billet. But I presume it was yours, Nash?'

'Well, sir,' said Nash, who was almost choking, 'I did think it was a good old Navy name.'

'Well done!' Admiral Boatwright said. 'But why the hell are you sitting on your duff now on this thing?' he added with a sudden thunder. 'What's holding you the hell up?'

'Well, sir,' Nash said, trembling, 'I wanted to figure all the possible Farragut Jones angles.'

'Angles!' the admiral exploded. 'Damn the angles! Let's open up with the sixteen-inchers!'

'Aye, aye, sir!' Nash said, just stopping himself from saluting.

'This Nebraska editor's suggestion of sending him on a tour of Navy war plants is four O!' the admiral boomed. 'I hope you've already got off a dispatch ordering Jones to Tulura before sending him to the States.'

'I was just preparing a dispatch to the *Ankletooth* not long ago,' Nash said weakly.

'Excellent!' Admiral Boatwright roared. 'Excellent! What a name, Boatswain's Mate Second Class Farragut Jones! The Typical Young Navy Man!'

' "The Typical Young Navy Man!" What a phrase!' Nash said, with a sudden, grinning smile. 'Admiral, you ought to be in Public Relations!'

The admiral banged his fist on his desk at the thought and turned an intense purple.

'Never mind handling my duty assignments, Nash!' he roared. Then, flushing the thought out of him, the admiral returned to the matter at hand.

'Boatswain's Mate Second Class Farragut Jones!' he boomed. 'Get him in here, Nash! Break out the sixteen-inch guns on this one! All engines ahead full! Flank speed!'

'Aye, aye, sir,' Nash said weakly, coming to his feet.

Lieutenant-Commander Nash walked, weaving and dazed a little, out of the admiral's office and back across the road to the Public Relations building. First he got off a dispatch to the *Ankletooth* in the name of ComFleets, ordering Jones to report to Tulura. Then he sent for Griffin and Siegel. While waiting for them he took out his *Naval Leadership* and sat reading, nodding his head in agreement from time to time: 'Tact is the lubricating oil of human relationships. The man who considers tact unnecessary in dealing with subordinates is probably the same man who hammers his sextant with a monkey-wrench to make it work ...'

When the two officers entered, the exec snapped the book shut and looked up, beaming. Siegel looked impassive but Griffin was greatly alarmed, both at the interruption of the days of luxury and at the prospective day of reckoning which, he gathered from the exec's joyous expression, was at hand.

'Sit down, Morey ... Max,' the exec said. 'You realize, of course, that I was only funning when I confined you to quarters.'

'Funning!' exclaimed Griffin, shaken.

'Heh, heh,' Nash chuckled. 'Even ranks like lieutenant-commanders have got to have their little practical joke, you know.'

'Practical joke!' Griffin exclaimed.

'Actually,' the exec continued rapidly, 'I consider the Farragut Jones series to be the best Navy Public Relations idea since I have been at it. Four O! Guess what? I've ordered Jones to Tulura before sending him to the States!'

The exec scratched his leg offhandedly while Griffin and Siegel looked on in stupefaction.

'Boatswain's Mate Farragut Jones!' the exec suddenly sang out. 'What a name for a Navy man! Probably from an old Navy family. Named for David Farragut and John Paul Jones!'

The exec paused for breath. 'We're going to really exploit this man,' he yelled. 'Open up with the sixteen-inchers! Flank speed ahead! All engines wide open! In other words,' he explained this to Griffin and Siegel, 'we'll use initiative! Imagination! The Typical Young Navy Man! That's the pitch I'm taking on Jones. The Typical Naval Joe Blow!'

'Why, that's what I've always thought he was,' said Griffin, like a man coming out of shock. 'That's what I thought from the beginning!'

'That's what old Griffin thought all right,' repeated Siegel impassively.

'That's all, Sailors!' the exec exclaimed. 'Except I want to say: Well done! Oh, and of course,' the exec added as an afterthought, 'you're released from confinement.'

MELORA 3 : *Hydroz to Jerem*

'History …' the Tuluran girl said. 'Do you happen to know how far the first automobile could go on a tank of gasoline, Mr Siegel?'

Ensign Siegel stopped swabbing the blackboard and looked at the girl bent over the teacher's desk behind him. 'Not offhand, Miss Alba,' he said. 'Put it on your list and I'll get it for you tomorrow.'

Siegel thought how formal they were with each other, even after a month of twice-weekly visits in the schoolhouse, which was the only place he ever saw her.

'History …' she said. 'Why was President McKinley assassinated, Mr Siegel?'

'It was by an insane man who didn't believe in government of any kind, Miss Alba,' Ensign Siegel said. 'So he just got this feeling off his chest by shooting the head of the government.'

'Thank you, I'll mark that one off,' the girl said. 'Literature ... What is a raven?'

'Literature?' Siegel said quizzically.

'We've been reading Edgar Allan Poe,' she explained.

'Oh,' Ensign Siegel said. He squeezed out the blackboard rag in the bucket of water and straightened up. 'Well, a raven is a bird, a black bird, about so big' – he laid the rag on the blackboard ledge and held his hands apart – 'or so big.' He kept moving his hands back and forth from seagull to sparrow while she watched.

'Well, how big, Mr Siegel?' she said.

'Well, it's so big,' Ensign Siegel said, moving his hands.

'Mr Siegel, I can see you've never taught children,' she said, a little impatiently. 'You've got to be much more definite than that or they'll push you right up against the wall and nail you to it.'

'Sorry, Miss Alba,' Siegel apologized, finishing off the blackboard, picking up his broom, and starting to sweep the room. He sighed heavily. 'Put it on your list. I'll look it up tomorrow.'

Ensign Siegel and the school-teacher Melora Alba were having one of their regular after-school sessions. The Tuluran girl had been making use of Ensign Siegel's visits to help her in the lessons she gave her seventh-grade students. She needed help because she was in an odd position for a teacher. Her total tools were three textbooks – a geography, a modern history, and a book of literature readings – which had survived the pre-invasion shelling of the original schoolhouse. The teacher had been appalled to find out how wide open to the most elementary questions a lack of reference books left you. With Siegel's help she had worked out a makeshift substitute for the reference books. When her pupils asked questions she couldn't answer, she took them down and told the pupils she would try to find out. Then, on Ensign Siegel's next visit, she went over the list with him. The ones Siegel didn't know – and he was himself flabbergasted at how he couldn't answer the most ridiculously simple questions, such as how does a refrigerator freeze ice – he looked up the next day in the well-stocked Fleet Library, where he found himself spending more time than he had in any library since Widener. His next visit, two or three days later, he brought the answers to the girl and received a fresh batch. It wasn't the best teaching system in the world, but it was the best they could do.

Ensign Siegel had experienced a spectrum of emotions regarding this task. At first it was a sort of duty. Then he became rather fascinated at looking up things like 'Automobile', 'Cotton gin', and 'Indians' in the Fleet Library's reference books, and reading the hosts of basic but intriguing facts. Then, as the questions from the girl's pupils gushed forth – it seemed that the more you satisfied their curiosity the more ravenous it got – Siegel found greater and greater chunks of library time gouged out of his life. Oft-times, while the other officers were frolicking at the bar with their rum sours, Siegel's nose would be buried deep in the Hydroz to Jerem volume of an encyclopaedia as he sought the answer to some question on the internal-combustion engine. Siegel not only had to read the whole long passage through – it was astounding the space that an encyclopaedia could devote to the internal-combustion engine – but he had to figure out an answer to the question in language a seventh-grader could understand. He began to weary slightly of this additional duty. But there was nothing he could do about it if he wanted to keep seeing the Tuluran girl. Which meant there was nothing at all he could do about it.

'Who are the members of the American Cabinet, Mr Siegel?' the teacher asked from her list.

'State, Edward Stettinius; War, Henry Stimson; Navy, James Forrestal; Interior, Harold Ickes; Labour, Frances Perkins; Commerce, Henry Wallace; Agriculture, Clyde Wickard; Treasury, Henry Morgenthau; Attorney-General, Francis Biddle; Postmaster-General, Frank Walker,' Ensign Siegel rattled off, like a proud schoolboy, happy to have a question he could answer.

The girl looked up in mild surprise. 'Now, if you'll give them to me a little more slowly, Mr Siegel ...' And Siegel, leaning on his broom, did.

'How big is Brooklyn?' the girl asked.

Ensign Siegel's big forehead wrinkled. 'One million ... two million. Put it on your list,' he said helplessly.

'How long is a dinosaur?' the girl asked.

'My God!' Siegel said as the girl looked at him reprovingly. 'Put it on your list,' he said immediately.

'What were the seven wonders of the world?' the girl asked from her list. 'I can think of the Colossus of Rhodes, the Pharos at Alexandria, the Tomb of Mausolus ...'

'The Temple of Diana at Ephesus ... the Hanging Gardens of Babylon ...' Siegel added, and then faltered.

There was a silence of thought, Siegel leaning on his broom and the girl tapping her pencil against her chin.

'The two missing wonders,' Siegel said disgustedly. 'Put it on your list.'

With brusque movements Ensign Siegel resumed his broom.

'The little creatures never stop, do they?' he said.

'Well, they're children,' the teacher said comprehensively.

Ensign Siegel finished his sweeping and stuck the broom in a corner. Then he got a dry rag and dusted down the desks. Then he took the blackboard water outside and emptied it, came back and stuck the bucket, the wet rag and the dry rag and the broom in a cleaning-closet off to the side. He was happy to have taken on this work, which he had discovered was the only way he could have his half-hour alone with her. Otherwise the children took turns staying after school and doing it, while their teacher corrected papers. Both the ensign and the children considered the new arrangement a good deal.

His chores done, Ensign Siegel took a seat at the pupil's desk closest to the teacher's desk. It was built for a twelve-year-old and he was obliged constantly to readjust his big frame in it. They made a strange pair sitting there. Ensign Max Siegel, a huge, ugly man. And the exquisitely formed Tuluran girl, whose beauty was an almost startling fact, with her flawless palomino skin, her long black hair.

The girl finished her list and looked up at the shining blackboard, the swept room, the dusted desks.

'You do a good job, Mr Siegel,' she said. She smiled at the sight of the big ensign in the tiny desk. 'Don't fall out of that. And not just the cleaning,' she went on. 'It's a big help, your getting these answers for me. I never imagined how hard it would be to teach without books to look things up in.'

'I'm always glad to further the cause of education, Miss Alba,' Ensign Siegel said, shifting himself in the child's seat.

'Mr Siegel,' 'Miss Alba,' he thought. Apparently, he was thinking, for a Tuluran girl of her family to call him anything else before she had known him for at least five years would have been an act of familiarity on the order of a Boston débutante sitting on a young man's lap at his introductory tea with her parents. 'Mr Siegel.' But still it was very, very nice to be here with her, whatever she called him.

'Education needs furthering here, Mr Siegel,' she said, with a rather discouraged smile, looking around the small, bare room. 'I'm glad your ships have such excellent marksmanship. But I do wish those particular shells had gone a little wide.'

The one-room, makeshift school building, which had once been a storehouse, had to do for eight grades since the pre-invasion shelling. The girl had something close to a mania, Siegel thought, for getting a new schoolhouse. She seemed to him a quiet, easy-going girl except when it came to one thing – education. Having been educated herself, she seemed determined to have every other Tuluran educated.

'Of course your ships good reason for doing it,' the girl said. 'After all, the Japanese were using the schoolhouse as a storage place for bombs. But it was a nice schoolhouse,' she added. 'It's hard to teach eight grades in one room.'

'Well, you'll get another schoolhouse after the war,' Siegel said, rearranging himself in the seat.

The girl shook her head impatiently. 'That isn't good enough. The children now in school will never catch up with what they're losing, Mr Siegel – two hours a day each grade gets, when it should be six.' She shook her head again and spoke in a quiet fervour. 'After the war all that schooling time will be lost for ever. You never get that kind of loss back. I'm sorry to sound angry,' she said abruptly. 'Only we need things. I see the children and what they need and I can't help getting impatient sometimes.'

'I know,' Ensign Siegel said. He sighed. 'Maybe you should have spoken to those congressmen that day about it, Miss Alba.'

The girl smiled suddenly, in spite of herself, remembering that day. 'You mean the day you gave me a husband and several children, Mr Siegel?'

'Well, I had to rescue you, Miss Alba,' Ensign Siegel said, readjusting himself in the child's seat.

'You're so chivalrous, Mr Siegel,' she said. 'Next time some more of those congressmen come out, tell them we need a new school-house, will you?'

She looked at her watch and stood up.

'Well, I've got to be going now, Mr Siegel. Here's the new list.'

'Oh, just a moment, Miss Alba,' Ensign Siegel said, leaping up. He took the list. 'I have a present for you – it's outside in the jeep.'

'A present?' she said, quite formally. 'Why, that's very kind of you, Mr Siegel, but I really couldn't accept any present.'

'But I sent clear to the States for it,' Ensign Siegel said, standing there, looking down at her.

'The thought was very kind, Mr Siegel,' she said, very correctly. 'I'm sorry. I can't accept a present from you.'

'Well, you can at least look at it. After all, I did go to a lot of trouble getting this, Miss Alba,' Ensign Siegel said, quite stiffly himself.

'I'm sorry about that, Mr Siegel,' she said, 'but I didn't ask you to ...'

'You didn't ask me to?' Siegel said, a little inflamed. 'Well, that's just too bad. Now you're going to look at this present,' he said firmly. 'You just wait.'

'Mr Siegel, I ...'

But Ensign Siegel had dashed out of the door. In a few moments he was back, staggering under the weight of a huge wooden box. He set it down with a heavy thump in the middle of the floor.

'Now, Mr Siegel,' the girl said, very firmly. 'I can't accept a gift from you. Is that clear? I know it's different in America, but here girls aren't allowed to accept gifts from men ...'

'Be quiet, Miss Alba,' Ensign Siegel said.

'Now, see here, Mr Siegel,' she said severely.

But he had dashed out again. He was back presently with the box's twin, which he slung on top of the other box with a longshoreman crash. The two boxes now came to about her waist. Before she could get out a word he pushed out again and brought in a third large box. He slammed it down by the other two. Thundering out of the school-house twice again, Siegel hefted in two more boxes. The five boxes now made quite a barricade in front of the teacher, whose anger was now being diluted with astonishment. Ensign Siegel, who was per-spiring heavily from his labours, ran out once more. This time he returned with a crowbar and without a word started in on one of the boxes.

Suddenly, with a loud screech, the top of the box flew open. Siegel dropped the crowbar resoundingly, and diving into the box with both hands, started throwing wood-shavings out right and left. Then he stood back.

'Go ahead, Miss Alba!' Ensign Siegel said. 'Just look! It doesn't violate any Tuluran customs just to look, does it?'

The girl gave the ensign the look she might have given one of her obstreperous children.

'All right, Mr Siegel,' she said then, in tones of tried patience, and perhaps also her curiosity was beginning to get the better of her. 'I'll look – but that's all,' she added stubbornly.

Stepping over to the box, she peered cautiously inside as if afraid something was going to jump out of it.

'Go ahead, Miss Alba!' Ensign Siegel said. 'It won't bite you! Take one of them out!'

Hesitantly the girl reached with both hands into the box and lifted out a heavy object wrapped in thick brown paper.

'Open it, Miss Alba!' Ensign Siegel commanded.

Slowly the girl tore the wrapper off. Suddenly she was staring incredulously at the object. Then the wrapper slipped out of her hands and fell to the floor.

'Why,' she said in awe, 'it's the *Encyclopaedia Britannica*!'

Ensign Siegel reached in his pocket, pulled out the list of questions, and stuck it in the volume she was holding. It was the BALTIM to BRAIN volume.

'You can do your own homework now,' he said.

Abruptly, hugging the big, shining, new volume to her with one arm, she reached down with her free hand and gave Ensign Siegel's hand a quick squeeze.

'The *Encyclopaedia Britannica*!' she said. 'Oh, Max!'

Four: Ultimate Fraternization

YEOMAN SECOND CLASS ADAM GARRETT, who was Ensign Max Siegel's yeoman, was a rangy, lean young man of twenty-two and as handsome as Siegel was ugly. His skin gleamed bronzely against his enlisted man's whites and a shock of blond hair rose above a high-boned bronzed face and sea-blue eyes. His broad shoulders tapered down to a lean, flat-bellied waist, and all of him was leanness and muscle. Every movement of his body seemed rhythmic, effortlessly so. He radiated maleness, virile maleness, but he had no self-conscious-ness whatever about it, hardly awareness. He should have been a Viking with Eric the Red, with Drake on the *Golden Hind,* or one of John Paul Jones's men on the *Bon Homme Richard.* Instead he was a yeoman who typed up correspondents' travel orders.

Yeoman Garrett was an entirely easy-going young man who spent a good deal of time reading from the Fleet Library, which was one of the best west of Widener. He had one enormous passion, which was to get out on a ship. He and Siegel liked each other. From Yeoman Garrett's side, Siegel was virtually the only officer in the place for whom he had the slightest respect, and his admiration for Siegel was complete to the point of extravagance. This feeling originated in two elements – he considered Siegel, as a man who had had sea duty, about the only true officer there. And he considered him a man.

Ensign Siegel, for his part, appreciated what he knew to be Garrett's very real desire to be out on a ship. One time when Siegel asked him, Garrett explained why.

'Why, sir, just look around you!' With a sweep of his arm, Garrett indicated the large Media room, with its batteries of desks, type-writers, and filing cabinets, the correspondents' room, from which the cacophony of typewriters and raucous talk could be heard, the adjoining auxiliary Public Relations buildings outside the screened windows. His gesture seemed to take in the whole meaning of the place to him. 'My God, sir,' he said in one of his few fervent moments, 'I want to be able to look people in the eye after the war!'

Ensign Siegel wanted very much to get Garrett sprung. But getting out of Tulura on to a naval vessel was harder than for a battleship to steam through the eye of a needle. And with some reason, as Siegel tried to explain to his yeoman.

'It would look funny as hell,' he said, 'if the exec let you go right at the time he's asked Washington for thirty-five more yeomen.'

'Thirty-five!' Garret exclaimed. 'What the hell are they going to do, sir?'

'Fill chairs,' Siegel explained. 'We've got another shipment of chairs coming.'

Ensign Siegel, with Garrett's concurrence, soon laid down a plan. This was to wait until Washington acted on the exec's manpower request – then to ask for sea duty for Garrett. The arrival of thirty-five new yeomen would give him a certain arguing point, Siegel figured. As it was, there were no arguing points with the exec, despite the prevailing idleness of most of the yeomen already aboard. The last man who asked for sea duty had ended up in the psycho ward of the Fleet Hospital. Lieutenant-Commander Nash had a perfectly reasonable explanation for sending him there.

'There must be something wrong up here,' the exec said, tapping his bald head, 'with any man who would prefer some old tossing tub to the lovely duty we enjoy at Public Relations Headquarters here. Besides that, the man should have realized how vitally we need every man we can get and not be so selfish as to want to be out on a ship.'

Meanwhile Yeoman Garrett, who by philosophy believed in making the calm, relaxed best of his situation, contented himself with going through the shelves of the Fleet Library. He was probably the only man on Tulura who ever checked *The Confessions of Jean-Jacques Rousseau*, Kant's *Critique of Pure Reason*, and Nietzsche's *Thus Spake Zarathustra* out of the library. Once when Ensign Siegel came into the Media Section and stopped to talk with Garrett at the yeoman's desk in front of his, he noticed that the book was Veblen's *The Theory of the Leisure Class*.

'Doing a little professional reading, I see,' Ensign Siegel observed.

'It's all about Tulura,' Yeoman Garrett said.

One day Yeoman Garrett was approached by Lieutenant (jg) Ross Pendleton with an interesting proposition.

Lieutenant (jg) Pendleton was a man accustomed to doing everything on the grand scale. 'There are two ways to live,' Pendleton used to say. 'A man has a choice in this world. He can earn forty thousand a year, have an apartment on East River, eat steaks Châteaubriant, drink Chivas Regal, and get his central heating from the prime ribs of Hollywood. Or he can be what a man like Griffin here is. Small time.'

'I made sixty dollars a week,' Lieutenant Morey Griffin said, framing his words carefully, 'and I've heard it said by others that I was one of the best rewrite men in San Francisco. It was an honest way, in any case, of making a living. Conversing with you and learning that fact which you drill into us so often, Ross, that you dragged twenty thousand a year – I discount everything radio people say by half – is a perfect proof of how dissolute radio is. No self-respecting newspaper would hire you as a copy-boy.'

'You're just small time, Griffin,' Pendleton replied. 'You always were and always will be small time. It's a free country and there's nothing to stop a small-time man from earning sixty dollars a week all his life.'

Pendleton saw no reason why the rigours of war, or at least of Tulura, should interfere with his concept of living. He was the Public Relations Headquarters' best drinking man and his preferred drink was the martini. For some reason, probably in the interests of getting on with the war, gin was the only beverage not in supply at the officers' club. But Ross managed to get regular shipments of gin and vermouth through a pilot who made the run to Honolulu. He also kept his private cellar well supplied by making fast friends, it was believed on a vague promise of post-war radio employment, with the one non-drinking officer in Headquarters, a practising Christian Scientist, and taking his monthly rations off his hands.

Regularly once a week a large package from Pendleton's wife arrived on Tulura, containing one non-edible item – Mexana heat powder – and otherwise crowded with such interesting delicacies as *pâté de foie gras*, pearl onions, Smithfield ham, small cured cheeses, tins of boneless Portuguese sardines and Swedish marinated herring, jars of Norwegian shrimp and spiced Spanish olives, anchovies, and cocktail sausages – an assortment which provided first-rate *matériel* for the frequent twosome picnics which Ross undertook to secluded beaches with various of his nurse companions in his ample leisure time. Ross was the only officer at Headquarters who actually had a selection of women, which were his hobby much as some men collect postage stamps. He used to name famous Hollywood and radio names he'd slept with, and seeing him operate on Tulura, the accounts could be believed. He looked the type, and with his wavy black hair and suave manner, which seemed incapable of being ruffled, was attractive and good-looking in a Radio City sort of way. Besides, he was of a profession, huckstering, traditionally successful with women. He was a great name-dropper.

'Did I ever tell you about the time I slept with – ,' he said, naming an international household word famous for her Florence-Nightingale-type roles.

Then he would relate at length all the details, including what Lieutenant (jg) Pendleton referred to as 'the moment of truth' – the instant at which the pillowed head underwent the metamorphosis from haughty movie star to desire-crazed female. At these times Morey Griffin, writhing in torture, threatened to put a bullet through his, Pendleton's, head if he didn't stop. Griffin always told Pendleton he didn't believe a word of it, but when Pendleton wasn't there, Morey admitted: 'The tragedy of it is that the son of a bitch has actually probably laid half of Hollywood. Why, all you have to do is watch him here – I'll swear to God I'll bet he's slept with most of the women on Tulura.'

In peacetime Lieutenant (jg) Pendleton had never felt the slightest impulse to restrict his charms to one individual woman, and even on Tulura he saw no reason to start being selfish. Increasingly of late, however, he had been aiming the bulk of his efforts at one nurse. Her name was Ensign Alice Thomas and she pursued her temporary naval career in the Fleet Hospital eighteen miles on the other side of the island from Public Relations Headquarters. Knowing Pendleton, and observing the inordinate amounts of attention and time he was beginning to devote to this one woman, the other officers concluded from this fact alone that Ensign Thomas must really have something.

Whatever it was certainly was not at all overwhelmingly apparent. She was a pretty little thing but not, from any appearances of manner or conversation, a great deal more. She seemed a quite average, unthinking, normally extravertish American girl. She was rather saucy, even haughty at times, with eyes that said she knew exactly what she wanted and that this was the hunting season – she would never land a

Ross Pendleton back in her job at Presbyterian Hospital in Manhattan. To anyone else in the Pacific she would probably have appeared endowed with the charms of Cleopatra, but it was something of a mystery why Pendleton, with his rich sources of women even in the Pacific, should be giving her such a whirl.

It was not long after he had begun to concentrate so heavily on Ensign Thomas that Pendleton made his proposition to Yeoman Garrett.

'Garrett,' he said, 'how would you like to do convoy duty when I have a date – pack the old ·45?'

There was an order on Tulura that no nurse could be taken out by an officer unless accompanied by a third, armed officer. This was for the protection of the nurse against the few Japs still in the bushes, though some claimed it was for the protection of the nurse against her date. Garrett had some reason for being quite surprised at the offer from Pendleton.

'Well, sir,' he said, 'that's a very interesting suggestion. But the rule, I believe, says that you have to have an armed *officer* along.' And Garrett pointed a forefinger at his yeoman's stripes.

'Oh, don't bother about that,' Lieutenant (jg) Pendleton said. 'I've fixed all that with Clinton.'

'Clinton?' Garrett said, perplexed.

'Commander Nash,' explained Pendleton, who would have firstnamed the President. 'He said if I preferred an enlisted man I could have an enlisted man.'

Lieutenant (jg) Pendleton did not mention to Garrett his reasons for preferring an enlisted man to an officer as the escort on his dates, though Garrett had a good guess. The reason, of course, was to prevent any other officer from casting lustful eyes or more on Ensign Thomas. With an enlisted man the protection on this count was as foolproof and secure as having a eunuch, under the ancient, unquestioned, non-fraternizing Navy code that an enlisted man cannot date an officer. For a Navy enlisted man to cast lustful eyes on a Navy nurse, or at least to attempt to do anything about it, is as forbidden and as dangerous as for the Sultan's batman to essay a similar course with his master's favourite harem-girl.

'Naturally, Garrett,' Pendleton went on suavely, 'I wouldn't expect you to do this for nothing. There's something in it for you.'

Lieutenant (jg) Pendleton leaned forward confidentially. 'A bottle of Paul Jones a month!'

For an enlisted man in the Pacific, whose only alcoholic beverage was beer, and a limited amount of that, this was golden payment, even though it was little strain on Pendleton with his extra liquor sources. Garrett was properly appreciative.

'I get more interested by the second, Mr Pendleton,' he said.

'I thought you would,' Pendleton said. 'However, before we close the deal there are one or two rather important details to get settled.'

Lieutenant (jg) Pendleton straightened up in his chair.

'There will be times, Garrett,' he explained carefully, 'when I'll want you to make yourself scarce. I don't want any Peeping Toms around when I'm telling Alice good night – or, I hope' – Pendleton grinned lecherously – 'showing her the beach by moonlight. In a word, I don't like *voyeurs*. You know what the word means and is that clear?'

'Affirmative on both counts, sir,' Garrett said. 'I'll wear blinkers if you like.'

Pendleton smiled smoothly. 'Well, that's hardly necessary. However, I'm glad to see you catch the spirit of the thing. Never mind the blinkers, but do keep your eyes in the opposite direction.'

'I won't observe it,' Garrett said, slightly emphasizing the last word.

'I'm glad to see you catch the spirit of the thing. Also,' Pendleton said, 'there is one other item of extreme importance. You are not,' Pendleton said, framing his words with incisive clarity, 'to tell her that I'm married. I have an instinct that Ensign Thomas has one of those old-fashioned blind spots about dating married men that you occasionally run into in a woman. And to put it perfectly frankly, something you might want to remember yourself, Garrett' – Pendleton spoke in the tones of an expert – 'I have a rule of thumb in these things which is, "What they don't know won't hurt me." Do I make myself perfectly clear?'

'A hundred per cent,' Yeoman Garrett said. 'I doubt if there'll be an opportunity – I mean occasion – for me to have two words with her, but if I do it'll be about when the war is going to be over.'

'That's a safe enough subject,' Pendleton said. 'Well, shall we consider that we've come to an understanding?'

'I'm all for it,' Yeoman Garrett said.

'And I hope,' Lieutenant (jg) Pendleton said, closing the deal, 'that you enjoy the Paul Jones as much, heh, heh,' he laughed lecherously, 'as I hope to enjoy Ensign Thomas. Good deal for both of us, eh, Garrett, old man?'

'Sir,' Garrett said, 'it looks like we've both got it made.'

' "Got it made," ' echoed Lieutenant (jg) Pendleton, with a glossy laugh. 'I couldn't put it better myself. At least I have high hopes on my end.'

Almost every night Yeoman Garrett would check out a jeep and a ·45 and drop by the BOQ for Pendleton. From there the two would drive the eighteen miles across the island to the Fleet Hospital. While Garrett waited in the jeep, Lieutenant (jg) Pendleton would go in and pick up his date. When they emerged from the hospital, Garrett would get out of the jeep, come to attention, and smartly salute Ensign Thomas. Lieutenant (jg) Pendleton and Ensign Thomas would sometimes go to the hospital officers' club and pass the evening drinking or attending a dance there, while Garrett waited outside in the jeep or went over and shot the breeze with some of the hospital corpsmen. Usually he would drive the two officers back to the ComFleets officers' club.

Yeoman Garrett had been convoying Lieutenant (jg) Pendleton and Ensign Thomas for some three weeks when he told his own officer, Ensign Siegel, that he had something he had to talk to him about.

'Mr Siegel, this escorting job' – Garrett came to the point – 'it's beginning to get on my nerves. Smelling her perfume, watching her part her lips to put on lipstick, watching her little teeth the way she smiles, and her little tongue, watching the way she smooths her hair back, watching the way she crosses her legs – all this out of the corner of my eye – hearing the rustling …'

'For Christ's sake, Garrett!' Siegel said.

'Believe me, sir, I earn that fifth!' Yeoman Garrett exclaimed suddenly. 'I need it when I'm through!'

Siegel looked in utter dumbfoundment at the animated yeoman. He was flabbergasted to hear this outburst from a man whose easygoing calm he had never seen disturbed.

'It's really beginning to get on my nerves,' Garrett repeated, rubbing his hand through his shock of blond hair.

'Well, why in the hell don't you simply tell Pendleton to get someone else?' Ensign Siegel said.

'Oh, no!' Garrett said, alarmed. 'I can't do that! I mean, I think
night and day about her. It's torture to be with her – with them – but
it's even more torture when I'm not! I live for the time when Mr
Pendleton will have another date with her!'

Before long Yeoman Garrett found himself taking Lieutenant (jg)
Pendleton and Ensign Thomas, not to one of the officers' clubs for
drinking or dancing, but, the two officers sitting in the back seat of
the jeep, just for a drive. As Lieutenant (jg) Pendleton's attentions to
Ensign Thomas made progress, Yeoman Garrett's usual equanimity
retrogressed in almost exact ratio. It was not too many nights longer
before, the day after one of them, Yeoman Garrett asked Ensign
Siegel if he could talk with him again.

'Mr Siegel,' the yeoman said, 'now we're to the point where I'm
sitting in the goddamn jeep while she and Mr Pendleton, saying
they're going for a walk, go off on a beach and have at it. Thirty
paces away! God, I can almost hear them, my ears are straining so!
It's almost more than a man can take, Mr Siegel!'

'Now, Garrett. Maybe they *are* taking a walk,' Ensign Siegel said
in an effort to be reassuring. 'How do you know – why, you can't see
them, you said yourself.'

'How do I know!' Garrett exclaimed with abrupt violence. 'Mr
Pendleton *told* me, that's how I know! Last night, after we'd dropped
Ensign Thomas at the Fleet Hospital about one a.m. and were driving
back here! "Well, Garrett," he said, smiling like a tomcat, "I finally
made it." Then he started in telling me how it was – all the eighteen
miles back to here he kept giving me all the exact details of exactly
how it was! Smiling like a tomcat! That's how I know!'

Ensign Siegel was alarmed, the way Yeoman Garrett appeared to
be almost trembling.

'And you know something else, sir?' Garrett said in sudden outrage. 'Mr Pendleton hasn't even told her he's married!'

'Now, Garrett,' Siegel said. 'You're not getting moralistic about
this, are you?'

'Why, it's obvious to anyone what she is to him!' Garrett exploded. 'She's just a *lay* to him. Nothing but a *lay*!'

'Well, I'm glad your own interests in the young lady are of such a higher order,' Ensign Siegel said. 'Such as the way she crosses her legs.'

Garrett's mind had soon formulated an odd rationale concerning the obvious relationship to which Lieutenant (jg) Pendleton and Ensign Thomas had now arrived. The rationale was that it was all Pendleton's fault. Yeoman Garrett cast Lieutenant (jg) Pendleton in the role of the seducing huckster and Ensign Thomas in that of the glamour-struck but innocent girl just come to the big city. The Pendleton part of this characterization was certainly accurate. The Thomas part would have seemed, at best, to be highly questionable. It overlooked the obvious fact that Ensign Thomas knew, and knew Garrett knew, the purpose of the jeep rides which continued almost every night of the week now. One didn't go jeep-riding along the most deserted roads on Tulura, which were selected ahead of time by Pendleton and passed on to Garrett, for the scenery. In the black boondocks it was impossible to see anything at night anyhow. It entirely overlooked the audible boldness on the part of the nurse when, from the back seat, Garrett would hear the articulations of preliminary love. And the boldness even more when Pendleton, as they reached some beach, at last spoke. 'Oh, say, Garrett. Why don't we pull up here, son? I think Ensign Thomas might like to see the beach.' And Ensign Thomas would giggle, and the two officers would disappear and see the beach for an hour or so while Garrett waited miserably in the jeep. In Garrett's mind all of this was Pendleton's doing, and Ensign Thomas as innocent, if not technically as pure, as the driven snow.

'Mr Pendleton,' Garrett exclaimed one day to Ensign Siegel, 'why, he's – he's just a Radio City glamour boy; you know that yourself, sir! And *her*. Well, sir, I think he takes advantage of her!'

'That's a very admirable, protective attitude, Garrett,' Siegel said. 'And I hate to disillusion you. But most Navy nurses I've had the privilege of knowing can take care of themselves, if they happen to feel like taking care of themselves, even with Radio City glamour boys. I doubt that Pendleton has to take her at gun-point.'

Garrett rubbed his hand across his forehead. 'But, sir! She's such a *nice* girl.'

Ensign Siegel looked for a long moment at his yeoman.

'Garrett,' he said, 'how long since you had a woman?'

Garrett waited a moment, rubbing his forehead.

'Two years,' he said miserably. 'I've been two years in the Pacific.'

'Man,' said Ensign Siegel, 'Battleship Mary would look nice to you right now.'

'Maybe so, Mr Siegel,' the yeoman said miserably. 'I don't know. I don't know anything any more. Probably you're right. Probably it's just plain sex. But ...'

Garrett looked across suddenly at the ensign.

'But you know something else on that very point, sir? I think *she* likes me. Lately I caught her looking at me once or twice when Mr Pendleton wasn't watching. Least I thought I did. Probably wishful thinking,' the yeoman added bitterly.

One night something happened that made Yeoman Garrett decide it was really no longer bearable for him.

'Last night, Mr Siegel,' Garrett told his officer, 'we stopped at what looked like a usable beach, but just to make sure Mr Pendleton went off to case it. It was the first time we – Ensign Thomas and I, that is – had ever been alone. We were alone for about five minutes. There I was, sitting in the front seat, and there she was, sitting in the back seat.'

'What the hell happened?' Siegel said impatiently.

'Nothing!' Yeoman Garrett said. 'That's just it. Not a thing happened.' Garrett buried his head in his hands. 'However, maybe something did happen. I'm to the point where the slightest thing, if it concerns *her*, has significance to me. Maybe if I told you about it, you could give me your interpretation.'

'For God's sake, what was it?' Siegel said.

'Well,' Garrett sighed heavily. 'We were sitting there, Ensign Thomas and me. For the first minute or two after Mr Pendleton had gone neither of us said a word. You know how quiet it can get on Tulura at night? Well, it was that kind of quietness, almost terrifying. And so black you couldn't see a thing. I probably couldn't have seen her if I turned around. I didn't turn around, but I certainly knew she was there ...'

'Garrett, if you don't get on with this,' Siegel said, 'I'm going to be sent to Portsmouth Naval Prison for striking an enlisted man.'

'I was just trying to give you the setting, sir.'

'I've got the goddamn setting,' Siegel said. 'What *happened*?'

'Well, as I say, neither of us said a word for about two minutes. Then I heard her speak. I guess it was the first word she had ever spoken to me.'

'What did she say – "Now it's your turn, Buster"?'

'By God, Mr Siegel!' Garrett said angrily. 'You're as bad as Mr Pendleton!'

'Sorry, Garrett,' Siegel said.

'She isn't *like* that,' Garrett protested.

'I know,' Siegel said wearily. 'All right, let's try once more. What,' Ensign Siegel almost shouted, '*happened*?'

'Mr Siegel, I didn't mean that about your being as bad as Mr Pendleton,' Garrett said. 'I lost my temper.'

'Garrett, for Christ's sake, what *happened*? What did she *say*?'

'She said,' Garrett said, and breathed a long, deep breath. 'She said, "Garrett, I just want you to know that I realize this is a little hard on you."'

'The bitch!' Ensign Siegel exploded. 'Christ Al-mighty! "I realize this is a little hard on you."' Siegel mimicked his idea of a nurse's voice. 'Holy Jesus, Garrett!' Siegel said. 'Why in the world do you want to go drooling off after a bitch like that for!'

'Oh, no, Mr Siegel!' Garrett cried out. 'She isn't *like* that at all. You know what that remark told me about her?'

'The way your mind is functioning,' Ensign Siegel said, 'I don't have the faintest idea.'

'It means she has a sense of *humanity*,' Garrett said. 'She thought about what all this was doing to *me*.'

Ensign Siegel looked directly at Garrett a long time, then sighed, a deep, heavy sigh.

'Well, Garrett, I don't have a thing to say. I don't think you have enough judgement left to distinguish between the motives of Joan of Arc and Madame Bovary.'

'And I can't even date her!' Yeoman Garrett cried out. 'No matter how *we* felt, I can't even date her.'

'It's probably the most ancient of Navy rules,' Siegel said. 'The last vestiges of discipline would disappear if enlisted men started laying officers.'

'Mr Siegel!' Garrett exploded.

'I know,' Siegel said wearily. 'Please don't tell me any more how Pendleton's raping her every night on the beach.'

'Mr Siegel!' Garrett said in outrage.

Then Yeoman Garrett went limp. All of him seemed to sag in his chair. He buried his head in his hands and slowly, over and over again, he rubbed his hand across his forehead.

'Mr Siegel, I'm going nuts! I can't date her! They won't let me date her!' the yeoman cried passionately.

Ensign Siegel, looking at his bent-over yeoman, thought of the traditional Navy rule against an enlisted man dating a nurse, the nurse being quite naturally an officer, rather than a woman, as far as the Navy was concerned. His eyes rested idly on the row of four clocks on the wall which gave the time in San Francisco, Denver, Chicago, and New York. The clocks were there for the benefit of correspondents' meeting deadlines, but Siegel had a pastime of sitting and watching them and wondering what the people in those cities were doing right now. In Chicago, he noticed, it was seven p.m. People were getting ready to go out on dates. As his eyes rested back on Garrett, something quite basic occurred to Ensign Siegel. If the processes of unnautical natural selection were permitted to take their course, he thought, any woman worthy of that title would deeply prefer Yeoman Second Class Adam Garrett to Lieutenant Junior Grade Ross Pendleton.

'Garrett,' he said abruptly, 'see if you can hold out for a few more days – I mean nights. Do you think you can do that?'

'What she said,' Yeoman Garrett, who had not heard the officer, said desperately, 'I'll never forget it. "I just want you to know that I realize this is a little hard on you." Nobody but a woman *full* of humanity could ever make a remark like that!'

It was two nights later that the Japs attacked. The attack shot a vicarious thrill through Public Relations Headquarters and for a few days the letters home had the quality of having been written from the D-day beaches of Iwo Jima. A real banzai attack on Tulura! Of all places.

The attack was made on Lieutenant (jg) Ross Pendleton, Ensign Alice Thomas, and Yeoman Second Class Adam Garrett. It occurred on the eighteen-mile road which led from Public Relations Headquarters to the Fleet Hospital, following the sea for the most part.

On those exposed stretches no Jap could have got at anyone even if he'd cared to. But at two or three points there were long rocky promontories which had forced the Seabees who built the road to cut it through thick jungle, no longer than a mile in any one stretch. It was in one of these jungle stretches that the Japs attacked.

It was a moonless night. Yeoman Garrett was cruising the jeep at only about fifteen miles an hour, his passengers warming up for a certain operating ground down the way, with a certain convenient and flat rock above the water where Lieutenant (jg) Pendleton and the nurse often stopped. Garrett was listening to the muffled noises from the back seat, when suddenly a rifle-shot cracked the still night. Ensign Thomas screamed. Simultaneously a hissing noise escaped from aft the three passengers. A tyre had been hit.

'Take her through!' Lieutenant (jg) Pendleton shouted at Garrett. 'Give her the gun!'

Garrett jammed down the accelerator, with the result that Ensign Thomas was almost thrown from the vehicle, which was now riding on a rim.

'For God's sake, Ross!' she screamed.

Another rifle-shot barked, followed by another hiss of air. The jeep was now rocking like a destroyer in a typhoon. Nevertheless Pendleton ordered Garrett to keep course.

'Take her through!' he shouted in tones of command.

'Stop, for God's sake!' Ensign Thomas screamed hysterically. 'You'll kill us all, Ross!'

'It's Japs!' Pendleton yelled. 'Hold on, honey! We can't stop! It's Japs!'

However, the jeep expired and stopped on its own. A jeep could probably ride along on the rims, but one rim had been mangled by the second shot.

'Hit the ditch!' Pendleton chattered.

Ensign Thomas was out of the jeep and into the ditch and Lieutenant (jg) Pendleton and Yeoman Garrett joined her, all three crouching low in the ravine. The nurse kept whimpering like a cold kitten, and Pendleton was no more help, his shaking voice jerking out various tactical manoeuvres.

'Listen, Garrett! You go one way and I'll go the other, and we'll encircle them.'

'And leave me here!' Ensign Thomas squealed. 'You won't do any such thing! Oh, Garrett, I'm scared!'

Pendleton looked sharply down at the nurse for addressing her fear to Garrett, instead of himself, and placed his arm assertively around her. She drew up against him.

'Garrett's got the gun,' Ensign Thomas explained.

'Yes, maybe you better give me that side-arm, Garrett,' Pendleton said. 'After all, I am senior in command here.' Pendleton said this so weakly, however, that Garrett chose to disregard it. Pendleton didn't want the gun anyhow, never having fired a ·45, and he didn't mention his command status again. The three naval personnel crouched and waited in the black stillness where the thickness of the jungle rose close and menacing around them.

'Why doesn't something happen?' Ensign Thomas shrieked.

It was as if the scream were the signal for a banzai. Suddenly almost at their backs came a medley of terror-striking yells of many men: 'Yankee soljer, you die!' just like the Japs did it, as Pendleton had heard in the radio broadcasts which he arranged. A score of small, Jap-sized shadows sprang from the bushes. A wild mêlée followed, with the girl's shriekings, Pendleton's yells 'Go away! Go away!' addressed to the shadows racing towards them, and a couple of ·45 pistol shots fired by Yeoman Garrett filling the air. Ensign Thomas was horrified to see several of the figures pounce on Pendleton. Moving as fleet as weasels they threw a blanket over the lieutenant junior grade's head, stifling his yells, and dragged him back into the jungle. They did not touch Ensign Thomas or Yeoman Second Class Garrett, who were now alone in the black night.

'Oh, poor Ross!' the nurse sobbed, her head in her hands. 'Poor Ross! Why did they take just him, Garrett? Why?'

Yeoman Garrett shrugged. 'I don't know, ma'am – senior in command, I guess.'

Ensign Thomas was hysterical enough to believe almost anything, but this sounded strange, and she took her head out of her hands and looked up at Garrett.

'Why, that's silly! They couldn't tell.'

'Couldn't they? They could certainly tell the difference between this pyjama suit' – Garrett indicated his enlisted man's clothing – 'and an officer's uniform.'

'Well, maybe they could,' Ensign Thomas said. But she repeated, 'Oh, why did they take poor Ross?'

'Hostage. They probably want him for a hostage. Anyhow, I don't think we should stand here and philosophize about it, ma'am. Frankly, ma'am, I think we better get the hell out of here.'

'Yes, let's go for some help for poor Ross,' Ensign Thomas said.

Yeoman Garrett and Ensign Thomas started walking down the road, choosing the way that led towards the Fleet Hospital. They figured they could be no more than six miles away and this was the last stretch of jungle. In the black night with the boondocks close on them from both sides, Ensign Thomas kept whimpering and looking over her shoulder. She gave a great sigh of relief when they emerged from the jungle and the road went along the sea again.

'Oh, Garrett, I'm so tired!' Ensign Thomas said. 'I know a rock ledge over there.'

'Yes, I know you do,' Yeoman Garrett said matter-of-factly.

'I'm so tired!' Ensign Thomas repeated. 'Do you think it would matter if we sat down and rested a moment before going for help? Or do you think we should go on right now?'

'Well, I don't think it would hurt to rest just for a moment,' Yeoman Garrett said judiciously.

Angling off the road, they found the ledge that jutted out above the sea, which was hitting in perhaps thirty feet below them. Suddenly the nurse buried her head in her hands, sobbing, 'Poor Ross! Oh, Garrett!'

'I'm sorry you're so upset, ma'am,' Garrett said formally.

'And I'm sorry to be such a cry-baby,' Ensign Thomas said. 'Not a very good example for an officer to set with an enlisted man, is it?'

'I wouldn't let that worry me, ma'am,' Garrett said. 'After all, I am a man – and you're a woman.'

Ensign Thomas looked up at Garrett. 'However,' she said, 'I'm also a naval officer.'

'Yes, ma'am,' Garrett said formally.

'So there!' Ensign Thomas said. 'I'll just stop crying. There! I've stopped.'

The yeoman and the ensign sat a moment listening to the sea, which, though so near, they could not see through the night's blackness, but could hear washing the rocks below them.

'Isn't it strange?' Ensign Thomas said. 'I mean the way you can't see a thing. I have such a strange feeling, Garrett. It's so dark I can't even see you.'

'I can't see you either,' Garrett said. 'But I can tell you're there. I can smell your perfume.'

'Oh,' Ensign Thomas said rather crisply. 'We better be going, Garrett.'

She had started to get up when Garrett said abruptly, 'Ma'am, do you love him?'

There was a long, cold silence on the rock. 'Garrett,' Ensign Thomas said quite crisply then, 'that's not a very proper question, is it?'

'No, it isn't,' Garrett apologized. 'I'm sorry, ma'am. It's none of my business,' the yeoman said. He was miserable. 'I'm sorry I asked it.'

Garrett heard the ensign move a little on the rock. 'That's all right,' she said, less officer-like. She waited a moment. 'Do you have anyone out here ... Oh, I'm sorry.'

'Don't mind it, ma'am,' Yeoman Garrett said. 'It's an old Navy rule.'

'Oh, I am sorry!' Ensign Thomas said. 'How thoughtless of me!' she put in. 'Because,' she said hesitantly, 'you ... you can't ...'

She waited a moment, then: 'How long have you been – out here?'

'Two years in the Pacific, ma'am,' Garrett said. He could feel his heart pounding.

'Two years!' Ensign Thomas said. There was a sudden pity in her voice. 'What a long time without ...'

'You have no idea, ma'am,' Yeoman Garrett said.

His whole body seemed to project towards her, everything that he was as a man, all the Pacific's deprivation of his manhood. While Ensign Thomas, though feeling a detached pity, otherwise felt that calmness which those for whom it was not two years, but one night ago, can so richly afford.

'Well, we better be going, Garrett,' she said. 'We really had.'

'They probably won't do a thing to Mr Pendleton!' Garrett said with urgent reassurance. 'They undoubtedly just wanted the jeep.'

'Maybe so,' Ensign Thomas said. 'But we don't know what might be happening to him. Come on, let's go,' she said firmly.

'Oh, ma'am,' Garrett suddenly burst out. 'You don't know how miserable I've been these past few weeks! I've gone almost crazy! Being around you. Looking at you! Watching you smile! The sounds of you, the smells of you! Oh, ma'am! You don't know the hell I've been through! It's like the worst kind of torture! I can't sleep for thinking about you. I wake up looking at you. The littlest thing about you makes everything jump up and down inside me. The way you brush your hair back with your hand, watching you part your lips to put on lipstick, watching ... Oh, ma'am, you're a naval officer, I know. But you're a woman, too ...'

Suddenly Yeoman Garrett stopped. In a terrible realization, it came over him. He was crawling! And suddenly, as in a searchlight, he saw a picture of himself over the past few weeks. Panting, babbling, drooling, and now, finally, right on this rock in front of her, like a dog sitting up for a bone, almost wagging his tail! A wave of self-loathing engulfed him. He hated himself. He hated Ensign Thomas. He hated being here. He hated everything about it.

A convulsion of fury and violence seized him. Abruptly he turned savagely on the rock towards Ensign Thomas. So beside himself was he that he forgot the rank-infested danger, and a torrent of rage emptied from him.

'None of this raid happened tonight,' he said savagely. 'You understand that? It was all a fraud. From beginning to end it was a fraud! A put-up job! A fake! You understand? Those "Japs" were Tulurans. You understand that?' he said viciously. 'The whole thing was arranged. You understand, Ensign Thomas? A fraud! A fake!'

Ensign Thomas sat flabbergasted at the outburst – and at the news.

'The raid didn't really happen?' she said slowly, incredulously. 'You mean ... it was all ... so you could ...'

'Come on!' Yeoman Garrett shouted in a spasm of rage. 'Let's get the hell out of here – ma'am!' he added, hurling the word bitterly at the ensign. 'Let's go get some help for poor Ross!'

With a furious push against the rock, Yeoman Garrett was on his feet and starting away. Not a sound came from Ensign Thomas.

'Come on!' he barked. He stood there trembling with rage. 'Get the hell up, Ensign Thomas, and let's go!'

Suddenly, in a moment of sanity, he realized the enormity of the evening – the way he, an enlisted man, was talking to one naval officer, how he had arranged the abduction of another naval officer. In a moment of absolute terror he saw a vision of himself at age eighty chopping rocks in a naval prison. Then his fury rushed back into him. The hell with it! he thought. Let them send me to Portsmouth!

'God damn it, didn't you hear me?' he shouted down to Ensign Thomas. 'I said come on!'

There was a soft rustling movement from the rock. And suddenly a hand touched his face. It froze him.

The hand, which was incredibly soft, began to move across his face. The tips of the fingers touched his nose, his cheeks, along his ear, his lips, slipped down around his neck. Yeoman Garrett felt he would swoon away.

'Oh, ma'am!' he said in a sudden wail, all of his self-respecting fury gone like the sheerest wisp of cloud.

'Adam,' Ensign Thomas said.

'Oh, ma'am!' Yeoman Garrett said.

'Stop calling me ma'am,' Ensign Thomas said, her voice a whisper.

Then Yeoman Garrett felt a small hand taking hold of his. He felt his hand being lifted and then placed on top of hers along her throat. He felt her hands make a couple of quick movements. Then he felt two small objects being placed in his hand.

'Throw them away, Adam,' she said.

With a flick of his fingers Yeoman Garrett sent first one, then the other, over the side of the ledge. The ensign's bars made two small clinks on the rocks below.

Near dawn next day a company of Marines was dispatched into the stretch of jungle where Pendleton had been taken. They never found anything. Pendleton himself wandered in later that morning, with a swaggering, wild-eyed tale of being held captive and blindfolded all night long. He said he guessed the Japs were after the jeep. He and Garrett were sort of heroes around Public Relations Headquarters for a few days and as a matter of fact some of the officers went over and got the Seabees to knock out a couple of huge tin medals bearing the legend: 'Second Battle of Tulura'.

That afternoon Ensign Siegel and Yeoman Garrett took a walk down the hill to the ship's service store.

'Well, did it go?' Siegel asked.

Yeoman Garrett was silent a moment, a silence of delicacy. 'It went,' he said quietly then, in such a manner that Siegel realized the man was in some sort of daze.

'I thought it would,' Siegel said dryly. 'She's got so much humanity.'

'Oh, indeed she has, sir,' said Garrett, on whom anything but adoration for Ensign Thomas was now lost.

They waited for a jeep to pass, then crossed the road.

'Those Tulurans!' Siegel said with abrupt enthusiasm. 'I tell you, they're a great people. So adaptable.'

Garrett seemed suddenly miserable. 'I know, sir,' he said, 'but I was just thinking. Even if they are your friends, we can't have them pull off a raid every night, can we?'

'No, I suppose not,' Siegel said. 'Pendleton would probably catch on after a dozen or so of them. However, now that we've started this historic violation of Navy manners, we can't chicken out and stop, can we?'

'I couldn't stop and still live,' Garrett said dazedly. 'I'm in love!'

'Yes, I know,' Ensign Siegel said with a patient sigh. 'Just remember, you've been in the Pacific two years.'

Shortly after that a development that rocked the officers of the Public Relations Headquarters took place. Ensign Alice Thomas stopped dating the glamour-glazed Lieutenant (jg) Ross Pendleton. No one was more astounded than Lieutenant (jg) Pendleton that any woman would voluntarily give him up. After that, Ensign Thomas was seen occasionally with Ensign Max Siegel. The very idea that any woman who had enjoyed the priceless privilege of his company could spend five minutes with Siegel so infuriated Pendleton that he almost stopped speaking to his fellow officer.

'Ross' – Siegel tried to make Pendleton feel better – 'you shouldn't be hurt about this.'

'Hurt!' Pendleton bellowed, enraged at the adjective.

'These things happen all the time,' Siegel continued benignly. 'Besides, you've got practically every other woman on the island sewn up. You can afford to be generous and let old Siegel have a date once in a while with Alice.'

'Take her! Take her!' Pendleton said furiously. 'Take the slut!'

'Careful there, old man,' Siegel said. 'You're speaking of the woman I might love.' Siegel let his eyes glow lecherously. 'My, what a lovely slut she is!'

'I'm warning you,' Pendleton said ominously.

'Ross, old man,' Siegel said, settling a detail, 'you don't mind if I use Garrett for the convoy duty, do you? You've broken him in, and after all he is my yeoman.'

'You can use ComFleets as far as I'm concerned!' Pendleton exploded. 'What you work out with the slut is your own business.'

'Ross, it's wonderful of you to be so big about this,' Ensign Siegel said graciously.

Suddenly Pendleton's eyes widened in an idea. 'Max,' he said in friendly tones, 'I feel I ought to warn you that she's a very calculating woman.'

'Why, thanks for mentioning that, old boy,' Siegel said gratefully. 'However, I'll take my chances. In the Pacific a man would take his chances on Lucrezia Borgia herself.'

'Okay, you son of a bitch,' Pendleton said.

When Siegel and the ·45-armed Garrett went over to the Fleet Hospital on the other side of the island, Garrett would wait outside while Ensign Siegel entered the hospital and picked Ensign Thomas up. As the two officers came out of the hospital, Garrett, standing by the jeep, would snap to attention and salute the nurse. Then she and Ensign Siegel would get in the back seat of the jeep. Yeoman Garrett would slip in behind the driver's wheel and drive the two ensigns to some deserted road. From his experience with Lieutenant (jg) Pendleton and Ensign Thomas, Yeoman Garrett knew like the back of his hand all the deserted roads on Tulura. By now night would be falling and Yeoman Garrett would pull the jeep up alongside the road. He would get out of the jeep. From the back Ensign Siegel would get out.

'Watch relieved!' Ensign Siegel would say, saluting Garrett.

Yeoman Garrett would then climb into the back seat alongside Ensign Thomas. Ensign Siegel would climb into the driver's seat and the jeep would continue as before along the deserted road. Sometimes the jeep would stop and Yeoman Garrett and Ensign Thomas would disappear on to a beach. Ensign Siegel, a man who was never lonely with his own thoughts, would sit contentedly for the hour or so before they came back. Returning to the hospital, Garrett would be in the driver's seat and Ensigns Siegel and Thomas in the back. Arriving there, Siegel would escort Ensign Thomas back inside.

'Thanks for a lovely evening.' Siegel, with a small bow, would bid Ensign Thomas good night.

'Oh, Max,' Alice said one night, squeezing the big ensign's hand for a moment and looking up at him high above her. 'If there was a Legion of Merit for helping the cause of love you'd get the first one, with crossed Cupids. Sometimes I feel almost like you're the officer-in-charge of this love affair.'

'I know, my little chicken,' Ensign Siegel said dryly. 'I'm always glad to do my bit for Love – capital letter, please – or for Humanity.'

Ensign Siegel noticed that Yeoman Garrett never said anything more about sea duty.

Yeoman Garrett could not date Ensign Thomas. He could not take her to dances. He could not even be seen with her. Nevertheless, their affair, thanks to Ensign Siegel's management of it, moved along – always under the protection of night – on a fiery course.

For his part, Yeoman Garrett was like a man who after a two-year hunger fast is suddenly led alone to a sumptuous table, brimming with delectable dishes, and invited to help himself.

For her part Ensign Thomas, who had started out with pity, for the first time in her life found herself really awakened. She had thought, since her arrival in the Pacific and the slavish attendance upon her by scores of naval officers of ranks ranging from ensign to captain, that she was in a female heaven. And when she got Lieutenant (jg) Ross Pendleton, whose Hooper rating among the nurses of the Fleet Hospital perhaps led all Tulura, she felt she had won her harp and wings. With Pendleton, who had breached the boudoirs of the stars, as he himself had informed her, she assumed that it must be good. Now she knew that Lieutenant (jg) Pendleton was a boy scout of love compared with Yeoman Second Class Garrett.

Pendleton, that *clinical* Pendleton! Yes, clinical as a hospital physical! But Garrett ... Adam! His love-making poured over her until every nerve-fibre in her tingled and seemed on fire, until she could have swooned in her ecstasy – and repeatedly did, on many a Tulura beach. She was in love, deeply, completely in love.

The reason Yeoman Garrett was a better lover than Lieutenant (jg) Pendleton was, of course, that he appreciated it infinitely more. The slightest thing about Ensign Thomas excited him wildly. It was this that really sent the ensign to a degree she felt she had never really known what a man was before.

But then Garrett underwent a critical metamorphosis in his emotions about Ensign Thomas. As the weeks passed, as his deprivation ceased so richly, the wildness began to dissipate itself. There came a time when Garrett knew that Ensign Siegel had been right – it was the two years in the Pacific. He had never really been in love with Ensign Thomas. He had been in love with Woman.

However, this discovery changed matters scarcely at all. With emotion out of the way, Yeoman Garrett sat back and enjoyed himself. He recaptured not only his former relaxed attitude but compounded it geometrically. Almost every night he sallied forth from Public Relations Headquarters for a beatific evening with Ensign Thomas. They lay for luxurious hours on beaches from one end of Tulura to the other. Ensign Thomas's storehouse of excitements seemed unending. Like no other enlisted man in the Pacific, he knew, Yeoman Garrett had it made.

Not being in love, Garrett was free to notice, as no man in love can, some of Ensign Thomas's faults. He was appalled at first, and then amused, over the fact that she had read practically nothing in her life. It seemed incredible to Yeoman Garrett that an American youth could reach age twenty-two without knowing such elementary facts as who Balzac was, without ever having heard of the Battle of Hastings, with thinking that Newton was a form of cookie.

'Alice,' he once told her as they lay idly and deliciously stroking each other on a beach, 'I swear, I don't believe you've ever thought beyond the-importance-of-the-lastex-girdle level.'

'Is that bad?' Ensign Thomas said open-mindedly. 'I mean – isn't the most important thing for a woman to be a woman?'

Abruptly Garrett smiled in the darkness. 'Honey,' he said, 'you keep right on being a woman.'

Yeoman Garrett began to like Ensign Thomas.

The danger of what they were doing, their breaking of an inflexible Navy rule, if anything gave a certain fillip to their affair, at least to Ensign Thomas.

'I like fooling them,' she told Garrett one night as they lay on another beach looking up at the star-lavished Pacific sky. 'Fooling all the admirals, all the officer brass, all the Navy code which says we can't be together. Isn't it lovely to fool them, Adam?'

'I hadn't thought about it,' Yeoman Garrett said.

But then he did start to think about it.

'Alice,' he said one night as her hand moved tantalizingly under his enlisted man's jumper. 'Has something ever occurred to you? We haven't ever seen each other in daylight!'

'Why, so we haven't,' Ensign Thomas said, surprised. She giggled. 'But aren't the nights nice?'

'Now, honey, be serious a moment,' Yeoman Garrett said firmly.

'Yes, darling,' Ensign Thomas said meekly.

'Isn't this ridiculous when you stop and think about it?' Garrett went on. 'Siegel goes into the hospital and picks you up. You come out and I salute you. Salute you! Then you two get in the back seat and I drive you out somewhere. Then I stop the jeep and Siegel and I change places. Then he drives us somewhere like here. Then he waits out there by the road for an hour or two, like he is right now. Then you two get in the back seat and I drive you back to the hospital. Then he takes you inside. What childishness!' Yeoman Garrett suddenly burst out.

'But, honey,' Ensign Thomas said reasonably, 'how else can we do it?'

'You mean I'm not good enough to walk right in the hospital in this goddamn little-boy pyjama suit and say, "Where's my date the ensign!"' Garrett roared the phrase.

'Now, honey,' Ensign Thomas said soothingly. 'You know I don't mean that. You know that the first time you did it they wouldn't let us see each other again.'

The very thought of this prospect put the fear of God into Yeoman Garrett for a moment.

'I guess you're right,' he said, suddenly subdued.

But, then, a couple of nights later, he was back at it. His fingers were moving gently over her face when they stopped suddenly.

'What's wrong, darling?' Ensign Thomas, who was probably a much wiser woman than her lover thought, could tell at once something was.

'I don't know,' Garrett said, almost pouting. 'Well, it's just that I'd like to *see* you.'

Then he exploded angrily. 'God damn it, I feel like a … like a goddamn weasel or something that can come out only at night!'

'I know,' Ensign Thomas said quietly. 'But, honey, why fight something we don't have to fight?' she said in an effort at reason. 'We're happy. We're having what we want – this. Why fight it when we've won already? Why not let well enough alone?'

It was a woman's advice and really excellent advice. But Yeoman Garrett was not the sort who could let well enough alone.

On her next day off, he finally decided, he would drive over to the hospital just by himself and pick Ensign Thomas up. He would wear bathing-trunks and a T-shirt, which would not reveal his lack of rank and which officers often wore anyhow when picking nurses up for daytime swimming dates. This struck a balance between being an obvious enlisted man and impersonating an officer. And they would be at least partly in the open.

Ensign Thomas tried to oppose this plan. She never had a chance.

'I'll pick you up Thursday at noon,' Yeoman Garrett firmly told her.

'All right, then, Adam,' she said slowly.

Thursday when Garrett stopped by for Ensign Thomas she was very nervous. Nervous when he came in for her, nervous as they started away from the hospital, Ensign Thomas walking faster than usual. This made Garrett a little angry and he deliberately slowed his own pace.

'What's wrong? Are you ashamed of me?'

'Do you like saying silly things?' she said in a low voice.

But as they got into the jeep and started away, Yeoman Garrett said, 'I'm sorry, Alice.' Then he looked over at her. And she looked at him. They had never really seen each other completely before. And each could only gain by daylight.

'My God, how lovely you are!' Yeoman Garrett said in awe.

'Oh, Adam!' Ensign Thomas said, feeling an equal awe.

Garrett swerved the jeep sharply, where he had wandered over to the left side of the road, to avert a three-quarter-ton truck bearing down on them.

Garrett, who was a superb swimmer, decided to try a new beach he had heard of situated on the remote side of the island, where the swimming was supposed to be particularly good. The beach, walled on three sides by the black boondocks, was of white sand so fine as to seem pulverized, and soft as a woman's hair. It sloped gently down to water of a blueness almost unreal and clear as a shined window. It was quiet water, shielded by the coral reef which rose whitely a couple of hundred yards out. They could hardly wait to get into it.

For a while they idled happily in the water, the warm contentment of the day lightly covering the excitement that swelled in anticipation in them. Ensign Thomas splashed water into Garrett's face, Garrett grabbed the ensign and lifted her into his arms as easily as lifting a puppy, then effortlessly tossed her, amid screams and giggles, into the water. Then she lay on her back, in the water, body and face to the sky, while he held her up with one hand flat under her waist and with the other traced her body, which he had never really seen before.

After a couple of hours Garrett left Ensign Thomas, whose swimming ability was limited to perhaps thirty furious feet, dog-paddling around inside, and struck out beyond the coral reef for a shot of real swimming. With long strokes he paced off about a half-mile one way in the deep water, a half-mile back. These long swims always made him feel exuberant, and today, probably from knowing what was waiting for him on shore, he felt he owned the sea. Coming back inside the reef, he waded out of the water and saw her lying in the sun, asleep. Silently he knelt by her. Then he lay down, and resting on one elbow, looked down upon her for a long time.

Then he took her into his arms.

'Adam!' His wet body against her own sun-heated body awakened her.

'Oh, Adam!' she said. 'Not here. It's broad daylight.'

'Nobody's in ten miles,' he said, drawing her to him. 'Yep, it's daylight!' he said suddenly, and joyously. 'Pure, broad, sunny daylight up there! Do you realize we've never ... we've never in the daylight! Never in the sun!'

Afterwards they lay in each other's arms, looking up at the sunny sky.

'I feel so free!' Yeoman Garrett said. 'Alice, I love you,' he said before he knew it. But then, surprised, he realized that it was true.

'Yes, darling,' Ensign Thomas said drowsily, since she had never known that he didn't.

Yeoman Garrett began to feel sleepy, too, from sun and love ...

Ensign Thomas came to with a start. She was still in Garrett's arms — and the sun had begun to pale in the sky.

'Adam,' she said, waking him. 'It's late. We have to hurry, honey. When I'm off in the day, I have the night watch, you know.'

Garrett picked her up and carried her through the stretch of underbrush to the jeep, where he set her down in the front seat.

'How I love you!' Yeoman Garrett said with an air of discovery, his lips moving across hers.

'Me, too,' Ensign Thomas said, her fingers touching his cheeks.

Yeoman Garrett felt very strange, quietly and nicely strange. All the way back to the hospital he kept thinking: How odd, to fall in love now. With *her*. With a very specific woman named Alice Thomas.

By the time they reached the hospital it was almost dusk.

'You better just drop me,' Ensign Thomas said as they drove into the grounds. 'And not come in. Let's not live too dangerously, darling.'

Garrett started to get out, but Alice squeezed his hand.

'Please, darling,' she said. 'It was ... it was. Let the ensign know best this time.'

Yeoman Garrett smiled. 'Okay, Ensign,' he said, drawing his finger under her chin.

She hopped out and he waited, watching her go up the walk. He sat a few moments longer, watching the door where she had disappeared. My God, how I am in love with her, he thought. This day!

He had just turned to start the jeep when he saw Lieutenant (jg) Pendleton sitting in a jeep about twenty feet in front of his and looking straight at him. Pendleton had a nurse with him. They somehow looked as if they had been sitting there a while. Then Pendleton started his jeep, and whirled into the driveway. As he passed Garrett's jeep, no more than a yard away, he slowed almost to a halt.

'Well, how was it, Garrett?' he said. 'Pretty good, eh?'

Then Pendleton gunned his jeep so suddenly that the spinning tyres almost spat gravel into Garrett's face. Yeoman Garrett sat there a moment. Then he started his jeep and drove slowly out of the hospital grounds. It took him a long time to cover the eighteen miles to Public Relations Headquarters. Most of the way, all he could keep thinking, bitterly, was the thing he had said out there under the sun when he had really just discovered her, 'I feel so free'.

'Sailors,' Lieutenant-Commander Nash said at the morning conference of Public Relations officers, 'one of the most serious things in all my naval command history has happened, and certainly one of the most *unusual* problems of all I've ever had to deal with.'

'What is it, Commander?' Lieutenant-Commander Arnold Gladney said solicitously.

'Love!' the exec said. 'By that I mean plain, raw, unadulterated sex.'

The officers' ears went immediately into general quarters.

'An enlisted man,' Commander Nash exploded, 'is dating an officer!'

'My God, sir!' Griffin said, appalled. 'I didn't know we had any of that kind in our midst!'

'No, no, it's perfectly normal!' the exec put in hurriedly. 'By that I mean stupendously abnormal.'

'How's that, Commander?' Griffin said, perplexed.

'An enlisted man is dating a nurse-officer!' the exec burst forth.

The rows of officers sat up with great interest in their chairs.

'Great Lord!' exclaimed Lieutenant-Commander Gladney. 'Who is it?'

'Yeoman Second Class Garrett,' the exec angrily let out the name, 'has been secretly dating one of the Fleet Hospital personnel!'

'Garrett!' Two or three officers repeated the name with various emotions.

'How in the world could that happen?' Lieutenant-Commander Wayne Hereford asked.

'How should I know?' Commander Nash said violently. 'I'm not Dorothy Dix. All I'm interested in is that one of our men has been violating one of the oldest of all naval laws. An enlisted man dating an officer! It's unheard of!'

'Who's the nurse?' asked Lieutenant Griffin. 'Anybody we know?'

'I wouldn't know whether you do or not, Griffin,' the exec said wearily. 'Her name is Ensign Alice Thomas.'

'Ensign Alice Thomas ...' Griffin said slowly. 'Why' – he turned slightly in his chair to look at Lieutenant (jg) Ross Pendleton in the row behind him – 'isn't that the babe you used to go with, Ross?'

'I know her,' Lieutenant (jg) Pendleton said. 'A real slut. I had a date or two with her myself before dropping her for something more interesting.'

This was a new explanation to the other officers as to why Ensign Thomas and Pendleton had ceased dating, and they looked at the radio liaison officer with interest.

'Well!' Lieutenant Griffin said. 'I always thought Ensign Thomas was pretty well stacked up.'

'I guess that's how Garrett got to know her,' the exec said. 'He carried the ·45 for Ross here when Ross had a couple of dates, as he says, with this Thomas woman.'

'A couple of dates?' Lieutenant Griffin turned in his chair. 'I seem to remember you were giving Ensign Thomas a hell of a rush, Ross. Well!'

'I wasn't aware you followed my personal affairs so closely, Griffin,' Pendleton said acidly.

'Well!' Lieutenant Griffin said happily. 'Ensign Thomas and Yeoman Garrett. So she stopped dating you, Ross ...'

Lieutenant (jg) Pendleton, a man eternally suave, unruffled and condescending, flushed.

'Well!' Griffin continued with a happy smile. 'So one of the yeomen's been dating Pendleton's girl.'

Lieutenant (jg) Pendleton gripped the arms of his chair until his knuckles were a bone-white.

'You listen to me now, Griffin ...' he said.

'Well,' Lieutenant Griffin said. 'So the great lover had a woman taken away from him – and by an enlisted man!'

Suddenly Pendleton leaped from his chair and stood glaring down at Griffin.

'I'm warning you ... I'm warning you, Griffin ...' he stuttered in a blind fury. 'I'm warning you ...'

The startled officers jerked around in their seats. They had never seen Lieutenant (jg) Pendleton's suaveness even slightly marred before. Tumbling to his feet, Lieutenant-Commander Gladney lumbered his plumpness between the two officers.

'Knock this off!' Lieutenant-Commander Nash was shouting. 'Knock this off! We've got enough of a problem here without two of my officers fighting! Jumping Jupiter, what's going on here? Knock it off or I'll have you both locked up!' the exec yelled – the first time he had ever spoken sharply to Pendleton.

Pendleton, his feathers still bristling, nevertheless was persuaded by Gladney to return to his seat.

'Jumping Jupiter!' the exec said. 'Naval officers!'

The exec allowed the room to quiet down slightly before proceeding.

'Now let's get back to it,' he said briskly. Suddenly he looked across the first rows to Ensign Siegel in the back. 'Siegel,' he said, 'it's your yeoman, after all. And, by the way, haven't you been dating this Thomas woman yourself? I don't keep up with these things, but I thought I saw you together a couple of times.'

'I've gone out some with this Thomas woman,' Ensign Siegel said. He shook his head sadly. 'To think that my own yeoman would do this behind my back. However,' Siegel continued more philosophically, 'if Pendleton here wasn't enough for her, I guess she'd be bound to consider me equally lacking.'

'Lacking!' Pendleton spat out. 'Boy, I can guarantee you that if any woman finds me lacking there has to be something wrong with her. Say!' Pendleton said with an air of discovery. 'I bet he started getting his licks in when all those Japs overpowered me that night. He probably made himself out a big hero.'

'Well, you've got to admit, Ross,' Siegel said, changing the subject quickly, 'that Garrett's a very good-looking boy.'

'Good-looking!' Pendleton exclaimed peevishly. 'I don't think he's good-looking at all.'

'For heaven's sake!' the exec shouted. 'What in the name of Jupiter do the *looks* of Yeoman Garrett have to do with the issue! Which is,' the exec shouted it in a furious scream, '*An enlisted man is dating an officer!*'

The exec's screams settled the room, which had been extremely restless and excited, first by the news, then by the Pendleton–Griffin tiff, down slightly.

'Now,' the exec said crisply. 'Siegel. It's your yeoman, after all.' The exec looked closely at Ensign Siegel. 'Have you noticed Garrett acting strange lately?'

'No more so than any of us,' Ensign Siegel said. He waited a moment, then added, 'Though when I stop to think about it, he has seemed a little more relaxed.'

There was a small chuckle around the room.

'Ensign Thomas would relax the hell out of me,' Lieutenant Griffin said.

'Mind your rudder, Griffin,' the exec said. 'You don't think it's a psycho-ward case, Siegel?'

'No, sir,' Siegel said. 'I know Garrett pretty well, and whatever he did, he certainly isn't nuts.'

'Then he's got something coming to him,' the exec said grimly. 'Such an outrageous flouting of the Navy! Probably laughing up his sleeve all the time at this mockery he was making of officers!'

'He probably just wanted a woman, sir,' Ensign Siegel said.

'A woman!' the exec exclaimed. 'He's taken a naval officer!'

'I think it's outrageous,' Pendleton said, pretty tautly.

'What gets me,' the exec said in baffled tones, 'is how *she* could do it. It's completely beyond me, how an officer could lower herself like that.'

'Well, maybe she just liked him,' Siegel said.

'Liked him!' the exec exclaimed. 'Liking enlisted men is one thing. But it's another to carry it to the point of ultimate fraternization like she's done.'

The exec opened his right top drawer and brought out his 7×50 binoculars. Striding to the screened window, he looked through them for a few moments down the hillside. He came back to his desk, replaced the binoculars, shut the drawer, and sat back in his chair.

'The punishment,' he said almost to himself. 'What shall the punishment be?' He waited in reflection. 'Jupiter, you could really throw the book at this man!'

'Commander,' Ensign Siegel spoke up. 'May I say something?'

The exec looked impatient at this interruption of his reverie. 'Permission granted,' he said wearily.

'Commander,' Ensign Siegel said. 'The Navy has its point about this, I'll admit ...'

'Well! That's nice of you!' the exec said sarcastically.

'But in spite of the Navy being right,' Siegel went on, 'I think we have to be careful here. I agree it has to be stopped …'

'Well, that's nice of you!' the exec said, inflamed.

'But anything like direct punishment,' Siegel went on, 'might really stir this up among the correspondents, Commander. This issue involves love, romance, sex, whatever you want to call it. If we give any drastic punishment to an enlisted man for dating an officer – well, you know what sentimental bastards the correspondents are, Commander. Can't you just imagine, if we did anything to Garrett, a correspondent like Gordon Ripwell rubbing his hands and going to town?'

'Ripwell!' the exec said, in fear at the mere mention of the name.

'Why, before Ripwell was through with it,' Siegel went on, 'he'd have it that the Navy was crucifying an enlisted man who hadn't seen a woman in two years for just looking at one. He'd build it up in his paper – and you know what a circulation and what influence the Chicago *Gazette* has, Commander – so it was a pure black-and-white case of the Navy versus Love. The page one banner headline in Ripwell's paper would probably read, "NAVY TORPEDOES CUPID", and the subhead, "ENLISTED MAN PUNISHED FOR FALLING IN LOVE".'

'Jumping Jupiter!' the exec said, appalled at these headlines. 'That's exactly what Ripwell would do! Those "sentimental bastards", especially Ripwell, would probably just blast the Navy without ever stopping even to think of the ancient, traditional, code-filled points involved. Ripwell!' the exec said, almost in terror. ' "NAVY TORPEDOES CUPID!" '

The exec spun around in his chair, then stopped it. For quite a long while he gazed at the 'Don't Give Up The Ship' legend dead ahead of him on the wall. Then he gave his head a grim, hopeless shake.

'It's a terrifying thing,' he said soberly, 'to let a man go scot-free for such an outrageous unprecedented violation of the Navy code. But we've got to be unselfish about this – we've got to think of the overall good of the Navy.'

The exec slapped the flat side of his hand on the desk. 'But one thing we can do. We can put the fear of God in this man! Siegel!'

'Yes, sir.'

'I want you to tell Garrett he's to give that nurse a wide berth, hear? You can tell him for me he's to knock it off instantly and that if he sees her again I'll really throw the book at him, good of the Navy or no. You understand, Siegel?'

'Yes, sir.'

'Just to make sure,' the exec said, 'his movements are restricted to the Headquarters area here. Is that a hundred per cent clear?'

'Yes, sir,' Ensign Siegel said. 'I'll tell him.'

That afternoon Ensign Siegel told Garrett. The yeoman was unsurprised.

'I thought so,' he said. 'I knew Mr Pendleton had seen us.' The yeoman put his head in his hands. 'Mr Siegel, I love her.'

'I'm sorry, Garrett,' Ensign Siegel said. He waited a moment. 'I've got to like Alice, talking with her on your dates.' The ensign waited again, then added, 'If you can think of anything I can do, let me know.'

Two days later Yeoman Garrett thought of something. He asked Ensign Siegel if he would try to get him sea duty, something he had not mentioned in a long time.

Five: The thousand-dollar bill

ONCE he turned his back on you, everyone knew his name and profession. Stencilled in bold red letters on the back of his khaki shirt, the legend was visible fifty paces away: 'Gordon Ripwell, War Correspondent, Chicago *Gazette*.' Rip wanted it thoroughly understood he wasn't in the Navy. He was dedicated to preserving the great American tradition of the ascendancy of the civilian over the military.

Hardly a conference of Public Relations officers passed but what one of Rip's civilian-like demands arose, and that morning was no exception. Ensign Christopher Tyson III brought the matter up.

'He isn't getting his sheets changed often enough,' Tyson said.

'Did you say sheets?' repeated Lieutenant-Commander Nash.

'Sheets, Commander,' Tyson repeated. 'Some day,' Tyson added thoughtfully, 'I am going to tell that man to double up his fist and stick it up his rostrum.'

'Oh, no!' Lieutenant-Commander Nash was alarmed at the concept. 'You mustn't do that, Ty. Any time you feel like telling a correspondent that, see me first.' The exec made a pacifying gesture. 'What's the problem precisely? Let us remember, I might say, that our central function out here is to service the correspondents. We ought never to forget that.'

'Ripwell never lets me forget it, Commander,' Tyson said. 'He even asked me the other day to get him a date with a nurse. Get him a date! In the Pacific!'

'Don't forget, Ty,' the exec said, 'that Gordon Ripwell is in a position to do the Navy a lot of good – or a lot of real damage. His emotional situation is pretty important to us.'

'Does that mean, sir,' Ensign Tyson asked, 'that I've got to pimp for him?'

The exec's face reflected displeasure at the small ripple of laughter around the conference of Public Relations officers.

'The trouble with Ripwell's emotional situation,' Tyson, encouraged by the laughter, went on, 'is that he's oversexed.'

This remark provoked further laughter. The executive officer, his face showing definite irritation, rapped his pencil firmly on his bald head for attention.

'Sailors, I think all of you realize by this time that I have as effective a sense of humour as the next man – officer, that is. But this increasing levity I've observed lately, even about the very fact we're out here, instead of at sea ... Frankly, Sailors, I don't like it, and I shall expect to see less of it in the future. Is that clear as I can make it? Now, let's look alive. What's this business about Gordon Ripwell and the sheets? We must let no problem be insurmountable where a correspondent is concerned.'

'It's very simple, Commander,' Tyson said. 'He thinks Tulura is the Hotel Plaza. He wants fresh sheets on his bed every day.'

'He *has* been getting them changed weekly?' the exec said.

'Yes, sir. Like everyone else. But that isn't good enough. Not for Gordon Ripwell. He claims he has to have them changed every day.'

'Any reason given?' the exec asked tentatively.

'Reason?' Tyson said blankly.

'I don't suppose you could ask him, though,' the exec admitted, selecting a paper-clip and aiming it for the wastebasket. 'He might resent it. Also, it might be something rather personal. Like a skin ailment. Lot of crud in the Pacific, you know.'

'Frankly, Commander,' said Tyson, 'I think he's trying to bluff us.'

'That's a rather negative attitude, Tyson,' the exec said. 'What do you say we look at it constructively? Ripwell is a *very* important correspondent. Roger?'

Ensign Tyson didn't say anything, and the exec, his eyes bulging into an agate glare, repeated, 'I said, "Roger?"'

'Oh, Roger, sir,' Tyson put in quickly.

'Roger,' the exec said decisively. 'I think we better go ahead and change them daily.'

'What if the radio correspondents hear about this?' Lieutenant-Commander Arnold Gladney objected mildly.

'The photographers will doubtlessly want theirs changed daily also,' said Lieutenant-Commander Wayne Hereford. 'Photographers always want everything that anyone else has – sometimes they want somewhat more.'

'We'll cross those bridges when we come to them ... Arnold, Wayne,' the exec said briskly. 'I see no reason why we can't put it in a "Top Secret" classification that Ripwell is getting daily fresh sheets. No one has to see them changed. It's all done behind doors, anyway. Of course, Ty, that means you'll have to handle the whole thing personally.'

'What do you mean "personally", Commander?' Ensign Tyson inquired suspiciously.

'The first thing for you to do is to go ahead and authorize the steward's mate to change Gordon's sheets every morning.'

'I authorized him, Commander. Andrew, the steward's mate, says he can't do it.'

'What did you say?' The exec flushed. 'Insubordination to an ensign from a steward's mate!'

'Not exactly, Commander. From a Marine colonel – Colonel Cannon, the Headquarters commandant. He says it'll upset his system – laundry dates, everything – besides setting a precedent. You can't imagine how much trouble I had getting him to even discuss it. You know how Marine colonels are. Even ComFleets doesn't get daily sheets, he said. Definitely no daily sheets for any goddamned, half-assed, 4-F'ing, frigging correspondent – Colonel Cannon's phrases.'

'Doesn't sound very public-relations-minded to me,' the exec said.

'Well, he's a Marine colonel, you know,' Tyson said.

'And is likely to find himself in front of a regiment if he's not careful!' Lieutenant-Commander Nash said tartly. 'What a short-sighted viewpoint anyway! It's just like a Marine! Good in their place – the fighting phase of the war – but shortsighted about the big picture! If daily sheets will make Ripwell write good press about the Navy ...' The exec jumped up excitedly in his chair. 'The issue,' he said, with an air of having at last isolated it, 'is precisely that: whether a few extra sheets are worth good Navy press in one of the biggest, most influential newspapers in the United States!'

'Commander,' Tyson said, 'I know Ripwell pretty well. Not by choice, but by unavoidable association. If you want my opinion, Ripwell's going to write what he feels like about the Navy even if we give his bed a daily change of Navy nurses. If anything, giving him the sheets will convince him we can be pushed around and he'll be worse than ever – if that's possible. He's that kind of man, Commander! If I know anything about human nature, you can't appease a man like Gordon Ripwell.'

'Human nature is one thing, Tyson,' the exec said briskly. 'The nature of correspondents is another. It takes trained experts to know it, and if you don't, it's no reflection on your ignorance. After all, you aren't very old.'

'Sir,' said Ensign Tyson, with a summoning of dignity, 'I don't know what that has to do with it. Anyhow, Colonel Cannon says he won't issue the extra sheets, so this is all academic.'

'Nothing is academic where a correspondent is concerned!' the exec suddenly shouted, yanking out Bowditch's huge *American Practical Navigator* and banging it cacophonously on the desk. 'Now, in view of Cannon's shortsighted attitude,' he said decisively, 'there's just one thing to do. We'll have to draw an extra supply of sheets from General Stores. That ought to handle it.'

'Colonel Cannon,' Tyson said immediately, 'says he won't launder any extra sheets.'

'Then that means,' the exec said promptly, 'that you'll have to take them down to that naval-base laundry and have them done there.'

This was a large laundry, unlike the comparatively small one run by Colonel Cannon at Headquarters, that did laundry for ships and all comers. A look of disbelief passed over Tyson's face as he comprehended what was expected of him.

'You mean m-m-me to take them to the laundry?' Ensign Tyson stammered a little when he got very angry. 'But I'm an ensign, Commander!'

'Belay that attitude!' the exec shouted. 'Tyson, you're a Correspondents' Aide. That means just what it says. You're here to *aid* the correspondents to do their jobs, so they'll write good Navy press, though to hear you talk one would think you were trying the hardest way possible to make them furious at the Navy. Jumping Jupiter, man,' the exec said with sudden, angry impatience, 'you'd jettison good Navy press in the Chicago *Gazette* for a few measly sheets! Also, since you mention it yourself, it seems to me you could have worked this little matter out in the first place without bothering me or the conference about it. I delegate responsibility and I expect to see it exercised. Even by ensigns!'

'Commander,' Tyson said with sudden intensity, 'I don't believe carrying a correspondent's dirty sheets to the laundry is in line of d-d-duty for an ensign of the United States Navy. ...'

'That's where you're wrong,' the exec snapped.

Suddenly the exec's hands shot impatiently forward and grabbed out *Navy Regulations* from his desk library.

'Chapter Thirty-one,' he said, finding a place in it, 'entitled, "Junior Officers of the Line", that is, ensigns, deals entirely with the subject you're talking about – their duties. Let me read you just a snatch or two.'

The exec lifted the book, which it was necessary to hold in both hands, and read loudly.

'Article 1119, paragraph (1), reads: "They shall perform such duty as may be assigned them." Article 1122, paragraph (1), reads in part: "In order to broaden their experience, they shall be detailed successively to as many different line duties as practicable."'

Shutting the book, the exec slammed it down on the desk.

'I guess that takes care of that,' he said with stern decisiveness. 'Now ...'

'Commander,' Tyson said, enraged to the limits of an ensign's allowance, 'how in the world does carrying Ripwell's d-d-dirty sheets broaden my n-n-naval experience...?'

'Knock it off!' the exec yelled. 'Knock it off! I've had enough of this foolishness! Not another word! What's next, Sailors,' the exec said stiffly, 'on the agenda...?'

At the end of the conference Ensign Tyson checked out a jeep. Bitterly he drove eight miles along the beautiful sea highway and then through the dust around the docks to general stores. There he drew two dozen new sheets and drove them the eight miles back to Headquarters and the correspondents' BOQ. He took the sheets in to the steward's mate, Andrew, whom he instructed tersely: 'Every day put a fresh pair on Mr Ripwell's bed. Every Friday bundle up the dirty sheets and leave them in my room over at BOQ 3. I'll take them to the laundry and bring back clean ones – you pick the clean ones up in my room on Saturday morning. You think we got this organized now, Andrew?'

'Organized on this heah end, Mistuh Tyson,' Andrew said. 'Just you pruhvide the sheets.'

'Never mind,' Ensign Tyson snapped. 'I'll provide the sheets, Andrew.' He was getting such a persecution complex he fancied even Andrew was ordering him around.

It was by now five o'clock, which was bar time, and Ensign Tyson felt in need of a drink. He left the BOQ and walked with a ruffled air down the road to the officers' club. He entered the bar to find Gordon Ripwell holding forth to a cluster of officers.

'... a point I sometimes have trouble getting over to these gold-braided, millpond Caesars. I'm nothing myself, I know that. But I do represent two million Americans ... two million *Gazette* readers. Two million ain't hay! I regard myself as the watchdog out here of the interests of those two million Americans. When they push Gordon Ripwell around they push around two million Americans! Who do they think they are! This country is a Democracy, not a naval oligarchy! As I told Bull Halsey: This isn't any private war! This war is the property of the American people! You people in the Navy are only their hired hand! Don't let's forget it! Say, if it isn't young Tyson! Get that item about the sheets squared away, Admiral?'

'It's all taken care of, Mr Ripwell. Sweet dreams.'

'Ha, ha. Call me Rip. Tyson's a good boy,' Ripwell informed the officers. 'Highest-ranking bellhop in the western Pacific – no offence, son. I really appreciate it the way you look after me. Even if it is your duty, and otherwise, heh, heh, you'd be at sea. Went to Harvard, didn't you, son?'

'Princeton,' Tyson said.

'Six of one, half a dozen of the other,' Ripwell said. 'Myself, I never got within spitting distance of college, and my experience in the actual world has taught me considerable suspicions about the whole field of so-called education. However, I'm broad-minded enough not to hold it against a man that he's been to college, though as a rule I don't care for Harvard – or Princeton – men. Usually I've found them little snotnoses, even when they're not pansies. But Tyson here' – Ripwell patted the ensign twice on the head – 'he's my boy! Say! Bartender! Rig the admiral with one of those whisky sours.'

An officer wearing coloured glasses walked in to the bar.

'Say. That reminds me, son,' Ripwell addressed Tyson. 'Pick me up a pair of those smoked specs tomorrow, will you? Broke my other pair, and this coral's driving me blind. Cheers, Admiral!' The correspondent lifted his drink.

'The basic choice a correspondent has to make,' Ripwell continued, 'is whether he's for the officers, in which case he can suck and get sucked, or for the enlisted man. I'm for the enlisted man, by Godfrey, and I don't care who knows it.'

Ensign Tyson thought of reminding Ripwell that the correspondent had been first in line when the Navy issued gold oak-leaves with a raised 'C' on them to all correspondents as visible testimony to their assigned rank of lieutenant-commander. This was an attempt on the part of the Navy to glorify the correspondent and at the same time top the Army, where a correspondent's assigned rank was a mere captain.

'I told MacArthur that to his face,' Ripwell was going on, '– how Gordon Ripwell is for the enlisted man. That's because the enlisted man is the American people.'

'Officers aren't?' Tyson said.

'Watch.' The correspondent slapped down a fifty-cent piece for the five-cent drink the Marine bartender was delivering up to Tyson, and the Marine brought change. 'Keep it, son!'

'Sorry, sir. It's against regulations.'

'See what I mean!' Ripwell said triumphantly. 'A poor Gyrene PFC can't make an extra quarter by way of a bar tip, and yet look at the way the brass here is living! Inner-spring mattresses! Take-home liquor rations! Besides all you can drink here at a nickel a throw! Say. Remind me to tell you sometime about a Wave ensign I laid in Frisco right before shipping out this last time. Her husband was a naval officer in the Pacific – none of you men, I trust, heh, heh – out two years he'd been, and say – was she ready for it! Reminds me. Tyson, how about that nurse you're going to fix me up with?'

'That's a little outside my line, Mr Ripwell.'

The correspondent slapped his hand on the bar. 'By Godfrey, your line's to help the correspondents! Don't let's forget it! Let's get the lead out, Admiral, and go scoutin' around over to that Fleet Hospital. Oh, I just remembered, son,' the correspondent said to Tyson, 'pick me up one of those Frank Buck helmets like Nash has been wearing around, will you?'

'Any special size, Mr Ripwell?' Tyson said.

'Seven and five-eighths. About the same size in nurses.' The correspondent let out a leering bellow. 'You be a good boy, Tyson, and I might let you have seconds, heh, heh.'

The correspondent leaned both elbows back on the bar. His eyes moved secretively around the circle of officers.

'Say,' he said. 'I got something here I think might interest you young brass-hats.'

Ripwell let the mildly expectant attention focus itself on him for a moment. 'Remember that B-29 raid I heisted on about a month ago? Well, just look here.'

Whipping his billfold from his hip pocket, the correspondent extracted a bill and snapped it loudly like a small-town bank teller.

'Gawd Almighty!' an officer exclaimed. 'It's a thousand-dollar bill!'

With a rustling movement, the officers huddled around the correspondent and stared incredulously at the bill he was holding.

Ripwell casually handed the bill to one of the officers. 'Want a feel?'

Tenderly and in awe the young brass-hats passed the bill around. It reached Tyson last, and even he stared at it a moment.

'Ever held one of those things in your hand before, son?' Ripwell said. 'Probably have – but I'll bet it belonged to your old man. You're obviously the inherited- as opposed to the earned-wealth type, Tyson. Go ahead! Look at the back!'

Tyson turned the bill over.

'Read it aloud!' Ripwell suggested.

Tyson read the inscription, written across the green bill: ' "To My Favourite War Correspondent, Gordon Ripwell. For service above and beyond the call of duty, to wit: a perilous, flak-fraught raid in a B-29 over Tokyo, Japan, resulting in the destruction of critical Japanese war industry. His bravery exceeded that of the crew in that they had to go on the raid and he didn't." '

The inscription was signed by Ripwell's famous publisher.

'That's the kind of guy I work for,' the correspondent said proudly. 'Ordinary publisher would have sent you nothing – or sent you a cheque. What does my man do? Sends an autographed thousand-dollar bill!'

'You gonna cash it here?' an awed lieutenant asked.

'Cash it?' Ripwell ejaculated. 'I'll never cash it, Junior. Not a souvenir like that!'

'Pretty expensive souvenir to keep,' the officer said. 'A thousand bucks!'

Ripwell chuckled. 'Frankly, fellows,' he said confidentially, 'and I told Lemay the same thing, I wouldn't make one of those raids again for ten thousand bucks.' He relieved Tyson of the bill and replaced it in his billfold and shoved the billfold casually into his hip pocket. 'Some publisher I've got, eh, son?'

'You said it, Mr Ripwell,' Tyson, by now on his third whisky sour, agreed. 'All I can say is, "You said it." Tell me, Mr Ripwell. What's a guy like who'll do a thing like that?'

'Call me Rip. What's he like?' Ripwell leaned back against the bar. 'Well, he's a funny guy. A newspaperman. Got that sixth sense of what the public wants. No lip from government big-shots – or brass. Personally an American Puritan. Doesn't smoke, drink' – Ripwell chuckled – 'once fired a hell of a good city editor for playing around with women and, I can assure you, any representative of the Chicago *Gazette* has to watch his step where morals is concerned – least make sure it doesn't get back to the old man. He's for the American home and all that,' Ripwell said, though not cynically. 'For the frontier and private enterprise – and for running his own business, taking no lip from nobody. He'll print a scandal about the daughter of a big advertiser, by Godfrey, as quick as about someone he's never heard of. And he's thrown more'n one advertiser out of his office for objecting. A *newspaperman!*'

The correspondent tossed off the rest of his drink and smacked his lips.

'What say we all have one more round before chow and then a spot of poker?' The correspondent patted his hip. 'With that G-bill battin' me on the fanny, I feel like a little stud!'

'Thought you weren't going to spend that,' an officer said.

Ripwell laughed heartily at the officer's walking into the trap. 'Don't expect to, men. Don't expect to! No, sir! Say!'

Several Public Relations officers were sitting around the Media Section next morning when the Chicago *Gazette* correspondent strode in. Rip always made his presence felt, but the word of the bonus for the B-29 flight was getting around and this morning the officers let their eyes rest on him a little longer than usual. Here was a man carrying a thousand-dollar bill in his pocket!

'Morning, Rip,' Lieutenant-Commander Nash, who was at a desk downstairs while a new fluorescent-light fixture was being installed in his own office upstairs, said cheerfully. 'Anything we can do for you?'

'Nothing especially, Nash,' Ripwell said. 'Anything going on I ought to know about?' he said, giving Nash a suspicious look.

'Why, I can't think of a thing,' the exec said frankly. 'An LST is carrying a load of C-rations to Gug-Gug, but I don't think a paper your size would be interested in anything like that.'

'Just always tell me, then I'll decide if we're interested or not,' Ripwell said curtly. 'You've got to be a newspaperman to really tell.'

'Of course,' Commander Nash said amiably. 'Anything else we can do for you?'

'I'll let you know if there is, don't you worry about that,' Ripwell said. He looked across the room at Tyson reading a newspaper. 'Tyson,' he said.

Tyson forgot himself long enough to snap his paper down sharply.

'How about that Frank Buck helmet and goggles?' Ripwell said.

'You need a Frank Buck helmet and some goggles, Rip?' Nash said in a perturbed voice.

'If I didn't need them I wouldn't have asked for them yesterday,' Ripwell said.

'Tyson!' Nash shouted. 'Fix Gordon up with a Frank Buck helmet and goggles right away!'

'Yes, *sir*,' Tyson said, rising in a military fashion.

'You might pick me up a pair of field-shoes while you're down there,' Ripwell said.

'And a pair of field-shoes for Mr Ripwell!' Nash shouted.

Tyson laid his paper down slowly. 'S-s-size?'

'Nine and a half,' Ripwell said.

Ensign Tyson walked erectly through the door and was back in thirty minutes lugging a Frank Buck helmet, goggles, and a pair of field-shoes. Ripwell stopped writing a story long enough to try the shoes on.

'Don't fit,' he said tersely. 'Too big.'

'We should have thought of that,' Commander Nash apologized. 'In the Navy you always take a size smaller.'

'In the Navy you do everything different,' Ripwell said.

'Tyson!' Nash waved at the ensign. 'See what you can do about exchanging these!'

The ensign took the shoes and left, carrying one in each hand. In another half-hour he was back carrying another pair. Ripwell put them on – they turned out to be the proper size for his feet – then, with a couple of guffaws, planted the helmet on his head and tried on the goggles.

'All fitted out for the rear echelon! What a life! Frank Buck helmet! Goggles! Plus field-shoes! Now wouldn't I have liked,' he said, looking down at the shoes, 'to have had a pair of these when I was slugging through the jungle with the 7th Division! By Godfrey! You Navy men don't know how lucky you are.'

'Anything we can do for you, let us know,' Nash said uneasily.

'I'll let you know, don't you worry about that, Nash,' Ripwell said. 'You got that appointment with the sub admiral set up for to-morrow?'

'Roger!' Nash said eagerly. 'Eleven hundred sharp. I had the admiral cancel a conference with his sub commanders to make it.'

'Tell the admiral *he* better be sharp. Heh, heh. Like to give the sub boys a plug now and then. Being as how they're about the only Navy boys who come within hollering distance of the war.'

'Ha, ha, ha!' Nash tried to take this as a joke. 'Now the aircraft-carriers, Rip. You'll have to admit they get in the thick of it.'

'In my book,' Ripwell said, 'no fly-boys are ever in the thick of anything except talk. I'm talkin' about fightin' the *war*, Commander. I've got to get back to this story,' he said, dismissing the commander.

That night the flight bonus was the subject of a breeze session in Lieutenant Morey Griffin's and Ensign Max Siegel's room.

'Imagine a man getting a thousand bucks for making an air raid,' Ensign Tyson said.

'Would you make an air raid over Tokyo for a thousand bucks?' Lieutenant (jg) Calvert 'Little Marblehead' Brownell said.

'You miss the point entirely, Brownell,' Tyson said.

'What point is that?' Lieutenant (jg) Brownell said blankly.

'Never mind, Calvert,' Tyson said wearily. 'I don't care what Ripwell gets for his air raids,' he went on, 'except I'd be pretty intrigued if he got a visitation of Jap flak up his jock. But I don't believe a commissioned officer ought to be carrying dirty sheets to the laundry for anyone – even a correspondent. Matter of fact, I'm not sure it's even legal.'

'Why don't you write your congressman?' Lieutenant Griffin suggested.

'You always have a funny remark, don't you, Griffin?' Tyson said bitterly.

Griffin laughed. 'Seriously, why don't you go to the captain and complain?'

'The commander might be pretty sore if you did that,' Lieutenant (jg) Brownell said. 'Going over his head. In fact, I'd guarantee he'd be sore. If I were you, sport, I'd just grin and bear it. Ripwell's not a bad sort really, once you get to know him.'

'You want to carry his dirty sheets for him, Calvert?' Tyson said.

'Well, it's better than being at sea,' Brownell said simply.

'Why did you get in the Navy anyhow, Calvert?' Tyson asked.

'Tell me that. When I got my commission it said the President of the United States reposed special trust in my patriotism, valour, fidelity, and abilities. It didn't say anything about being laundry boy to a correspondent. This isn't what I got in the Navy for. Not to pimp either. If he asks me once more to get him a date with a nurse, I'm, I'm … I'm going to do something!'

Tyson scooted back on the innerspring-mattress bed. 'You know, last night I just wanted to take that thousand-dollar bill and tear it up in his face!' he said magnificently.

'Really?' said Brownell, surprised. 'Why?'

'You wouldn't understand, Calvert,' Tyson said wearily. 'That's what I wanted to do. Tear that thousand-dollar bill up in little pieces right in front of him!'

'Who's tearing up thousand-dollar bills?'

It was Ensign Max Siegel, coming in the door.

'How're the people's chosen representatives doing, Max?' Griffin asked.

Siegel set down a box he was carrying and took a heavy seat on the bed. He had been out the day long shepherding a party of congressmen around the island.

'We got individual pictures of all of them standing on men-o'-war – at camera angles such as not to disclose the fact that the ships were in port,' Ensign Siegel said. 'Also, we photographed them heavily over at the Seabees jabbering with their constituents, pictures of each congressman with each of his constituents. My God, I wonder where Eastman stock is these days.'

'What's the box, Siegel?' Tyson asked. 'A portable congressional bar?'

'That comes next,' Siegel said. 'This one's a recording machine. Nash's idea. Wire-recorded interviews between the congressmen and their Navy constituents. The congressmen can take 'em home to play during their campaigns to prove they've been to the wars – and are looking out for their voters. Some of the interviews are on ships with guns going off for sound effects. Little trouble laying that part of it on.'

'It's a big idea of the commander's,' Brownell said eagerly. 'Gets the Navy good public relations with the congressmen. I bet they liked it, didn't they, sport?'

'Calvert, I've yet to meet the man who doesn't like the sound of his own voice,' Siegel said. 'Even congressmen. What's this about Ripwell and a thousand-dollar bill? I been away.'

Tyson filled his fellow Correspondents' Aide in on this matter and in general on his problems with Ripwell.

'Did he really get a thousand bucks for making a B-29 raid?' Siegel asked.

'Yep, and 's carrying it around flashing it to everyone like it was the Congressional Medal of Honour. Sickening,' Tyson said. 'But of course I'm prejudiced about the man. As Calvert here says, he may be the arsehole-buddy of the earth, once you get to know him. I probably just don't know him,' the ensign said. 'Don't want to either,' he added bitterly.

'He ought to take that thousand-dollar bill down and show it to some of those PFC B-29 crew-men who make the same raid ten times a month for a hundred bucks,' Griffin said.

'Listen, Siegel.' Tyson raised himself petulantly on his elbow. 'Why do I have to get stuck with Ripwell? You haven't had him any.'

'I *did* have Ripwell on a tour of the island when he first came,' Ensign Siegel said. 'All he was interested in was whether I knew any Tuluran lays.'

'That's it!' Tyson exclaimed triumphantly. 'Over-sexed! He's dangerously over-sexed. I wouldn't be surprised if he had a criminal record of rape.'

'Everybody in the Pacific is dangerously over-sexed,' Griffin said. 'I'd rape a woman right now if I got a chance.' When no one said anything, he bellowed, 'Anybody in this room wouldn't?'

Regularly once a week Ensign Tyson checked out a jeep, dropped by his BOQ, picked up a bundle of fourteen dirty sheets, drove them down the hill, along the sea-coast highway and through the dust of the docks eight miles to the laundry. He returned with a week's supply – change-daily-rate – of fresh sheets.

For a couple of weeks an air of preoccupation enveloped the young ensign. Then the third week he asked Max Siegel, who was sitting in the Media room reading papers that afternoon, to accompany him on his weekly laundry safari. With Siegel in the jeep beside him, Tyson stopped at his BOQ.

'I'll be right back,' he said bitterly, 'soon as I pick up the b-b-bastard's used sheets.'

Ensign Tyson was back in a moment with the big bundle. He tossed it grimly in the back seat, started the jeep, and headed away from Headquarters on the eight-mile drive.

It was a lovely Tulura day as Tyson eased the jeep down the long hill. The sea lay shimmering below the two ensigns and the breeze coming through the valleys gently caressed them. They drove along the sea road to the naval-base laundry down by the docks. Tyson took the bundle of dirty sheets inside and was presently back with a large package of clean ones. He slammed the package angrily in the back seat of the jeep.

The two ensigns started back to Headquarters. Presently Tyson slowed the jeep to where it was lazing along at only a few miles an hour.

'You know, Max,' he said, 'I don't like to complain – especially when there are men out on that ocean fighting the war – but the fact is, I've had all I can take of carrying Ripwell's dirty sheets. Funny, isn't it, that it should come down to that? I mean, you go along in this war doing a lot of things you don't like and then suddenly you do one more and that's it.'

Tyson slowed the jeep even more.

'I don't want to sound dramatic,' he said, 'but this is it. I mean, I'm not going to carry these sheets any more. I don't care what they do to me, I won't do it.'

Ensign Siegel laughed mildly. 'You mean you're going to walk into the captain's office and say, "Captain, I refuse to carry Ripwell's sheets any longer even if it's a direct order?" Naval ensigns don't do things like that with naval captains. You been in the Navy long enough to know that.'

'No, I'm not going to do that, Max,' Tyson said quietly.

Tyson pulled the jeep off the road on to the shoulder and clicked off the ignition. Only a few feet from them the Pacific washed in sweetly on the island's shores.

'Max,' Tyson said, 'do you mind taking a look at a letter I've written?'

Ensign Tyson reached into his shirt pocket and pulled out a piece of paper and handed it across to Ensign Siegel.

'Read this, will you?' Tyson said.

Siegel unfolded the paper, which was an 8×11 sheet of typing paper, and read it to himself. It read:

From: Ensign Christopher Tyson III, USNR
To: The Secretary of the Navy
Via: ComFleets
Subject: Proper duties of commissioned officers; clarification of
References: United States Navy Regulations, Article $76\frac{1}{2}$ (paragraph 3)

1. Three weeks ago, I was assigned to the duty, in addition to my other duties, of once a week carrying the soiled sheets of a civilian correspondent attached to this Headquarters to the Naval Operating Base laundry eight miles from said Headquarters. This assignment originated in the desire of the correspondent to have a daily fresh change of sheets for unspecified reasons. The correspondent's insistence on this service was itself in contradiction to existing practice at this Headquarters, where all other officers and correspondents are given only a weekly change of sheets. Nevertheless the demand was acceded to by the executive officer of this Headquarters Public Relations Unit, to which I am assigned as a Correspondents' Aide. Headquarters laundry being geared and equipped only to provide weekly fresh sheets it became necessary to issue extra sheets for this correspondent and once a week to carry 14 of his soiled sheets to the Base laundry. This additional duty was assigned to me. In accordance with this direct order, I have now been engaged for three weeks in carrying out this duty.

2. Questioning whether the duty is a proper one for a commissioned officer of the United States Navy, I have appealed to the executive officer of my unit to be relieved of it. The executive officer, however, has ruled that such an assignment is in fact in line of duty for a commissioned officer.

3. Reference article grants to officers of the Navy the right to appeal directly to the Secretary of the Navy for 'instructions or explanations as to the force, meaning or effect' of any Navy law or regulation. In accordance with this authority, I request a ruling from the Secretary of the Navy as to whether the duty of carrying the soiled sheets of a civilian correspondent is proper duty for a commissioned officer.

4. If the Secretary of the Navy should rule negatively on this question it is further requested that the executive officer of the Public Relations Unit of this command be directed to order me to cease and desist from any further exercise of this duty.

Christopher Tyson III

Ensign Siegel finished reading the letter and looked over incredulously at his fellow ensign. He saw something in Tyson's face that convinced him his friend meant it. Tyson promptly pulled out another piece of paper.

'In case you're wondering what Article 76½, paragraph 3 is,' he said, business-like, 'it reads as follows: "Any officer who may be required to take official action under any regulation of the department, or any law governing or referring thereto, who may desire instructions or explanations as to the force, meaning, or effect of such law or regulation, shall address his communication of inquiry through the proper official channels to the Secretary of the Navy."'

Ensign Tyson shifted in his seat. 'You know, Nash himself gave me this idea. Since he was flummoxing around in Navy Regs about the duties of ensigns I decided I would just have a little look myself about a phase of ensigns he didn't bother to mention – namely, their rights, if any. I was very interested to discover,' Ensign Tyson said confidently, 'that we have a right to appeal anything right to the top. Doesn't it reassure you to know that basically the Navy is a democratic organization with rights of appeal?'

Ensign Siegel said nothing for a few moments, looking thoughtfully at Tyson. 'Not particularly,' he said then.

Siegel turned a little in his seat towards Tyson. 'Listen, Ty,' he said, 'you realize this has to go through Nash?'

'What of it?' Tyson said promptly. 'He has to send it on. He can endorse it "approved" or "disapproved". But he has to send it on to SecNav. That's another Navy regulation.'

'Listen, man,' Siegel said firmly, 'regardless of all that mythology, it's a highly serious thing for a Navy ensign to appeal directly to SecNav. Not to mention Nash, who can make it really rough for you if you do anything like that.'

'No rougher than I've got now!' Tyson said immediately. 'Can you think of anything rougher than having to carry Ripwell's dirty sheets?'

'Listen,' Siegel said strongly, 'you better think this over. This could lead to … Listen, man, you really better think this over.'

'I'm through th-th-thinking it over!' Tyson exclaimed furiously. 'I'm giving Nash exactly one week to stop this ow-ow-outrage! If he doesn't, this letter goes off!'

Suddenly Ensign Tyson started up the jeep.

'That thousand-dollar bill from that famous great-newspaper-man, American-Puritan publisher of Gordon Ripwell's!' he exclaimed abruptly.

'American Puritan?' Siegel fielded the phrase as they came on to the road again.

'Ripwell's description,' Tyson said. 'His publisher doesn't smoke or drink – and fires reporters who play around with women.'

Tyson rammed the jeep swiftly back to Headquarters. He slammed into the drive of his BOQ and stopped with a jerk that bounced Siegel in his seat. He got out, reached over into the back seat and grabbed out the package of fresh sheets. He stood a moment holding them.

'Disgraceful, isn't it?' Ensign Tyson said. 'I must look like a delivery man for the S-S-Sanitary Laundry!'

Turning savagely, he took the sheets inside. Returning, he drove with Siegel back up to the Public Relations Section. They went inside and Siegel went to his desk and phoned naval air transport for ETA information on a plane due in tomorrow with a correspondent he was supposed to meet. He hung up the phone and sat a few moments looking up at the row of four clocks on the wall. It was now ten p.m. in San Francisco, he noticed. The Top of the Mark would be filling up ...

He went up, checked out a jeep, and drove across the island. It was the day for one of his regular twice-a-week visits to Tanalolo, and as always on this day he felt full of comfort and anticipation. Also, driving over to the village, he kept thinking about his friend Ensign Tyson's problems with the sheets, and the action Tyson had decided on. Siegel visualized the letter arriving in SecNav's office. Suddenly he shuddered at the thought of the possible action they would take. But then, before he knew it, he was driving up to the schoolhouse. He got out and started inside and automatically he forgot all about Ensign Tyson, sheets, the Navy and about everything except the fact that he was about to see Melora again.

Ensign Siegel dipped the rag in the bucket of water, squeezed it out, and started scrubbing the blackboard.

'I don't know, Melora,' he said. 'Maybe the intensity is necessary.'

The Tuluran girl looked up from where she was correcting papers at the teacher's desk just behind him. 'But the great trouble with American writers, Max – you take Fitzgerald, take Wolfe – has always seemed to me to be that their intensity is not balanced by anything.'

Ensign Siegel soaked his rag, squeezed it out again, finished off the last section of blackboard, picked up his broom, and started sweeping the schoolroom.

'You mean in what they wrote, or in a personal sense?' he said.

'Oh, I mean in a personal sense,' Melora said. 'I think their writing – what they did of it – was good. I think American writers are doing the best writing in the world today. But they burn themselves out before they even live to the time when they would have written their really great novels.'

'Well, of course,' Ensign Siegel said dourly, 'there were those two non-Americans, de Maupassant and Tolstoy, both of whom went nuts.'

'Tolstoy was eighty at the time,' Melora said. 'A man has a right to go nuts when he's eighty.'

Ensign Siegel swept across the room, brushing the boards with long, swirling strokes.

'Anyhow, I don't see anything wrong with intensity,' he said. 'There's something more than soaking up sun on a Pacific beach.'

'Oh, intensity is fine,' Melora said. 'But only if it has something to balance it. And I think it has to be the concept that life takes place over a period of time, not just now. I think that's what gives you a contentment inside.'

Ensign Siegel finished sweeping the room and stuck the broom in a corner. He got a dry rag and started dusting the desks.

'Not much dust out here,' he said. 'Now this would be a real job in New York. Well, I don't know, Melora,' he said. 'A cow is a very contented animal, but I haven't heard of any writing *Boule de Suif*. I don't know if a man can have all that "balance" and turn out anything. I don't think many of them have.'

'Oh, lots of them have, Max,' Melora said. 'Only they've been Orientals, most of them. Confucius and lots of the Japanese and Chinese poets – lots of them have been quiet men, and thousands of years later people are reading what they wrote.'

Ensign Siegel put his cleaning tools away and took a seat in the pupil's chair closest to the teacher's desk. For a few minutes Melora worked at correcting her papers. Looking across at her and adjusting his huge frame from time to time in the tiny desk, Siegel thought how these visits, these talks had become his one contact with civilized reality. He thought of the limited scope of Navy conversation out here – gripes and women. It was a wonder the mind didn't atrophy and flake off. He felt he had begun to use his mind for the first time in years. And he was also glad they had got around to calling each other 'Max' and 'Melora' now.

In a moment she had finished her papers. Looking up, her eyes rested almost worshipfully on a bookcase against the wall in which twenty-four large volumes gleamed brightly.

'Max,' she said, 'you don't know what a difference it has made in my teaching since you brought me the *Encyclopaedia Britannica*. The lessons are so much better now – we've got some place to go to when we want to know something. You don't know what a difference it has made.'

'Oh, yes, I do,' Ensign Siegel said. 'I don't have nearly so many questions to look up now. I even have time now to have an occasional drink in the officers' club.'

'It was very good of you, Max,' she said, smiling.

'Well, I almost had to cram them down your throat,' he said.

She smiled, remembering her anger a month ago when she had resisted the gift, not knowing what it was.

'Well, we do have our customs out here,' she said. 'I couldn't have accepted any Vol de Vent perfume.'

'Would you like some Vol de Vent?' he said.

'Now, Max,' she said.

She sighed, looking again at the encyclopaedia.

'Now all we need is a schoolhouse,' she said. 'I'm tired of looking at this old room,' she said abruptly. 'Let's go outside and sit on the steps.'

They went outside and sat for a while, not talking, looking down across a lagoon which spread out below the hilltop schoolhouse. The water was very blue and the hills rising up from it a brilliant green.

Ensign Siegel laughed suddenly. 'You know, there's a funny thing over at our Navy Headquarters right now. One of our young officers is very upset because he has to take a correspondent's dirty sheets to the laundry.'

Ensign Siegel sometimes told Melora about his Navy experiences, and now he related the matter between Ensign Tyson and the correspondent Gordon Ripwell.

'Do Navy officers have to do things like that?' she said, genuinely surprised.

'Well, that's the question Ensign Tyson has been asking himself – and thinking about asking certain other people,' Siegel said. 'He's pretty upset about it. He's not too fond of this correspondent Gordon Ripwell, anyway.'

'I don't think I would be myself,' Melora said. 'He doesn't sound like too attractive a person.'

'Oh, he isn't bad,' Siegel said. 'He just likes to have naval officers wait on him.' Siegel laughed again. 'Funny thing about Ripwell. He has this thousand-dollar bill he's been flashing around.'

'Thousand-dollar bill?' Melora said curiously. 'What would he be doing with a thousand-dollar bill out here?'

'Well, his publisher sent it to him for accompanying one of our B-29s on a raid over Tokyo.'

'A thousand-dollar bill,' Melora repeated. She laughed abruptly. 'I was just thinking, what a strange thing! That – a thousand dollars, I mean – is just about what it would take to change' – a gesture of her hand indicated the shabby, one-room schoolhouse behind them – 'this. At least it would pay for most of the materials.'

'Well, that's a very interesting thought,' Siegel said. 'But I don't think Gordon Ripwell would fancy himself as the patron of Tuluran education.'

'Why not? He probably doesn't need the money, does he?' Melora said.

Ensign Siegel, looking down at the girl beside him, laughed shortly. 'Listen, you don't think it's as simple as all that, do you? My goodness, there's about as much chance of Gordon Ripwell donating that thousand-dollar bill of his to put up a school as there is of me being made an admiral tomorrow. A thousand bucks is a thousand bucks – Anyhow,' Siegel added, 'his publisher autographed it, and it's a souvenir he wants to carry around for the rest of his life.'

'Then that means he doesn't really need the money,' the girl said promptly. 'Don't you think a schoolhouse is more important than a souvenir?'

'For heaven's sake,' Ensign Siegel said, irritated at such a simple line of approach, 'what difference does it make what *I* think? I don't have the thousand bucks.'

'Well, it wouldn't hurt to ask him, would it?' the girl persisted.

'For heaven's sake, Melora!' Ensign Siegel said, highly irritated. 'I'm sorry I ever mentioned the subject. You don't walk up to Gordon Ripwell and say, "Listen, how about forking over that thousand-dollar bill you treasure so infinitely, just so we can put up a school?" For heaven's sake, Melora! If you knew Ripwell you'd know how ridiculous it is even to think about it. I'm sorry I ever mentioned it,' Ensign Siegel repeated, in a temper. 'Now tell me what you've been doing lately …'

'What kind of man is this man?' Melora said. 'Might he be the kind of man who is interested in education?'

Ensign Siegel sighed wearily. 'No, I'm afraid that education would not be Gordon Ripwell's favourite hobby. Now, Melora …'

'Maybe we here in the village could do something for him in return for the thousand dollars he would give us,' the girl said.

'Melora …' Ensign Siegel said, pressing his lips together. 'What in the world could you do for a man who gets thousand-dollar bills that he doesn't have already …'

Suddenly Ensign Siegel stopped. 'Christ Almighty …' He was so startled by his thought that he had forgotten momentarily she was there. 'I'm very sorry for my language, Melora,' he apologized.

'What in the world is it?' Melora said.

Ensign Siegel shook his head again. 'No, I'm afraid that's out of the question.'

The girl turned in irritation towards the ensign. 'Max, what in the world are you talking about?'

Ensign Siegel gave a long, long sigh. 'Well, maybe it isn't,' he said slowly, more to himself than to her. He turned towards her. 'Melora,' he said, definitely embarrassed, 'may I be very frank with you about something?'

The girl said with real delight, 'Why, Max, I don't think I've ever seen you blush before. What in the world is it?'

'Do you know what Puritanism is?' Ensign Siegel blurted out.

Suddenly Melora started laughing. She held her face in her hands. Siegel had never heard her laugh so much.

'What's so funny?' he said, a little annoyed.

'Max,' she said, putting her fingers against two tears of laughter that were coming down her cheeks. 'The way you said it, it sounded exactly like the questions we used to go over that my pupils ask. "Do you know what Puritanism is?"' she repeated, starting to laugh all over again.

'All right, all right,' Ensign Siegel said, annoyed. '*Do* you?'

'Yes, Max,' she said, in mock soberness. 'I know what Puritanism is.'

'All right now,' Ensign Siegel went on, turning more towards her. 'This is a little complicated, but just listen, and it's going to be pretty frank, too.'

'Yes, Max,' the girl said, mocking him a little.

'Ripwell's publisher,' Ensign Siegel went on, 'is probably the most formidable Puritan in the United States, certainly the most formidable powerful one. That's Fact Number One. Fact Number Two is ...' Ensign Siegel hesitated, swallowing.

'What in the world is Fact Number Two, Max?' the girl said mockingly.

'Fact Number Two,' Ensign Siegel blurted out, 'is that Ripwell wants – wants a girl!'

Melora waited a moment. 'What an interesting Fact Number Two,' she said then.

'I have just thought,' Siegel hurried on, embarrassed, 'of one very remote possibility. Now, just listen to me ...'

'I'm listening, Max,' the girl said, her eyes still smiling.

For perhaps four minutes Ensign Siegel talked, rapidly, for fear he wouldn't get it out if he stopped. At the end he gave an exhausted sigh.

'Well, that was what I was thinking about,' he said. 'It would get Tyson out of carrying those dirty sheets and at the same time get you a schoolhouse.'

'Well,' Melora said in amazement. 'Well! Possibility Number One. And Possibility Number Two.'

'But I don't think that it's very,' Siegel said, with a fresh rush of embarrassment, 'practical.'

'But it *is*, Max!' the girl said. He had never seen her show such enthusiasm. My God, he thought, she really wants that schoolhouse. 'I think you're very clever to think of it,' she said wooingly.

'No, I don't think we should do it,' Siegel said grimly.

'Yes, we should, Max!' the girl burst out again. 'It's something it would be wrong not to do. The children really have a right to that money, and we'd be doing wrong if we didn't get it for them! Now,' she said, as if it were all settled, 'how shall we proceed …?'

Siegel sighed. 'Well,' he said tentatively, 'I could …' He hesitated, self-conscious. 'I could,' he went on, 'speak to Mr Seguro about getting somebody … getting a girl,' Ensign Siegel added, flushing all over.

They waited a few moments in a silence which was definitely embarrassing to Ensign Siegel and which he assumed must be equally embarrassing to her.

'No, the whole idea is – well, going too far,' Ensign Siegel said, looking down at the lagoon.

'It isn't at all,' Melora said quietly. Actually, he could see then, looking at her, she seemed as matter of fact as if considering some practical problem like getting books for the children. 'I think it's an excellent plan,' she went on. 'I've told you. But why some other girl? Why take the risk of somebody else?' she said simply. 'It's too important. Why not me?'

'You?' Ensign Siegel whipped around, as if stung. 'Why, it couldn't be you. Your father …' Siegel stuttered. 'Your family … they …'

'But I'm not going to do anything wrong,' she said simply.

Ensign Siegel sat for several moments, incredulous, stunned, and with all sorts of other strange emotions rushing around in him.

'You really want to do this?' he said then.

'Max, I just think we shouldn't take a chance on anybody else. It means a new schoolhouse, which is something I want more than anything else in the world. And I'm not going to do anything – wrong.'

It was quite a long while before Ensign Siegel said, 'All right, then.'

They talked a few moments longer, in a planning which Siegel found it quite difficult to talk about but which she took in an entirely offhand manner. Then she stood up to go. Suddenly he had turned towards her, was looking down at her.

'Melora,' he said, unhappy, uncertain.

'Yes, Max.'

'You've got to promise me one thing. You'll be ... you'll be ... you'll be extremely careful ...'

'Yes, Max,' she said, looking up at him. 'I'll be very careful.'

They waited a few moments longer.

'The thousand dollars would buy the materials,' she said, then, reflectively, 'and my own people can build it. Maybe it won't be the best-looking schoolhouse in the world – we don't have many skilled workers. But it'll be wonderful,' she said happily, 'whatever it *looks* like.'

Suddenly Ensign Siegel, who was starting to walk her the few steps to the road, stopped. 'I just thought! Why, Tulura has some of the best engineers, carpenters, bricklayers, and plumbers in the whole world. It has my friends the 357th Construction Battalion. The Seabees! I'll talk with the Seabees! The Seabees will put you up the snappiest-looking schoolhouse in the whole blooming Pacific. You know what the Seabee motto is?'

'I'm afraid I don't,' the girl said.

'"Can do!"' Ensign Siegel said. '"Can do!"'

A lot happened in the following week. Ensign Tyson decided to put off for a while sending his letter to the Secretary of the Navy. Ensign Siegel was busy with comings and goings. He made a couple of extra trips to the schoolhouse. He made three trips over to the 357th Construction Battalion and had several talks with the Seabees he knew so well. Then, towards the end of the week, Siegel drove the correspondent Gordon Ripwell through Tanalolo and slowly by the schoolhouse without, however, stopping.

The next night Ripwell came alone to the schoolhouse. It was well after dark.

The next day Ensigns Siegel and Tyson made it a point to be away from Headquarters all day, showing other correspondents than Gordon Ripwell around. In the late afternoon Siegel went over to the schoolhouse. He stayed perhaps a half-hour. Then he returned and repaired to his room, where Tyson soon joined him. The two ensigns broke out a bottle of Paul Jones.

'To mellow if possible,' Ensign Siegel said with a wry smile, 'the great confrontation.'

They had barely taken a first shot when Ripwell burst into the room without knocking. He stood there several moments in the doorway, a very photograph of fury, his eyes darting furiously from ensign to ensign.

'All right, you two smart-aleck, one-striper twerps,' he said finally in a savage burst of fury, 'what gives?'

Eloquent surprise embraced Ensign Siegel's face, as he looked up slowly from his chair at Ripwell planted in the doorway.

'You need something, Rip old man? We're Correspondents' Aides.'

'Don't you Rip-old-man me!' Ripwell shouted in trembling tones, storming into the room. 'You know what I mean! Last night. What's the idea of ...'

'Mr Ripwell!' Ensign Siegel's big frame came to its feet and a booming voice that would have made an admiral pop to by reflex crashed through the room. 'There is much you don't understand! But shortly will! Sit down and listen to a recorded announcement!'

The astonished Ripwell let his knees bend and sit him down on the bed.

'Ensign Tyson!' Ensign Siegel boomed. 'Shut the door and rig this correspondent with a double slug of Paul Jones! The better to prepare him!'

'Yes, sir!' Ensign Tyson said. He slammed the door, poured out a big drink, and shoved the glass into Ripwell's hand.

'And now,' Ensign Siegel said, switching to a voice not unlike that of the March of Time announcer's, 'as a public, or at least a private, service we present: "The Adventures of Richard Harding Davis Jacques Casanova Ripwell!"'

Stepping smartly to a box in the corner – it was the wire-recording machine used for congressmen–constituent interviews – Siegel made some rapid adjustments. Suddenly a girl's voice in very broken English emerged: '*Goordoon Reepwell. Foony name.*'

The correspondent jerked up on the bed like a man tickled by a flame-thrower. 'What's that? What's that?' he babbled.

Fresh noises came from the machine.

'*What's funny about it?*'

'*Joost foony.*'

'*If it's so funny, call me Rip ...*'

'*What work you do, Reep?*'

'*Correspondent, baby … Reporter, writer …*'

'*Where'bouts in States?*'

'*Chicago. Biggest goddamn paper in Chicago. Chicago Gazette. Best goddamn paper in the United States. And Gordon Ripwell's the Gazette's best goddamn correspondent, by Godfrey.*'

'*Have heard of Cheecago.*'

'*Ha, ha. Baby, if they could hear this back home! The Chicago Chamber of Commerce could use you. "Have heard of Cheecago." Ha, ha! Baby, you're the sweetest-looking thing I've seen since my last Miss America contest. Where you been hiding yourself, baby? That skin of yours! That hair! That … Baby, you've certainly got 'em upstairs there, too! How old are you, baby?*'

'*Joost seven-teen. Seventeen year old.*'

'*Godfrey! Do I like 'em just seventeen!*'

Ripwell had stood up. He set his untouched glass of whisky on the floor. His hands and body were quivering in anger and he seemed about to lunge at the machine. Ensign Siegel, smiling happily, slowly moved his towering hulk between the machine and the correspondent.

'Want to hear the rest of it, Reep?'

The correspondent's mouth moved, but said nothing. Sweat-beads of temper stood out on his face, and some fell off it. Almost, it was so quiet you could hear the drops of sweat hitting the floor. In his anger the correspondent kept closing and opening his hands.

'Rip, old sock, I think you better hear just a little more,' Ensign Siegel said. He spun the wire forward rapidly, then put it on playing speed again.

'*… Reep,*' the girl's voice came from the machine. '*What you want?*'

'Heh, heh. What do I want? You, baby. All I want is you.'

'*What that, Reep?*'

'Come on, baby. Let's stop horsing around.'

'*Horsing around, Reep?*'

Ripwell's voice, a little impatiently: '*Let's get the duds off, baby. I didn't come here to sit all night gabbing. Seventeen years old! Heh, heh. Come on, baby, let's see what's under that dress. Upstairs and downstairs, heh, heh!*'

There was an interval of several seconds, a sound of movement, then the girl's voice switched into perfectly modulated, exquisite English: '*Before we do anything, I should warn you to be a little careful, Mr Ripwell. I have not quite recovered from a mild disease we sometimes have on the island. I don't know what you call it in Chicago, but on Tulura it is called social disease.*'

The correspondent, on the recording, let out an outraged yell. And now a curious thing happened. As the girl switched into perfect English, the correspondent switched to a broken, pidgin or even Biblical English: '*Let me out of here. TOUCH ME NOT. Didn't say anything about that. Away from me get! TOUCH ME NOT!*'

Now the girl's voice switched back to broken English. '*But, Reep, don't you ... me?*'

'*Get away. Don't touch! TOUCH ME NOT!*'

Ensign Siegel snapped the machine off. An enormous silence filled the room, broken only by the sound of the correspondent's wet hands clenching and unclenching. Suddenly he roared a question:

'What in the hell are you one-striping bastards up to?' His voice vibrated like an infuriated, over-aged electric fan. 'What's this all about, you two-bit, one-stripe bastards...?'

'Well, you see,' Siegel said with an offhand laugh, 'we do want something from you, Rip, and well ... the simple fact is we intend to use this recording to get it.'

For a moment the correspondent said nothing, just breathing a little hard.

'Okay,' he said finally, giving Ensigns Siegel and Tyson the blackest of looks, but his anger now modified by a certain cool caginess. 'What do you one-striping bastards want?'

'I don't want to have to carry any more of your filthy sheets,' Ensign Tyson said promptly.

Ripwell breathed deeply. 'Okay, Junior. Is that all?' His hand reached forward. 'Now let me have that recording!'

'Uh, just a moment ...' Ensign Siegel slowly raised a hand, policeman-like. 'You haven't asked me what I want. ..'

Ripwell laughed hollowly. 'All right. What's yours?'

Ensign Siegel smiled gently. 'You know that schoolhouse you had your romantic interlude in? Pretty shabby to hold eight grades, isn't it? You see, our shelling knocked out the former school building. Did you know that?'

'What's that?' Ripwell ejaculated. 'How the hell should I know? What the hell do you think I am, a wet nurse to the Tulurans?'

'Materials for a new school can be had – the Seabees have agreed to do the work free,' Siegel went on, 'for almost exactly the wages of one B-29 raid. Isn't that interesting? Chicago *Gazette* correspondent wages, that is,' Siegel explained.

'Why, that's, that's ... blackmail!' the correspondent sputtered, all his fury returning in a rush.

'Yes, I believe that's what they call it,' Ensign Siegel said with utter casualness. 'Blackmail.' He smiled happily.

'Just plain little old blackmail,' Ensign Tyson added with a fond smile.

'Blackmail!' The correspondent's voice burst the word in enraged incredulity. 'I'll see ComFleets! ComFleets'll be happy to know you're using Navy recording machines to blackmail correspondents! ComFleets'll be so happy he might dream up a court-martial!'

With elaborately easy motions Ensign Siegel closed the Navy wire recorder. 'He probably will at that. But meantime that great American Puritan, the publisher of the Chicago *Gazette*, will be happy to know the adventures of his ace Pacific correspondent with seventeen-year-old Tuluran girls. He might dream up another correspondent. You do like your job, don't you – uh, Reep?'

For a full minute the correspondent did not speak, but stood there, legs a little apart and closing and opening his wet hands. His rage at having been tricked and trapped by two mere ensigns seemed to have deprived him of all speech. He waited, his eyes burning into the big ensign. Then he picked up his glass and swallowed the double slug of Paul Jones in one gulp. He slammed the glass down.

'What a couple of smart ensign twerps! You think you've got me by the short hairs, don't you?'

Ensign Siegel smiled softly. 'Yes, old man, that's where we think we got you.'

The correspondent laughed mirthlessly. 'So do I – this time. Why, you little one-striping sons a bitches!'

With shaking hands he pulled out his billfold and extracted the thousand-dollar bill. But for a moment he held on to his precious souvenir.

'Tell me, you bastard twerps – for a thousand bucks I got a right to know – where did ya hide the mike?'

Siegel opened the machine and spun the wire until it came to the line: '*Baby, you've certainly got 'em upstairs there, too.*'

Ensign Siegel handed the spool across with one hand and with the other received the thousand-dollar bill. For several moments Ensign Siegel, holding it in both hands, looked at the bill with a gaze of tender endearment. Then a smile began slowly to spread across his face, enveloping it in a total beneficence.

Next morning Tyson, who had torn up his letter to SecNav, reported to the conference of Public Relations officers that Ripwell no longer needed fresh sheets daily. It seemed that the exec was right. It was a skin ailment that necessitated them for a while, but now the infection was cleared up.

'I hope in the future that you'll mind your rudder,' Nash said briskly, 'and not be so quick to judge, Tyson.'

'Commander, you've convinced me,' Tyson said humbly, 'that our central function out here is to service the correspondents.'

The school ground-breaking ceremonies were held only a month later. It was a great holiday for the village of Tanalolo, and the entire citizenry gathered in front of the temporary platform which the Seabees who were to build the school had erected. On the platform sat a number of dignitaries, including a senator from Illinois who happened to be junketing the island – he owed his election to the publisher of the Chicago *Gazette*; a tubby Seabee chief carpenter's mate decked out in whites; the leading Tulurans and schoolteachers of the village; eight school-children of ages six to fourteen, representing the eight grades which would occupy the new schoolhouse; and, in the middle of the front row, the guest of honour, Gordon Ripwell.

Ensign Siegel had laid on an elaborate programme with himself as master of ceremonies and translator. Siegel had never been in better form. First he introduced the senator from Illinois, who, with a sonority that echoed through the surrounding palm trees, delivered a lengthy oration consisting almost entirely of a godlike eulogy of the publisher of the Chicago *Gazette*. The Tulurans could hardly have understood the references to 'that leading American citizen of the Midwest and the world who from the great bastion of Chicago has successfully, and ofttimes with an aloneness comparable only to the eagle on the distant crag, resisted all foreign encroachments and entanglements'. Nevertheless they clapped vigorously on the cues which Siegel, immediately after each paragraph of his own translation, added in Tuluran, 'Applause, please.' When the senator, deeply gratified by the enthusiasm, had at last finished, Siegel introduced the mayor of Tanalolo, who in brief but warm words expressed the Tulurans' overwhelming gratitude for the schoolhouse. Then, representing the Seabees, Ensign Siegel introduced the chief petty officer, who, his stomach sticking out comfortably, told how pleased the Seabees were to do this sort of work and mentioned how he had six kids at home himself and would be having more but for the war. To this the Tulurans gave out with some very honest, lusty applause. By the time the chief had sat down, a warm, folksy glow filled the air.

'And now,' Ensign Siegel said, 'there remains the chief figure of all to hear from. The man but for whose sublime generosity none of us would be here today. That dedicated representative of the American free Press,' Siegel's voice rose resonantly, 'who risked his life – voluntarily, mind you – to accompany one of our B-29s on a dangerous raid on the common enemy, Japan. No one asked him to risk his life! No one ordered him to risk his life! And if you ask me the natural question of why he did it, I can only answer, "That is the kind of man this man is!"'

After each sentence or two in English, Ensign Siegel paused to translate himself into Tuluran. The last translation contained a slight variation, coming out as, 'That is the kind of man this stupid fool is!' This brought from the Tulurans a burst of laughter which perplexed the Americans, who could only attribute the laughter to the quaint Tuluran sense of humour.

'... Rewarded for his dauntless daring,' Siegel continued, 'by the magnanimous publisher of the great Chicago *Gazette* – himself one of the great pillars of our precious heritage of free Press that we Americans all, you and ourselves, so cherish, and pretty free with his money, too – this man kicked in the entire sum to the building of this school. In a moment I am going to ask this selfless correspondent to step up here. First, however ...'

Turning to the school-children, Ensign Siegel made a motion. One by one they trooped up to the correspondent and with small bows made their offerings. The first-grader presented Ripwell with a highly imaginary drawing of the new schoolhouse which appeared to be modelled on a picture of the Empire State Building in his teacher's geography book. The second-grader presented him with a bunch of bananas. The third-grader, with some difficulty, hung an enormous garland of white frangipani around the astonished correspondent's neck. The fourth-grader presented him with a live coconut crab in an old cigar-box. The fifth-grader brought him a basket woven of aggay plant. The sixth-grader presented him with a watch-fob made of land snail-shells. The seventh-grader gave him a large hat of woven palm fibre. And the eighth-grader presented him with a huge jug of palm toddy.

'And now,' Ensign Siegel said, 'will you step up here, Rip?'

Gordon Ripwell, frangipanied, the big straw hat on his head, and almost staggering under his load of gifts of palm toddy, snail-shells, restive coconut crab, and the rest of it, rose and walked to the speaker's stand. Ensign Siegel placed his arm affectionately around the correspondent.

'And now,' Ensign Siegel said, 'I take great honour in something I am sure will come as a surprise to this benefactor and which I do on authorization of the Tulura Board of Education. I hereby christen this edifice the Gordon Ripwell–Chicago *Gazette*–357th Construction Battalion Grade School!'

A mighty roar, for which no cue was necessary, burst from the crowd, and flash-guns popped. Siegel had seen to it that the occasion was well covered for state-side papers by other correspondents and a dozen or so Public Relations photographers shooting from all angles. Gordon Ripwell waited for the tide of applause to subside. Then he made a short speech.

'I had thought,' he said, 'of keeping as a lifelong souvenir the magnificent memento sent me by the great publisher I am proud to serve. Then, however, I happened to hear indirectly of Tanalolo's need for a schoolhouse. Nothing except the cause of education, which has ever been near to my heart, would have persuaded me to part with my souvenir. But better souvenir even than a thousand-dollar bill is' – he pointed to the broken dirt symbolizing the new edifice – 'a building for the education of youth.'

Gordon Ripwell waited for the fresh tides of applause to subside.

Then, raising his hand, he created the hit of the day with the people of Tanalolo.

The best goddamn correspondent of the Chicago *Gazette* turned to a very beautiful girl who had been seated next to him.

'But the real credit for this school,' Rip said, 'goes to this charming maiden – one of your teachers, who worked harder than anyone else for its fulfilment. No one knows that – by Godfrey – better than I.'

At Rip's insistence Melora arose and took a shy bow to more violent applause. Then the entire citizenry of Tanalolo, full of emotion, surged forward, and lifting Gordon Ripwell to their shoulders, carried him gratefully through the streets of the little village.

Back home in Chicago, everyone soon learned from the clippings, the story made a great smash. Ripwell's picture was plastered all over the *Gazette*, led off by a four-column page one picture of the correspondent, garlanded with frangipani and holding on to his big straw hat, aboard Tuluran shoulders. All the wire services carried the story, too. Later on there was talk of Rip's receiving some special sort of journalistic award for giving a school to the Tulurans.

Then, a couple of weeks after the ground-breaking ceremonies, the publisher of the *Gazette* sent his own characteristic token of appreciation. Rip brought it over and showed it to Ensigns Tyson and Siegel.

It was another thousand-dollar bill.

'My God,' Tyson said, 'how many of these does he have?'

'Turn it over and read it, Admiral,' Ripwell suggested to Tyson, who complied: '"To My Favourite Correspondent, war or peace: For selfless devotion, even in the midst of bloody war, to the ennobling cause of educating our distant backward brothers."'

Gordon Ripwell was not a bad guy. He smiled and said, 'That's the sort of publisher I have. Oh, say, Tyson. Do you know where I can get a girl – and would you pick me up a pair of sheets to go with her? And oh, say, Admiral. I like my girls like I like my sheets. Clean.'

Six: The typical young Navy man

'BOATSWAIN'S MATE Second Class Farragut Jones of the U.S.S. *Ankletooth*,' Lieutenant-Commander Nash exclaimed in the tones he reserved for the most important visitors, 'will hit Tulura tomorrow!'

The exec sat back happily in his chair, leaning his bald head into his cupped hands, and beamed at the morning conference of Public Relations officers.

'I've never seen Admiral Boatwright so enthused about anything connected with Public Relations,' the exec said, all in a glow. 'Why, hardly a day has passed but what the admiral has asked me, "When does the Typical Young Navy Man arrive?"'

'Well, I certainly thought it was a great idea,' said Lieutenant Morey Griffin. Such had been the exec's complete expropriation of the Farragut Jones idea that Griffin had been experiencing an enormous amount of trouble keeping alive the fact that the original Jones concept, though certainly when he started filing the Jones dispatches to his home-town paper he had not thought of it as a concept, was his.

'I don't mind saying,' the exec continued unhearingly, 'that already I rate the Farragut Jones idea as one of the best two or three ideas I've cranked up during my entire career in Naval Public Relations.'

'Commander ...,' Griffin said.

'Now on to the Farragut Jones plan,' the exec said as if his ears were stuffed.

From the centre of his desk the exec pulled forward a folder labelled 'Farragut Jones'. He lifted out a sheaf of six sheets of paper stapled together.

'This is the Jones itinerary,' he said proudly. 'First we have Jones here for a few days of familiarization and orientation on the purpose of his trip, which in broad terms is to sell the Navy story back home. The basic idea, the central concept, is that Jones will *epitomize* everything the Navy is. He will *be* the Navy to the home-fronters, who will need only to look at him to think, "This is the Navy".'

The exec looked up. 'That means that as many people as possible must see Jones. And in particular the workers in Navy war-plants who are making the guns, ammunition, paint, and such things which keep the ship part of the Navy going. I figure that laying eyes on the end product of their work, so to speak, that is, a flesh-and-blood sea-going man named Farragut Jones – named for two of the greatest naval heroes – will give them a thrilling dose of morale. Can you imagine what a morale problem there must be in Navy war-plants where the workers never see what happens to their work? Farragut Jones,' the exec said decisively, 'will correct all that.'

The exec returned to the sheaf. 'But before he hits the war plants we have numerous other concepts in the frying-pan for Jones, whom we intend to milk to the last drop. First, we have the big home-town celebration for the Typical Young Navy Man in his typical Joe Blow town of Appleton, Nebraska. Bands, community dinner, and other such folksy trimmings. The governor of Nebraska will be on hand in Appleton to greet Jones. Photographs.'

The exec flipped a page. 'From Appleton, Jones goes to New York to hold Press conferences, newsreels, etcetera, appear on "We The People", get the key to the city from the mayor, photographs, etcetera.'

The exec flipped another page. 'After that we take him to Washington, where he will go down to Congress and meet the senators and congressmen, and be photographed right and left.'

The exec looked up from the itinerary. 'I suggested to Washington that Jones might address a joint session of Congress, but they thought this might be a little hard to lay on, even for an idea as big as Jones. My guess is that the Air Force' – the exec said the two words with sudden anger, almost a hissing sound – 'heard about the Jones joint-session address and enviously scuttled it. However,' said the exec, resuming his glow as he returned to the sheaf of pages, 'Farragut will be going to the White House to meet the President. More photographs.'

The exec flipped a page. 'This page is devoted to Farragut Jones in Hollywood.'

'Hollywood!' Griffin exclaimed.

'At the Hollywood airport,' the exec continued from the itinerary, 'Farragut Jones will be met by the top movie stars. Actually,' he said, looking up, 'I hated to bring him in to Hollywood in a plane, but it would have taken weeks to send him in a ship from the East Coast, through the Panama Canal, and up to California. So I sacrificed the ship idea after getting an ironclad promise from Washington that it won't be an Air Force' – the exec said the phrase angrily – 'plane which flies him in. It would be just like the Air Force' – he said the phrase furiously – 'to try to horn in on the Typical Young Navy Man.'

The exec returned to the Hollywood page. 'After being greeted at the Hollywood airport by the élite of the movie colony, Jones is paraded down Sunset Boulevard, sitting amongst a bevy of movie queens and atop a floral float fashioned in the shape of a ship. Numerous photographs. Then follow several days in Hollywood, visits at the homes of the stars, who will vie with each other to entertain the Typical Young Navy Man … Well, Sailors' – the exec breathed deeply – 'there's more of this, but those are the highlights.'

The exec laid the sheaf of papers down.

'Initiative! Imagination! That's what we want to show on Jones. The sixteen-inch treatment! Flank speed!'

'Commander,' Griffin said.

'All right, what is it, Griffin?' the exec finally recognized the lieutenant.

'Now that we've got the initiative,' said Griffin, 'we want to keep it. Hollywood! What a wonderful idea for Jones! It occurs to me, however, that it's absolutely vital that some officer from here accompany Jones back to the States. See that the tour's run right, make sure Jones is really used Navy-wise, that outsiders like the Air Force don't try to horn in.'

'You may have something there, Griffin. We want to keep control of our own idea.' The exec sat for several reflective moments. 'Yes, I'll decide it right now! I'll send one of our own officers to accompany Jones.'

'And it ought to be,' Griffin said enthusiastically, 'some officer who's really been on fire for a long time about this Farragut Jones idea. …'

'But unfortunately I can't take the time off,' the exec said, laughing. 'I'm not going to decide the officer now. But I will put it in my tickler file. And you may be sure that I will give the gravest thought,' he said menacingly, 'to who we do send with Jones. Incidentally, it'll be a nice trip for the officer, won't it? The States! New York! Hollywood!'

The officers' mouths all almost visibly watered.

The exec leaned forward. 'So Farragut Jones arrives tomorrow! Right now we need an officer to chaperon Jones around here, be sort of his aide. Siegel! I'm appointing you to be with Jones here,' the exec said by way of explanation that this did not necessarily mean Max would accompany Jones clear back to the States, 'to be his aide-chaperon.'

'His aide-chaperon?' Ensign Siegel said.

'I know what you're thinking, Max – that he's only an enlisted man. Well, he's not!' the exec said, reproving Siegel. 'He's the one Typical Young Navy Man! From the moment Farragut Jones arrives on Tulura, I want you to give him the complete red-rug, big-wheel, VIP treatment that you're so clever at, Max!'

The C-47 fetching Boatswain's Mate Second Class Farragut Jones to Tulura set down at the airfield at a little after 2100 next evening. Ensign Siegel, who had waited there many times to welcome senators, congressmen, publishers, businessmen, and correspondents to Tulura, leaned against the door-jamb of the Operations building waiting for Jones and thinking of the tasks the United States Navy could think up for an ensign to perform. He watched the passengers file in, keeping his eyes not on their faces but on their sleeves. Near the end of the parade he sighted a pair of crossed anchors and a couple of stripes, and before he looked into the face above, intoned: 'Boatswain's Mate Farragut Jones?'

A voice that sounded as if it belonged to a sea-lion with a head cold responded: 'Farragut Jones here!'

Ensign Siegel looked and his mouth came open, then closed without a word. Then it opened again, and for quite a while it stayed open.

A big man himself, Siegel was looking up at the boatswain's mate, who towered at least six feet five inches and must have weighed 240 pounds. He looked like some fearsome sea monster come to shore. His flesh suggested scales and barnacles. Even his breath smelled of salt water. Through the V-neck of his faded jumper could be seen, penetrating a black and tangled forest of chest hair, evidences of a great tattoo. Beneath his pushed-up sleeves his hairy, bulging muscles were engraved with more thoroughly visible tattooes of naked women. His sailor's hat pushed back on his head, he stood there looking fierce and rock-like, carrying a ditty-bag in one hand, and over his shoulder, as lightly as if it were a woman's evening purse, a full sea-bag. His eyes watched the officer as a natural enemy, animal-like. Now his voice, rumbling up from deep down in his chest, burst forth threateningly:

'What's this here all about?'

Ensign Siegel swallowed, tried to say something, nothing came out, breathed deeply, and finally was able to say, 'You mean the dispatch didn't say?'

'The —er,' Jones roared fiercely, giving out that breath of the sea, 'said to report here to Tulura, that was all the —er said!'

'That stupid Marblehead,' Siegel said.

'What'd you say?' Farragut Jones said threateningly.

'Not you,' Ensign Siegel said quickly. 'Our executive officer.'

'I got rights!' Jones suddenly let go a terrifying clap of thunder. 'I got rights to know what goes on about me! I been in this Navy a long time, I ain't no —ing reservist! I know me rights!'

'Yes ...' Ensign Siegel started.

'If it's about that time I told the skipper to jam the bow anchor up his ass,' Jones bellowed, 'well, it weren't my job to paint the —er, and besides I already done a month in the brig for that one. Besides, our skipper don't know an anchor from a goat's balls and the —er hisself belongs in Portsmouth. I know me rights!'

Ensign Siegel gave the boatswain's mate a long, probing look. He breathed a while, then spoke again.

'That's fine,' he said. 'Come along with me and we'll have a long talk about your rights.'

On the way in from the airfield in the jeep, Ensign Siegel drove slowly. Then with extremely cautious gentleness, as much for per-sonal protection as anything else – since for some reason, driving through the black boondocks with what was beside him, Siegel felt a considerable personal sense of unsafety – he began to explain to Jones what they were going to do to him. The boatswain's mate sat like some huge, wary animal, suspicious and unbelieving. Then, his voice bursting like a tempest over his ensign-driver, he said tentatively,

'Well, whatever it is, it couldn't be worse than the *Ankletooth*! That there is the worst fouled-up —ing bucket in the Yew S. Navy. That —er we got that calls hisself a skipper ...'

'The idea,' said Ensign Siegel gently, 'is that you'll go back to the States and go around to the Navy war-plants.'

'What's them —ers?' Jones said.

'That's where they make Navy stores, Navy equipment, naval guns, Navy paint,' said Siegel.

'Maybe I can find the —er that made the paint we been using on the *Ankletooth*!' said Jones with his first real eagerness. 'I'd like to castrate the —er! The —ing stuff won't dry.'

Ensign Siegel soberly watched the road unreel through the boon-docks.

'The main idea of the trip,' he said quietly, 'would be for you to give the workers in the war-plants a talk on how they are helping to win the war. That's to increase their morale. They're even talking about taking you to Hollywood.'

'Hollywood!' Jones said gutturally, in an abrupt burst of enthusiasm. He scratched his chest, making a noise like two pieces of sandpaper rubbed together. 'That mean I get laid?'

'I imagine that's on the itinerary,' Ensign Siegel said. 'I don't know why else anyone would go to Hollywood.'

'Hog-tie me and lead me to the —!' Jones roared, laughing lasciviously. 'I'm as horny as a barrel of toads in June. You know how long since I been ...'

'Listen, Farragut,' Siegel said, slowing the jeep. 'I hope you don't mind me calling you Farragut. We're pretty informal around here, not much caste. Incidentally, where did you get that name?'

'My old lady never knew who my old man were except that he were a Navy man,' Jones said informationally, and almost proudly. 'One of three or four Navy men off the *Farragut*, a destroyer which was hanging around Boston a lot in them days. Listen here,' he said, his suspicion returning, 'is this on the level about me getting to — around in Hollywood? I ain't just intendin' to be trapped into nothin'! I know me rights!'

Siegel, sighing quietly, speeded up the jeep. 'I tell you, why don't we just talk about it later, okay? You had chow?'

'Yeh,' said Jones, loudly scratching his chest, 'but I could use a few beers now that you mention it. We hear how you've got the —ing Pacific division of Budweiser on this here island, and I'm dry as a virgin's balls.'

'Nicely put, Farragut,' the ensign said, producing a laugh. 'Well, we got just about everything on this here island. Maybe you'd rather have some hard stuff.'

'You mean drinkin' whisky?' Jones said enthusiastically.

When they had crested Headquarters hill, Ensign Siegel headed the jeep directly to his own BOQ. He remembered gratefully that his room-mate Griffin was out with a Red Cross girl. He led Farragut Jones hurriedly upstairs to his own room. He shut the door and locked it.

'Make yourself comfortable, Farragut,' he said.

While Jones sat down heavily on one of the two beds, Ensign Siegel opened the closet and broke out a fifth of Four Roses.

'I'll be a hog-tied —ing son of a —ing bitch!' Jones's eyes bulged. 'Haven't *seen* any of that —ing stuff for three —ing years!'

Ensign Siegel poured a third of a glass and passed it to the boatswain's mate, who drained it off in one gulp as if it were a coke, wiped his mouth with his sleeve, and held the glass back to Siegel. 'Seconds.'

This time the ensign filled the glass half full and Jones promptly drained it again. Then Siegel handed him the bottle.

'Mind if I take off this —ing jumper?' Jones said, pausing from drinking straight out of the bottle and pulling the jumper over his head as he asked. 'I'm not used to wearing the —er and I feel stinking as a Honolulu whore on Sunday morning.'

The gesture unveiled a blockbuster of a chest jungled with black hair framing and lapping over into a massive tattoo depicting a ferocious sea battle, ships sinking, guns firing off, and waves heaving up and down as Jones breathed. Siegel looked on in fascination.

'Battle of Lake Erie,' the boatswain's mate explained proudly. 'Had that one done in Boston. Lookee here.'

The boatswain's mate, rising massively to his feet, turned around, revealing, across his plateau-like back a brilliant red, foot-long tattooed cross, jutting up from a rock and with a sailor clinging to the cross.

'Rock of Ages,' Jones explained. 'Long as you have one of these

—ers you'll never go down at sea. You'll notice I'm still afloat. New Orleans.'

As he cut down the Four Roses, Jones ticked off proudly the significances and places of execution of his 'Mother', naked girls and other tattoos which almost entirely covered his torso, arms, thighs, and calves, front and back. Ensign Siegel was thoroughly absorbed by the catalogue. Over each of the boatswain's mate's nipples was a tattooed word – one 'hot', one 'cold'.

'Seattle –' he pointed to his left. 'San Diego –' he indicated his right, and took a long pull on the bottle. 'The West Coast Twins, I call the pair of them,' he said in sober exposition. 'You know,' he said suddenly, scratching his chest, which gave off the sandpaper noise, 'this here U.S.A. business might be all right at that! It's about time somebody went back and told off those —ing 4-F's!'

'That's not quite the purpose of the trip,' Siegel said in a fresh effort. 'However, let's don't discuss it tonight. We're probably both bushed. Anyhow, I am.'

Ensign Siegel had planned to take Jones down to the enlisted men's barracks. But deciding definitely that he had better not let him out of his sight, he waited until Jones had emptied the fifth of Four Roses, then told him to sack out for the night in the extra bed in his room. He left an urgent note on his door telling Griffin to sack out somewhere else tonight, that he had an important guest staying with him. Then he locked the door again.

Next morning Siegel, who was hard to awaken, jumped up in his bed to what he first thought was a violent tropical thunderstorm. Resting on his elbow, he watched for a while, and listened, hypnotized, to the long rumbles through the boatswain's mate's chest, the foghorn blasts and the expelled breath rushing through the hair on his chest like a stiff breeze through a field of tall grass. He got out of bed, dressed, and, leaving Jones alone with his snoring, locked the door and went up to the Public Relations building to report to Nash.

'Well, Max,' the exec said happily as he came in, 'how's our young VIP? Does he have much stage-fright?'

'Commander' – Siegel came right to the point – 'I'm afraid we haven't got quite the Typical Young Navy Man in Farragut Jones. At least I hope not.'

Siegel furnished the exec a takeout on the boatswain's mate, his appearance and attitudes.

'Jumping Jupiter!' Nash said, alarmed.

'He has the notion that he's going to go back to the States and tell all the 4-F's off,' Siegel said.

'Jumping Jupiter!' Nash said. 'What have we got ourselves in for?'

Ensign Siegel described the tattoos, including the West Coast Twins.

'Hot and cold!' Nash said, his mouth puckering. 'Jumping Jupiter, right there that eliminates any pictures by the swimming-pools with Hollywood movie stars.'

'That's the least of our troubles,' Siegel said. 'We could always keep him clothed. I'm more worried about his mouth. Every other word that comes out of it is —er.'

'Jumping Jupiter!' Nash said, revolted. 'Does he really use expressions like that?'

For a moment neither officer said anything, and Nash sat, appalled. 'Well, of course he's been to sea a long time,' he finally said hopefully, clutching at the explanation. 'A few days here on Tulura will make him more wholesome. One of our main Public Relations plays was going to be on his name. We've still got that, anyhow,' he said cheerfully. 'You might ask him how he happened to be named Farragut. Old Navy family or whatever.'

'It's an old Navy family all right,' Siegel said, and explained where Farragut had got it.

'Jumping Jupiter!' the exec exclaimed. 'This is serious!'

The exec fished his binoculars out of his desk drawer, walked to the screen window and for a few moments gazed through the powerful glasses at something down the hillside. He marched back to his desk, stuck the binoculars back, sat down and started tapping his bald head with a pencil, filling the silence with a resonant, staccato sound. It was a sound Siegel knew as evidence that the exec was beginning to take on a strain.

'Well, we can't change course now, Siegel!' he exclaimed. 'That's for sure. We've told the Navy Department all about this great idea of ours and they've directed us to cast off. Appleton, Nebraska, is all alerted for Jones! The itinerary from Washington to Hollywood is all laid out! Jones has got to be on his way out of here in' – the exec fumbled over his desk for a dispatch – 'ten days. Ten days! Not a second to lose!'

The exec eyed the ensign closely and desperately. 'Listen, Siegel, you're pretty good at these things. You can talk to anybody. I want you to start getting Jones in condition for the United States. Sort of freshen him up, you know what I mean? You've got ten days.'

'Commander,' Siegel said, 'this isn't a case of freshening up. This is a case of complete overhaul. Even a first-rate school takes four years just to do a simonize job.'

'I just told you, we can't change course now!' the exec shouted. 'There's no direction for us to go now but forward! We've got our backs to the bulkhead on this thing! I wish I'd never heard of Farragut Jones!' Nash said, irritated. 'Look alive! Do something! Work on him! Meantime just keep him rooming with you. I'll put Griffin somewhere else.'

'Rooming with me!' Siegel said. 'Commander, I'm not ordinarily finicky, but I'd as soon room with a water-buffalo. They don't snore – at least not so loudly.'

'For the time being we've got to keep him out of sight,' the exec said, ignoring the objection. 'Work on him day and night! I'll give you a couple of days off when you're through. For now I'll have chow sent in for both of you. How about that? Room service,' Nash said. 'The only way to do it is to have him living with you. Rub off a little of your Harvard education on him.'

'Commander,' Siegel said, 'this just isn't realistic. Even George Bernard Shaw gave Eliza Doolittle several months.'

'Don't get fancy with me, Siegel!' Nash sputtered. 'What I want is action! Jumping Jupiter, man, can't you realize we're caught in a first-class bight? We're like a submarine being depth-charged in Tokyo Bay, and you sit here making fancy talk! If we don't produce a decent Farragut Jones, the Navy Department will think we're all looney as a jay-bird out here. They'll have a board of admirals out here to investigate us all. Not to mention what Admiral Boatwright, who mistakenly thinks none of us are too vital to the war effort any-how, will do. You especially will be in trouble. Don't forget, Siegel,' the exec threatened, 'you and Griffin started this. I'm trying to be decent and give you a chance to redeem yourself, but not unless you mind your rudder, hear? Work on his language especially. I don't suppose we can have those tattoos taken off. Tattoos won't come off, will they? One thing I've never been able to understand,' the exec added thoughtfully, 'is why a man will let himself be tattooed.'

'One of them keeps him from drowning,' Siegel explained.

Ensign Max Siegel began at once to undertake to work over Boatswain's Mate Second Class Farragut Jones in his BOQ room. Siegel found out almost immediately that he had an enormous initial block to get over in the simple fact that Jones appeared to believe that there was some trap behind it all, such as enticing him back to the States in order to clap him in Portsmouth Naval Prison. At the outset Siegel therefore attempted to explain to the boatswain's mate that such things as Navy stateside tours did exist and, moreover, were important.

'Farragut,' he told him, 'there are many kinds of naval duty these days. Things have changed a lot in the Navy in the last few years, particularly in the last twelve months or so. Ships are no longer everything in the Navy. ....'

It took a full day, with several sessions of about two hours each, before Siegel considered that Jones was even registering a word he said. Then, beginning on the second day, Siegel went more directly to work.

'Now for one thing,' he told Jones, 'you're never to use the word —er in the continental limits. Is that clear?'

Farragut Jones made an uncertain sound.

'Now try to talk for a minute without using that word,' Ensign Siegel said. 'Talk about anything.' He looked at his watch. 'All right. Get set! Go!'

Jones looked at the ensign dumbly.

'Say something!' Ensign Siegel said. 'Don't just sit there!'

'What the —er am I supposed to say?' the boatswain's mate asked.

Ensign Siegel breathed heavily. 'Farragut,' he said, 'do you like the Navy?'

'I never thought,' Jones said, 'whether I like the —er or not.'

At the end of the second day, Ensign Siegel, who felt he was standing completely still, sent a request, or demand, to the exec for some supplies. The exec authorized a case of Four Roses to be drawn from the officers' wine mess and delivered to Siegel's room. Siegel opened a bottle and placed it on a chair between himself and Jones. Whenever he passed a test, the ensign explained to the boatswain's mate, he would get a reward – a shot of Four Roses.

'Now,' Ensign Siegel would try again, 'listen to this sentence. "The *Ankletooth* is a great ship." Now say that after me. "The *Ankletooth* is a great ship."'

'"The *Ankletooth* is a gr ..." —er!' Jones exclaimed. 'I can't say that! It's a —ing lie!'

'Don't use that word!' Siegel said with sudden viciousness. 'And don't be so finicky!' He picked up the opened bottle and moved it back and forth under Jones's nose. 'Now say after me: "The *Ankletooth* is a great ship."'

'"The *Ankletooth* is a ... great ship."' Jones, sniffing, got it out.

'Swallow,' Siegel said, handing him the bottle.

Jones gulped a slug down. 'Christ,' he said happily, 'this —ing stuff tastes good!'

'Jones!' Siegel screamed, grabbing the bottle. He sat back on his bunk, limp. It was hopeless, he decided.

Then one more idea, following the line of much of Jones's talk, occurred to him. It was the last thing he could think of, and if it didn't work he was ready to toss Farragut Jones back into the sea.

'Look here, Farragut,' Siegel said on the third day. 'Lot of people I know out here'd give their right eyeball for a lay in Hollywood. Now if you don't really want to learn this and go to Hollywood and screw around, just let me know and I'll have them get someone else off one of the ships.'

The boatswain's mate made an indefinite sound, somewhat like a grunt. Ensign Siegel leaned forward and spoke into his ear.

'Think of all those dames in the States,' he said, almost in a whisper. 'How'd you like to be sitting on a couch by one right now? Someone about nineteen with long blond hair and wearing one of those tight dresses that fit like it was her skin and smelling all nice, and then you pull her up against you on the couch and open the top of that dress, and there they are, like cherries on a marshmallow sundae. ...'

Farragut Jones gave a croak.

Ensign Siegel leaned over until his mouth was about a half-inch from the boatswain's mate's ear. For some time his voice droned graphically on: 'And finally she starts to pant, wanting you – you, Farragut!'

Jones let out a noise like a bull walrus. The sweat poured river-like off his brow and down his naked chest, wetting the hair and the Battle of Lake Erie.

'No nineteen-year-old girl for you to play around with,' Siegel whispered, 'no silk panties for you to pull off, Farragut, unless you get this and get it fast, unless you get in line.'

'I'll get in line, sir!' Jones croaked. 'If you'll just show me how! What you want me to do? I'll do it! I'll do anything!'

'Now if you say the word —er just once more, you're through,' Siegel leaned over and bellowed suddenly in the boatswain's mate's ear. 'You understand? You're through!'

'Aye, aye, sir!' Jones said, sweating profusely. 'I understand.'

'Just once more, Jones, and it's all off! I'll have the admiral send out to another ship for someone else to go back to the States and — all those ...'

'You just used one of them words yourself!' Jones said, outraged.

'Never mind what I used!' Siegel shouted in the boatswain's mate's face. 'I'm not going to the States. And don't talk back to me!'

'Aye, aye, sir; I'm sorry, sir,' Jones said humbly, and scratched his chest.

'All right now,' Siegel said gruffly. 'Let's stay in line. Now, another thing. You're never to take your jumper off in public, you understand? You've got it off right now!' he said violently. 'Put your shirt on!'

Jones meekly put the jumper on, covering up the majority of his tattoos, particularly the hot and the cold.

'You promise never to take your jumper off in public in the States?' Siegel roared.

'Aye, aye, sir,' Jones said meekly. 'But, sir, what about when I'm with them silk panties,' he croaked, sweating. 'Can I take my jumper off to ...'

'That's not in public, you idiot!' Siegel said. 'Or at least I hope not. Jones, you're probably the stupidest man in the whole United States Navy! I don't think you're good enough for this assignment!' Siegel started to his feet. 'I'm going up right now to the admiral and tell him to get someone else!'

'Don't do that, sir!' Jones pleaded. 'I'll do anything! I'm trying, sir!' the big boatswain's mate whimpered.

'All right; this is your last chance,' Siegel said, sitting back down. 'No jumpers off in public, understand?'

'No jumpers off in public!' Jones swore.

'No words like —er any more.'

'No words like ... that word any more!' Jones swore.

'The *Ankletooth* is a great ship!'

'The *Ankletooth* is a great ship!' Jones swore.

'Say, "I'll be nice to the war workers."'

'I'll be nice to the ... nice to the ... nice to the war workers,' Jones got it out, vigorously scratching his chest under his jumper.

'And stop scratching your chest!' Siegel roared furiously. Jones dropped his hand as if a bullwhip had flicked it. 'Say, "I'll never scratch my chest in the States."'

'I'll never scratch my chest in the States!' Jones swore.

Siegel sighed, exhausted. 'Have a drink. I think I'll have one myself.'

In another day Ensign Siegel had brought the boatswain's mate along to where he was able to talk a full minute without using the word, and in two more days, his room littered with empty Four Roses bottles, a full five minutes. Siegel was red-eyed and haggard from loss of sleep, but he felt slightly encouraged.

'Now, Farragut,' he sighed, rubbing his hand through his hair, 'I've written up a speech I want you to memorize. You can give the same speech everywhere, at all the war plants.'

The speech was the most difficult part of all – it was 500 words long, beginning, as Siegel now read it aloud, 'Fellow War-Winners, I'm not much at making speeches. I just want to tell you how much we're countin' on you, out on the ships, to keep the supplies comin'...'

'What does that ... what does that there mean?' Jones interrupted.

'Never mind what it means!' Siegel roared at the boatswain's mate. 'Just say it!'

For several days more Jones worked on the speech, sitting up far into the night, memorizing it and repeating it over and over to Siegel.

By the eighth day Ensign Siegel had begun to feel it was possible. He devoted that day to laying actual traps for Jones. He tried to lead him on to say the word, to take off his jumper, to scratch his chest, to castigate the war workers. The boatswain's mate didn't bite.

'Mr Siegel,' he said, 'you can't fool me! I'm gonna take them silk panties off like they was barnacles on the *Ankletooth*! Hog-tie me, Mr Siegel, and lead me to the panties!'

Siegel considered this was a sufficient improvement on Jones's previous term of woman identification that he could let it pass.

On the ninth day Ensign Siegel went up to report to a specially assembled conference of Public Relations officers. He looked beat.

'Well, fingers-crossed, Commander,' he sighed wearily. 'But I think we could be in. At least he doesn't say —er every other word.'

Nash shuddered. 'I feel like we're playing with dynamite. But we've got to take the chance. We're past the point of no return.'

'Remember my idea, Commander,' Griffin said, 'of sending an officer with him. If he's got a good officer who'll stay right with him he'll be all right.'

Nash sat back reflectively. 'Yes, I've always thought that was a superb idea,' he said. 'The natural officer to send would be Siegel. But of course we couldn't send an ensign on an assignment like this. Since Jones is a Home Town News story, the next natural officer to send is Noah,' he said matter-of-factly.

'I'll be happy,' Lieutenant Noah Pratt said very loudly, 'to undertake the assignment.'

'Undertake the assignment!' Griffin said furiously. 'But, Commander, I thought up the whole idea of Farragut Jones!'

'Morey,' Nash said patiently, 'you had your chance to be Joe Blow officer, and turned it down. This ought to teach you to look alive. He, if I may paraphrase Captain John Smith, who does not work shall not go to Hollywood. Besides, we can't spare you,' he said inconsistently.

'Can't spare me!' Griffin cried. 'But I'm not doing a damn thing!'

'Oh, you're not?' Nash said. 'Very interesting. That's what I've been thinking for a long time now. Then you can take over Noah's Home Town News job for a month while he's in Hollywood and the rest of the States.'

'Take over Home Town News!' Griffin said, appalled.

'And don't forget to go through channels next time on things like Farragut Jones!' Nash said.

'All Joe Blow stories ought to be sent through channels,' Noah Pratt said loudly.

'But it was my idea. Farragut Jones was my idea from start to finish!' Griffin exclaimed, enraged.

'I haven't forgotten that,' Nash said meaningfully.

The exec turned instructionally to Lieutenant Pratt. 'Remember, never leave his side, Noah! Never leave Farragut Jones alone, any more than you would the secret torpedo sight. Especially with the Press. And now,' he said, 'Siegel and I have arranged a dry run. Max?'

Ensign Siegel left and brought Farragut Jones in. It was the first look the officers had had at him, and they stared intently up at the specimen. Jones, all shaved, bathed, aqua-velvaed, and with a fresh set of whites and a T-shirt which kept in most of the hair on his chest, and his sleeves rolled down to conceal the tattooed naked women, looked passably civilized, though still rugged. He stood before the officers, shuffling his huge frame from one foot to another in a winning way, and gave his speech, beginning, 'Fellow War-Winners …'

The performance was so flawless – winning, in fact – that at the end of it the officers broke into spontaneous applause. Farragut Jones beamed.

'Thank you, Officers,' he said smoothly.

'Jones,' the exec said, 'let me commend you. Just stick to that speech, Jones. Try not to say anything else at all while you're in the States except the words of that speech, Jones, and the Navy will appreciate it. Do I make myself clear, Jones?'

'Aye, aye, sir,' said Farragut.

'And otherwise do whatever Mr Pratt tells you, Jones. Do anything he tells you and don't do anything but what he tells you. You understand?'

'Aye, aye, sir.'

'Well, that's all, then. You may shove off. Steady as you go, Jones. And don't let the Navy down. As your namesake said' – the exec looked at the eye-level legend on his wall – 'Don't give up the ship!'

'What's that, sir?' Farragut said.

'Never mind,' the exec said.

'Sir,' said Farragut, lingering, 'I wonder if I could say one word of my own.'

Nash looked alarmed at the idea of the boatswain's mate speaking his own words. 'All right, Jones, permission granted,' he said nervously.

'Sir, I just want to give all the credit of this where credit is due,' he said, 'to Mr Siegel. That is the best ...' – Siegel almost cried out, but Farragut had swallowed the word – 'that is the best officer I ever served under!'

'Those are nice words, Farragut,' the exec said, sighing. 'I think we all realize that Ensign Siegel has demonstrated the true quality of an officer – leadership.'

Jones's state-side trip was a great success, Lieutenant Pratt brought word back to Public Relations Headquarters. Farragut made a nice hit with everyone, from congressmen to the workers at the Navy war plants. In Hollywood Farragut did so well that he stayed on. Public Relations, on Lieutenant Pratt's recommendation, decided he could now be trusted alone among the civilians, and so granted MGM's request for him to serve as technical adviser on a motion-picture on APA's entitled *The Battling Ankletooth*. Also, Ensign Siegel was notified personally of the boatswain's mate's real success in Hollywood. Siegel got a letter almost daily from him, relating in some detail how Farragut Jones was stripping the movie colony port and starboard of its many silky barnacles.

MELORA 4: *I went to Harvard College, sir!*

HE couldn't, Ensign Max Siegel was thinking, have felt better. Everything was going along magnificently. Here he was in Melora's home, and had been for a half-hour, having an eminently pleasant tea with her father, who had shown himself extremely charming. And then there was that happy permission, which he hadn't acted on yet, having just finally got it from Lieutenant-Commander Nash – permission for him to bring Melora to the officers' club.

It had taken considerable persuasion on Ensign Siegel's part to achieve this permission.

'A native girl in the officers' club?' Lieutenant-Commander Nash had expressed amazement at the suggestion. 'Why, I don't believe she would be too comfortable in such a sophisticated atmosphere, Max. I mean, they're used to more primitive forms of entertainment than a Navy officers' club.'

'Well, sir, I think there's enough primitivism there to satisfy most of them,' Siegel had said. 'Besides, some of the Tulurans are pretty sophisticated themselves.'

'Now, Max,' Lieutenant-Commander Nash said, 'you're not practising your sense of humour on the executive officer, are you?'

'No, sir,' Ensign Siegel said firmly. 'Now, you take this one girl I know. She's really a sort of "Navy brat" herself, as our Annapolis colleagues say. She's in the family of Admiral Ruiz de Mendoza.'

'Who's that?' the exec said, annoyed. 'What Navy's he in? Doesn't sound very American to me.'

'No, sir,' Ensign Siegel said. 'Ruiz de Mendoza was an admiral even before there was a U.S. Navy. He was an admiral in the Spanish Fleet during the days of its highest flowering.'

'H-m-m,' Nash said, a little suspiciously. 'It's funny I never heard of him.'

'Mendoza was chief of staff to Admiral Magellan,' Ensign Siegel explained.

'Well, I have heard of Magellan,' the exec said.

'If it weren't for Magellan and the ancestor of this girl I know, Ruiz de Mendoza, we wouldn't even be here today, Commander,' Ensign Siegel went on. 'Actually, the existence on Tulura of today's great U.S. Navy installation, the Headquarters of ComFleets, is, in a certain sense, traceable directly to Magellan and Ruiz de Mendoza.'

'How the hell do you figure all that, Siegel?' the exec said irritably.

'Why, they discovered the island,' Ensign Siegel said, 'and got Navy things going here.'

'How's that, Siegel?' the exec said impatiently.

'Ruiz de Mendoza's Navy,' Siegel explained, 'are fifty per cent of the ancestors of the present Tulurans. The Tulurans' well-known friendliness to the U.S. Navy is unquestionably derived from the early Navy bias the native girls got from Admiral Ruiz de Mendoza and his men. The way I figure it, we ought to preserve that Navy bias by doing everything we can to be friendly to Tulurans, and one way we can do this is by letting a Tuluran girl who is a direct descendant of Magellan's chief of staff come to the officers' club.'

The exec finally agreed. 'Well, permission granted,' he said. 'As long as she's descended from an officer.'

Then he added, 'But only as an experiment, understand? It depends on how this native girl conducts herself. We don't want any rowdy element in the officers' club.'

'I can guarantee you, Commander,' Ensign Siegel reassured the exec, 'that this girl knows which fork to use.'

Ensign Siegel, as the tea-drinking came to an end in the living-room of the Albas' home, reflected that the Albas certainly knew which fork to use. It had been an exceedingly proper and most pleasant tea. Melora had poured out of a beautiful silver teapot into cups of a delicate, paper-thin fragility. Mr Alba, a handsome, fit-looking man of about forty-eight and of entirely aristocratic bearing, was wearing a linen suit which had obviously not been tailored on Tulura. He had been a charming conversationalist and Siegel felt brimming over with satisfaction. Mr Alba had made only the most general talk, proper to a proper tea. And he had remarked, even if formally, that Melora had mentioned to him Ensign Siegel's help in the new schoolhouse. It was this help, indeed, that had triggered the invitation to tea, though what the help was, and what his daughter's part in it had been, Melora and Siegel kept rigorously from her father. Ensign Siegel, who gave almost no thought to uniform, had come to the tea more shined up than at any time since he had entered the Pacific. He wore long creased pants instead of the usual shorts, polished black shoes instead of his usual dirty boondock shoes, and, most extraordinary of all, he wore a tie that he had dug out of the bottom of his sea-chest.

'Yes, we rather like it here, even all year round,' Mr Alba was saying as a maid removed the teacups. 'Before the war we used to stay here only about three months a year, in the hot months. But since our house in Palan was destroyed during the shellings,' he said un-complainingly, ' – actually, in a way, I was glad to see it happen, since it meant our liberation was at hand – we live here the year round. We find it quite pleasant.'

They should, Siegel thought. It was the loveliest Tuluran house and one of the loveliest houses of any kind he had ever been in, with large, flowing rooms, the house set in groves of trees on a rise which afforded a splendid view of the Pacific. Down below the rise, the

Albas – that is, Melora and Mr Alba, for she was an only child and her mother had died when she was a young child – had a nice three-mile stretch of beach.

With the tea-things removed, they all slightly readjusted themselves in their chairs, in the customary after-tea stirrings – Ensign Siegel in his chair, Melora in her chair across from him, and Mr Alba in the chair between them. Siegel was sitting back happily when Mr Alba said to him, 'And what part of the United States do you come from, Mr Siegel?'

It was a routine enough question. Ensign Siegel was struck by it mainly in the realization that it was the first question of any kind Melora's father had asked him. It was in entirely friendly tones.

'From Boston, sir,' Ensign Siegel said. 'I grew up in Boston. Actually, I was born in Ohio, but before I was a year old my parents had the good judgement to remove to Boston. Boston is somewhat the Athens of America,' he said informationally, '– that is, its cultural centre.'

'Is that so?' Mr Alba said with an easy smile, which none the less made Ensign Siegel feel slightly uncomfortable for the first time, and a trifle like a child for having made the remark.

'Yes, sir,' he stammered, crooking his neck a little and straightening the uncomfortable tie. 'There are two or three U.S. cities that like to call themselves the American Athens, but I believe Boston has the best claim to the title.'

'It sounds rather like a contest of football,' Mr Alba said, smiling easily, and Ensign Siegel felt himself feeling more uncomfortable. 'Well, it's interesting that you grew up in one of the several claimants to the title of Athens of America.'

Mr Alba rose and stepped over to a chest on the other side of the room. He was back presently with a humidor.

'Would you care for a cigar, Mr Siegel?' he said, holding the lid open. 'Melora won't mind, will you, dear?'

'Papa, I've been breathing your cigar-smoke all my life now,' Melora said with a sigh, smiling a little at her father.

Ensign Siegel certainly did not care for cigars, but he felt somehow that it would be imprudent to refuse. He took one and lighted up rather awkwardly, while Mr Alba gently drew in on his own cigar.

'I don't know Boston well,' Mr Alba said easily.

'Oh, you've been there, sir!' Ensign Siegel blurted out before he could catch himself.

Mr Alba's clear brown eyes gave the ensign a casual glance over his cigar. Then he inhaled and blew out a small wreath of smoke.

'Only once,' he said. 'And even then I was really only through there. One year I returned from Spain by way of the United States instead of down through the Suez, as I usually do. I went up to Boston with the remote thought that I might put Melora for a year or two into one of those schools, Radcliffe or Wellesley.' Mr Alba inhaled easily on his cigar. 'I decided not to.'

Ensign Siegel now feared to ask Mr Alba why he had decided not to. Somehow he had the feeling that this question was precisely what Mr Alba wanted. Siegel realized he would not have felt any hesitation a quarter-hour ago in asking. Uncomfortably he wondered exactly what turn the conversation had taken. He knew beyond any doubt that it had taken some definite turn.

'Well, I was never too fond of Radcliffe myself,' he did venture, feeling slightly toadying and even a little disloyal. 'And Wellesley appealed to me even less,' he could say honestly, without explaining that the reason was that by the time you took a girl the twelve miles there and got back, it was quite an operation, besides which you almost never got a thing for it, while with Radcliffe …

'It's interesting to get your viewpoint,' Mr Alba said with a thin smile, 'even though you didn't go to Radcliffe or Wellesley yourself. Though from the looks of some of the girls there, I wasn't entirely sure whether it was co-educational or not. I remember having a strange thought while watching them, that one of the purposes of that complex of women's colleges in the eastern region of the United States is to change American women into men.'

'I've sometimes had a thought like that myself,' Ensign Siegel said. He drew in on his cigar and coughed.

'Is the cigar too strong for you?' Mr Alba said.

'No, sir,' Ensign Siegel said, coughing again and fingering his tie. 'I think it's probably one of the most enjoyable cigars I've ever had.'

Sticking the thing firmly in his mouth, Ensign Siegel inhaled a basketful of smoke. Immediately he was coughing violently.

'Would you like a drink of water?' Mr Alba said solicitously.

Ensign Siegel finally managed to get control of himself, though he felt his eyes smarting.

'No, thank you, sir,' Siegel said. The tie which he was not accustomed to wearing felt like a noose closing on his neck, but it was unthinkable to loosen it. 'I guess it's that I'm not used to such good cigars. The cigars I get over at the Navy ship's service aren't of such excellent quality.'

'Possibly these are milder,' Mr Alba said, with that smile. 'So since you didn't go to school at Radcliffe or Wellesley ...' Mr Alba picked up smoothly.

And suddenly Ensign Siegel knew. He knew what the turn was that the conversation had taken. He was being dissected! That was it! Mr Alba was going through him critically, piece by piece. Mr Alba had felt, because of his help with the new schoolhouse, that he had to invite the ensign to tea. But it was plain that Mr Alba considered this did not for a moment exclude an exhaustive analysis and classification of the specimen who was seeing his daughter.

'I went to Harvard College.' Siegel heard himself, for the first time in his life, say the name of his school almost resoundingly.

'Oh, of course, Harvard,' Mr Alba said, rotating his cigar easily in his fingers. 'It's perhaps one of the better schools – American, that is.'

'I've even heard people in Europe say it's a pretty good school,' Melora said.

'There are many charitable people in Europe,' Mr Alba said, smiling softly through the cigar-smoke.

He certainly seems to enjoy a cigar, Siegel thought, and thought also that he never imagined he would have to defend Harvard's academic reputation. As a matter of fact, he decided it would probably be better not to defend it at all, and felt pretty disloyal indeed now.

'Speaking of Europe,' Mr Alba was saying. 'What years were you in Europe, Mr Siegel?'

'Europe?' Ensign Siegel said, and felt he said it blankly. 'Well, sir, I regret to say I haven't been to Europe.'

'Is that so?' Mr Alba said in tones of slight surprise which none the less suggested to Siegel his judgement that this alone identified this Ensign Siegel as a barbarian.

Melora laughed. 'Well, there is a war on, Papa,' she said. 'Ensign

Siegel's plans to go to Europe were probably interrupted by the war.'

'Yes, that was it,' Ensign Siegel plunged in gratefully. 'You see, sir, I didn't get my degree from Harvard College until not too long before I went in the Navy. I had anticipated going directly to Europe for a period – but then,' he sighed, 'this dreadful war came along, interrupting my plans for a protracted European stay.'

'Is that so?' Mr Alba said, and Ensign Siegel felt confident this was being translated, 'Ah – that is a pretty lie.' He felt extremely uncomfortable.

There was a pause, before another question came.

'How do you find Tulura, Mr Siegel?' Mr Alba said.

'I think it's probably the greatest place I've ever been!' Ensign Siegel said in a burst of enthusiasm.

'I find it rather boring not to be able to leave here at all because of the war,' Mr Alba said, and Ensign Siegel knew, horribly, that Mr Alba looked upon such enthusiasm as gross at the worst and childish at the best. 'I have a deep love for Tulura, and certainly my family are and always will be a part of it,' he said with what Siegel felt was meaning. 'But the love is better preserved if mixed with fairly frequent stays in Europe. It was interesting to have someone from the Navy call on us.'

The last came so suddenly, yet so smoothly and with such formal courtesy, that Ensign Siegel was startled. But it was obviously his dismissal, especially since Mr Alba was making motions of rising from his chair.

Suddenly Ensign Siegel felt a sense of panic. It seemed years ago, that actual half-hour ago, when he had felt such contentment after having tea with Melora and Mr Alba. Now he knew that Mr Alba, having completed his analysis, had found him sharply wanting. He felt like a Scollay Square barkeep who had been seeing a Back Bay society girl on the sly and had just finished his first tea with her parents. He felt also an overpowering desire in some way to recover some of his position before he got out of this house.

Suddenly, with a spurt of inspiration that cut through his panic, he remembered that permission he had secured with such difficulty from Nash – to let him bring Melora to the officers' club.

'Oh, Mr Alba,' he blurted out as he stood up to be shown out.

'I wonder if you and Melora would be my guests tomorrow night – or any night that's convenient for you – at the Navy officers' club?'

Mr Alba looked at Ensign Siegel. 'Why, that's very thoughtful of you, Mr Siegel,' Mr Alba said. He smiled his thin, courteous smile. 'But I'm afraid I don't allow Melora to go to public places.'

Seven: The Budweiser Mutiny

THE trouble began when the rumours got started so early, tipping off the enlisted men.

Everybody knew, of course, that there would be some sort of new officers' club going up. The present temporary bar in a Quonset hut, inferior even to the enlisted men's recreation centre, if that was possible, would naturally not do for long. But until the rumours started flying, no one had the remotest idea of what the club would be like. Later Lieutenant-Commander Clinton T. 'Marblehead' Nash, whose inspiration the club was, made a large effort to find out who had let it out. He never did find out, or at least if he did he never mentioned that it was his own assistant and the Public Relations Headquarters 'office manager', Lieutenant (jg) Calvert 'Little Marblehead' Brownell, a model officer with one flaw. He was incapable of not letting his fellow junior officers know that he was privy to secrets not visited upon their lowly likes.

On the evening of a ration day several junior officers were lounging in Lieutenant Morey Griffin's BOQ room attending to their rations when a young man crystallized in the doorway. He was an arrestingly neat and trim-looking officer. His hair was slicked back neatly and his sleek cheeks exuded Mennen's after-shave lotion. He wore a set of freshly pressed khaki shorts and shirt, with the collar of the shirt folded neatly back, exposing a couple of inches of Rinso-white T-shirt, and the pleats of the shorts bearing a blade-like crease. His socks fitted snugly on his ankles and his black shoes shone like a Cadillac's hubcap. In his manicured hand he carried an unopened bottle of Paul Jones and his newly brushed teeth gleamed.

'Gentlemen!' he said humorously, switching on his electric-light smile. 'I thought my sonar gear detected the sounds of merrymaking down this way.'

'By cracky, Calvert, you are the nautical one,' Griffin said. He yanked up from where they rested on his hips the old, stained pair of khaki shorts which were all he was wearing. 'Come on in and drop anchor. We are glad to have you and your Paul Jones aboard. Here, give me that, before you torpedo someone with it. Heh, heh, heh.'

Griffin, his hand shooting out, relieved the lieutenant junior grade of his bottle, opened it, and filled his own empty glass halfway up.

'Help yourself to a depth-charge, Calvert,' he said, passing the bottle back. 'Take those old dirty toothbrushes out of the glass on the medicine shelf and recharge your batteries. Heh, heh.'

Lieutenant (jg) Brownell ran the washbasin full of hot water and washed the glass thoroughly, poured himself a couple of careful fingers, filled the glass with cold water, sat down erectly on the edge of a bed, and crossed his polished legs.

'We were just discussing the next operation, Calvert,' Griffin said. 'Wondering if one of us might be the lucky man.'

'Well, I know the exec is thinking it over,' Brownell said mysteriously. The office manager glanced coyly around the circle of officers, which included Ensign Christopher Tyson III, Lieutenant (jg) Ross Pendleton, Lieutenants Noah Pratt and Woodrow Shoemaker, and the correspondent Jerry Wakeley. His lips parted in a precise, cat-like smile. 'I wouldn't be surprised if there *is* one officer in this room that's going.'

'By cracky,' said Lieutenant Griffin. 'So one of us is going into action with the fleet, you say, Calvert? Now I just wonder who?'

The office manager smiled cagily. 'The commander may ask for volunteers,' he hedged.

'Then Pendleton here's your man,' Griffin said genially. 'What was that you were saying the other night, Ross? "I'd dearly love to feel the deck of a ship under my feet for a change."'

'If you'd really like to look-see a little combat, sport,' Brownell said as Pendleton glared at Griffin, 'I'd be happy to put in a plug for you with the commander.'

'That's awfully white of you, Calvert.' Pendleton forced a smile. 'But right now I've got an extremely important Navy radio project cooking that I didn't anticipate when I said something of the sort.'

'Yes, you probably said it for the benefit of that nurse you were with,' Griffin said succinctly. 'Besides the fact that Pendleton is going on the next assault, Calvert, what else of an operational nature is Marblehead dreaming up for us?'

Brownell paused, looking down narcissistically at his polished shoes.

'Morey, that's not a very respectful term to use for our executive officer.'

'Why, all these old naval leaders have nicknames like that,' Griffin said earnestly. 'Halsey, for example, is known universally as "Bull". Why, it's a term of endearment.' Griffin smiled pleasantly. 'Come on now, Calvert; don't be sore. Give us the poop.'

'I just don't like to hear him called by that name,' Brownell said sulkily. 'It just isn't loyal. After all, he is my boss – and *our* executive officer.'

'I said I was sorry, Calvert,' Griffin whined, realizing he was on the verge of cutting off an excellent source of information. 'Hell, you know what I think of Nash, boy. For my money, he's the Clausewitz of Public Relations, and I don't care who knows it. I've never run into an officer, ashore or afloat, who has such a grasp of naval language. Here, have a drink.'

He poured Brownell some of Brownell's Paul Jones. Then he poured himself some of Brownell's Paul Jones.

Suddenly Brownell smiled generously. 'Forget it, sport. This isn't exactly operational but' – his voice lowered – 'the fact is, I had a look-see today at the blueprints for the new officers' club. The next two weeks will see the keel, heh, heh, laid.'

In the dead, waiting silence Brownell sipped his drink delicately. He recrossed his legs and leaned forward.

'I tell you for a fact, gentlemen,' he said with a confidential air, 'we're going to have the best darned lash-up in the Pacific Ocean Area. The site will be the choicest and most picturesque on the island – on the ridge beyond the BOQs, overlooking the ocean. The club will be of low-slung, ranch-type architecture with the seaward side completely glass, to afford an unparalleled view of the sea and the ships passing by. Anywhere you stand or sit in the club, even from the bar, you will be able to see the sea. The club will be divided into two parts by a two-sided bar. One for flag rank, one for non-flag. Fanning out from each will be not just ordinary tables, but a network of low-slung cocktail tables, each with its own red bankette seat against the wall and soft facing chairs. Just about the only rank distinction in the place,' Brownell said parenthetically, '– and there really has to be *some* such distinction – will be that the flag side of the bar will have cushioned stools, while the non-flag side will be a stand-up proposition.' He went on: 'There'll be soft indirect lighting on both sides. The Marine bartenders will wear red jackets. Opening out of the glass sides will be two terraces, flag and non-flag, each equipped with round tables, canvas beach chairs, and umbrellas, so you can bring your date and look out over the Pacific. There'll be an orchestra playing nightly for dancing on the terraces. And – *pièce de résistance*,' Brownell said excitedly, 'between the terraces will be a swimming-pool, oval-shaped. Flag and non-flag rank will share the swimming-pool. You won't be able to tell them apart anyhow when they're in bathing-trunks.'

The officers sat for several moments in a silence of wonderment, staring at the source of this intelligence. Expressions of great beatitude filled their faces.

'I thought you'd like it,' Lieutenant (jg) Brownell said, beaming as if the entire set-up were his personal gift. Then he quickly added in fairness, 'The whole thing is the exec's idea, stem to stern.'

'Incidentally,' said Griffin, 'how did the exec get mixed up with the officers' club? It isn't exactly a Public Relations problem.'

'He's got such imagination,' Brownell said, 'that when the board to plan the new club met – the exec is on the board – his ideas so exceeded everyone else's dreams that he more or less took over. He volunteered to plan and direct its building in addition to his other duties. How he gets time for all of it, I don't know.'

'You aren't the only one,' said Griffin. 'Didn't I tell you he was a Clausewitz? What a conception!'

During all this rhapsody the correspondent Jerry Wakeley had sat silent and watchful as an owl, and like an owl in the midst of a perch-load of happy parakeets he suddenly became noticeable for his silence.

'How about it, Jerry?' Brownell said. 'I guess this is a pretty good example of how the Navy takes care of its own. What do you think? Incidentally, this is all off the record.'

Jerry Wakeley was a wiry, rather weatherbeaten man of 140 pounds, thirty-eight years old, with thinning hair, a mild manner, wearing spectacles, and in his mouth a dead cigar which was almost as much a part of his face as his nose. He could speak pungently, but he seldom raised his voice. He never used the first person in discussing the war. You would never know it to read his dispatches, since he had the habit of writing about the men doing the fighting and the invading rather than about himself, but he had seen, close up, more actual war than almost any half-dozen correspondents on Tulura. Being on a command ship off Tarawa or hitting the beach with the early waves can be made, with no outright lying, into seeming the same thing to a reader 5,000 miles away. For example, a correspondent on a command ship may begin his story, quite truthfully, 'I watched the Marines hit bloody Tarawa today', but omit to mention that he watched them through a pair of 7×50 binoculars from the ship's bridge a mile off. Jerry Wakeley made his invasions without binoculars.

Wakeley had an odd way of drinking whisky, which was to pour about a third of a glass – three jiggers about – every hour or so, drain it off as expressionlessly as if it were milk, then touch nothing for another full hour, when he again would drink off a big slug. It had been an hour since his last shot, so he poured himself a third of a glass and swallowed it in a gulp. He replaced his cigar and answered Brownell's question.

'I think,' he said, 'that the Navy must be trying to hang itself with a gold-plated anchor chain.'

Lieutenant (jg) Brownell recrossed his legs and pulled up his socks. His eyebrows arched upwards, then down, retractably.

'I'm afraid I don't get it, Jerry.'

'You don't?' the correspondent said. 'Nelson's butt, I can see the headlines now. "Navy Goes Palm Beach in Western Pacific." "Lavish Country Club Rises on Tulura." You can't throw up a casino like that out here and get away with it. Especially when all the enlisted men have is what they've got.'

'What's wrong with what the enlisted men have?' Brownell said.

Wakeley shifted his cigar across his mouth. 'Well, it's a decent enough shed, I guess, but those saw-horse tables are going to stand out against those red bankettes like a settlement house against Park Avenue.'

'Aren't you forgetting,' Griffin said, 'that old saying about what rank hath?'

'It's going to hath a lot more if that castle goes up.' Wakeley chewed on his dead cigar. 'I'm telling you, your tits are headed straight for the Bendix.'

Brownell stood up importantly. 'Sorry to leave this excellent gathering, but I've got a lot of work to catch up on – planning for the Public Relations phase of the next operation.'

He turned to Wakeley and slapped him affectionately on the shoulder. The correspondent winced.

'If you don't mind my saying so, sport, I think you're over-alarmed,' Brownell said. 'I don't see anything at all exceptional about it. After all, officers have always had officers' clubs.'

In twenty-four hours there wasn't a man or officer on the place who hadn't heard of the forthcoming club, embroidered even beyond reality with air-conditioning and two alternating orchestras – one regular, one rhumba. The enlisted men were talking of nothing else by the time a detachment of bulldozers from the Seabees mobilized one morning on the ridge and started moving dirt around. Even Yeoman Second Class Adam Garrett, who lately hadn't shown much interest in anything, mentioned it to Siegel, who had been told all about it by Griffin.

'I hear there's going to be a pretty nice installation up there on the ridge,' he said. And Garrett furnished Siegel a description of the club which was remarkably close to Brownell's.

'You don't have a personal copy of the blueprints, do you?' Siegel asked.

Garrett smiled. 'Well, these things get around. That sounds pretty familiar though, flag and non-flag rank using the same swimming-pool.'

'Well, we have to let the bars down a little in wartime, you know,' Siegel said.

Garrett fidgeted a little in his chair. 'Any word on those thirty-five yeomen, Mr Siegel?'

It was the question Garrett asked every day. It had been over a month now since the yeoman had been sealed off from seeing Ensign Alice Thomas, eighteen miles across the island. That affair which had flowered so spectacularly for a while was now but a memory with the Public Relations officers, something they thought of every time they saw Garrett but mentioned only occasionally, at night in officer breeze sessions in the BOQs. 'That time we had an enlisted man secretly dating a Navy nurse,' it would be recalled, in the tones in which sea-going officers recall a famous naval engagement in which their ship took part. Garrett himself had gone back to reading his books from the Fleet Library, doing what work was required of him, being a little more withdrawn than before, and asking Ensign Siegel repeatedly what news he had on those thirty-five additional yeomen the exec had requested from Washington and who represented possible sea duty for him.

'There's no word yet on the reinforcements,' Siegel said. 'It should be along soon.'

Garrett moved a little impatiently in his chair.

'Anyhow, if you stay around a little longer,' Siegel said, 'you'll get to see the new edifice on the ridge. You wouldn't want to miss that, would you?'

Garrett smiled. 'No, I guess not. That club's going to be one of the seven wonders of the world, isn't it?'

As the Seabees swarmed over the ridge, a joyous anticipation spurted through Headquarters – through, that is, the officer part of Head-quarters. Through the enlisted men's part coursed something sullen, almost ominous.

Then in the afternoon two days after payday something extra-ordinary occurred at the Disbursing Office down near the enlisted men's barracks.

Starting shortly before 1430, when the office opened after noon chow, a line of enlisted men began to form outside. When the office opened, the first man in line stepped up to the counter and said to the officer on duty, Lieutenant (jg) Arthur Ditmore, 'I want to cancel my war-bond allotment.'

Enlisted men were for ever changing their pay-roll allotments, taking a larger one out for their wives on getting a series of sweet letters or cancelling it altogether on receipt of a letter from a friend that their wives were helling around back home; making an allotment for a war bond or cancelling one; cancelling or taking out National Service Life Insurance. This enlisted man's bond-cancellation request being so usual, Ditmore had no more than a vague sense of irritation, plus an unpermitted desire to ask him where his patriotism was. He got out the man's pay-roll jacket, wordlessly completed the transaction, curtly said, 'Sign here', and the man moved on.

The next man stepped up to the counter and said, 'I want to cancel my war bond.'

Two in a row! Ditmore grimaced and completed the transaction.

A third man stepped to the counter. 'I want to cancel my war bond.'

By the time the sixth man had stepped up with the same request, Lieutenant (jg) Ditmore, looking at the line of a couple of dozen men behind him, decided that something was going on.

But there was nothing he could do about it. There was no law against a man's cancelling a war bond. It was, after all, his money. Ditmore left the counter momentarily to report the fact of the line to his boss, the chief disbursing officer, and returned to handle more cancellations, sulkily.

By night the news had rampaged through Headquarters, and the officers passed the evening talking about it. No one could explain it. Then around ten o'clock word was passed to the Public Relations officers that there would be a special meeting immediately. Poker games and breeze sessions dissolved as the officers found their way through the night up to the building on the hill. They filed in to find a solemn Lieutenant-Commander Clinton T. Nash waiting for them. When his office was full the executive officer took a seat at his desk and looked out gravely over the pack of officers. He picked up a pencil and started tapping his bald head with it, a barometer to the officers that something serious was up.

'Gentlemen,' he said, 'this is an emergency session, so I'll come right to the point. Something terrible, from a public-relations viewpoint, has happened.' The exec paused dramatically. 'I suppose all of you have heard about the enlisted men cancelling their war bonds?'

A murmur of affirmations crooned back to the exec.

'Naval Intelligence,' said the exec soberly, 'first informed me of it at 1610. Every moment since then we've been trying to get to the bottom of it. We haven't hit bottom yet, but we're on our way.'

The commander opened his desk drawer and flushed out a legal-size sheet of paper.

'We have picked up one deadly piece of evidence which reveals the instigation of it all. Ready your ears: "To All Hands: As Confucius said,"' the exec began to intone from the sheet, '"Rank Has Its Privileges. It certainly Has. We do not begrudge the officers most of these privileges. They get inner-spring mattresses and the enlisted men get cots. Okay. They sleep two to a room, one to a room for lieutenant-commanders and above. We sleep fifty to a room. Okay. They are privileged to wear shorts in this climate, we have to wear long pants. Okay. They have cover over them at the movies when it rains, we have to sit out in the wet. Okay. The coral reef around their beach has been blasted, while ours right next to it has not. They even have to have their beaches different, i.e. with surf. But okay. They get all the whisky they can drink at five cents a shot plus two bottles of it and one of wine a month in their ration. We get no whisky at all. Okay. BUT ...

'"On the ridge beyond the BOQs,"' the exec continued reading in tones of contempt and fury, '"bulldozers of the 357th Seabee Battalion are erecting a new, world's wartime record for privilege. This privilege is to have everything but Turkish baths – for the officers. It will even have a swimming-pool – is this necessary on an island where the officers possess one of the finest beaches in the Pacific? – and an outdoor terrace for live-orchestra dancing. This important naval installation is the crowning, chocolate-covered, whipped-cream layer to a system which allows the officers limitless whisky and beer, the enlisted men a tyrannical two beers a day. We suggest that with this new Palace of Pleasure the chasm between officers and enlisted men, which we accept, has been opened a shade too far.

'"As enlisted men we have little recourse without the peril of Portsmouth. But there is one way we can at least say that they go too far. We can cancel our war-bond allotments. They cannot send you to Portsmouth Naval Prison for that. We can just walk in and cancel our war bonds. Is privilege licence? Is rank a blank cheque to debauchery? We ... can ... just ... cancel ... our ... war ... bonds. Men of the

Navy! Are we only enlisted men or are we men? (Signed) Joe Blow Paine.'"

Lieutenant-Commander Nash, his face and bald head purple, flung the sheet down on his desk and spat a word: 'Mutiny!'

A long, sober silence held the room.

'Joe Blow Paine!' exclaimed Nash. 'We've searched the roster of enlisted men. No one name of Paine.'

'I doubt if he would sign his real name,' Ensign Siegel said. 'It's probably a pseudonym from Thomas Paine.'

'Who's that?' shot out Nash. 'I just said we don't have anyone name of Paine aboard! Thomas, Dick, Harry, or anyone else Paine.'

'Thomas Paine is dead,' said Siegel. 'He was a revolutionary.'

'Might have known it,' said Nash.

'You know,' Lieutenant-Commander Hereford said thoughtfully, 'I have a feeling there's some article of war that's been violated here.'

'My God, Hereford,' Nash said violently. 'Where's your IQ? I just told you. Mutiny! The most serious of all articles of war!'

'Sorry, Commander,' Lieutenant-Commander Hereford said humbly.

Nash picked up the document and his voice lowered. 'Gentlemen, I haven't told you the worst yet.'

The officers waited, wondering what could be worse than mutiny.

The exec held the document by the top with both hands, so that it was facing the officers.

'Gentlemen! You notice anything in particular about this insidious thing?'

The officers all leaned forward and looked.

'It's mimeographed,' said Siegel.

'Precisely!' the exec said triumphantly. 'Very clever, Siegel.'

'You mean ...' said Hereford slowly.

'Precisely!' said Nash. 'The Public Relations Section's eighteen mimeograph machines are the only mimeograph machines in this Headquarters.' Nash flung the document down. 'Gentlemen! I hate to say this worse than I ever hated to say anything, but here goes!' The exec took a big swallow. 'There is every evidence that the ringleader of the mutiny is one of our own Public Relations men!'

In the silence the exec said, 'Awful, isn't it?'

'Incredible!' said Lieutenant-Commander Hereford.

'Impossible!' said Lieutenant-Commander Arnold Gladney.

'But true,' said Nash, looking from one to the other of the Echo Twins.

The exec placed his hands, fingers spread, over his marble-bald head. 'I never thought I'd live to see a Public Relations man heading up a mutiny,' he said glumly.

'Ding! ding! ... Ding! ding! ... Ding! ding!'

Startled, the exec snapped his head around towards the ship's bell on the wall.

'Six bells!' he exclaimed irrelevantly.

The exec stood up and planted his feet in a posture of determination. His protruding eyes moved from the 'Don't Give Up The Ship!' legend on the wall to the rows of officers. 'Gentlemen! The captain, as you know, is off on an inspection tour of the islands, so we're going to have to quell this ourselves. Naval Intelligence has a crew on it, but I don't want to leave it to them. We've got to fumigate our own house. I want you to drop everything else and comb your sections, fore and aft, scupper to scupper, to root this snake out. Interrogate and question every man in your respective sections! Hear? The mutineer has got to be found! By 1100 tomorrow at the latest, gentlemen!' the exec said grimly. 'Go out there and get him!'

The cross-examinations of the Public Relations enlisted men by the Public Relations officers got under way early next morning. At 1100 the officers assembled with their reports in Commander Nash's office, where the exec went from officer to officer.

'Hereford?'

'None of my men wrote it, sir,' the photographic chief said.

'Gladney?'

'All my men deny it vehemently, sir. Vehemently,' the radio chief repeated for emphasis.

'Randolph?' the exec asked the chief of the Media Section.

'No mutinous authuhs in mah section, Commanduh,' Lieutenant-Commander Junius Randolph, the former Georgia editor, replied.

All the answers were similar.

Nash sighed heavily. 'Gentlemen, I'm more disappointed in you than you can imagine. Of that, more later. Right now something else terrible has happened. When it rains, it pours. But let's don't make jokes about this!' he said in angry reproval. 'The correspondents – at least one of them, Gordon Ripwell, wouldn't you know it? – has got hold of a copy of that mutiny sheet, no doubt from an enlisted man, and – this is awful – written a story.'

The executive officer jerked a piece of paper with carbon writing on it off his desk.

'Here's a copy of Ripwell's story. Listen to this libellous garbage.' And he read:

'While angry enlisted men rebelliously cancelled war bonds and got out circulars in furious protest, I witnessed ground being broken here today on a spectacular new U.S. Navy installation: a swank officers' club and recreation palace, including a large, glass-walled clubhouse with red leather bankette seats, soft indirect lighting, orchestra pit, two terraces with matching hilltop sea views and two spacious bars – one for "Ordinary" rank, one for flag rank – and an oval-shaped, tile-lined swimming-pool.'

'That's an outright lie!' Nash threw the story furiously on his desk. 'The swimming-pool is to be lined with cement!'

'The rest of it sounds pretty correct, though,' Lieutenant-Commander Hereford said glumly.

'That Ripwell!' Nash said. 'After all we've done for that meathead.'

'Like you having his sheets changed daily,' Tyson said in a quiet voice.

'Mind your rudder, Tyson!' the exec snapped.

'What do the censors say about Ripwell's story?' Lieutenant-Commander Gladney inquired. 'Can't we stop it? What are censors for anyhow if not to stop something like this? There's no doubt in my mind that it's harmful to Navy morale – at least, to officers' morale.'

'The censor says,' and Nash quoted curtly, '"No naval security violated."'

'It doesn't involve ship movements, that's true,' Gladney said.

'We've got to *do* something!' the exec said. 'We're caught in an incredible bight! Navy for the worst kind of trouble. If we can't keep good Press in our own house, what kind of Public Relations officers are we? That's what Washington is going to be asking itself – and maybe us – as soon as they hear about this. Which they will any moment now – now that security's been broken,' he said, waving Ripwell's story violently. 'The man has absolutely no gratitude! No gratitude at all!'

'He's not the grateful type,' said Ensign Tyson.

'None of them are!' the exec exploded. 'You may be sure that when we get the club a naval officer won't be able to get to the bar for the mobs of correspondents!'

The exec hit his head hard, giving a sharp report of skin against skin.

'Damn it to hell, officers have a *right* to have a club! It's small enough return for the added responsibility. I can't imagine what would happen to officers' morale without a club. Why, you might as well be an enlisted man!'

'Commander,' Hereford said, 'I've got an idea.'

'Well, don't just sit there loving it up all to yourself!' Nash said violently. 'Look alive! If we ever needed ideas it's now.'

'Maybe,' Hereford said quickly, 'we could give up the swimming-pool part of the club. That might appease the enlisted men. Anyhow, we'd still have the beach.'

'"Appease the enlisted men!"' the exec exploded. 'That isn't the object of an officers' club! Let the enlisted men bluff us out of our rights – is that what you're suggesting? Not as long as Clinton T. Nash is exec! We've got a right to a swimming-pool. We're officers, aren't we?'

'That's true, I guess,' Lieutenant-Commander Hereford said uncertainly.

'Any other ideas?' Nash said.

'Nash!' An angry voice broke through the corridors outside.

'The commander is in a conference, Mr Ripwell.' The dignified voice of Lieutenant (jg) Brownell could be heard through the door. 'I'll be glad to let you know when he's through – or give him a message for you.'

'Conference! Message!' the first voice raged. 'Why, you impudent young lieutenant *junior* grade. Do you know who I am? Do you know I represent two and one-half million readers who are getting goddamn sick of all these conferences you're eternally having here on God knows what. Conference! They will call a two-hour conference in this place to decide whether to use white or baby-blue paper on the mimeograph machines. Now you listen to me, Little Lord Fauntleroy. Fetch your precious little brat up out of that chair this second and march right in there and tell your master that Gordon Ripwell wants to know' – and the voice rose to a crashing bellow – '"When are we going to have a statement from the Navy about this glorified boondoggle, the officers' bathhouse–swimming pool–dance hall–night club-bar! Two bars!"'

'Gentlemen,' said Nash, 'that will be all for today.'

The officers filed out and by the Chicago *Gazette* correspondent cursing out Lieutenant (jg) Brownell. Behind Ripwell stood several other correspondents.

'A convention!' Ripwell stormed, watching the officers march by. 'A convention they're holding when a correspondent is trying to do a story. Why do they think they're all here, anyhow, instead of at sea – to attend conventions or to help the correspondent?'

Nash stood in the doorway of his office.

'It's always good to see you, Rip,' he said genially, his voice giving off frightened tremors. 'Won't you come in?'

'"Come in"!' Ripwell shrieked. 'I'm not "coming in" anywhere. I've got a deadline to meet. Do you know what a *deadline* is, Nash? Tell me, do we or do we not have a statement on what the Navy is going to do about this officers' club–swimming pool–dance hall, etcetera, and this enlisted men's rebellion, or do I file a story saying the Navy refuses to comment?'

Before Nash could stutter out an answer, Ripwell turned on his heel and stormed downstairs. Ensign Siegel followed him down to the correspondents' room and saw Ripwell go to his typewriter, slam in a sheet of paper, and start furiously pounding out a story. Then Siegel went in through the swinging door to his desk in the next room. Jerry Wakeley was using his typewriter, so he sat down at Garrett's desk in front of his.

'Well, the rockets are flying,' Siegel said. 'The masses are in revolt. I know, you told us so.'

Wakeley removed his cigar. 'Max, why don't they do something? Nelson's butt! At least they could tone the club down.'

'Appeasement, eh?' Siegel said, slapping the desk. 'Let the enlisted men bluff us out of our rights, eh? Is that what you're suggesting?'

'So that's the way Marblehead's playing it,' Wakeley comprehended.

'Officers are entitled since God knows when to have an officers' club, Jerry. An old naval historian like you ought to know that.'

'Those men aren't kidding,' Wakeley said, chewing on his cigar. 'I just came from down at the Disbursing Office. It looks like bingo night. I counted forty-seven more in line.'

Ensign Siegel felt suddenly weary of it all, detached from the air of rather frightened tension that hung over the Public Relations office. He looked up at the row of clocks on the wall. In New York, he noticed, it was 8.40 in the evening. In the theatres the lights had just dimmed and people were watching the curtains go up. ... He leaned forward on Garrett's typewriter and rested his head on his crossed arms. He must have dozed off. When he awakened, Wakeley had gone.

He rubbed his eyes, still resting his head on the typewriter. Then, as he started to raise his head, his eyes caught some words on the typewriter roller. Someone must have been hitting pretty hard on those words. He leaned closer and read them.

'*Is rank a blank cheque to debauchery?*'

Startled, Ensign Siegel drew back up. Instinctively he glanced around him to see if anyone was in the room. No one was. He hesitated a second and then moved the roller down until the words were in line with the key punch. Then he 'x-d' through them. He 'x-d' through them three times until only x's could be seen on the roller. Then he got up and went to his own desk.

Why, that stupid son of a bitch, he thought. What the hell is he up to?

Wonder where the hell Garret is now? Siegel thought. Then he remembered. Garrett had said he was going down to sick-bay to get something for a case of fungus on his feet.

Ensign Siegel went to his own typewriter, settled back, and wrote a couple of letters. Then there Garrett was, coming through the swinging door from the correspondents' room.

'What's wrong with Ripwell?' Garrett said. 'That typewriter of his sounds like a five-inch gun gone berserk.'

'He's covering this revolution us officer class have on our hands here.'

'Oh, the revolution,' Garrett said. 'What's Ripwell doing about it?'

'Filing hourly bulletins on the progress of the club – and the latest tabulations on the number of war bonds cancelled. There hasn't been so much excitement on Tulura since Magellan sailed into the harbour and dropped anchor.'

Garrett sat down in his chair, facing the officer. He took off one shoe, pulled out a pocket-knife, and started cutting a hole in the shoe.

'The Doc's prescription for fungus,' he said. 'I wonder if Magellan started the first officers' club here.'

'Probably, but I don't guess it had a swimming-pool. But of course we've advanced enormously since then.' The ensign slumped his big frame deep in his chair. 'I suppose you've seen that inspiring manifesto?'

The yeoman rounded off a hole in his shoe. 'Yes, sir, I have.'

'A beautifully written document, I'll say that.'

Garrett continued working on his shoe.

'That Joe Blow Paine signature,' Siegel said. 'That was a good touch.'

The yeoman finished up one shoe and started cutting a piece of leather out of the other one. 'Yes, sir. I guess whoever wrote it had read a little American history.'

Ensign Siegel stretched his legs out distantly.

'Garrett,' he said suddenly, 'I've got an idea about your sea duty.'

Garrett glanced up at the officer. 'Yes, sir?'

'I thought maybe we should make a pitch for it now, and not wait on those thirty-five yeomen,' Siegel said. He waited, thinking Garrett would ask him why he had changed his mind on the timing of the request. He didn't, so Siegel added, 'If you're willing to take a chance on the exec getting so worked up that he sends you over to have your head examined.'

'I'll take that risk,' Garrett said, smiling softly. 'I'm wide open.' He waited, then added, 'For any kind of sea duty, including a garbage scow. But what I really want, like I've told you before, is a destroyer.'

A nostalgic grin fanned across Ensign Siegel's face.

'A destroyer,' he said. 'That's a respectable place to be when there's a war on.'

Siegel straightened up, and pushing his hands on his knees, stood up. 'The first opening I get from the exec I'll wade in.'

'I'll leave it to you, sir,' Garrett said.

Siegel wandered out through the correspondents' room. The place was jumping with several correspondents batting out stories on the mutiny. He went on upstairs, just thinking, Garrett had better be getting off this island, fast. He belonged off it before, but now he really better get the hell off it. Brownell wasn't there, so he knocked at Nash's door. He thought he heard someone jump inside, then a tremulous, 'Who's there?' He opened the door. Nash looked bug-eyed and frantic, as if he were scared it was Ripwell. His desk, usually so neat, was a scene of wild disorder. It was covered with sheets of paper, each of which appeared to contain only three or four lines of heavily x'd typing.

'Commander,' Siegel said, 'can I see you a minute?'

'I'm trying to get out a statement!' the exec exploded. 'The correspondents are yelling for a statement. Whatever it's about, I'm too busy to see you now.'

Siegel mused for a moment how high the exec would jump if he told him he had the name of the man who had started it all – and especially that Joe Blow Paine was the same man who had been involved in another major breach of Navy regulations, dating a Navy nurse. Then, just looking at the exec, he knew, all at once, that the worst thing he could do right now was to ask for sea duty for Garrett. It could arouse suspicions, and anyhow the exec wouldn't give an enlisted man anything right now. Siegel knew he would have to let matters calm down quite a bit before asking.

'I understand,' Ensign Siegel said, withdrawing.

'No, you don't,' the exec said curtly. 'Nobody could understand what I have to go through. You know what I wish at times like this, Siegel? I wish I was back at Merrill Lynch, Pierce, Fenner, and Beane!'

When Siegel had left, the exec stuck a fresh sheet in his typewriter. He started typing furiously: 'Background Memorandum to the Correspondents Concerning the Minor Incident of the Bond Cancellations ...'

He stopped and looked at what he had written. Then he tore it out of the typewriter and threw it on the pile on his desk. He sat back, limp, in his chair.

His roaming eyes lit upon *Naval Leadership* in his desk library. Hopefully he took it out and opened it at random. He read: 'Ability to ride a horse is a most desirable accomplishment of any officer.'

Grimly he shut the book. For a minute or two he sat uncertain. Then the thought occurred to him that the best thing to do might be to get his mind entirely off the problem of the mutiny for a few minutes. He took his sextant out of the drawer and, clearing a space for it, placed it on his desk. Then he pulled out Bowditch.

He opened the big book and began to read studiously:

'Select two clearly defined objects whose angular distance must be not less than 90°; bring the reflected image of one object into exact coincidence with the direct image of the other at the inner wire; then, by altering slightly the position of the instrument, make the objects appear on the other wire. ...'

Baffled, the exec reread the passage. He glanced around the room at its various fixtures. With determination he came to his feet, picked up his wastebasket, and placed it at what he hoped was the right relationship to the wall barometer. He came back, moved the sextant to the edge of the desk, and bending from the hips, began to peer through it in the direction of the barometer and the wastebasket. Shaking his head in confusion, he commenced to move the sextant around the desk, with no success. Finally, with a deep sigh, he gave it up after marking his place in Bowditch. He sat back at his desk and for quite a time gazed earnestly at the sign on the wall 'Think Big!'

Abruptly it came to him. He sat up, galvanized, grabbed up his phone and spoke to Lieutenant (jg) Brownell in the outer office.

'Calvert,' he said, 'I have come through! Pass the word there'll be another emergency conference at 1400.'

The arriving officers were surprised to find the exec entirely calm, his feet anchored on his desk, and happily sighting at different objects on the wall through his sextant.

'Gentlemen,' he opened the conference, 'how are the Chinese and naval officers alike?'

The officers looked surprised at this conundrum and none could solve it.

'Face!' the exec said. 'To both, face is an important value.'

The exec, looking intently through his sextant, paused for this similarity to sink in.

'Face,' he repeated. 'Gentlemen, you're probably wondering what I'm talking about. Gentlemen, I have given this matter long and probing thought and have dredged up a piece of daring strategy. Something that will get us off the hook and still not cause us to lose face with the enlisted men by retreating from what, after all, naval officers have traditionally had – a real officers' club.'

The exec paused, then, lowering the sextant, spoke in a tone of vision:

'How would it be if we, the officers, did most of the building of the club ourselves?'

'What's that?' the words popped out of Lieutenant-Commander Gladney's mouth.

'I know, Arnold,' the exec said. 'That sounds pretty drastic. But in my estimation it will belay all opposition and criticism. No one can object if we build our own club, now, can they?' he said cagily.

'You mean to have the officers actually put the club up with their own hands?' Lieutenant-Commander Hereford said incredulously.

'The Seabees have already done the groundwork,' the exec continued. 'So all we have to do is borrow their tools,' he said simply. 'The actual putting up of the buildings – well, I used to drive a pretty fair nail myself, and to get the Navy off the hook I'd be willing to lend a hand. I imagine there'd be plenty of other volunteers besides me.'

The exec paused meaningfully.

Two officers spoke.

'I'd be willing,' said Lieutenant-Commander Hereford. '– For the good of the Navy.'

'Count me in,' said Lieutenant-Commander Gladney. But both of the plump little 'Echo Twins' seemed appalled at the prospect of physical labour.

'It's a pretty desperate measure for officers to build their own club,' the exec said. 'But we're in a pretty desperate situation. We'll start tomorrow morning. I'm getting out a release for the correspondents, pointing out that this unusual step is being taken in the interest of conservation of manpower.'

The exec, removing his feet from his desk, and putting his sextant down, leaned forward and set his lips sternly. 'I want every officer to continue his search, as is Naval Intelligence, for the man who started all this,' the exec said, breathing hard. 'I'm all for the enlisted man, I'm a Joe Blow man from stem to stern, but,' the exec, almost panting, said, 'that man, if he's ever found, is going to be handled in a way that never again on this island will the enlisted men try to take over the ship.'

Suddenly the exec was on his feet: 'Gentlemen! All officers who volunteer to lend a hand tomorrow – and I trust,' the exec said, looking threateningly around the circle of officers, 'that that includes everybody – will report in fatigues at 0800 at the club site. We Public Relations officers should set such a bang-up example the first day that (A) the enlisted men will be ashamed of themselves, seeing the officers work, and (B) most of the other officers in Headquarters will be out there next day wild to turn to with us. Gentlemen! Look alive! Go get rested up!'

That evening the officers readied themselves for the unusual morrow by unusually heavy drinking in the BOQ rooms.

'I think Gladney and Hereford ought to volunteer their backsides for bulldozers,' Lieutenant Griffin said. 'They've got the size.'

'But not the cutting edge,' Siegel said.

'I wonder who Joe Blow Paine is,' Griffin mused. 'I shudder to think what Nash will do to the poor bastard if he ever catches him.'

Yes, Siegel thought again, he was right in deciding not to approach the exec now about sea duty for Garrett.

'I can guarantee the commander will throw the book at him,' Brownell was saying grimly. 'After all, you've got to have discipline in the Navy. Well, I'm turning in. I'd suggest you men do the same. We've got a hard day tomorrow.'

The next day was more than hard. It was complex. That evening, Lieutenant Griffin, Ensign Siegel and Correspondent Jerry Wakeley stood in the Quonset bar trying to unravel the day's events.

'I have been covering naval matters for some six years now,' Jerry

Wakeley said, sticking a fresh cigar in his mouth, 'but today has been a new experience for me.'

'You aren't the only one,' Ensign Siegel said. 'They never prepared me for anything like this back in midshipmen's school.'

'It was an experience which I shall always treasure in my Navy memory book,' Lieutenant Griffin said nostalgically.

The door of the bar opened to admit Lieutenant-Commander O. S. B. Badgett, His Majesty's Navy's Public Relations liaison officer. The U.S. naval officers didn't see how the Badger could endure so much beard on tropical Tulura. 'On the contrary,' the Badger would explain, stroking his foresty red-black growth. 'It keeps the heat *off*. Ever hear of a shade tree?' Now the Badger, striding forward, joined the three Americans at the bar.

'I'll have one of those five-cent rum sours,' he told the Marine bartender. 'Something strange here,' the Badger said, gazing around thoughtfully. 'Where are all the Public Relations officers? Those massed legions that customarily block all access to the bar?'

'Where in hell have you been?' Siegel said.

'I was messaged this morning that H.M.S. *Vainglorious* had put in to Muranu. I rushed down to set up liaison – with the vessel's inventory of Scotch.'

'Well, you picked a hell of a day to do it,' Siegel said.

'Something happen today?' the Badger said. 'Well, what do you say we don't keep our British ally on pin-cushions?'

'Wakeley,' said Siegel, 'you sat there on your ass and got the total picture. Suppose you give the ally a run-through.'

'Well, I may need help,' the correspondent said. 'It was a bit confusing.'

Wakeley took his dead cigar out of his mouth and drank off an ounce and a half of straight whisky.

'Not long after first light this morning,' he began professionally, 'the commissioned officers attached to the United States Navy Public Relations Section on Tulura assembled in fatigues at the site of the new Navy officers' club on the ridge overlooking the Pacific.'

'A dedication?' said the Badger.

'It was the concept of the Public Relations executive officer, Lieutenant-Commander Clinton T. Nash,' Wakeley continued, 'that certain resentments among the enlisted men over the construction of this Pacific version of the Savoy Lounge, to visualize it for you, would vanish overnight if the officers were to build it with their own delicate hands.'

'What an extraordinary idea!' the Badger said in amazement. 'So American.'

'At the club site,' Wakeley went on, 'Commander Nash ...'

'... formerly of Merrill Lynch, Pierce, Fenner, and Beane ...' said Griffin.

'Who's that?' the Badger said.

'An American brokerage house,' said Griffin.

'... took charge,' Wakeley said. 'Commander Nash, in the best naval tradition, deployed his forces to engage the various problems. Lieutenant-Commander Hereford, the chief of the photographic section, was put in charge of cement-mixing. Lieutenant Commander Gladney, the radio chief, ran the wheelbarrows, assisted by a task force of three ensigns. Lieutenant Commander Randolph, the Media chief, headed up a crew of concrete-block layers.'

The Badger's eyes gleamed with interest above his chest-length beard.

'The commissioned workers fell to with varying degrees of ardour.' Wakeley stuck his cigar in his mouth momentarily. 'Soon various developments ensued.'

'Various developments ensued,' repeated Ensign Siegel happily.

'Lieutenant Noah Pratt, the Home Town News officer, was aiming for a nail,' continued Wakeley, 'when instead he struck his finger, fracturing it. Lieutenant Pratt left for the dispensary.'

'Casualty Number One,' said Lieutenant Griffin, holding up a finger.

'Then,' continued Wakeley, 'Lieutenant-Commander Hereford passed out from the heat, which by that time was beginning to crystallize on the ridge. First aid revived him, but he was removed to the hospital for observation.'

'He should have been long ago anyhow,' Lieutenant Griffin said, and held up two fingers. 'Casualty Number Two.'

'Then,' continued Wakeley, 'Ensign Christopher Tyson started sneezing violently over the cement-bin. It developed that the ensign had an allergy to wet cement. Commander Nash demanded irritably how he had ever been able to get a waiver for his commission with

218

such a disability. Tyson replied insolently that the stupid Navy doctors probably never visualized that an ensign would be mixing cement. Commander Nash sent him to his room.'

'In disgrace,' Lieutenant Griffin said, holding up three fingers. 'Casualty Number Three.'

'Next,' continued Wakeley, 'Lieutenant (jg) Pendleton, who was stacking concrete-blocks on top of each other, stopped stacking them. He withdrew from the scene after telling Commander Nash that he had suddenly remembered an urgent appointment he had with an NBC correspondent.'

'That was almost certainly a lie,' Griffin said.

'Casualty Number Four,' the Badger said eagerly, holding up four fingers.

'The work,' Wakeley went on, 'continued in some confusion. Then, after a break for chow, an altercation broke out. It began when the Seabee officer came over and spoke to the Public Relations officers who were building the concrete block wall. They were, the Seabee officer said, doing it wrong. This officers' club, the Seabee officer said, was going to look like the leaning tower of Pisa. And while he was about it, he said, he might as well say, which he did loudly, that he considered this whole idea the stupidest thing he had heard of in eighteen years of pre-Navy construction experience and three more in the Navy. Loudly enough that Commander Nash heard him and strode over to where he was facing the Seabee, whom he ranked by a half stripe.'

'The position is important. At the top of the wheelbarrow runway,' said Lieutenant Griffin eagerly, 'the Public Relations commander stood talking to the Seabee lieutenant.'

'Commander Nash,' continued Wakeley, 'told the Seabee that he had not heard anyone ask his opinion as to whether anything was stupid or not. He took down the Seabee's name, rank, and file number. Commander Nash, while speaking, began to shake his finger at the Seabee officer. Then, having quenched this impertinence, Commander Nash turned on his heel to go back to bossing the project. In his anger over the Seabee's remarks, I would guess, the commander was not watching too closely where he was going.'

'His eyes were blinded in his fury and excitement,' said Ensign Siegel resonantly.

'His whole face seemed to be pulsing,' intoned Lieutenant Griffin.

'What in God's name happened?' cried the Badger.

'Just as the commander turned,' Wakeley continued, 'it was unfortunate that Lieutenant-Commander Gladney should be urging a wheelbarrow of fresh cement up the runway at the top of which Commander Nash stood. Turning abruptly, Commander Nash stumbled on the wheelbarrow. He plunged head first into the cement.'

'Oh, no!' the Badger said incredulously. 'Oh, no!'

'Wheelbarrow, executive officer, and radio officer,' Wakeley went on, 'all crashed headlong into the excavation which the Seabees had previously dug out for the swimming-pool. The executive officer and the radio officer, though conscious, were removed to the hospital with multiple lacerations and contusions, requiring several stitches in both of them.'

'And in the case of the executive officer,' said Lieutenant Griffin enthusiastically, 'requiring the scraping off, by the medics, of the cement before it hardened. Casualties Five and' – Griffin put down his glass – 'Six.'

Wakeley carefully laid his cigar down by his glass and hitched himself up a little against the bar.

'Left without a commanding officer,' he said, 'the remaining Public Relations officers stood around for a while in uncertain clusters. They made a few stabs at going back to work, but gradually, in twos and threes, they began drifting off to their BOQ rooms, where I understand most of them are still asleep. At 1400 only Lieutenant (jg) Brownell, the executive officer's assistant, remained, a lone figure loyally and conscientiously stacking up concrete-blocks. Finally at 1500 Brownell walked off down the road towards the BOQ,' the correspondent said softly. 'The ridge above the Pacific stood deserted.'

The Badger stood a moment in respectful silence.

'It's very moving,' he said. 'It reminds me a little of Dunkirk.'

The British liaison officer took a swallow of his rum sour. 'And how is it you two are here?' he said to Siegel and Griffin.

'Somehow,' said Siegel, 'I couldn't whip up too much enthusiasm for the project. I think I took about a half-hour to drive each nail.'

'I stirred cement,' said Lieutenant Griffin. 'As with stirring martinis, I discovered, you can control your own pace.'

The Badger finished his drink and set the glass down crisply. 'I must see the devastation,' he said.

'It's probably very moving by moonlight,' Griffin said. 'I'll give you a conducted tour.'

'Not me,' said Wakeley, picking up his cigar and biting down on it. 'I've seen enough.'

'I'm really pooped from that nail-driving,' said Ensign Siegel. 'I'm not moving.'

When Griffin and the Badger had gone, Wakeley turned to Siegel. 'I wonder where Nash goes from here.'

'It'll be interesting to see,' Ensign Siegel said happily. 'Personally I'm enjoying myself.'

'Well, I tell you one thing,' Wakeley said, 'if this place doesn't get a hold on itself in damn short order, there's going to be a board of about sixteen admirals out here raging and roaring and the heads will be rolling from fo'c'sle to fantail.'

'Maybe they'll close the shop up,' Ensign Siegel said, unworried. 'With this man-power freed to take part in the war, we'd probably get it over six months earlier.'

The correspondent ordered a straight shot of whisky and drank it off. Suddenly he chomped down on his cigar. 'Has anyone in this hothouse,' he said, 'thought of talking with the enlisted men?'

'No, no one's appointed a mediation board,' Siegel said. 'This isn't the Longshoremen's Union, old man.'

'Maybe they don't know it up there, Max, they're so in the clouds up there,' the correspondent said, 'but all hell is about to break loose.'

'I thought it already had,' said Siegel.

'It hasn't even started,' Wakeley spat out a piece of his cigar. 'I was talking to Gordon Ripwell this afternoon.'

'You mean the celebrated correspondent for the Chicago *Gazette*?' Siegel said. 'Well! That must have been quite an honour for you. What were you doing, asking for some criticisms on your copy?'

Wakeley tapped his shot-glass on the bar.

'Ripwell, so he was telling me,' he said slowly, 'has his tentacles out among the enlisted men. In two days at the most he expects to have the name of the man who wrote that manifesto which started this whole nightmare. When he gets it,' Wakeley said softly, rotating his cigar in his mouth, 'when he gets it, he intends to write a story making a hero out of him.'

Siegel turned sharply to the correspondent.

'A hero?'

'That's what Ripwell said. "A hero all over the United States," he said, and, in Gordon's own minted words, a "symbol" of the caste system.'

'My God,' Siegel said, as if to himself, 'they'll crucify the bastard. The last thing that guy wants to be is a symbol.'

Wakeley, pulling his cigar out of his mouth, looked quietly at the ensign.

'You know who he is?'

'Yeh, I know,' Siegel said. He waited, then said, 'Between you and me, it's Garrett.'

'Well, Nelson's butt,' the correspondent said. 'Garrett. What the hell's eating him?' Wakeley considered a moment. 'Oh, I get it. Isn't he the yeoman who was mixed up with that Navy nurse before they stopped it?'

'That may have helped put Garrett to commanding this thing,' Siegel said. 'But I'd bet my little stripe the enlisted men are really browned off about the club, Garrett, too, and he's not the kind to hesitate about sticking his neck out if he really believes something. Maybe because of the nurse he's sticking it out a little more, that's all.'

Wakeley chewed his cigar. 'Well, whatever his reasons are, you better do something or they're going to chop his neck off right at the collarbone.'

'You know, that was a pretty good job of writing he did, wasn't it?' Ensign Siegel said.

'Nelson's butt!' Wakeley said. 'What has that got to do with it?'

Ensign Siegel looked at the correspondent and grinned. 'Okay, Jerry. What do you say we have a talk with Garrett? I'll go get him.'

'I'll meet you in my room,' Wakeley said. 'That's about the safest place I can think of for a closed-door kind of conference like this.'

'What's your interest in this exactly?'

Yeoman Second Class Adam Garrett's question was entirely matter-of-fact. He looked completely at ease, where he sat on the edge of the bed in Wakeley's room, despite his knowledge of the last few minutes that a correspondent knew, as well as Ensign Siegel – he had already suspected that Siegel knew.

'His interest,' Ensign Siegel said, 'is somewhat in the same category as one of your reasons for wanting to get to sea. He's interested in the Navy being the Navy.'

'After today I see what you mean,' Garrett said. 'Another correspondent is interested, too, but I judge for a different reason. Gordon Ripwell. He's been doing a lot of talking with the enlisted men. He's making us all into heroes. We're not heroes.'

'No, you aren't,' Siegel agreed.

Garrett moved his rangy frame on the bed.

'Ripwell had a long talk with me,' he said. 'I think he suspects I did it all right.'

'I'll say this,' Wakeley said, rotating his cigar in his mouth. 'You don't seem worried. Don't you know they can really let you have it for that interesting piece of writing you turned out?'

Garrett smiled softly. 'I guess maybe they can. Anyhow, it's too late to worry about that, isn't it?' he said practically.

'Then let's convene the arbitration board,' Ensign Siegel said. 'Garrett, do they just want the club stopped or made more, shall we say, modest? Or do they *want* something?'

Garrett leaned forward easily with his elbows on his knees. 'Well, first of all, sir, I think – this is my opinion, I'm not the bargaining representative for the enlisted men's union – I think that in return for one consideration the enlisted men wouldn't care if the officers built ten bars and fifty swimming-pools.'

'One consideration?' Ensign Siegel said. 'Liquor rations? The right to wear shorts instead of long pants? Officers' surf on their beach? Thirty days' leave apiece in the States?'

Yeoman Garrett smiled. 'Well, those things sound pretty nice but, actually, our desires are a lot more modest.' The yeoman straightened up a little on the bed. 'The men like beer a lot,' he said quietly. 'With beer you'd have a lot of negotiating power.'

'Beer?' Ensign Siegel said. 'Let's see. You get two bottles a day now. You mean you want that increased to a case?'

'No,' Garrett said, 'it isn't a matter of increasing it. It's the timing of the beer.'

'What's that?' Wakeley popped out. 'What in God's name is "timing of the beer"?'

Garrett scratched his toes through the hole in his shoe. 'Fungus,' he said. 'It's this way. As it is now we get two bottles of beer a day, but they have to be drunk that day. Some days a man wants only one beer, but some days, every now and then, a man would like all he can drink in one day – six, seven, a dozen beers.'

'That's the way some days are out here,' Siegel said.

'Some days,' Garrett said, 'a man would like to get loaded. You can never get loaded now. They dole you out those two beers a day and you drink them that day or lose them. In other words, the men don't like two bottles of beer a day – but they might feel entirely different about fourteen bottles a week. It's the timing of the beer.'

Wakeley looked incredulously at the yeoman. 'You mean,' he said slowly, 'that the men are satisfied with the fourteen bottles of beer a week. Only they want to drink them when they want to – fourteen bottles in one day if they want. And that if they got this they'd call off their war-bond cancellations?'

'I couldn't swear to it,' Garrett said. 'Nobody's appointed me spokesman for anything. But I wouldn't be surprised. I wouldn't be at all surprised.'

'You mean that something as simple as that would settle it?' Wakeley said in awe. 'Siegel, why doesn't anyone ever ask anybody anything around here?'

'This is the Navy, Wakeley,' Ensign Siegel said.

'But what can you do about it, Mr Siegel?' Garrett said. 'After all, you're only an ensign,' he said factually.

'Nobody ever lets me forget that,' Siegel said. 'I don't know, frankly. The exec has got himself in a position where any move is a retreat. But I can try. Meantime, if I were you I'd try to avoid Mr Gordon Ripwell for a couple of days.'

Garrett laughed abruptly. 'Ripwell,' he said, shaking his head. 'He told me if I'd play ball with him and give him an exclusive he'd see to it personally that I was protected, and what was more' – Garrett laughed again – 'he'd get me on something like "We The People".'

'Why, that vulturous son of a bitch,' Wakeley said. 'What'd you tell him?'

'Well,' Garrett said quietly, 'I told him he could jam "We The People" up his ass.'

'Well!' Ensign Siegel said happily. 'I'm sorry I wasn't there to hear you tell him that.'

Garrett got up to go. 'Mr Siegel,' he said, 'would you tell me one thing? How did you find out?'

'That you're Joe Blow Paine? You hit the typewriter keys too hard.'

'I'll be damned,' Garrett said softly. 'So that was how. Thanks, Mr Siegel.'

'Oh, by the way, Garrett,' Siegel said. 'I figured we better let matters soothe down a bit before we took up that matter of sea duty for you with the exec. I figure that the less he hears your name right now the better.'

'Yes, I guess that's a good idea,' Garrett agreed.

When the yeoman had gone, the ensign and the correspondent sat in silence for a moment.

'That Garrett,' Wakeley said. 'Too bad about him and that nurse. But he ought to be pretty good on a ship.'

Siegel sighed and heaved himself to his feet. 'Well,' he said. 'I guess the next item on the agenda is for me to make a sick call.'

'Nelson's butt,' Wakeley said. The correspondent sat there shaking his head over and over. 'Nelson's butt! The Budweiser Mutiny.'

The executive officer, sitting up in his bed at the hospital, had the aspect of a man who had tangled with one of the Seabee bulldozers. His body was cross-hatched with bandages and his face and the top of his bald head were red and raw as a Tartar steak from where the medics had scraped off the rapidly hardening cement. He was reading *Naval Leadership* with absorbed attention. He came to a passage: 'It is a good idea to retain a copy of what Paul Jones wrote. Read it over from time to time – especially when you have been taken down a peg or two – then ask yourself: "Am I measuring up to his standards?"'

The exec shook his head doubtfully and continued to read. There was a knock on the door, which then opened quietly.

'May I come in, Commander?'

'Well, Max! Nice of you to drop by. Good thing you came to-night because I'm going to be out of here in a couple of days,' the exec said bravely. 'We'll lick this thing yet. I may be dead in the water but I'm far from foundered.'

Ensign Siegel pulled something out of a musette bag he was carrying.

'I took the liberty, sir, of dropping by your office and getting this. I thought you might want it while you're in the hospital here, with lots of time on your hands.'

'My sextant!' the exec said, seizing it joyously. 'Why, Max! That was very thoughtful of you.'

'Glad to do it, sir.'

Siegel took the sextant back from the exec and placed it on the chest of drawers. He drew up a chair beside the bed.

'Commander,' he said in confidential tones, 'I've got important news. Do you know what? I heard something today that I think might get us out of this *contretemps*.'

'What's that?' the exec said irritably.

'Off the buzzsaw we're on with the enlisted men about our club.' Nash looked at the ensign almost supplicatingly.

'Commander,' Siegel said, 'you know, don't you, that the enlisted men are allowed two bottles of beer a day?'

'I've forgotten,' said the exec. 'Something like that. What is this, a quiz show? Get to the point, Siegel.'

'Fourteen bottles a week they're allowed. I think they're satisfied with the total ration.'

'They ought to be,' the exec said. 'An Egyptian camel should be satisfied with, let's see – two a day, seven hundred and thirty bottles of beer a year. Working at Merrill Lynch made me pretty good with figures,' he explained, in a moment of pride.

'Very clever, Commander,' Ensign Siegel congratulated the exec. 'Fourteen bottles a week they get,' he continued. 'But no more than two bottles in any one day. Get the difference? What they want, I believe, is to be able to drink as much of that week's ration in one day as they'd like.'

'So they can get drunk?' Nash snapped.

'You've got right to the heart of the matter,' Siegel said. 'Isn't it odd that even enlisted men like to get drunk once in a while? The point is, that a simple memorandum not even increasing their ration but allowing them to drink as much or as little of that ration in one day as they'd like – hell, sir, that wouldn't be any concession at all for the officers to make. And I may be wrong but I'd bet my stripe on it that it would make them forget about their bond cancellations and let us, the Seabees, that is, go ahead with the club.'

Nash was so desperate for a solution, he didn't even ask Siegel how he knew this, so that Siegel didn't even have to use his prepared story that it was scuttlebutt.

'Personally,' the exec said, 'I could never stand the taste of beer. Do you like beer, Max?'

'Not particularly,' Ensign Siegel said. 'Why?'

'That proves my point.'

'What's that, Commander?'

'You've got to be an enlisted man to really like it.'

'Also, beggars can't be choosers,' Ensign Siegel said. 'You wouldn't believe how important beer is to the enlisted men. And, Commander,' Siegel said softly, 'Ripwell's writing a lot more stories.'

'He is?' the exec said, starting to look frightened.

'He's stirring the whole thing up as much as possible,' said Siegel. 'Which is a lot.'

'You know,' the exec said, trembling with rage, 'I believe that's the only man I ever really hated.'

'Good for you,' Siegel said.

'I'm becoming convinced he's a dangerous man,' said the exec.

'Right now,' said Siegel, 'I'd rather have a time-bomb under our Headquarters.'

'I wish he were an enlisted man!' the exec said violently. 'I'd ... I'd keelhaul him!'

'I wouldn't mind doing that myself,' Siegel said pleasurably, 'but unfortunately the Navy doesn't allow us to keelhaul correspondents. So we've got to outsmart him.'

'Roger,' the exec said, his eyes bulging. 'Outsmart him!'

The exec scooted up painfully in his bed. 'Hand me my sextant, will you, Max? Max, let me ask you something,' the exec said, beginning to peer through the sextant at the hospital ceiling. 'Say we did that – let the men drink their fourteen bottles of beer whenever they pleased. ... Say we do – and I'm not saying we're going to – would you consider we'd lose face with the enlisted men?'

'Face?' the ensign said. 'Why, sir, I think we'd *gain* face. The beauty of this, sir, is that you give them something but you don't give them something. They'd still have only fourteen bottles a week. Besides that, it would be a big thing to do,' Ensign Siegel said huskily. 'A big, big thing.'

The exec lowered his sextant. 'I attach a lot of importance to face. Face is very important in dealing with enlisted men,' he said educationally. 'You've got to run a taut ship. "A taut ship is a happy ship." Who was it said that?'

'John Paul Jones, I believe,' Siegel said. 'Or Oliver Hazard Perry, I forget which.'

'I don't want anyone to get the idea I'm soft, you understand,' the exec said.

'Soft!' Siegel exclaimed. 'Why, Commander, the handmaiden of toughness is magnanimity. I think Admiral Farragut was the one who said that.'

'Did he?' said the exec. 'That's an interesting statement – especially coming from an admiral.'

'The higher the rank the bigger the man, I've always found,' Ensign Siegel said. 'Though it may have been Mahan instead of Farragut.'

'Who?' the exec said.

'Mahan – the conqueror of the Spanish Armada,' Siegel said. 'Anyhow, the point's the same. No one considers you soft, I can guarantee you that, sir. And giving the men their beer when they wanted it wouldn't make you soft at all. It would just make you big. It was Admiral Dewey who said, "A good officer always sees that his men are fed before he eats himself."'

'Dewey?' the exec said. 'That's a funny thing for a Navy man to say – on a ship, where there's always plenty of chow. I think you're wrong about that, Max. It must have been some Army man.'

'Commander, you're right! It was Jeb Stuart, now that I think about it. Anyhow, the point's the same. You might apply the same idea to liquids: "A good officer always sees that his men are drunk before he gets drunk himself."'

'It's not that I don't like enlisted men,' the exec said, raising his sextant for a fresh look at the ceiling. 'Why, I was the one who thought up the whole idea of the Joe Blow Department to let people know the enlisted men are fighting the war, too.'

'Commander,' Ensign Siegel said, 'I think everybody knows that you're one of the best friends the enlisted men have. And if you let them drink fourteen bottles of beer a day, why, sir, they'd worship you.'

'You really think so?' the exec said, looking intently through the sextant.

'Why, it'd be like you were the enlisted men's patron saint,' Siegel said. 'I happen to know they have pretty clear thoughts about you already. Only today I was reading some of their mail home' – Ensign Siegel's duties included censoring enlisted men's mail – 'in which they mentioned you in the most outspoken way. And if you gave them that beer ... well, sir, they'd idolize you, that's all I can say. Idolize you!'

Nash lowered the sextant and set his lips decisively. 'In that case we'll try it.'

Ensign Siegel closed his eyes.

'It takes a big man to do a big thing,' he said. 'It was Horatio Lord Nelson who said that. Commander, you've done the big thing.'

'I always try to,' the exec said.

Three days later the executive officer presided at the first conference since the officers' ill-fated attempt to build their own club. The officers looked like the survivors of a fierce naval engagement. Lieutenant Noah Pratt's finger was in a splint. Lieutenant-Commander Hereford still looked pale from his heat-stroke. Ensign Tyson, his nose red, continued to sneeze occasionally from the exposure to his cement allergy. Lieutenant-Commander Gladney had several patches from his fall with the exec and the wheelbarrow of cement into the swimming-pool excavation. The exec himself was the most bandaged officer of all, mainly because of the unprotected expanse of bald head when he dived into the cement. A huge bandage almost covered his head, like a white wig. Nevertheless the exec was jubilant.

'What a change from the last time we met!' he said happily. 'Today I've got nothing but good news, which we could stand a little of around here for a change.'

The exec smiled benignly. 'First and foremost, the mutiny has been put down. Isn't that nice?'

'It makes me very happy,' said Lieutenant-Commander Gladney. 'It's hard to get any real work done when you have a mutiny.'

'It's certainly nice to have the enlisted men speaking to you again,' Lieutenant-Commander Hereford said.

'I might say, Wayne,' the exec said acidly, 'that that very attitude is what led to a lot of our trouble. However' – he brightened – 'I want to get on with the good news.'

Using both hands, the exec tenderly pressed the edges of his toupee-like bandage down more securely.

'The club is once more going up speedily on the ridge, where the Seabees are busy as bees. Heh, heh. I guess that was a joke on me, thinking we could build it – that you could turn a silk purse into a sow's ear. No reflection on the Seabees.'

The exec's face glowed bountifully as he continued counting the many blessings.

'Yes,' he said, 'the enlisted men have finally seen the light of day and have withdrawn their war bond cancellations. Mr Ripwell and his kind,' he snapped, 'will have to navigate other seas for anti-Navy scandal.'

The exec resumed his glow. 'This concession was brought about, just as I insisted from the first, with no loss of face on our part. The enlisted men have no more than they had before and we can feel a sense of generosity – of bigness – which a naval officer should have towards the men – in letting them drink their beer when they want to.'

The exec's eyes slipped to an officer in the last row. 'Oh, by the way,' he said, 'I want to give a small commendation to one of our ensigns who gave me an assist in this matter. I can't specify it any more than that due to the secret nature of much of this whole thing – as you know, Naval Intelligence has been in from the first on this, and still are. But I do believe in giving credit – publicly – where credit is due. Siegel, you have shown some of the best qualities of a naval officer.'

The exec, his commendation out of the way, returned to the overall picture. 'All you have to do, gentlemen,' he summed up with mellow self-satisfaction, 'is not lose your heads. Keep calm. Not get small. Be big about things, and you'll always find there's a mine-free channel through. Even if it's a mutiny. And if there's any greater test of naval command than how to handle a mutiny I don't know what it is.'

'Don't you think matters have calmed down enough now, sir?'

It was two weeks later and Yeoman Garrett and Ensign Siegel were walking down the hill, Garrett to small stores to pick up a new pair of shoes for his de-fungused feet, Siegel to ship's service to pick up some candy for a visit that afternoon to a Tuluran village.

'I guess so,' Siegel said, looking beyond him to where the new officers' club was beginning to take striking shape on the ridge.

'I've tried not to think about it,' Yeoman Garrett said, 'but those eighteen miles …'

Involuntarily Garrett's eyes looked up to where, beyond the buildings, the boondocks stretched away across the island to the Fleet Hospital.

'If it were eighteen hundred miles I don't think I'd mind so much,' Garrett said. 'But eighteen – a half-hour in a jeep. What do you think about hitting them for sea duty for me now?'

'I certainly think it would be to the Navy's advantage to get you out of here,' Ensign Siegel said. 'Dating a nurse, leading a mutiny … You weren't a professional anarchist before the war, were you, Garrett?'

Yeoman Garrett smiled. 'No sir, the only time I ever got to vote, it was for the Republican ticket.'

'Well, Tulura has certainly brought you out,' Ensign Siegel said. 'We'd all have a little more peace and quiet if you got the hell out of here. I don't think the chances are very good, but if you want me to, I'll talk with the exec.'

'I wish you would,' Garrett said rather grimly. 'I'd feel better if we at least tried.'

'Okay, then,' Siegel said. 'I'll do it soon as I get back.'

After loading up his musette bag with Tootsie Rolls, chewing gum, gumdrops, Hershey bars, Mounds, Heath bars, Baby Ruths, peanuts, and six different flavours of Life Savers, Ensign Siegel went back up the hill to the Public Relations Section. He walked over to his desk and saw a note from Lieutenant (jg) Calvert Brownell that the exec wanted to see him right away.

Siegel walked on upstairs, stopping to gas with a couple of correspondents on the way, and was told by Brownell to go right in. The exec was buried so deeply in his copy of *Navy Regulations* that he didn't see Siegel enter.

'Well, sir,' Ensign Siegel said amiably, to draw his attention, 'this is a coincidence because I wanted to see you about something.'

The exec looked up suddenly and, seeing Siegel, jerked himself up explosively in his chair.

'You wanted to see *me*!' the exec shouted. '*You* wanted to see me!'

'Yes, sir,' Siegel said, 'I wanted to ask you ...'

'You don't want to ask me anything!' the exec roared. 'And what the hell is that haversack you've got on your back!' the exec suddenly screamed, as if personally affronted by the sight of it.

'Tootsie Rolls,' Siegel said. 'Would you care for one, sir?'

'Tootsie Rolls!' the exec shrieked.

'They're for the Tuluran children,' Ensign Siegel felt he'd better explain.

'The Tuluran children!' the exec yelled. 'If you'd been paying less attention to Tootsie Rolls for the Tuluran children and more to you own crew, you wouldn't be in the trouble you're in now.'

'Am I in trouble, sir?' Ensign Siegel inquired.

'Are you in trouble!' the exec repeated in a shout. 'I'll say you're in trouble.'

Suddenly the exec slammed *Navy Regulations* deafeningly on his desk.

'It's your yeoman!' he began to shout. 'It's your yeoman! Your yeoman! Your yeoman!' accenting each 'yeoman' with another crash of *Navy Regulations*.

'Once a trouble-maker always a trouble-maker!' the exec shouted in fury. 'First he flouts the Navy by dating an officer! Then he flouts it by starting a mutiny! Jumping Jupiter, if ever a man ought to be in Portsmouth!'

'What is this all about, sir?' Ensign Siegel stalled.

'I'll tell you what it's about,' the exec yelled. 'Naval Intelligence informed me an hour ago that Yeoman Second Class Adam Garrett wrote that scurrilous letter, started that mutiny!'

A sinking feeling passed through Ensign Siegel's chest. 'How did they find that out?' he asked.

'What difference does that make?' the exec shouted. 'They've got invincible proof.'

The exec slapped his hand on the desk. 'You don't seem to see what this tells about *you*, Siegel.'

'No, sir,' Ensign Siegel said blankly.

'Why, it shows you're entirely lacking in the foremost quality of a good officer – naval leadership!'

'Yes, sir,' Ensign Siegel said absently.

'How any officer could let a man under him get so out of hand is incredible to me!' the exec exclaimed. 'But I can't waste time on your problem right now. I've been sitting here going through *Navy Regulations*. Reading the various articles on crimes and mutinies, on discipline and punishment. Why, it's incredible what we could do to this man! Twenty years in Portsmouth wouldn't be an unusual sentence for a court-martial to hand down for such a crime.'

Ensign Siegel felt a sense of urgency seize him, a desperation to think of something or say something to head off the exec from making, in his fury, some terrifying decision about Garrett.

'Sir,' Siegel said, 'may I say something?'

'You may not!' the exec shipped out. 'There's no end of punishments we could give this man. I've been reading up for a full hour on it and I know!'

'Sir,' Siegel said, 'as this man's officer …'

'I haven't forgotten that!' the exec shouted. 'But I can't use a court-martial,' he went on. 'Those blasted correspondents, for one thing! They'd start it all up again and we might end up losing our club after all. Besides that, you can't be a hundred per cent sure what a court-martial will do, and it would take weeks anyhow. I want,' the exec said ferociously, 'to fix that man right now.'

'Sir,' Siegel said urgently, 'I feel I do have the right …'

'You have no rights at all!' the exec shouted. Suddenly a canny smile crossed his face. 'So I've figured out one of the worst punishments I know of for this man.'

The exec's voice rose. 'I am putting this trouble-maker where he will toss many a night longing for a comfortable cot to sleep on, where his tongue will hang out wishing he had one beer a week, where his bitterly hard work will leave him no time for trouble-making.'

'Commander,' Ensign Siegel said, his own voice rising for the first time, fervently, 'I believe I may almost insist on the right to speak for this man …'

'Belay it, Siegel! I've made my decision!' The exec came to his feet triumphantly. 'I am ordering this man immediately to sea – and to the roughest duty of them all, a destroyer.'

The exec waited a moment, calming himself down, then turned to Ensign Siegel.

'The Garrett matter is closed,' he snapped, 'and we won't discuss it, you understand? And now, Siegel, what was it you wanted to see me about originally?'

MELORA 5 : *Queen's Pawn Opening*

'Let's skip the cleaning today,' Melora said as soon as Ensign Siegel arrived at the schoolhouse. 'It isn't so important to keep this place clean any more anyhow. Let's go over and take a look at the new schoolhouse. It's really going up!' she said excitedly.

They walked around a grove of palm trees, and there in a clearing on the hilltop they could see the framework of the Gordon Ripwell–Chicago *Gazette*–357th Construction Battalion Grade School.

'Isn't it beautiful?' Melora said in awe.

The schoolhouse was in a pretty raw state now, but the evidences of the fine workmanship that was going into it were plainly visible. Above the perfectly laid concrete block foundation rose the firm lines, the handiwork of top craftsmen, of the frame skeleton.

'They certain know how to build things, your Seabees,' Melora said.

'The Seabees,' Siegel said with some pride on behalf of his friends, 'are without doubt the finest bricklayers, carpenters, bulldozer-men, and plumbers in the entire world.'

The ensign and the girl inspected the new building for a while, climbing over the concrete blocks and walking around what would be several schoolrooms before long. Melora led the way through what would shortly be a wall, and stood in the middle of empty space.

'This will be my schoolroom,' she said. 'Isn't it wonderful?'

'I guess it's going to be,' Siegel said, smiling at her pride.

After the inspection they went on out to what would be the front of the schoolhouse and sat down on the concrete-block foundation, their legs hanging down.

Below them spread a scene beyond all enchantment, the village of Tanalolo, like something plucked out of sweet imagination. The village square was a blue lagoon, with the houses set here and there along it amid the palm trees. From the scimitar of white beach the green hills rose gently upwards on all sides, shutting the village away.

'Look down the hill there, Max. The frangipani are in bloom.'

'Never mind the frangipani,' Ensign Siegel said.

'What did you say?'

Ensign Siegel laughed. 'I was just thinking about the day I had so much trouble getting Mr Seguro to tell me anything about you. He kept talking about everything else – including the frangipani.'

'He's nice, isn't he?' Melora said, smiling.

'I guess he is,' said Ensign Siegel. 'He's got good palm toddy. But he certainly was protecting you that day.'

Melora smiled. 'I never knew.'

'Oh, he was certain your father would be very angry if I got within a mile of you,' Ensign Siegel said. He added, 'And I guess he was right.'

'Oh, now, Max,' the girl said. 'Papa is just – well correct. He's a very interesting man, really.'

'Yes, I guess so,' Ensign Siegel said. 'He certainly asked me some interesting questions.'

'Oh, now, Max,' Melora said. 'I've always liked so much sitting here watching the water and the village,' she said, changing the subject. 'I used to come up to this hilltop when I was a pretty small girl even and do the same thing. Did you ever just sit, when you were a boy, and watch things?'

'I never had a blue lagoon,' Ensign Siegel said. 'But pretty days my father used to buy me a bag of peanuts, walk me over to Harvard Yard, and sit me down to feed the pigeons for an hour until his class was over. Only sometimes I cheated on the pigeons. Sometimes I gave myself every other peanut and the twenty or thirty pigeons every other one.'

'Your father,' Melora said. 'He sounds like a nice father. I mean, to take you and sit you down on the campus there with the peanuts and the pigeons.'

'He always seemed to me the most thoughtful man I ever knew,' Siegel said. 'But he could be strict about things. Reading, more than anything else. He wanted to see me looking into books. I think by the time I was fifteen I had read more books out of Widener Library than three-fourths of the students there. But I liked them. The way he made books sound, you couldn't help but like them.'

'I think I would like your father,' Melora said. 'It's strange, but my father was the same way. He made books sound so I couldn't stay away from them. You know, I think probably your father and my father are a lot alike. I think they would like each other.'

'Maybe so,' Ensign Siegel said. He grinned at the picture of the two men together. 'But I think some sparks would fly. I think my father is a – well, less ceremonious man.'

'But ceremony is a superficial thing,' Melora said.

'I'm not so sure,' Siegel said. 'Ceremony, with some people, can be almost the beginning and end of everything.'

'What did you do besides feed pigeons and read books?' she said, changing the subject.

'Well, in the winters we used to find ponds and go ice-skating. Boston is cold in the winter, lots of ice and snow. Have you ever seen snow?'

'In Switzerland one year when Papa took me on a trip. I liked it to see, but I didn't think it would be the best thing to live in.'

Ensign Siegel looked down at her, wearing the garments of Tulura. He tried to visualize her in the snow. Then he was thinking of himself again on the ice-ponds around Boston. His memory seemed to him a strange and unreal thing, with this girl by him and looking down at the lagoon – he got a picture of snow falling slowly out of the skies on to the soft blue water. He felt mixed up and he shook his head a little.

'Excuse me,' he said.

Ensign Siegel got up and walked to the jeep that was sitting a few yards away from them under a palm tree. He got something out of it and came back and sat down by her.

'A present for you,' he said, handing her a package wrapped in brown paper.

236

'Oh, Max!' she said, taking the present.

'Unwrap it, Miss Alba!'

'Yes, Mr Siegel.'

And she opened it unhesitatingly.

'Oh, Max!' she said.

It was a volume of the plays of Calderón, which Siegel had sent off for to a rare book shop in Boston he used to patronize when he had some money saved up.

With great care Melora opened it as something fragile. She read the inscription on the flyleaf: 'Miss Alba – Hoping you will accept this in defiance of Tuluran customs – Mr Siegel.'

She laughed and then looked through the volume, treasuring it, for several minutes.

'I'm already in love with this, Max,' she said. '*La Vida Es Sueño* is one of my favourite of all writings. To me Calderón is next to Shakespeare.'

It was getting a little late, and presently she turned to him.

'Max,' she said. 'Why don't you come back and have tea with Papa and me?'

Ensign Siegel was a little surprised at the abrupt invitation. What was more, he was not at all sure he wanted to accept it. He didn't care to be put on the grill again by Mr Alba. It hadn't been a particularly pleasant thing for him and also he just saw no point of his going there.

'Well, I don't know,' he hedged. 'I probably ought to be getting back.'

Melora looked directly at him. 'Well, I've never known you to be in such a hurry before,' she said, a touch of petulance in her voice. 'You don't have the watch tonight, do you?'

Ensign Siegel smiled, at how she had picked up Navy terms so quickly from him.

'No,' he said, 'I don't have the "watch".'

'In that case,' she persisted, 'what's to keep you from having tea with Papa and me?'

It occurred to Ensign Siegel, in a happy moment, that she had never at all persisted with him before. However, he still did not say yes, nor tell the reason. But in a moment she said it herself.

'Is it because of Papa?' she asked. 'Max, actually he's a very interesting man. I think the two of you might really like each other in time.'

It would take at least fifty years' time, Ensign Siegel thought.

'He's a very interesting man, really,' his daughter repeated. 'Max, come along – please.'

Nothing on earth could give him strength to say no after that.

They went over and he helped her into the jeep.

'I've never ridden in one of these before,' she said delightedly.

Siegel drove down the road for a couple of miles. He drove slowly, wanting his time with her more than his time with 'Papa' and her. The road was meant for water-buffalo-pulled carts. It was bumpy and barely wide enough for the jeep, and the forests pressed closely on them from both sides, in great pools of blackness.

One bump lifted Melora quite off the seat.

'Sorry,' Ensign Siegel said.

'It's fun!' she said. 'It's like a carnival ride Papa took me on once in Paris.'

Papa! he thought.

After a while Siegel pulled off into a small clearing. They got out of the jeep and started walking up a path just wide enough for two persons to walk alongside. Once they bumped accidentally against each other.

'Sorry,' Ensign Siegel said.

'It's a very narrow path,' she said.

Soon they could see the lovely house looming up through the trees. It was an astonishing thing to see sitting there in the remote forest. Ensign Siegel followed the girl up the steps and inside.

'Papa!' she called out. 'Mr Siegel's here!'

Siegel reflected that this announcement surely would not give Mr Alba the greatest thrill of his life.

However, Mr Alba, emerging from a room in the back, greeted Ensign Siegel with a courteous smile.

'I've just been sitting out on the terrace, just looking out over the water,' he said. 'The usual occupation of an old man.'

Ensign Siegel pigeonholed this remark as the luxury of a man who was about forty-eight and didn't look a day older.

'Not just old men, Papa,' Melora said. 'We've been at the new schoolhouse – which Ensign Siegel got for us,' she added pointedly, 'doing the same thing. Watching the lagoon.'

'Is that so?' Mr Alba said, a phrase which Siegel had come to associate with the idea that Mr Alba was dissecting him.

'It's always been one of my favourite places to sit, you know, Papa. But let me see to the tea things.'

The few minutes Melora was out of the room seemed severely long to Ensign Siegel. It was not that Mr Alba was brusque. He would never be brusque, Siegel thought. He would have considered it gross. Actually he was entirely courteous, a good host, chatted with Siegel and asked him no more questions. He didn't need to, Siegel thought. He had found out all he wanted to know before. And Ensign Siegel was not in the least comfortable.

He felt a little better when Melora came back. Soon the maid came in with the tea-things. Melora poured, and over the tea-cups, father, daughter, and U.S. ensign made polite talk.

Ensign Siegel's eyes must have been wandering around the room – he found it difficult to keep them on Mr Alba, with his relaxed gaze which none the less seemed to suggest, in those clear brown eyes of his, that Ensign Siegel was a trespasser. In any case Siegel's eyes suddenly rested on a glass case that sat on the far side of the room. It was a beautiful piece of furniture, of teakwood, Siegel would have guessed from where he sat. The case was partly in shadows, but Ensign Siegel was blessed with 20–20 vision and, his eyes focusing, he made out there were objects sitting on the shelves inside. Then, with a certain feeling of emotion, he became aware of what the objects were.

'Excuse me,' he said.

Abruptly he rose and walked over to the case. As he stood before it, seeing the objects clearly, a definite emotion welled up in him.

For inside the case were at least a dozen of some of the most exciting sets of chessmen Siegel had ever laid eyes on. One, of gleaming elegance, was of chased silver and silver-gilt. Another was a group of about forty small Egyptian stone and turquoise-glazed clay chess-like pieces. There was an impishly carved Balinese wooden set, each piece with a little pointed face and hands on hips – it made Siegel chuckle happily to see it. There was a rare Greek set made of leather. There was a vivid set of German porcelain Huns and Teutonic knights, the Hun king with flowing black moustaches. There was a Spanish wood and ivory and a German amber and ivory set. And there were four of carved ivory – French, German, Chinese, and one, Flemish, the most exquisite Siegel had ever seen.

'Blessed heaven!' Ensign Siegel let out an exclamation of pure awe.

He must have been standing for several minutes before the case before he became aware that Mr Alba had come over and, respecting Siegel's concentration, was standing to the side and slightly behind him. For at least a couple of minutes more neither man spoke a word.

'I've never seen more beautiful ones,' Ensign Siegel said.

'You know chess sets?' Mr Alba said.

'My father – whatever spare money he ever had he spent it on chess sets,' Siegel said. 'He had several fine ones – though never anything to match these. He once took me down to New York just to see the collection of sets at the Metropolitan when they were on display.'

'Is that so?' Mr Alba said. 'Do you know I once travelled five thousand miles just to see that same collection?'

'Did you, sir?' Ensign Siegel said, in an interest which instantly considered such a trip entirely natural.

'Would you like to see them more closely?' Mr Alba was saying.

'I would consider it a rare privilege, sir,' Ensign Siegel said.

Mr Alba took a key out of his pocket and unlocked the case. Carefully he opened the glass door. For a few moments both men looked at the treasure of exposed sets in deep and silent pleasure. Then Mr Alba's hand went out and picked up the white bishop of an ivory set.

'This,' he said, 'is French, eighteenth-century. You recognize him?'

'Why, it's Voltaire!' Ensign Siegel exclaimed.

'So it is,' Mr Alba said, pleased at Siegel's recognition.

And he handed the bishop to Siegel, who took it with great care. It was a bust on a tiny pedestal. Despite its two-inch height the features were as detailed as on a statue, with a large grin covering Voltaire's face.

'Now look here,' Mr Alba said.

He reached in the case and took out the other white bishop. This one was also Voltaire, but here he had a highly displeased expression. Siegel and Mr Alba, looking from one to the other of the bishops, smiled.

'The two moods of Voltaire,' Ensign Siegel said.

'Exactly,' Mr Alba said, pleased.

Siegel carefully handed the two small busts back.

For perhaps twenty minutes Mr Alba showed Siegel several other sets, furnishing their history, where known, and their particular points of excellence. Finally, with his greatest pride, he came to a set on an ivory chessboard that stood about six inches high, with a bas-relief in each side and a griffin on each corner.

'This,' he said, 'is undoubtedly the best of the collection. It's seventeenth-century Flemish. It was done just after the Thirty Years War. The sides are scenes of Wallenstein in battle.'

The two men bent, engrossed, over the magnificent set. The pawns, about two and a half inches high, were soldiers of the period completely detailed from head to foot – one side wearing cavalier-type hats with plumes, hip-length coats, and carrying guns; the other side with helmets, steel vests, and javelins. The rooks were towers with balconies, resting on boulders. The knights were delicate horses rearing on their hind legs. The kings and queens were obviously portraits of actual royalty.

Mr Alba picked up one of the queens. 'This,' he said, 'is the master-piece of the set. This is Marie de' Medici, and she closely resembles the Rubens portraits in the Louvre done at the same period. Here, take her.'

'Oh, no!' Siegel said. 'I wouldn't dare to touch her.'

'Not at all,' Mr Alba said. 'It's all right for you to touch her.'

Ensign Siegel's huge hand, taking the three-inch-high little figure, turned her about with the utmost gentleness, admiring the series of puffs in the sleeves and the delicate folds in the skirt, the rounded breasts in the neck of the low-cut gown, the minute necklace, the tiny fan which she held against her side, and the minuscule curls on top of the diminutive head.

'She's absolutely enchanting, isn't she?' Ensign Siegel said in com-plete awe. 'To get such perfection in such a tiny space! I've never seen anything like it.'

Mr Alba put the ivory queen back, shut the door of the case and locked it.

'Well,' he said. 'Well.'

Abruptly he turned to Ensign Siegel.

'Do you play, too?' he said casually, but with an unmistakable hope in the under layer of his voice.

Ensign Siegel waited a moment. Having been unable to get a game since coming to Tulura, he was very anxious for one. But deliberately he made his voice casual. 'Yes, sir, I do,' he said impassively. 'As a matter of fact, I was chess champion of my college – Harvard College,' he added rather loudly.

'Is that so?' Mr Alba said, a quiver of excitement in his voice.

'Oh, Max!' Melora said, for she had come over. 'Papa has been dying for a chess game for four years – ever since the war has kept him on Tulura. I used to accuse him of making trips to Europe just to play chess – no one does here. He plays these games by mail – but the mail is so slow these days that it takes six weeks to find out his opponent's move. He tried to teach me but I never could get good enough to make it interesting for him – Papa's good. He hasn't had a real game in four years …'

'Mr Siegel,' Mr Alba interrupted impatiently, his voice almost trembling, 'why don't we step over here?'

It was no more than five minutes before Mr Alba and Ensign Siegel were seated on opposite sides of a table, their heads bent, with the most absolute concentration, over the detailed animal figures of a beautiful contemporary chess set.

'So you're using the Queen's Pawn Opening,' Mr Alba said with keen interest. 'Oh, Melora' – he looked up for a moment – 'tell Maria we'll have a guest for dinner. You will stay, won't you, Mr Siegel? We will continue afterwards.'

Eight: The Lacy Battle Flag

THERE were some Navy people who bitterly resented women correspondents, claiming the war would be over years earlier if they stayed at home. It was true that they added a number of man-hours' labour in the Navy's push to the Japanese home islands. Once a detachment of five men from the Seabees, the famous Navy 'Can Do!' outfit, had to put in a full day building a special head for a correspondent who decided her coverage of the war required her to visit Gug-Gug, and there was considerable complaining over this. It was difficult to have any sympathy with such complaints. After all, a war is no excuse to add to the discriminations women already endure. Besides, some of the women correspondents went above and beyond the call of duty to make themselves useful. On Tulura there was one correspondent, a fifty-five-year-old woman who represented a chain of Texas papers, who put in every Saturday afternoon in the main Public Relations building sewing on buttons and darning socks for all comers. She was a kindly if somewhat concupiscent lady who probably had more suitors than any fifty-five-year-old woman in the world. It was necessary to date her up three weeks in advance. Being a woman correspondent in the Pacific put you in a really distinctive class. The ratio of woman correspondent to military men was about 1:250,000. The Pacific needed more, not fewer women, and it was worth building an extra head here and there for them.

A few of the women correspondents flaunted the ratio. But they could hardly be blamed for obeying the oldest law (supply and demand). Some also paraded that envied mobility which derived from profession rather than sex. One war correspondent for a true-confession type of magazine used to pop into the Media Section and plant herself, legs apart, in front of a map of the world which obliterated the entire wall. Her eyes would ravage the great map as if it were a tray of French pastry and she couldn't make up her mind which piece to select, all of it being so mouth-watering.

'I wonder where I should hit next,' she would think out loud. 'Guadalcanal – but things must be terribly dull down there by now. Bombay – there *would* be Gandhi to interview. Sydney – we could use a little down-under stuff. Tahiti – I wonder if anyone's ever thought of asking those gentle Tahitians what *they* think about the war …'

The island-stuck officers would sit at their desks and look at her menacingly out of the corners of their eyes. Ensign Christopher Tyson III would be seething. The Princeton odd-job ensign was a very handsome young man who was not accustomed to going without sex. Back in Rye, Ty had had succulent débutantes standing in line ready to give him their most precious possession. But he was a long way from Rye. When the true-confession woman would flutter out of the room after a few minutes of map-gazing, Tyson would storm to his feet.

'The b-b-b-bitch. The fanny-shaking b-b-b-bitch.' And he would mimic her, mincing around the room, hips shaking and hand to the back of his head. 'Now I wonder if I should go to Tahiti ... or Sydney ... or Bombay and get the true confessions of Mahatma Gandhi. I'd like to catch the b-b-bitch some dark night down in the boondocks and r-r-rape her from here to Sydney. Women correspondents! I don't see why we can't fight a war without women correspondents.'

Tyson was always talking about fighting the war, always itching for sea duty.

Any woman correspondent in the Pacific became a very special person, if for no other reason than the oldest law. But the most upsetting woman correspondent ever to reach the Pacific was Debbi Aldrich. For one thing, she represented a publication of a type which until then had not been sending correspondents to the Pacific. Most of the women correspondents were with newspapers or wire services. Debbi Aldrich represented *Madame*.

When the dispatch that a *Madame* war correspondent was on her way to Tulura arrived, there was a lot of speculation as to what angle of the war she was going to cover, *Madame* being a magazine of great tone, best described by its subtitle: 'The World of Women – Décor and Cuisine, Beauty and Fashion.' There was certainly not a great deal of subject material for these matters in the Western Pacific. 'I hear she's going to do a takeout on what kind of drawers ComFleets wears,' Lieutenant Morey Griffin said. There were many guesses along this line.

Debbi Aldrich turned out to be quite a dish. The critical faculties of Pacific Navy men about women were almost pathologically warped, of course, but Miss Aldrich could have held her own in Radio City. She made a spectacular entrance into the Pacific. Lieutenant Morey Griffin said later he was too embarrassed to get up from his desk for an hour. As a Correspondents' Aide, Tyson had gone out to meet her, and he followed her into the Public Relations building like a cocker spaniel with its tongue hanging out. All his resentment against women correspondents had evaporated sometime between his departure for the airfield and the trip back. He was staggering under a load of three brand-new, bright-red lizard-skin bags, including a hatbox wedged under his arm. In the surroundings the hatbox looked sensational.

'May I present Miss Debbi Aldrich!' Ty exclaimed to Lieutenant-

Commander Junius Randolph, the Media chief, in his excitement making a *faux pas* in introduction etiquette unusual for a Rye boy.

She was very beautiful. She had a sculptured face which must have had a kind of wistfulness to it before she got into the magazine business. Now there was no wistfulness, but an air of being in complete command of any situation. She was very clean-looking and as smart and tailored as an illustrated ad from her famous magazine, even in her khaki slacks and shirt, and with her face faultlessly made up, her lipstick precisely modelling her small mouth. She had a junior-model body, boyish hips, and her hair, just peeking out from under a baseball cap, was cut almost as short as a man's. In fact, if one had looked at her just from the neck down, one might have had trouble, except for one feature, deciding for sure whether she was a boy or a woman. This feature left no doubt, and if the ancients were right, that it is really woman's crowning glory and a woman desirable in direct ratio to its shape and prominence, then Debbi Aldrich was certainly a queen. They were magnificent and incontestably all her own. One other tiny but startling feminine detail appeared below the neck – half-inch of black brassière just visible in the V of her khaki shirt.

She crossed the room briskly, held out a hand to Lieutenant-Commander Randolph, and came right to the point.

'I'm sure it's going to be a pleasure working with you, Commander,' she said in a husky, just slightly bored voice which, like her whole appearance, stepped right out of the pages of her magazine. 'I'm out here to do a job. I'm not on a junket. *Madame* is anxious to bring off some really different material from the Pacific. We have a feeling it hasn't been really covered – I mean, of course, as *Madame* wants it covered –' and she made a graceful gesture with her free hand. 'I'm after the off beat, if you know what I mean.'

It was quite an inaugural speech, and the officers could feel the uncovered Pacific all around them, right here in this room, waiting to be covered by Debbi Aldrich.

Griffin gave a gulp from across the room. 'Well, anything we can do,' he said with a forced laugh, '– that's what we're here for, Miss Aldrich.'

'Yes, I'm sure you are, sweetie,' the *Madame* correspondent said, giving Griffin a polar one-second smile before turning back to

Randolph. 'Right now, before I get to work, Commander – may I call you Junius? – I really could use a shower.'

'Tyson!' snapped Lieutenant-Commander Randolph, who before the war had run a paper in Georgia. 'Give – I mean get – Miss Ahldrich a showuh right away!'

'Yes, sir!' Tyson said, coming to attention.

It was the nearest to a military exchange the Public Relations Headquarters had ever seen.

Debbi Aldrich created a major upheaval in the Public Relations Section. So many officers were for ever sniffing around her, volunteering assistance, to the neglect of correspondents of the opposite sex, that some of these began to grumble that, after all, the Associated Press, United Press, International News Service, New York *Times*, Chicago *Daily News*, CBS and Time, Inc., as well as *Madame*, were covering the war and had been for years before that goddamn fashion sheet decided it wasn't really being covered.

Before long, Debbi Aldrich was both the most hated and most sought-after person in the western Pacific. She was hated and sought after for the same reason: for being an aloof, tantalizing, and beautiful woman in the midst of many men. She would come into the Media Section to use a desk and sit there tapping out her copy on her new Hermes, her body lithely erect in the chair, that half-inch of black bra showing in the V of her khaki shirt. No brave bull was ever more violently disturbed by a red muleta than the officers of the Public Relations Section by this minute strip of cloth. No work ever got accomplished while she was present, except by herself. As she typed, absorbed in what was going on on her Hermes, the officers would sneak glances at her and writhe in hellish frustration, at night go back to their BOQs, and over poker hands bicker endlessly as to her accessibility.

Ensign Tyson came very near to going crazy. 'She knows that little piece of black b-b-bra shows,' he would rage. 'You know what she is? She's a sadist! That's what she is! I know these b-b-black-underwear kind of women!'

Tyson was probably entirely wrong, for Debbi Aldrich seemed oblivious of the effect she created and interested solely in her work, which she was at almost constantly. She was all over the place, interviewing Seabees, submariners, admirals, amphibious crews, fly-boys –

everybody. She filed reams of copy to her magazine. Tyson knocked himself out getting jeeps, arranging interviews, even changing type-writer ribbons for her. It was obvious to everyone but Tyson himself that he would never get to first base with Debbi Aldrich. She accepted all he offered politely but with the condescension that said it was all her right both as Debbi Aldrich and as correspondent for *Madame*, and that anyhow he was just a boy, and an ensign boy at that.

For her escort, Debbi Aldrich looked around and tapped Admiral Boatwright's assistant. Captain Thornberry was fiftyish and grey-haired. It was Thornberry who took her to the beach for swims – she carried her two-piece black bathing-suit (anything closest to her skin was always black, it seemed) in the red lizard hatbox – Thornberry who took her to the dances at the Island Base officers' club. Tyson was enraged at the idea of her going around with an ageing, homely cap-tain when there was a pretty ensign like himself so available. 'I can' figure her out,' he fumed, 'I don't see what she g-g-gets out of it. It's downright p-p-perversion. I've got it figured out! She's a lesbian!' Really, for all his looks, Tyson didn't know the first thing about women.

Debbi Aldrich had not been long on Tulura when she announced her plans to do what no woman correspondent had ever done: make a combat operation. The Media officers were sitting at their desks shuffling papers one day when she walked in and gave the word to Randolph. Ship assignments for the invasion of Nanto Shima had been relayed to the correspondents a half-hour earlier. Debbi Aldrich sauntered up to Randolph's desk and cocked her hands on her hips. Randolph looked up and saw her standing there and got quickly to his feet. Lieutenant-Commander Randolph was a Georgia gentleman who had been reared to stand up in the presence of women, even those who wore pants.

'Junius, I haven't heard yet what ship I'm going on,' she said, as if it were mere oversight on his part.

'But ... theh's no arrangement on ships,' Randolph mumbled in Georgian. 'Theh's no arrangement for carryin' women, Miss Ahl-drich. You see, that is ... that is, it isn't customary for women corre-spondents to go along on combat operations. Women stay back heah, and, ah, well, one subject the women correspondents covuh frequently is the wounded when they come back to the fleet hospitals ... ah, that is, how the nurses and the wounded are doin' … Ah, the women's angle, the nurses as related to the wounded.'

'But, Junius, *Madame* isn't in the slightest interested in doing the customary,' Debbi Aldrich said crisply. 'I've come five thousand miles, Junius, to do something that's not customary. The fact a woman correspondent has never made an operation is precisely why *Madame* wants me to do it. Isn't that logical?'

'But Miss Ahl-drich, ah just don't see … Much as we'd like to, we can hardly refit an entah ship, knock out bulkheads and that sort of thing, to, ah, accommodate a woman. It's relatively easy on an ahland, putting up a separate, ah, cottage and that sort of thing – we've got plenty of Seabees to do that sort of thing – but on a destroyuh … Ah, you see, theh are not separate facilities and the officers use, ah, things in common. Besides, the Bureau of Ships has to approve any structural changes in a naval vessel. Next destroyuh we build, we'll try to blueprint in a compahtment for women. …'

Randolph gave a forced laugh, in which Miss Aldrich did not join.

'Junius,' she said crisply, 'please don't talk to me as if I'm a retarded child. I don't know what kind of women you're used to in Georgia, but I assure you, I can take care of myself – even on a destroyer.'

Lieutenant-Commander Randolph looked forlornly into Debbi Aldrich's flawlessly made-up face. 'Ah'm suah of that, Miss Ahl-drich. But on a Navy ship theh's …'

'Now, Junius, be a good boy and write me up those orders. If nothing else, my conscience wouldn't let me stay on Tulura during the operation. This isn't the nineteenth century, you know, sweetie. Women are emancipated – or haven't you heard? – and we've got to do all the things the men do, and all that. That's what I'm out here for. Really, Junius, I wish you wouldn't try to give me special consideration.' She reached out and touched Lieutenant-Commander Randolph's hand resting on the desk, and Randolph's hand blushed violently. 'I want to be treated just like anyone else.'

'Puhsonally, Miss Ahl-drich,' Lieutenant-Commander Randolph said soothingly, 'ah'd be happy to write those ohduhs up right this minute, but, you see, it's not in mah powuh …'

Randolph turned to his desk. The Media chief had foreseen, in the short time he had known the *Madame* correspondent, that such a demand might arise, and he had done his homework well. He had been relieved to discover that the all-encompassing *Navy Regulations*, which provide for almost every conceivable contingency, had also provided for this one. With complete assurance Randolph picked up the volume and, opening it to a marked place, turned to his last and sure resort.

'Y'see, Miss Ahl-drich, Article 116 of *Navy Regulations*, entitled "Women on Board Ship", reads in full as follows: "Officers commanding fleets, squadrons, divisions, or ships shall not permit women to reside on board of, or take passage in, any ship of the Navy in commission except by special permission of the Secretary of the Navy."'

There was a moment of silence while Randolph, closing the book, stood ready to soothe Miss Aldrich's disappointment.

'Why, you mean,' Debbi Aldrich said slowly, with an air of incredulousness at the simplicity of it, 'that all I have to do is ask Jim Forrestal? Why, Junius, why didn't you say so in the first place?'

And Debbi Aldrich was gone, her narrow hips swivelling her across the room and through the swinging doors.

'Commander,' Lieutenant Griffin broke the awed silence when she had gone, 'I'll be happy to have Miss Debbi-all share my stateroom on the U.S.S. *Campfollower*.'

'Oh, be quiet, won't you? Women in trousuhs, anyhow! Damn it all!' Lieutenant-Commander Randolph said. That was rather astonishing, too, for the Georgian had never before been known to lose his temper.

What exactly happened no one ever knew, but Captain Thornberry was credited with the leading role in the outcome. The outcome was that Debbi Aldrich was assigned to a ship for the Nanto Shima operation. She didn't get a destroyer, but she did get a cruiser. The roster of vessels for the operation was searched and a heavy cruiser, the *Seattle*, turned up which was used ordinarily as a flagship but had no admiral aboard for the operation. The *Seattle* was to take part in the bombardment of Nanto Shima. Debbi Aldrich was to pick up the ship at Muranu, stay with her during the operation, and return with her. She was dispatched to the *Seattle* and put up in the admiral's cabin.

At the same time Ensign Tyson, who had never got anything but the odd jobs nobody else wanted at Public Relations Headquarters, got the sea duty he had so long sought. It was still an odd job, but this one happened to be in great demand, for the sea duty was with Debbi Aldrich. Tyson was assigned as Public Relations officer-in-charge of Miss Aldrich for the Nanto Shima operation. There was scuttlebutt that Debbi Aldrich had arranged this, too, through Thornberry. Tyson just smiled when asked about it. 'Men, I'm the obvious choice for the assignment with Miss Aldrich,' he said. 'You guys should have got on the ball and changed a few typewriter ribbons instead of sitting around torturing yourselves.' Of course Tyson never gave anyone else a chance to change her typewriter ribbons.

The captain of the *Seattle*, Ty later related, almost had apoplexy when he and Debbi arrived aboard. The captain was a non-public-relations type. He was outraged at the idea of a woman occupying flag quarters on his ship during an assault operation.

'He couldn't say anything to Debbi,' which was what Tyson called her after the operation, though he had always called her Miss Aldrich before, 'though you should have seen the look on his face when she and her three suitcases, including that damn red hatbox, were piped aboard. But soon as she was settled in the admiral's quarters and I in the non-admiral quarters – well, I'd no sooner unzipped my duffel bag than a Marine orderly came down and said the captain wanted to see me at the double.'

The captain banged on the table and shouted at Tyson. 'What are you trying to do to my ship? What kind of war do they think we're fighting out here?'

'Sir, it wasn't I who assigned her. I'm just in charge of her.'

'Don't tell me who assigned her out here, you impudent pup. So you're "in charge of Miss Aldrich",' the captain sneered. 'What duty for a commissioned officer of the United States Navy!' The captain fixed his eye on Tyson. 'Do you know how many men there are on a heavy cruiser?'

'Sir, the *Seattle* carries a complement of 1,712 officers and men,' said Tyson, who had boned up on the ship on Tulura before putting out to sea with the *Madame* correspondent.

The captain was irritated that Tyson should know the answer so exactly. 'And do you realize how long this ship has been in the Pacific?' he snapped.

'Thirty-one months and thirteen days, sir.'

'All right,' the captain said furiously, 'do you realize something these secret documents they let you read but shouldn't on Tulura don't tell you: do you have any notion what just the sight of a woman, any woman, but especially this woman, has on these men who haven't seen even a white woman in thirty-one months and thirteen days?' The captain banged the table. 'Do you?'

'Yes, sir, I minored in psychology at Princeton. Besides, I have something of a notion myself,' Tyson said truthfully.

'The hell you do!' shouted the captain, whose concept of Tulura was of officers boozing all day and wallowing in orgies in the boondocks with nurses all night. 'I'm placing a twenty-four-hour Marine watch on the admiral's cabin!' the captain said. 'No one is to be allowed up there. That goes for you, too,' the captain said suspiciously.

Tyson was dismayed. 'But, sir! There are certain coverage problems on which it is essential for me to confer from time to time with Miss Aldrich.'

'Coverage problems!' the captain bellowed. 'What does that mean in English?'

'Well, sir, I mean, what stories she would like to do, transmission problems, deadlines, censorship problems, that sort of thing,' Tyson said mysteriously. 'You'd be surprised, sir, how many problems these correspondents can come up with. ComFleets is most anxious that they come away with a favourable impression of the Navy, and that means we've got to take care of their problems.'

Tyson's discreet dropping of 'ComFleets' did the trick. Really it infuriated the captain even more, this ensign pulling ComFleets' rank on him. But there was nothing he could do about that, for the woman correspondent did come from ComFleets. However, his eye gleamed as he thought of something to do.

'All right, then,' he said, pushing his lips together, 'you can "confer" with her in her cabin. Incidentally, have you ever been aboard a ship before?'

'No, sir,' Tyson said shyly.

'I thought not. Well, we've no room for deadheads on the *Seattle*. Starting with the first watch you'll stand regular watches in communications in addition to conferring with that woman.'

ComFleets Headquarters Public Relations officers were not

supposed to be given additional duty during their visitations aboard ship, but far from being displeased, as the captain had expected, Tyson was overjoyed. He had always wanted to be aboard ship, and here he was standing watches, just like a naval officer! Of course, the work in the communications shack, consisting of sitting at a desk and coding and decoding messages, wasn't particularly nautical, but still he was standing regular watches. They couldn't very well have made him a junior officer of the deck. The captain of the cruiser was not so angry at Tyson that he wanted his ship run aground.

The crew took a different attitude from their skipper's towards Debbi Aldrich. They were happy to have her aboard. They talked of little else. Fresh scuttlebutt was piped down almost hourly from the admiral's quarters by the Marine guard. Once Miss Aldrich asked a big Marine corporal from Oklahoma named Donahue if he would get her some Ivory soap-flakes to wash out some 'things'. The *Seattle* had a fine laundry, but the clothing it handled required somewhat more powerful soap-flakes. But Donahue got a case of Ivory bar soap and got one of the carpenter's mates to shave it into fine pieces on his lathe and there were Ivory soap-flakes for Miss Aldrich.

'She had them "things" soaking in the admiral's basin when I took the soap-flakes in,' Donahue reported, 'and Jesus Christ what "things"! Yow-ee!'

For days the crew would talk about how Debbi Aldrich was washing out her 'things' in the admiral's basin. God damn!

The moment one of the Marines came off watch he was pumped for new Aldrich poop, Donahue especially because he always acted mysteriously. A swarm of sailors would surround him in Marine quarters and Donahue would hold court.

'What about that damned officer who goes up there?' a sailor with a ravenous look in his eye would ask Donahue. 'You hear anything when he's inside?'

'Hell, you can't hear through them bulkheads,' Donahue said. 'You swabbies ought to know that.'

'You sure you don't hear no noises?' the sailor said suspiciously.

Donahue would look as if his sense of delicacy had been offended.

'God damn, you swab jockeys can't never think of nothing else, I'll swear to God.'

'Listen, you Gyrene bastard; we said noises. You hear any *noises*?'

Donahue shrugged. 'To tell you the truth, men, I heared one or two noises. But it's been so goddamn long since I even *heared*, I just can't tell for sure if it's *them* noises.'

As the ship cruised towards Nanto Shima, Debbi Aldrich's very presence aboard began to give a certain spirit, a lift, to the ship. This spirit was typified by an incident just before the bombardments.

D minus eight, as the ship was preparing to manoeuvre into position for the first bombardment, the captain came on the bridge, and glancing skywards, noticed a flimsy piece of cloth fluttering from the mast.

'What the hell!' he muttered and flicked his binoculars to his eyes.

Studiously the captain examined the delicate and magnified fret-work. Still looking through the binoculars, he addressed the officer of the deck:

'Hepburn, am I getting old or are we flying from the mast a pair of something no one on this ship has seen for thirty-one months?'

'Yes, sir,' Hepburn said nervously. 'I mean no, sir, you're not getting old and yes, sir, you have correctly identified the object.'

The captain snapped the binoculars down, looked quietly at Hepburn, who was standing twelve inches away, then suddenly let out a roar: 'Well!!?'

'You see, sir,' the officer of the deck said, his voice trembling a little, 'I believe we're the first ship in naval history to carry a woman into combat, and the crew had the idea of, well – flying her pennant!'

'Anyhow, sir,' piped up the boatswain of the watch, boldly flinging a hand towards the transparent strip of cloth, 'that's what we're fighting for!'

The crew had noted Debbi Aldrich's half-inch of black in the V-neck of her shirt. They had correctly gauged that anyone representing a magazine like *Madame* would be wearing a matching colour below. They had requested and Debbi Aldrich had supplied the pennant. She was delighted that her colours – the panties were a lacy black – should lead the U.S.S. *Seattle* into battle.

The captain looked mastwards again, his face reddened and swelled. Then suddenly he burst into laughter, a phenomenon many of the crew had not witnessed during three years under his command.

'Okay, Hepburn. Let's go in and give 'em hell!'

The pennant stayed up. The cruiser *Seattle*, incidentally, was credited with the deadliest bombardment of any of the ships in the Nanto Shima operation.

Then one day – D plus two, it was – Debbi Aldrich disappeared from the ship. Vanished. Flick! Like that.

There was unprecedented consternation on Tulura when that first message, marked 'Urgent', came in and was decoded:

031955. Originator: U.S.S. *Seattle*. Action: ComFleets. Miss Debbi Aldrich, correspondent for *Madame* magazine, disappeared at 031910 from *Seattle*. Miss Aldrich was last seen by a Marine orderly who left his post at her quarters in flag cabin to go to ship's service and purchase her a package of cigarettes. When orderly returned, Miss Aldrich was no longer in the cabin. The officer of the deck, ship then being anchored in Nanto Bay five miles offshore, immediately instituted search. Exhaustive search of all ship spaces fails to turn up Miss Aldrich. Search of flag cabin reveals two of three pieces of luggage she brought present and accounted for but one – a red hatbox believed to be made from lizard skin – missing. All ships in area and all ground forces on Nanto Shima being notified to be on lookout for woman with red hatbox. Disciplinary action being instituted against Marine orderly and Ensign Christopher Tyson III, OinC Miss Aldrich.

ComFleets' answer was prompt and hot:

ComFleets stupefied by your 031955. Dispatching immediately Airtrans Rear Admiral B. G. Pumphrey, chief of intelligence, to supervise search for Miss Debbi Aldrich, correspondent for *Madame* magazine, and conduct exhaustive investigation into startling laxity of *Seattle* whereby VIP passenger can quote disappear unquote from ship five miles from shore. You are hereby directed meantime to conduct relentless and unceasing search of ship ballast to bridge. Signed (Personal) ComFleets.

Viewed from the *Seattle* the whole operation on Nanto Shima, where the Marines and Army had landed and were pushing respectively north and south, ground to a halt. It was not true that the Army's search for Miss Aldrich was responsible for its temporary failure to progress southwards. The Japs were to be blamed for that hold-up. But all Marine and Army units were repeatedly reminded to be on the lookout for the *Madame* correspondent and supplied with detailed descriptions of the missing woman – including her red-lizard hat-box, as if there might be several similar creatures, but perhaps not equipped with red-lizard hatbox, wandering around the battle area – and all ships in the area were searched. For a while the Navy communications system carried almost as many Debbi Aldrich as operational dispatches. The Navy Department in Washington was putting the heat on ComFleets, which was burning up the air-waves to the *Seattle* off Nanto Shima. War or no war, you just don't lose a correspondent, at least a *Madame* woman correspondent, by 'disappearance'. Admiral Pumphrey directed all search operations from the *Seattle*'s newly vacated admiral's quarters, which at least were again rightfully occupied by flag rank.

Seven days after Debbi Aldrich vanished, Tyson, who was a prisoner-at-large awaiting his disciplinary action for losing her, was standing forlornly on deck leaning over the rail and thinking seriously about jumping in. It was a beautiful, clear day with a sea smooth as a summer pond where the *Seattle* remained at anchor in the spot from which she had not budged since Miss Aldrich disappeared. She had been ordered to remain there, like a homing-pigeon's loft. Squinting shorewards, Tyson saw an LCVP bobbing its way towards the cruiser. As the boat came closer, he could see what appeared to be a rather grimy Marine sitting, legs crossed, on the engine-cover. His eyes moved casually over the boat, then fetched up. The Marine's hand was resting on an object which, though grimy itself, looked familiar. It looked like a red hatbox.

By the time Tyson had rushed down to the gangway, the boat was alongside. Peering over the side – he almost fell overboard – he was just in time to see the Marine wave goodbye to four other Marines and the LCVP crew and hear a familiar husky voice.

'Thanks awfully, you darling Leathernecks,' the voice said. 'It couldn't have been lovelier.'

Tyson tore down the gangway past the startled officer of the deck.

'Debbi!' he yelled. 'My God, Debbi. You've had the whole U.S. fleet looking for you! The war's almost stopped since you left! Where in the name of God have you been?'

Debbi Aldrich, correspondent for *Madame*, brushed a wisp of hair back under a Marine fatigue cap which came down over her ears. She hitched up her Marine combat trousers and pulled down her Marine jacket. They were so big for her that the sleeves came over her hands, and half the pants legs had been rolled up. Her face was caked with dirt – her lips, however, were properly lip-sticked. She looked up at Tyson and said, easily, 'Where have I been? Why, to the wars, sweetie. Be a good boy and help me with this hatbox, will you?'

Stunned, Ty preceded her aboard with the hatbox. By this time the captain and Admiral Pumphrey were striding rapidly down to the quarterdeck. The captain was practically a stuttering maniac. But Pumphrey retained the coolness that had made him an admiral. His voice rammed like a torpedo across the quarterdeck.

'Miss Aldrich, you will be confined to your quarters until the first available air transportation to Tulura. I hope you know what this means. You're headed back to the States, Miss Aldrich.'

Grimy-faced, Debbi Aldrich stood there on the quarterdeck, her body almost swallowed up in the Marine fatigues, hands on hips and cocky as a sparrow. She pushed back her hat, gave her pants another hitch, and suddenly reached forward and chucked Admiral Pumphrey under the chin. The admiral drew back, startled.

'Sweetie,' Debbi Aldrich said, 'it was worth it.'

Then she looked up slowly at the mast. The black pennant was still there. It just looked a little limp, it being a windless day.

'Happy to see my panties are still flying.'

And with an insolent swagger Debbi Aldrich started to her cabin, the hoarse echo of a violent command from the admiral – who had looked mastwards with a startled air – following her.

'Take those goddamn things down! What is this, a United States Navy vessel or the Pacific office of *Madame*?'

'Haul down those panties!' the captain boomed.

Down came the panties and up went the two-star flag of Rear Admiral Pumphrey, which in the confusion of the search had not previously been hoisted.

Debbi Aldrich wrote her story under confinement in the admiral's cabin. Rear-Admiral Pumphrey furiously sent two Marines to empty the cabin of his gear after Debbi Aldrich had scribbled him a note: 'Sweetie, are we *both* going to stay here! I do need a bath more than anything in the world. If you don't mind, I don't.' Her story was a good story, of its kind, beginning: 'I have just become the first woman in American history to accompany an infantry patrol into battle.' She wrote how simple it was. One evening around dusk she had looked out of the port-hole of her cabin and seen an LCVP alongside the ship. It had come out for some supplies from the cruiser. She quickly threw some 'things' in her hatbox. Then she sent the Marine orderly for some cigarettes, pushed her hair up under her cap, and stepped out of her cabin. While the deck watch was seeing to the supplies, and in the confusion of men passing back and forth between cruiser and LCVP, she simply went down the gangway and got aboard. LCVP crews are used to carrying everything. They didn't bother to ask questions. Ashore she hitched a ride with a Marine jeep headed for the front. She stayed with a front-line Marine outfit for four days. The Marines never ask questions, particularly of women.

Then she came back. It was as simple as that.

Of course they had to send her back to the States, even though she was a correspondent for *Madame*. It was probably worth it to her, for she had a real exclusive. Tyson said he thought it was a pretty shabby thing to do, sending her back, in view of the fact that she probably had a lot to do with the *Seattle*'s brilliant bombardment record. Really, he said, Debbi Aldrich was a great inspiration to the whole crew, and maybe the Navy Department in Washington knew what it was doing, after all, and should send a couple of hundred women correspondents out here. Ty said he thought those black panties should be preserved in one of those glass cases at Annapolis where they keep famous naval battle-flags.

An odd thing was that when he returned from Nanto Shima, Tyson had completely lost his stammer. Though there were cases of combat operations giving stammers to men, this may have been the first time such an operation actually cured a stammer.

MELORA 6: *New York is a very great excitement*

Ensign Siegel and Melora sat on the terrace of Melora's house finishing a cool tall drink that was made with three parts of the milk of the coconut and one part papaya. It made a delightful drink and it had been a pleasant Sunday, Siegel was thinking. There was not much more of it, for it was around six o'clock and the sun was beginning to descend the lower reaches of the sky towards the Pacific down the hill below them.

A most pleasant Sunday, Ensign Siegel thought, sipping his coconut and papaya. Shortly after arriving about noon he and Mr Alba had had a three-hour game of chess. They had played three or four times a week since discovering this common interest. They were interesting opponents for each other, of the twelve games Mr Alba having won seven and Siegel five. Today's game had been particularly satisfying, lasting sixty-four moves before Mr Alba, playing the white pieces in a Three Knights opening, mated. After the game the three of them had had a late Sunday lunch on the terrace; then Mr Alba, happily satiated with chess, had gone inside for his siesta, and now Ensign Siegel and Melora were alone on the terrace.

'You know, Max,' Melora said, 'I think Papa really likes you.'

Siegel could not, he told himself, contradict this without false modesty. He felt that Mr Alba probably did like him, and not just for the chess. The chess had removed Mr Alba's suspicions sufficiently to give him and Siegel a chance to get at each other. The two men had come upon a host of communications, ranging from the world of philosophy to the world of five per cent convertible preferreds – Mr Alba, Siegel discovered, was Tulura's chief banker, and Siegel, Mr Alba had been quite interested to discover, had worked a spell in his uncle's New York brokerage firm before entering the Navy. They could discuss the concepts of Kant and the future of certain industrials on definitely shared wave-bands, and Siegel was to the point of enjoying the company of Mr Alba a great deal.

'He's a very interesting man,' Ensign Siegel commented, as Melora had used to reassure him about her father. He sipped his coconut and papaya with an extraordinary feeling of contentment, almost luxury. 'If he likes me, I am very glad of that.'

'He does,' Melora said, 'but don't sound so smug about it. He told me the other evening, very seriously, that perhaps he had underestimated American education. Then I think he probably felt this was going a little far, because he added that more likely you were the exception to the rule. He still thinks more of you came from your father than, for example, from Harvard College.'

'He's probably got something there,' Siegel said with a sigh. 'Though the place isn't so bad as he makes it out. It is an accredited institution.'

When they had finished their drinks Melora said, 'Max, why don't we take a walk? You've never climbed down to the beach with me.'

'Fine,' Siegel said.

They went off the terrace, across the yard, and, entering the woods, climbed down a path to the beach. It was a very white beach and stretched for empty miles in either direction.

'Let's take off our shoes,' Melora said. 'You want to feel this sand.'

When they had them off she said, 'I want to show you my rock.'

Way up the beach Siegel could see something sticking out into the sea. They started walking barefoot up the beach, Melora a little ahead of him. He felt the sand squishing between his toes and he thought he had never felt anything so soft – it was like the finest powder. Then, looking ahead, he thought, what an erect body she has, and he thought, quite abruptly, what a body she has. Then he watched her narrow footprints in the sand and his own obliterating them.

They must have walked almost a half-mile in the sand, saying almost nothing, when they came upon it. It was a huge, shiny boulder, flat on top, that sat on the otherwise unmarked beach as if it had been brought there and dropped. It entirely filled the beach – to continue, one would have had either to climb over the rock or go into the water. Melora promptly scrambled up it, and Siegel, with somewhat more difficulty, followed her up and saw her sit down, with her legs under her, as if sitting down in a familiar chair in her own living-room.

'This is my rock,' she said. 'I always come here.'

Sitting down by her, Siegel could at once see why. He had seen many nice views on Tulura and in the Pacific, where striking views were the common thing. But surely, he felt, he had never seen anything quite like this. Both ways from them stretched the miles of white, gleaming beach. Behind them the lush hills rose like a green wall. Then in the distance on either side of them the hills curved inward, into twin promontories. In front of them the sea was laid out, bigger than anything that ever was, and utterly blue and quiet, almost soundless. Nowhere was there the slightest sign of man or habitation, or slightest sign that man had ever, in his thousands of years, been here. It represented the Pacific, its vastness and its loneliness and its beauty, like nothing Siegel had ever seen. It gave Siegel, perched as he was on the rock, like a Buddha regarding it all, an immense sense of being alone. He found the feeling greatly satisfying, for the feeling really was of being completely alone with Melora.

'In Europe,' she said, 'when I was in school, I missed this rock more, I think, than anything else.'

For a few moments they silently watched the red ball of sun move steadily down towards the sea. Strange things had been happening to Ensign Siegel lately. A definite restlessness and preoccupation quite unusual for Siegel had begun to come over him. First, for the only time in his life, he had begun having a little trouble sleeping. Then he had begun to enjoy the officers' bar sessions less and even on occasions to get quite irritated at the sameness of the conversation. Then a couple of weeks ago he had spoken sharply to his astonished room-mate Lieutenant Griffin about Griffin's habit of dropping his clothes all over the room. Siegel had entirely forgotten that until not long ago he himself had been probably the unneatest officer at Public Relations Headquarters – lately he had been like the model in the display win-dow of a naval tailor. A week ago, on an orientation tour, a congress-man had to ask him three times the date of Tulura's liberation before he heard him. And two days ago he had had the startling lapse of leaving a picture of Robert E. Lee hanging on the wall of the Palan town hall when he had meant to replace it with Herbert Hoover for the visit of a New York congressman.

Turning a little on the rock, Ensign Siegel looked at the cause of it all.

'How long were you away?' he asked.

'Four years – four long years. It's unusual for a girl in our family to go to school in Europe more than a year, and usually the year the girl went, there wasn't much studying to it, but I' – she laughed briefly – 'really had to study. Including subjects I wasn't interested in. Like mathematics. I'm still not too good at it – but I passed.'

'Why all this torture?' Siegel said.

She smiled. 'Well, you see, there have always been Albas on this island, and they've always had responsibility towards it. Papa never let me forget this. Ordinarily this wouldn't be so important where a girl was concerned – but he had no sons. So Papa brought me up as he would have a son. The schooling was a part of that. He wanted me to do things. That's how the school-teaching got started. And he wants me to do other things some day, simply because I'm the only one of my generation.'

Ensign Siegel looked at her, beginning to understand things he hadn't understood before.

'What is man's most precious possession supposed to be,' he said, '– freedom of choice?'

'I know what you mean,' she said thoughtfully. 'But it happens that I like what I'm doing. And I love the island. It's my island.'

He looked at her on the rock. Ensign Siegel had enjoyed Melora's company so much in the past months that he had forgotten how truly beautiful she was. Now the fact of her great physical beauty suddenly rushed over him. Her features, exquisite to perfection, the smoothness of her flesh, the long blackness of her hair, the shape of her body beneath her dress ...

'I got very homesick away from the island,' she said. 'In 1941 Papa put me in school in Spain, where my family has always gone to school, because of the Spanish blood we've got in us, and their culture has always been an important part of our culture, though this time Papa hesitated about sending me there, since he wasn't too fond of the Government. In fact, he might even have sent me to France, but the Germans were there. I feel close to the Spanish – they're my own people in a way, really – but I missed this. Then America got in the war and the Japanese were on Tulura and I couldn't come back even in the summers. Those four years away – at times I thought I couldn't stand it unless I got back here tomorrow. Then the Americans were back on Tulura, and after a lot of arranging that I thought was going to go on for ever, and how happy I was when it was over, I crossed over into Portugal and got on that boat.'

She looked down the length of beach, then back at the sea. 'How I missed this! Maybe it's because I grew up with it. If you grow up with it, anyhow, you'll always miss it.'

Siegel suddenly became aware of a keen depression in him. For a while he could not place the source of it. Then he knew. He was depressed because she was talking about her ties to Tulura.

'I missed this,' she repeated, looking at the sea. 'Doesn't it seem to go on without any ending – right out to the skies?'

Ensign Siegel smiled softly. 'Well, it has an ending. You go far enough one way over it and you come into San Francisco. That's a nice city. Then you go on from San Francisco across the land and you come finally to New York. Now, that's a city.'

'Oh, yes, I liked New York very much,' Melora said with excitement. 'Papa took me there once when I was about fourteen. That so much could be taking place in such a small space! I had the feeling that the people and the things almost had to stand on top of each other, that there were so many wonderful things going on that you couldn't get them all on just the space that there was on the ground.'

Ensign Siegel realized that he was listening with enormous interest to her excitement about New York.

'There's no city like New York,' he hurried to keep up this line of thinking. 'It has everything, that city,' and he realized the phrase was trite, but he went on: 'That sense of something being just around the corner that's very wonderful and that's going to change your whole life,' he said, feeling quite trite but convinced he believed it.

'Oh, yes,' she said excitedly.

'The feeling of things happening in that city!' Siegel burst out, feeling every second more and more like the world's champion cliché-maker. 'Plays! Concerts! Clubs! People! All kinds of people! There's no city like it.'

'Oh, there isn't!' she agreed.

'You know, I worked in New York after college for a while before the Navy,' he said. He waited a moment. 'And undoubtedly it's the place I'll go back to after the war.'

The three-word phrase suddenly spread a strange chill through Ensign Siegel. He was fairly astonished, and he felt a quite uncomfortable emptiness.

'I want very much to go to New York again!' she said in excitement.

Ensign Siegel suddenly felt a good deal better again.

The sun had disappeared into the sea and around the sky the light was beginning to fade.

'We'd better go, Max,' she said.

They climbed back down the rock. Ensign Siegel wished he could have helped her, but she was so sure-footed it would have been as ridiculous as helping a squirrel.

They started out single file again down the beach, but they had not gone very far when, almost simultaneously, it seemed, he quickened his pace a little and she slowed hers a little and they were alongside and abruptly they were holding hands. We've never done this, Siegel thought with a jumping-around feeling inside him, and immediately was trying to remember whether he or she had started the gesture.

He was able to convince himself that she had – or at least that it was simultaneous. Ensign Siegel felt such a rush of pleasure that he was almost dizzy. All the rest of the way down the beach they walked holding hands.

They came to where their shoes were parked alongside, looking very isolated on the carpet of white sand. Melora laughed.

'Don't they look funny there,' she said.

Which they did, Siegel's huge black shoes coming close to doubling Melora's sandals in size.

They sat down and started putting their shoes on. Melora, with her sandals, had hers on somewhat before Siegel, who had the problem of socks and laces. He had tied the left shoe and was tying the right one when he stopped.

'Melora,' he said.

'Yes, Max?'

All through him Ensign Siegel felt warm with the pleasure of the hand-holding walk down the beach.

'Melora,' he blurted out, 'do you think you would like living in New York?'

'Living in New York?' she said. 'Why do you …?'

Suddenly they were looking at each other and Melora did not complete the sentence. But she knows, Ensign Siegel thought. She knows why I asked.

'To visit in New York, yes – that is a very great excitement,' she said slowly. 'But to live there …' She paused. 'No, I couldn't live there. I could never live anywhere but here.'

Ensign Siegel turned back quickly and finished tying his shoe. He stood up, rather abruptly. She got up and stood by him. She put her hand on his arm.

'Max …' she started to say, and stopped.

'Melora …' he started to say, and stopped.

Then, his head moving, he looked for a moment up the lonely beach, where the shadows were coming on so fast now, and out to the darkening sea.

Then he turned, so suddenly that her hand fell off his arm.

'Well, I guess we better get on back up the hill,' he said.

Nine: The day the bomb fell

BEFORE the war Lieutenant Woodrow Wilson Shoemaker, who had a long, pale face and a long, pale body, and a sense of history and was a thinking man, had been an editorial writer for a Mid-western newspaper with a circulation of half a million. On Tulura he commanded the Historical Section of the Public Relations branch. He kept ships' histories up to date, on the rare chance that any of the naval correspondents should care to do a story on a ship, and prepared background material on islands to be invaded. Lieutenant Shoemaker's background documents, being given out to correspondents shortly before an invasion, were real gems, sparkling with detail. The Okinawa Press release included the information that the island had two snakes for every one human being. These tasks filled at the most three hours a day, leaving Shoemaker ample time for a history of political thought in sixteenth-century Siena which he was writing – his 'Naval Guggenheim', as Woodrow contentedly called it. He was a stable and sedentary man, satisfied in his naval job and anxious neither for the war to be over nor for it to continue. On the day that the word flashed back to the island, Lieutenant Shoemaker had been updating the history of the U.S.S. *Missouri* by adding an item on her most recent bombardment of the Japanese home islands: 'Two freight cars at Yokoje disabled.'

The news came through as most of the officers were getting back from noon swims, sets of tennis, and siestas. Shoemaker was probably one of the first to hear it, for he was in Lieutenant-Commander Nash's office when a communications messenger arrived with a copy of the President's message. The exec was checking through the personnel of a VIP junket that was due on Tulura soon, trying to decide which of three top-ranking names – Gene Tunney, John P. Marquand, or Roy Howard – should occupy the one extra guest bed currently available in the admiral's quarters.

'Damned if that isn't a real Solomon's problem for you! One bed with the admiral and three wheels like Tooney, Roy Howard, and Marquand steaming in here. What do you think, Woodrow?' the exec tossed the problem to Shoemaker, who because he had once written editorials was considered a sort of one-man brains trust around Public Relations Headquarters.

The exec selected a paper-clip from the three-inch shell on his desk and leaning back in his chair cocked his arm and tossed it for a pinging bull's-eye into his wastebasket. 'I'll make up my own mind, of course, but say you had the helm like I do – how would you navigate this one?'

'That's a tough one, all right,' Shoemaker hedged. 'A famous prize-fighter, a famous novelist, and a famous publisher. That's an unusually tough one.' Shoemaker had found such hedging profitable: if he made these problems seem really difficult, Nash would figure he had helped more and so not bother to inquire what he did with all those hours when he wasn't researching ships, snakes, and invasion islands. The fact was, he knew instantly which of the three visitors ought to get the bed with the admiral.

'Incidentally,' said Nash, a little embarrassed. 'I know who Tooney and Roy Howard are, of course. But Marquand … it's slipped my mind. Isn't he the joker who wrote something about an artist who went to the South Seas? I have a feeling I saw a movie about it.'

'I believe you're thinking of Somerset Maugham, Commander. The Britisher. A novel called *The Moon and Sixpence* …'

'That was it!' the exec exclaimed happily. 'George Sanders played in it.'

'Marquand wrote a very good book too.' Shoemaker said. '*The Late George Apley.*'

'Never heard of it. No movie, was there?' the exec applied his yardstick.

Lieutenant Shoemaker pondered momentarily. 'No, but there were some movies made of some of Marquand's other stories,' he tactfully gave the exec a point of reference. 'Did you ever see any of the *Mr Moto* movies?'

'Of course!' the exec exclaimed happily. 'Peter Lorre played in them. So! Marquand wrote those, did he? You know what! We ought to try to get one of them to play while he's here. He'd probably be very flattered and give the Navy some good public relations sometime in one of his novels instead of this unfavourable officer type that's always getting into novels for some reason that's beyond me. Why, you'd think that no one but enlisted men ever wrote books!

Incidentally,' the exec said with sudden suspicion, sitting forward in his chair, 'Marquand wasn't ever an enlisted man, was he?'

'I'm just not sure, Commander,' Lieutenant Shoemaker said. 'Anyhow, I think he's old enough that if he was he's got over it by now.'

'Understand, I'm not opposed to the enlisted man, Shoemaker,' the exec said. 'Why, I was the one who thought up and commissioned the Joe Blow Department to glorify the enlisted man.'

'Yes, sir,' Shoemaker said.

'It's just that I just don't happen to think all officers are unfavourable people.'

'No, I guess we've got to have officers,' Lieutenant Shoemaker said.

'You might try to get that viewpoint across to Maugham while he's here.'

'Marquand,' Shoemaker said. 'I'll see what I can do, Commander. But I don't think you need to worry too much about Marquand. He's a very distinguished man of American letters, and I doubt that he's coming all the way out here just to smear officers.'

'Good!' the exec said happily. He anchored himself back again in his chair and parked his hairy legs on the desk. 'Well! Let's stop wasting time,' he said rather reprovingly to Shoemaker, 'and get back to the problem of the one bed in the admiral's quarters. Try this one for size. Bat it around! I'd be inclined to give that bed to Tooney. He's the biggest name by far.'

'H-m-m,' said Shoemaker. 'I guess Tunney is a lot bigger name than Marquand or Howard, but – if you did that, and suppose Howard was a little miffed at a prize-fighter getting the bed …'

'That's true,' Nash said thoughtfully, 'but somebody's got to be miffed. We can't put all three of them in one bed, now, can we? Suppose Marquand is miffed and we don't get that favourable Navy novel? Somebody's going to be miffed, no matter what we do.'

'Yes, sir,' Shoemaker said, 'but say Tunney was miffed – that wouldn't hurt the Navy very much anyhow, would it? Not too many people he could tell. Prize-fighters aren't the most articulate persons in the world as a rule.'

'What's that? what's that?' Nash said suspiciously.

'Prize-fighters aren't usually very good with words,' Shoemaker interpreted, 'so that Tunney would probably be somewhat handicapped even if he should be miffed and want to tell people.'

Nash soberly selected a fresh paper-clip. 'I believe you've got something there,' he agreed.

'And Marquand – even if *he's* sore, it'll take him a couple of years to write a book, even if he wants to mention it. By that time the war may be over. But Howard – he's got *daily* papers he can be miffed in the day after he doesn't sleep in the admiral's bed, if he feels that way.'

'Woodrow,' Nash said decisively, tossing the paper clip firmly into his wastebasket, 'I'll say one thing. You're a wonderful guinea-pig to try an idea out on. The fact was, I had settled on Howard myself. It's good to get it verified.'

A messenger entered with a dispatch. Nash scanned through it but, being absorbed in the Howard–Marquand–Tunney problem, failed to grasp its significance. He picked up his phone.

'Put me through to the billeting officer,' he told the operator. 'Here …' He tossed the dispatch to Shoemaker. 'Something about a new type of bomb. Damn! That Air Force propaganda mill is really something to keep up with … Hello? Billeting officer? Commander Nash, executive officer of the Public Relations detachment, speaking! About that billet in the admiral's quarters. I've got the name you're to put down for it …'

Shoemaker, reading rapidly at first then slowly through the President's announcement, could hear Nash's voice, two feet away, only as from afar.

'Put down Roy Howard … What's that? … I don't care if Lieutenant (jg) Brownell in my office did tell you Gene Tooney would get it, that's wrong! … Brownell works for me and I ought to know … If Tooney's already down, move him out of that bed …'

Lieutenant Shoemaker read it through again, word by word.

'That's what I said!' the executive officer was saying wildly. 'Let's look alive down there, Lieutenant! Kick Gene Tooney out and put in Roy Howard! However, give Tooney and Marquand the two most comfortable non-admiral beds you've got …'

Shoemaker, finishing a third reading, looked up from the dispatch.

'Well! That's taken care of,' Nash said, hanging up crisply. 'Say! I wonder if we might use Tooney in some Navy publicity do. Maybe we can get him to take on a couple of Navy men at the same time in the ring.' The exec's marble-bald head wrinkled in doubt. 'Wouldn't look so good for the Navy, though, if Tooney knocked the Navy men out, would it? Come to think of it, wouldn't look so good if the Navy men knocked Tooney out. It would leave Tooney with some pretty unfavourable memories about the Navy ...'

'Commander,' Shoemaker said, 'this is quite an announcement.'

With no further ado, Shoemaker started in reading it aloud. He read very slowly: '"That bomb had more power than twenty thousand tons of TNT. It had more than two thousand times the blast power of the British 'Grand Slam', which is the largest bomb ever yet used in the history of warfare ... With this bomb we have now added a new and revolutionary increase in destruction ... It is an atomic bomb. It is a harnessing of the basic power of the universe. The force from which the sun draws its powers has been loosed ..."'

More from the way Shoemaker read it than anything else – he had never heard this quiet-mannered officer speak words with such deliberateness, almost awe – Nash gathered that something unusual was afoot.

'The Infernal Air Force,' he said, as if that were the title of the flying organization.

'This is more than just that,' Shoemaker said. 'This is nuclear fission.'

'What's that gibberish?' Nash said. 'What's that? what's that?' he said impatiently.

'Splitting the atom. Getting at the basic source of energy of the universe. The simplest way I know of putting it,' Shoemaker said slowly, spacing the words, 'is that we've arrived at the time when one bomb can destroy the largest city in the world and everyone in it.'

'This is serious,' Nash said. 'We better get a conference together. Yell the yeoman to pass the word, will you, Shoemaker? Just for the hell of it, let's make it an all-officers-invited conference. We'll see just how serious this is.'

Shoemaker walked out and told the yeoman. He went downstairs to the correspondents' room. By this time a copy of the President's announcement had been posted on the bulletin board. Officers and correspondents, wandering in from after-lunch siestas, stopped and read it, and turned to discuss it. A yeoman stood downstairs telling arriving officers to report upstairs for the conference. Shoemaker went into his own office, where he saw lying on his desk the history of the

U.S.S. *Missouri* on which he had been working. He picked up and read the latest item on the ship's bombardment which he had been adding. 'Two freight-cars at Yokoje disabled.' He crumpled the sheet of paper and dropped it in the wastebasket, then paused a moment and picked up the sheaf of several stapled pages containing the ship's complete history and dropped this in the wastebasket, too. He went on out and walked back up the outside staircase.

The greatest concentration of officers Shoemaker had seen outside the bar was waiting outside Nash's office. Soon Nash sent word out to Lieutenant (jg) Calvert Brownell to herd them in. Brownell looked pretty grim.

'All right, gentlemen,' he said. 'The Commander's ready.'

The officers walked in to find the executive officer playing with his sextant. The higher ranks, the lieutenant commanders and lieutenants, took seats, and the jgs and ensigns stood. Some sat on the floor.

'Sailors,' said the exec, when the officers were settled, 'something called nuclear fission, whatever that is, has just rammed the Navy below the belt. You've all read the announcement by now. There'll be Press conferences later by the admirals to place this thing in its proper perspective. Meantime let's don't let this incident throw us. Don't let it let us lose the public-relations war after all our months and years of work. I've been trying to get details on this new-fangled thing. Can't find out a thing about it! Fantastic secrecy! Typical of how the Air Force doesn't trust its sister service. The meatheads,' he muttered.

The exec gazed sombrely at the 'Don't Give Up The Ship!' legend on the wall dead ahead of him.

'We've got to use a little imagination here,' he said, 'to counteract whatever it is.'

The exec, cocking his crossed feet on his desk, commenced to sight on his 'Golden Dragon' diploma with his sextant. 'All right, Sailors,' he said. 'Let's look alive. My hatch is open for ideas.'

'We could lay on a bombardment and carrier raid on Tokyo and adjacent cities,' suggested Lieutenant-Commander Wayne Hereford, 'to counteract this thing.'

'Heavens, Wayne,' the exec said irritably, 'we've been doing that for months. Let's try to be a little original.'

'Yes, sir,' Lieutenant-Commander Hereford said humbly.

'I don't guess the whole thing is a gag, is it?' Lieutenant-Commander Arnold Gladney said.

The exec, lowering his sextant, looked sharply at Gladney. 'Is this your idea of humour, Arnold?'

'Humour?' Gladney said blankly. 'No, sir, I was just thinking how we've caught the others – like the Air Force – exaggerating before. Matter of fact, I think the Air Force has a standing rule to multiply everything by ten. If they knock out one oil storage tank it's ten, a hit on a city block becomes a "devastated mile", one ...'

'Belay it, Arnold,' the exec said impatiently. 'Can't you see the announcement comes from the White House? Are you accusing the White House of exaggeration?'

'No, I guess it's on the level, then,' Gladney admitted doubtfully. 'I guess the White House wouldn't exaggerate.'

'I wouldn't be at all sure of that,' the exec said reprovingly.

The exec looked intently through his sextant. 'Nuclear fission!' he said in a baffled manner. 'I never even heard of the blamed thing.'

'Maybe it'll turn out that a Navy man helped invent this new contraption,' Lieutenant-Commander Hereford suggested. 'The Navy has a lot of research people. I know, because I've got a brother-in-law who's a chief sectional accountant at the Naval Research Laboratory in Washington ...'

'Maybe so, maybe so!' Nash cut off Hereford's take-out on his relatives. 'Maybe a seaman second invented the damn thing for all we know, but that's sheer speculation right now. We've got to take a position on something firmer than speculation.'

Suddenly the exec leaned forward, gesturing with his sextant.

'I've got it! Right now,' he said, 'we'll just take the temporary position that there have always been new weapons ... And there's always been a Navy! These things come and go and still there's the Navy. There'll always be a Navy!'

'Send Navy down the field!' came a singing whisper from the back of the room.

'What's that? What's that?' the exec said, startled.

He couldn't be quite sure he'd heard it – the room was so crowded he couldn't even see everyone from where he sat – and he chose to ignore it.

'There have always been new weapons,' he said. 'That'll be the Navy's official position on this thing.'

'This weapon is really different though,' Shoemaker said. Everyone looked at the historical research man and former editorial writer over in one corner. 'It means one bomb can destroy a whole city. One bomb!' he said with uncharacteristic fervour. 'That's a different weapon!'

The exec stared rigorously at the eye-level 'Don't Give Up The Ship!' legend.

'Like I said ...' he repeated slowly, firmly, 'there have been different weapons before, and you notice we're still around. I'm going to get out a directive on how, if any, this incident affects Navy Public Relations policy. Meantime it doesn't affect it at all. Meantime we're right out there sailing our ships, above and below water, and our planes in the sky. Meantime the Navy goes on carrying the war to the enemy. Sailors!' the exec said, raising his sextant high. 'Steady as you go!'

'We'll never change our course!' sang out a louder whisper from the back of the room. The composer of these chords, Ensign Max Siegel, was seated on the floor and well hidden behind several other officers. Nash looked very startled, but by this time the conference was breaking up and it was too late to catch whoever it was. He sensed that the news about the bomb was breaking – for some reason he couldn't be sure of – into the ranks of discipline. If this continued, he would damn well see that those ranks were reclosed damn firmly.

'Where's Nash?' a loud nasal shout from outside his door cut into these plans of discipline. 'What's that? Another "conference"! God damn it to hell, this is no time for frills. I'm a reporter! I've got a story to do! You people around here know what a *reporter* is?'

In terror the exec recognized the voice of Gordon Ripwell, and presently Ripwell himself brushing past the alarmed Brownell and ploughing his way through the outgoing stream of officers.

'Anything I can do for you, Rip?'

'Do for me! Why weren't we notified ahead of time about this business in Hiroshima?' Ripwell roared. Nash realized now that Ripwell was just back from a trip to the harbour to interview a carrier admiral who had put in to the island or he doubtless would have been in sooner. 'I want to know,' he shouted to Nash in tones of command so that all the officers could hear him, 'why we weren't notified ahead of time …'

'Why, it's very simple, Rip,' Nash explained. 'It was an Air Force show. I have no doubt that if the Navy had been running it, the whole thing would have been handled differently. You know our policy of letting you boys in on everything – ahead of time.'

'Yeh, I know all that guff,' Ripwell said. 'What's wrong with your liaison? This is a perfect example of why I'm for unification!' the correspondent roared. 'But meantime I want to fly over Hiroshima. Right now!'

'Fly over Hiroshima!' Nash said in a spasm, appalled at the project. 'Why, I'm afraid we have no facilities for that, Rip.'

'Facilities! What about all those Navy planes you're always getting out thousands of Press releases on …?'

'A carrier-plane can't quite make it to Hiroshima from here, I don't believe,' Nash said. 'And even if it could, you'd have to ride piggy-back on the pilot – rather uncomfortable for both of you for fifteen hundred miles, I should imagine. Heh, heh …'

'Of course a carrier-plane can't make it! And don't make jokes with me!' Ripwell was outraged. 'I'm talking about all those PBYs you've got up at Guam …'

'Let me look into it, Rip,' Nash said, exhausted, almost panting. 'I'll let you know.'

'Damn quick, too!' Rip said, flinging out of the office. 'Come downstairs the instant you find out!' he flung over his shoulder.

Shoemaker, catching most of Ripwell's conversation, wandered on out. He went to his BOQ and took a shower, then walked over to the new officers' club. It stood beyond him, a beatific, low-slung masterpiece against the Pacific sky. The club always had a nice crowd soon after opening, but this was the first time Shoemaker had ever seen officers standing around waiting for it to open. Twenty or so were gathered outside the locked door. It was embarrassing to see Navy officers waiting like that outside a bar. He wished he had not timed it so closely himself. Fortunately, just as he arrived one of the Marine bartenders opened the door and the officers swarmed in.

The shine of newness was still on the lovely club, and the officers happily took up positions on the luxurious red bankette seats, at the bar and on the terrace outside, by the swimming-pool, under the striped umbrellas which rose smartly above the tables. The officers tended to stay incestuously in their sectional cliques even while drinking – the Communications officers at one table, the Intelligence at another, the Public Relations officers and correspondents at several, there being so many of these and all exceptionally fine club customers. Shoemaker's table out on the terrace was soon full. They drank their rum and whisky sours and watched the picture-postcard view, the Pacific water far below gently jostling the island's shores. Shoemaker drank very little, watching the sun go down.

The correspondent Jerry Wakeley lifted his double shot of whisky and drank it off. 'Two thousand times more powerful than the biggest bomb ever dropped!' he exclaimed. 'Nelson's butt!'

The table lived with the fact a few moments before Harry Knight, a Chicago *Tribune* correspondent, said, 'I'd have given plenty to have been on that one.'

'Yeh, wouldn't we all, Harry?' said Jerry. 'Wouldn't we all?'

Shoemaker wondered what kind of editorial he would be writing on this one if he were back home. He felt very restless, an emotion quite strange to him. Infected partly, he guessed, by the air of restlessness that the news had brought over the Headquarters: the correspondents wanting to be where the story was but being pretty resigned, except for Ripwell, that on this one they just couldn't get there. The Navy officers wondering what next? Is the war about over now? But Lieutenant Shoemaker felt his own restlessness was something more.

After a while Wakeley and Knight got up to go off to dinner. Shoemaker said he believed he'd stay there.

'Never known you to miss the trough at slopping time,' Wakeley said.

'I'm just not hungry, Jerry. Damned if I know why. I'll stick around for a while.'

He was still there after dinner when Lieutenant (jg) Ross Pendleton wandered out to the terrace carrying a drink, and, seeing Shoemaker alone, joined him.

'What a really enormous thing,' Pendleton said affably, slumping into a chair, '– that bomb today! Well, this does it, I guess. Brother, just to think. One month from now, more or less, I'll tell the Navy to stick it and cruise back to Radio City to a man's work again.' Pendleton kissed his fingers. 'Oo-là-là!'

The radio liaison officer turned enthusiastically to Shoemaker. 'Let me tell you about this new show I just completed yesterday for Ivory Flakes,' he said. 'Isn't that marvellous timing? It's called "Ensign June Judson of the Fleet Hospital" – I got the idea right here in the Pacific, so that maybe my Navy duty won't have been a total loss to me. It'll be a psychological drama dealing with the threatened personality changes in a drab little girl who suddenly has thousands of men asking her for dates every night ...'

The former editorial writer turned savagely on Pendleton. 'That's all it means to you, isn't it? That you're back in Radio City. That's all it means to you, isn't it?'

Pendleton was startled.

'What the hell does it mean to you?' he said, getting up in a pet and stalking inside before Shoemaker could tell him.

For a couple of hours Shoemaker sat at the table, as the officers came to the club and went, mostly staying inside now, so that he had the darkening terrace largely to himself. Beyond the swimming-pool he could see, through the huge glass windows, the partitioned-off admirals' bar and lounge. He could see a few figures moving about.

'I wonder what a man who has devoted his whole life to naval strategy and whose whole future lies in it is thinking about now?' he said aloud.

'Promotion boards!' a voice boomed behind him.

Shoemaker jumped. It was Ensign Max Siegel.

'Damn you, Siegel!' Shoemaker said, irritated. 'You scared the hell out of me.'

'You're supposed to be one of those calm types, Shoemaker,' Siegel said, taking a seat and stretching his big legs out far in front of him. 'A double whisky sour, Matey,' he said to the Marine waiter. Siegel noted Shoemaker's empty glass. 'Seconds?'

'No, thanks.'

'What the hell's wrong with you?' Max said as the Marine waiter went off. Shoemaker was known as a man who held his own in the rum sour department.

'You never wrote any editorials, did you, Max?' Shoemaker said abruptly.

'Christ, no!' Siegel said, appalled.

Shoemaker pulled himself up in the chair and crossed his legs, long and white under the khaki shorts. 'I had a pretty good job,' he took off, talking as much to himself as to Siegel. 'Mostly my editors let me write anything I wanted to and my own opinions. For this privilege they exacted what I didn't think an excessive price: every once in a while I had to write an editorial I didn't entirely agree with. That didn't bother me much at the time. I mean, they were so generous in other ways – letting me write generally whatever I liked and giving me a good salary and nice working conditions – that it didn't seem much to ask. But suddenly, since hearing the news today, I find myself very bothered by having written things I didn't fully believe.'

Siegel, surprised at the windy take-out, looked studiously at the Historical officer.

'Well, there was probably very little harm done,' he said, taking the double whisky sour from the Marine, and giving him a dime for it – no tips were allowed. 'I don't want to disillusion you, but not many people I know read editorials. Now, if you'd been writing the copy for Orphan Annie, that would have been something else again.'

'But it's the idea of it!' Shoemaker said. 'You know, this damn bomb today,' he went on. 'You know what Gordon Ripwell's main concern about it is? That President Truman didn't notify him ahead of time. Pendleton – all it means to him is that he's going back to Radio City with a new monstrosity called "Ensign Hotpants Judson of the Fleet Hospital". And Nash – you know what he's worried about? That the Air Force has come up with a public-relations gimmick that's going to be very, very tough to top. Great God! Can't they see?'

Shoemaker leaned almost all the way across the table. 'Brother, you know what happened today? The goddamn world turned inside out, that's what happened. Moses threw the Ten Commandments down off a cloud, a mushroom cloud, and they busted into a million pieces, that's what happened!'

'Busted into a million pieces,' Max said like a refrain. 'Oh, the Ten Commandments, they done bust into a mill-yon pieces ...' He hummed it to a little tune, keeping time on the table with his drink.

'I don't see how any man can look at himself in the mirror from here on unless he's doing something about this,' Shoemaker said.

'Well, you can write a series of editorials on it when you get back.' Siegel beat time on the table. 'Go down, Moses,' he sang to the tune of the spiritual, 'and bust them Ten Commandments. ...'

'Editorials!' Shoemaker exclaimed it like a dirty word. 'I'm finished writing editorials. I'm going up tonight to get off a letter resigning my civilian job. You're absolutely right. Nobody ever reads the damn things. I've got to do something, Max! Something that counts!'

'You might start by going up and shooting Marblehead,' Siegel said, tasting his drink.

'No, no!' Shoemaker exclaimed. 'That's the wrong approach. You've got to *understand* people.'

Shoemaker told Siegel, who was looking quite studiously at him, how Nash had got the news while trying to figure out sleeping arrangements for Tunney, Marquand, and Howard.

'You've got to try to understand what it is that makes a man like Nash more concerned with where Gene Tunney is going to sack out than with the meaning of the atom bomb. We've got to do something to stop the world from going up in a chain of mushroom clouds!'

Siegel yawned. 'As between those two projects I don't know which would be the more difficult – understanding Nash or stopping all those mushroom clouds.'

Shoemaker gave a shudder through his long body. 'Max, how you can sit there and be flippant about nuclear fission is beyond me. I'm really quite surprised at you.'

Siegel sipped his drink. 'Woodrow, what the hell's wrong with you? You know what? You're probably the only person on this whole island who's worried about this damn thing.'

'No thinking man ...' Shoemaker began.

'No, Woodrow. You're beginning to sound like one of your editorials.' Siegel leaned across the table. 'Woodrow,' he said conspiratorially, 'I tell you. I'll bet you we can't find another soul in all Tulura who's worried about what happened up there.'

'If I believed that' – Shoemaker's eyes were missionary-like – 'if I believed that, I'd go out and shoot myself.'

'No thinking man,' Siegel said absently.

Siegel swallowed the rest of his drink. 'Woodrow, I tell you. I'll bet you a month's ration of whisky we can't find another soul!'

Ensign Siegel stood up and his voice rang with sudden spirit across the deserted terrace. 'Oh, bust the Ten Commandments!' Siegel's big hands pulled at Shoemaker's arms, yanking the Historical officer to his feet. 'Come on, Lieutenant! Let's search the joint!'

As they started off, Siegel said, almost as if he hoped it would be that way, 'Let's prove Max Siegel is sour, perverse, cynical – in a word, wrong.'

The two officers bounded their way off the terrace and around the clubhouse. They crossed the tennis-courts and the handball courts, heading vaguely for the BOQs beyond.

'Handball!' exclaimed Siegel. 'Our British comrade's game. Let's see how the Badger's standing the shock!'

Presently the two Americans were bursting into the BOQ room of Lieutenant-Commander O. S. B. Badgett, of His Majesty's Navy. They found him propped up comfortably in bed, with his walking-shorts on and his shoes and shirt off – reading some American funny papers. The Badger was fascinated by this form of U.S. culture, and always gathered the funnies up in the Public Relations Section, which subscribed to dozens of U.S. newspapers, and brought them back to his room to pore over. He never threw any away, but had an enormous stack beside the wall, reading old ones whenever he ran out. He looked piously at the two intruders over the luxuriant red-black beard which fell to his navel and above which he had to hold the funny papers.

'Hail, fur-bearing Briton!' said Siegel, raising his arm.

'Come in, ye American bastards,' the Badger, who was a rather unorthodox liaison officer, said. He laid the funnies aside. 'Just catching up on my professional reading. And a ho-ho-ho. Who said the British don't have a sense of humour? Ho-ho.'

The Badger dug through his beard to scratch the big blob of hair on his chest. Body and head, including face, he probably had more hair on him than any human being, and most animals, in the Pacific.

'We expected to find you on your knees,' Siegel said.

'But it isn't Sunday,' the Badger said. 'And a ho-ho-ho. Besides, can I help it if you heathen Americani don't have a proper Anglican cathedral and order of worship on Tulura? It's a choice between the Romans and The Roll Is Called Up Yonder. I'm too old and civilized to change to either.'

'Nevertheless,' Siegel said, 'we expected to find you on your knees praying for mankind's deliverance from the mushrooms. Funny papers! How can you read funny papers on a night like this! That's what Shoemaker here wants to know. He's just too stunned by the repulsive sight of you to ask it himself.'

'W'y, Gov'nor, there no plice on this h'island where h'a man can get 'is wick properly dipped,' the Badger said, 'h'and that's w'y h'I'm with these papers, Gov'nor.'

Shoemaker cut in impatiently: 'Badger, what was the first thing you thought of when you got the news?'

The Badger pondered a moment. 'Well, frankly, lads, I wondered if we Limeys had been cut in on this deal, too – that is, did we have the blooming thing also – or were you Yanks keeping them all up your own bloody sleeves?'

'There you have it, Shoemaker,' Siegel said triumphantly. 'The nationalistic attitude. Pretty soon he'll be quoting Rudyard Kipling to us.'

Siegel suddenly burst into a tempestuous rendition of 'The Road to Mandalay', the Badger joining in eagerly on the final bars.

'I just hope you Americans leave us something as fine as that from your term of totin' the white man's burden,' the Badger said.

'Briton,' Siegel said, 'enough of this chauvinism. Tonight we're on a treasure hunt. We're trying to find one soul who's worried about the bomb. Besides old Shoe here, that is. Fetch your ass along.'

The Badger instantly put on his British woollen half-socks, which came to just below his knees, his shoes, and a shirt, and stuck a couple of bottles of Johnny Walker black label, of which he had private sources from British ships, in a musette bag and flung it over his shoulder.

'Let's go call on Frank Williamson,' said Siegel. 'He was with Dewey at Manila and is as wise as an old owl, or should be.'

Frank Williamson was a great oddity among correspondents. He had actually been on Admiral Dewey's flagship in 1898, and in 1905 he had covered the Battle of Tsushima in the Russo-Japanese War – from the decks of a Jap man-o'-war. He had been covering wars since. He gave his age as fifty-three, which meant he would have had to be six years old when he was with Dewey. He looked about ninety, but was probably only seventy-five. The Public Relations Section lived in eternal terror that something would happen to him – like a head cold or twisted ankle, either of which might kill him off. Public Relations didn't want Frank dying on their hands out here. It would look as if they weren't giving correspondents the proper care. The slightest sign of a minor ailment and Nash sent steaming over to his room a whole task force of Navy doctors, whom Frank promptly threw out with a volley of insults, suggesting they mind their own business. Nash finally appointed a lieutenant (jg) as officer-in-charge of Frank Williamson. The jg's sole duty was to keep an eye on Frank and give the exec a daily report on his welfare. The jg had to be as stealthy as a private eye, since Frank would have blown the roof off if he had known about him. The Public Relations people really wished he hadn't come to this war, but you couldn't tell him he was too old.

The trio of Allied officers made their way across the ridge to the correspondents' BOQ. They found Williamson's room, but it was dark inside – though he wouldn't admit it, Frank had to go to bed early to keep up what little energy his ageing body supplied him. Nevertheless they gave the door a respectful knock, and an uncertain noise, like a croak, came from inside. Siegel opened the door and turned on the light. An old man wearing a nightcap sat up in bed. He looked at least a hundred. A nightcap! The tableau of three officers gazed at the old man. He stared back at the tableau: the bearded Britisher, that incredibly ugly young man Siegel, and the pale-faced, long-faced Shoemaker who turned out that research on the number of snakes on Okinawa.

'Mind if we come in, Frank?' Siegel asked politely.

Frank resented anyone calling him 'Mr Williamson', which everyone naturally would have, as a suggestion he was old.

'You already have,' Frank said brusquely. 'What do you want?' he demanded.

He sat up in bed. Now the officers could make out he had no clothes on. The ribs showed through his thin chest, furred with clumps of snow-white hair. He really looked like Father Time.

'How extraordinary, Frank!' the Badger could not help remarking. 'You mean you sleep in a nightcap and nothing else?'

'Did you wake me up to ask me about my sleeping habits?' Frank croaked acidly. 'What the hell are you doing in my room?'

'Frank,' Siegel said diplomatically, 'we just wanted to bat the breeze a little about the old days.'

The old correspondent's face brightened. As possibly the only living naval correspondent from as far back as Dewey, and certainly the only unretired one, he liked to be asked about those days.

'What was the Navy like in Dewey's time anyhow?' Siegel asked in a friendly manner.

'A real Navy,' Frank intoned benevolently.

'It must be something,' Siegel said respectfully, 'to have seen it grow from the little thing it was then to today when it's bigger than all the navies of history put together.'

'Bigger, yes,' Frank said briskly. 'But I never did put much stock in quantity. The quality of your officer corps is what counts.'

'Well, you take ComFleets,' Siegel began. 'I'd say he's doing a brill …'

'He's a promising young officer, I'll admit,' Frank cut in. 'I'm personally very fond of the lad. But he'll never be the man Dewey was.'

'A great naval commander, Dewey,' Siegel hurried to agree. 'No question about that.'

'Dewey would never have tolerated a travel agency like this around him. Also' – Frank looked keenly at Shoemaker – 'Dewey would never have tolerated giving a commission as a United States naval officer to research assistants, or' – he looked at Siegel – 'hotel clerks.'

'Well, a big Navy does have to be specialized,' Shoemaker objected mildly.

'Specialized hell!' Williamson's voice suddenly shook. 'Dewey didn't have to know how many snakes were in the city of Manila in order to sink the Spanish.'

'How did they do it in the Russo-Jap War, Frank?' the Badger asked, as both Shoemaker and Siegel seemed momentarily at a loss for something to say. 'What was that war like?'

The old correspondent's face shone again. As possibly the only American correspondent who had seen that war, he liked to be asked about it, too.

'Good fighters, the Japs,' he said affably.

'Did you foresee then,' said the Badger, 'that you Americans would one day be fighting them?'

'No, I'd be bragging if I said that. Using hindsight, which I never use. I did use to think the whole Orient was going to rise up and throw the white man right out of Asia. Especially the British. Which still may happen, may I be permitted to observe?' Frank said, looking keenly at the beard.

'A good thing, too,' Siegel said. 'It's high time the British got the hell out of here.'

'You don't mind if we keep Scotland, do you?' the Badger asked.

Now Shoemaker leaned forward to ask his question and to hang on the old correspondent's answer, like a man seeking the great wisdom.

'Frank,' he asked, 'what did you think of the bomb?'

'Which bomb?'

Shoemaker squinted. 'The one dropped today, Frank. The atomic bomb.'

'Oh, that bomb. Well, I have seen many new weapons come along,' Frank said. 'I saw the tank first used, and I saw the aeroplane used for the first time in war ...' His words fell so sagelike, one almost expected him to say, 'I saw the bow and arrow first used.' He went on: 'I would like to have seen that bomb dropped, too. I don't guess any outsider did, though, did they?' he said vaguely.

'No, I guess not,' Siegel said kindly. 'Just the crew, so far as we know.'

'Frank, listen,' Shoemaker said earnestly. 'You've seen a lot of wars. You saw the tank and the airplane introduced, as you say. You've seen dozens of new weapons, I suppose. But can't you see that this is different?' Shoemaker spoke hopefully. 'Can't you see it isn't just another weapon? Can't you?'

Frank started going under the covers. The impudence of this young fool, questioning his estimate on a military matter! 'Actually,' he said curtly, sliding down in bed, 'there is nothing new under the sun. When you've lived longer you'll know that. I think Ecclesiastes may have been the first to say it.'

'But this *is* new, Frank!' Shoemaker was a little desperate now, wanting to make the old man see it. If he, who had seen so many wars and weapons, could see it, it would mean much. 'It's different. We've got to do something about it! Something to stop it!'

'You never change human nature, young man,' old Williamson said, pulling his nightcap down over his ears, as if to shut out the noise, and the covers up under his chin. 'I hope to live to cover one more war.'

'Cover one more war!' Shoemaker exclaimed, outraged. 'Why, Frank, that's positively ghoulish.'

Frank Williamson looked intently over the covers at the lieutenant. It was time to put him in his place. 'I never talk with do-gooders at this hour,' he said. 'I bid you good night.'

'But, Frank ...' Shoemaker began again frantically.

Siegel pulled at Shoemaker's arm. 'Let's go,' he said, 'and let Frank get some sleep.'

The old man stuck his head out of the covers like an ancient turtle out of its shell. It was a hot night, but he had three Navy white wool blankets over him. 'The first sensible words I have heard since my sleep was disturbed,' he snapped. 'Turn out the lights as you leave.'

As they closed the door the officers heard a sneeze, or wheeze.

'Hope we didn't make the old boy catch cold,' the Badger said. 'A single young germ would probably kill him off, especially if British.'

'And Nash would court-martial us all for manslaughter,' Siegel added.

'Even old Frank Williamson!' Shoemaker exclaimed. 'He's just sorry he didn't see it, like he saw the first tank and the first airplane. That's all it means to him! And he's old enough to know better!' he said, discouraged.

'He's old enough, all right,' Siegel said.

'Don't let your chin drag in the bloody gravel, Woodrow,' the Badger said as they came outside.

The officers stood for a few moments, uncertainly, on the grass apron of the BOQ.

'You know,' Shoemaker said, 'maybe we ought to get a woman's viewpoint. Women – they've got a bigger stake in this than men.'

'How the hell do you figure that?' Siegel said.

'Well,' Shoemaker said, 'they bear the children.'

'I can't argue with that,' Siegel said.

'How about Janey of the all-healing American Red Cross?' the Badger said. 'Why don't we drop in on Janey?'

'He said a woman,' Siegel said.

'She's much more so than you'd think,' the Badger said mysteriously. 'Nothing homelier than an oyster shell, but inside there dwell sometimes glistening pearls.'

'You Limey whoremonger,' Siegel said.

'Just doin' my bit to spread the joy around,' the Badger said.

The Badger–Janey romance must have been one of the strangest love affairs in the history of war, which brings on a lot of strange love affairs. The Red Cross employed some very pretty girls during the war, but most of these went to the ETO. The left-overs got sent to the Pacific. Janey was a broad-shouldered, big-thighed, red-faced creature to whom the Badger, for some odd reason, was attracted and went out with regularly. No one could quite understand it. Maybe this huge character was the Badger's idea of American womanhood and he wanted to try it. Even more strangely, Janey was Boston Irish and violently anti-British, a fact which she never attempted to hide from her British paramour.

Picking up the jeep which the Badger had permanently assigned to him, the three officers drove down the hill to the nearby Island Command area and around a corner to a Quonset hut, where the Badger pulled up.

'All dark in there, isn't it?' the Badger said, getting out. 'Just stand by, chaps; I know where her cage is.'

Sidling down to almost midway in the Quonset, the Badger pulled one of his Johnny Walker black labels from the musette bag and started drawing the neck of it across the Quonset screen, making a rasping, penetrating noise.

'What the hell's going on out there?' a guttural voice soon came from inside.

'You'd never guess that was a woman, would you?' Siegel said to Shoemaker in the jeep.

'Me, Turtledove,' the Badger's high British accent emerged from a shadow down the way.

'It's the Limey!' said the basso voice inside. 'What do you think you're doing here, Lord Nelson?'

'Just paying a friendly social call,' the Badger said, 'turtledove. Slip on something and come on out here. I've got a couple of chaps with me.'

'A couple of chaps?' Janey did a British-accent mimic. 'What do you take me for, you Limey bastard?'

'Now, Turtledove,' the Badger said. 'We just want to chit-chat.' In the half-moon dark the Badger held up something. 'Also we've got a little Johnny Walker black label to take the chill off.'

'Black label!' the guttural voice said enthusiastically. 'Why didn't you say so?'

Presently the front door of the Quonset opened and a largish hulk of a rumpled figure in a Red Cross uniform stepped out, pulling down her skirts. The Badger, whom she dwarfed, led her over to the jeep.

'You know these chaps – Max Siegel and Woodrow Shoemaker – don't you, Janey?' the Badger said, helping her, as she hoisted her shovel-like hips into the front seat, from where the two officers in the back quickly became aware she had been doing a little drinking already.

'Oh, yes, I know these chaps,' Janey said, mimicking the Badger's British accent with her own virile Boston–Irish tongue.

The Badger slid in behind the driver's seat, uncorked a bottle of the black label, and passed it to Janey. From the back seat Siegel and Shoemaker heard three long gurgles. The three males in turn lowered the level.

'One of the few nice things about associating with Limeys,' Janey said, starting the second round, 'is that where drinking whisky is concerned they always have the finest. Their finest hour,' she said.

'Turtledove,' the Badger said forgetfully, leaning towards her slightly, 'you always say the sublimest things.'

'Turtledove!' said Siegel from the back seat.

'Not here, for Christ's sake, you fur-bearing Limey!' Janey said, giving the Badger a push that sent him slapping back against his seat.

'Pardon my natural British sense of affection,' the Badger said.

'Don't I know it!' said Janey.

'Actually,' said the Badger, 'we're gathered together here for something much less intimate. Janey, you're two things – a woman and a representative of a bloody humanitarian organization, the American Red Cross. Isn't that right?'

'Don't bloody me, you hairy Limey bastard,' Janey said. 'Get on with it.'

'As both,' the Badger went on, 'but mainly as a woman, we have a question we want to ask you. It's this. What was your reaction' – the Badger belched – 'when you heard the news today about the new bomb – the atomic bomb?'

Janey waited a moment, turning the bottle in her hands.

'You know, I felt like going out and getting drunk.'

'You did?' popped up Shoemaker eagerly from the back seat.

'So I did just that. Me and Ross Pendleton and Morey Griffin and, gee, there must have been seven or eight men there and just me.'

'I think it's wonderful it hit you that hard, Janey,' Shoemaker said.

'Yes, sir. I heard about that little old bomb dropping, and I just felt like getting drunk – and crying,' she said softly.

'I knew it,' Shoemaker said happily. 'I knew a woman would get it.'

'That bomb ...' Janey went on, 'it meant the war was going to be over two years before I thought it was. It meant I was going home.'

Suddenly she gave a loud sniff, which sounded like a sow snuffling.

'No more Morey Griffins and Ross Pendletons! No more Badgers!' she said, touching him hesitantly on his beard. 'No more just little me and all these thousands of men, men, men!'

'Now, now, old girl,' the Badger said.

'No more turning men down for dates!' she sniffed. 'No more chance to, even!'

'Dates! Men!' Shoemaker suddenly turned on her savagely. 'The bomb means you aren't going to have any more dates and that's why you're sorry about it! Why, that's outrageous! You ought to be thinking about humanity!'

'Humanity!' Janey turning around in her seat, spat back at the Historical officer. 'What do you think *I* am! You bastards make me sick. You blabber about humanity, and all you think about is laying us,' she said incisively.

She took another stiff drink from the bottle and suddenly laughed gaily.

'Why the hell do I want a husband, anyhow? I'll be damned if I know. All they do is order you around and make you mop up after them,' she summed up the relationship. 'Still, I'd liked to have caught one of the bastards,' she said nostalgically. 'That's why I hated to see that damn thing dropped today.'

'How selfish can you get?' Shoemaker said.

'Listen, old man,' the Badger said. 'How about layin' off Janey? How would you like it if you'd just lost all your girl friends?'

'He probably hasn't got any,' Janey said. She leaned over affectionately against the Badger, then with her ham-like hands parted his beard and kissed his lips. 'You old hairy Limey,' she said, yanking his beard. 'You old ...'

Suddenly her head slipped down and, as the Badger caught the bottle from her hands, she was out cold in his beard.

The Badger patted her head a moment, then gave orders.

'All right, mates,' he said. 'Let's lend a hand here.'

The three of them, straining somewhat, carried the weighty Red Cross load inside the Quonset and to a room which the Badger seemed able to find in the dark with no difficulty. There they gingerly deposited her on a bunk. For a moment the Badger stood tenderly watching the huge sprawled form. Then he reached into his musette bag, pulled out the unopened bottle of Johnny Walker, and placed it on the bureau above her.

As the three got back in the jeep the Badger said, 'It may seem strange, but that girl has a curious attraction for me.'

'You keep talking like that, chappie,' Siegel said, 'and little Janey's Pacific quest will not have been in vain.'

'But she doesn't care much about the atomic bomb,' Shoemaker said sadly.

'I don't care much for it myself,' Siegel said. 'I tell you, let's go get the official word. I have in mind that we ought to interview Admiral Boatwright.'

'Admiral Boatwright!' Shoemaker exclaimed.

'Yes,' Siegel said, 'let's go call on the brains of the Pacific War. Or perhaps instead of a personal call we might be able to communicate with him more effectively by telephone – that way our rank would be a little less of a barrier to him. We might borrow the telephone setup in Lieutenant-Commander Nash's office.'

The three officers drove back up the hill to the Public Relations building and walked, weaving somewhat from the black label, up to the darkened second floor and into the office of the executive officer. Ensign Siegel switched on a light.

'Don't give up the ship, I frequently say,' he said, reading the legend on the wall in front of the exec's desk. 'Now, Sailors, let's look alive! Latch on to a couple of those phones out there ...'

Leaving the door open, the Badger and Shoemaker arranged themselves at connecting phones. Siegel, reaching into Nash's drawer, took out Nash's binoculars and slung them around his neck. He noticed the Bowditch on the desk with several bookmarks in it and reflected on the exec's long course of study. He got out Nash's sextant. Settling back comfortably into the exec's chair, he planted his crossed legs on the desk and commenced expertly bringing images into contact in the horizon glass, bringing the ship's bell down to the wastebasket under it, the Merrill Lynch citation down to the top of an armchair. Presently he laid the sextant down, picked up Nash's phone and dialled the quarters of Admiral Boatwright. A gruff, sleepy voice answered.

'Admiral Boatwright there?' Siegel said in a blast. 'Sorry to get you out of bed, old man.'

'Who the hell is this?' the admiral said irritably.

'Roy Howard here!' Siegel said enthusiastically. 'Gene Tunney, Jack Marquand, and I just blew in.'

'Well!' a suddenly cheerful voice came from the other end. 'Welcome aboard, Mr Howard! I hope you had a nice flight out.'

'Well, Marquand and I did all right, but Tunney got airsick as usual. Just between you and me, Admiral,' Ensign Siegel said, lowering his voice confidentially, 'I don't understand how he ever won the championship. Aside from that, Admiral, I suppose you've been wondering why I'm calling you at this ridiculous hour.'

'Oh, not at all, Mr Howard,' the admiral said genially. 'Anything we can do for you any time.'

'A friendly attitude!' Ensign Siegel said. 'A friendly attitude indeed, and one I'm not likely to forget next time I write something about the Navy. Yes, sir! As a matter of fact, there is something, Admiral,' Siegel said in confidential tones. 'I'm doing a rush-job think-piece for my papers to be printed in my whole chain – circulation thirty-five million – on this business up at Hiroshima and I'd like to get your views, such as they are. In the first place, Admiral, what are your feelings about the bomb off the top of your head?'

'Well, the reports are still coming in,' Admiral Boatwright said cagily. 'But it looks like a very interesting weapon.'

'Then I can quote you, "Admiral Boatwright says atomic bomb is 'fascinating weapon'."'

'No, no, I don't believe you'd better do that,' Admiral Boatwright said uneasily.

'All right, then; let's begin all over,' Siegel said a little impatiently. 'I'll ask you this one: Do you think this new bomb will revolutionize the art of warfare?'

'Well, sir ...' Boatwright hedged. 'War principles have always been the same, however weapons changed. In general, I'd say the Navy would be able to adapt it to its own uses, though as to the revolution part – well, as I say, war principles remain the same. In any case, I'd say it was too soon to tell. After all it was only dropped yesterday morning.'

'Then I'll just say you don't know a damn thing about it,' Siegel said curtly. 'All right, Boatwright, this is your last chance: Do you or don't you think the Air Force dropped the atomic bomb for the sole and exclusive purpose of stabbing the Navy in the back?'

'See here, Mr Howard ...' said the admiral.

'Admiral, I'm afraid that's all the time I can give you,' Siegel cut in, signalling frantically to the Badger at the phone outside the door. 'But here's Gene Tunney wants to say hello to you. Don't mention what I said about him getting airsick,' Siegel whispered. 'He's a little sensitive about it.'

'Good morning, Admiral,' the very British voice spoke loudly into the telephone. 'How's about a few rounds of sparring – just you and me? I'll do it with one hand tied behind my back. Ho-ho-ho.'

'Did you say this was Mr Tunney?'

'I know what you're thinking, Admiral. But I'm direct from an exhibition bout in London, and some of that blooming Limey gloss is still on me. Those bastards, the Limeys, I fixed their bloody arses,' the Badger said, chuckling. 'Put three of them in dreamland in one round each, ho-ho.'

'That's enough, Gene,' Siegel cut in quickly on the phone. 'Isn't Tunney a bore, Admiral? Thinks he has a sense of humour, but I can tell you it wears pretty thin after five thousand miles with him. However, Marquand is very anxious to speak to you, Admiral, and I know you are to him. I realize you don't read much, Admiral' – Siegel lowered his voice to a confidential whisper – 'but at least have the decency to pretend you've heard of one of our most distinguished men of letters. I'd hate to see you embarrassing the Navy. Also, he's a little shy, like most writers, so try to put him at ease, if you know how to do such a thing. Here's Marquand!'

In the suspicious silence on the other end, Siegel clapped his hand over his phone and yelled out the door to Shoemaker, who had been sitting in a thoughtful daze:

'Shoemaker! Admiral Boatwright wants to talk to you.'

'To me?' Shoemaker said, grabbing the phone. 'Sir,' Shoemaker said into the mouthpiece, 'it would mean a lot to me if you, as a man who knows warfare, would tell me your true opinion of the atomic bomb. I'm sorry to disturb you, sir, since I'm only a lieutenant ...'

Dropping his own phone like a hot grenade, Siegel made a flying tackle through the door and landed squarely on the conversing Shoemaker with a horrible crash. As Shoemaker lay sprawled on the floor with the breath knocked out of him, noises came through the dangling receiver.

'Operator, operator!' Admiral Boatwright was saying.

'Yes, sir,' another voice came in.

'Where is this call coming from?' the Boatwright voice demanded.

'Commander Nash's office, sir.'

'Nash!' Boatwright bellowed.

Simultaneously Siegel and the Badger scooped up the gasping Shoemaker and dragged him outside and into the jeep. With Siegel driving, the jeep sped down the hill, stirring up a high gust of wind.

'I guess he didn't get it either, did he?' Siegel said.

'You know he really didn't,' Shoemaker said thoughtfully.

'He got too bloody much, if you ask me,' the Badger said. 'I suggest we get as far away from this installation as possible. You don't know of any ship leaving for Australia or other friendly soil, do you?'

Keeping the accelerator fairly flattened, Siegel started bounding them across the wild-seeming island, along the ridges, and down through the boondocks where the road wound its way. Shimmerings of light were beginning to trace the sky. Suddenly they were ascending a long hill so steep that Siegel had to shift into second and finally into low as they neared its crest. Then they were over it and what they saw below brought Siegel's foot automatically off the gas-feed and sliding the jeep to a stop over at the side of the road.

There lay the island, spread out greenly below them, mile upon mile of dew-glistening trees and vegetation thick enough to give the illusion that one could walk across the green carpet top to the sea beyond, and the clean, clean smell of earth and morning rising up to them. Siegel said, as in a spell, 'Look.'

Over to the left side, and close enough to them it seemed they were looking directly down upon it, was a small fishing village. On the beach some fishermen were shoving their boat out, and the faint echoes of their shouts rose happily to the three naval officers on the hill.

'Nice, isn't it?' Siegel said.

Siegel, suddenly realizing he had Nash's binoculars around his neck, lifted them to his eyes and for a few moments watched the fishermen going about their tasks. Through the powerful binoculars Siegel could make out the most minute details – the faces of the fishermen and the veined pattern of their nets. He passed the binoculars to the Badger, who also sighted for a while.

'Charming,' said the Badger, who started to give the binoculars to Shoemaker, but, seeing he was in such a daze, returned them to Siegel.

Ensign Siegel looked again, and this time let his binoculared eyes rest on a smaller hilltop, where, amid the thatched-roof houses, stood out a gleaming, brand-new building of wood-and-concrete block construction. To Siegel it looked greatly beautiful sitting there. A smile began to come across his face. The Seabees, he thought, certainly did a fine job on that schoolhouse.

Now down the hill in the distance they saw a silhouette move upwards. It came on slowly and Siegel, peering through the binoculars, could make out a cart drawn by a water-buffalo, and driven by someone he knew. The cart disappeared around a curve, then came on steadily, strongly, and crested the hill.

'Morning, Mr Seguro!' Siegel called out.

'En-sine!' Mr Seguro shouted happily, pulling his beast to a stop. 'What're you doing up here this time of day? Pretty early for Yewnited States Navy to be out of bed.'

'We haven't even been in it, Mr Seguro,' Siegel said in Tuluran. 'I'm just showing these tourists what a nice place you've got here. Mr Seguro, this is Commander Badgett, one of our British friends, and Lieutenant Shoemaker.'

The two officers and the Tuluran said hello, each in his own language. Ensign Siegel and Mr Seguro chatted for a while before Siegel asked, 'Did you hear the news about the bomb, Mr Seguro, the big bomb?'

'Big bomb?' Mr Seguro said. 'What bomb would that be, Ensine? Would that be the bombs your B-29s are dropping all the time on enemy Japan?'

'No, Mr Seguro ...' Siegel started.

'You can't tell me anything about the B-29s,' Mr Seguro said, drawing himself up with dignity on his cart. 'I see them fly over all the time – dozens of them. Why you would think I don't know about the B-29s. ..?'

'No, Mr Seguro ...'

'I know everything about the B-29s!' Mr Seguro said huffily.

'Mr Seguro,' Ensign Siegel said hurriedly, 'this is an entirely new type of bomb ...'

And Ensign Siegel, speaking rapidly to get it in, gave his Tuluran friend a brief fill-in on nuclear fission. When he had finished, Mr Seguro smiled and shook his head.

'What'll they think up next?' he said. 'So you were out to Melora's house three times last week, En-sine?'

Siegel was a little startled both at the abrupt change of subject and at the detailed nature of Mr Seguro's information.

'Well, I've been playing chess with Mr Alba,' Siegel felt he had to explain.

'How did you like the walk along the beach?' Mr Seguro said acutely.

Siegel felt quite exposed. 'Well, Melora and I just thought we'd take a walk,' he said lamely, and then he felt unhappy, remembering the end of that walk. Melora, he thought. Melora, Melora, Melora.

'Well, En-sine,' Mr Seguro said, having reasserted his knowledge of everything that went on in Tanalolo, 'I've got to get to the coconut grove. We're making a new batch of palm toddy today. It'll be ready next week. You come by.'

'Thank you, Mr Seguro,' Siegel said, and he felt quite unhappy. 'I'll do that.'

When Mr Seguro had pulled away, Ensign Siegel started up the jeep. As he eased it slowly down the hill, he started giving the Badger and Shoemaker a rough translation of Mr Seguro's reaction to the big news.

'He didn't get it either,' Lieutenant Shoemaker said dejectedly. 'But of course he hasn't had much education.'

'Oh, I don't know,' Siegel said, watching the fishing-boat moving out to sea now. 'Maybe he's the only one who did get it. "What'll they think up next?"'

Ensign Siegel drove very slowly through the village of Tanalolo listening to the first stirrings of day in the houses. He felt strangely depressed. It was still early by the time, a while later, they ascended another hill, leading to Navy Headquarters.

Lieutenant Shoemaker, who seemed thoroughly dejected now, asked Siegel to stop at his BOQ. He went inside and returned carrying two bottles of whisky and one of burgundy, which he held out to Siegel.

'Congratulations,' he said.

Siegel didn't seem to see the whisky. Shoemaker wrapped it in an old Navy blanket which was crumpled up on the floor of the jeep and put it against the seat.

'Would you mind dropping me at Headquarters?' Shoemaker said. 'I've got a little work to do.'

The Badger gazed in astonishment at Lieutenant Shoemaker. 'At this time of day?' he said. 'Bloody Mary, don't you Americans ever stop? Personally, I'm going to hit the sack for the duration, which shouldn't be long.'

Siegel and the Britisher deposited Shoemaker at Headquarters. They started back down the hill to the BOQs. Suddenly Ensign Siegel spoke. 'Badger,' he said, 'could I borrow your jeep? I want to go see somebody.'

'Bloody Mary, you, too?' the Badger said.

Lieutenant Shoemaker watched the jeep spin down the hill and then walked slowly into the Public Relations building. He went back into the Historical office and sat down at his typewriter. It was eerily quiet. He got out a sheet of bond paper and typed a salutation to the editor of his paper. He wrote the first line: 'I have decided not to return to my position with the paper after the war ...' Then he stopped, folded his arms across the typewriter, and rested his head. He remained that way, fearfully awake, for at least ten minutes. Suddenly he lifted his head, pulled the embryo letter out of his typewriter, and crumpled it.

What the hell? he thought. If they don't care, why should I? Why should I do anything but go back and write editorials that nobody reads? He reached into the wastebasket, pulled out some other papers he had crumpled yesterday afternoon – it seemed a century ago. He smoothed them out and put them in the centre drawer of his desk. Then he went outside and walked down the slope and into his room and pulled off his clothes. For the first time in his life Lieutenant Shoemaker felt old. He stood a moment, long, white, and naked. Suddenly, for no reason he could think of, he felt a lot better. I think I'll sleep all day, after all, he thought as he climbed into his sack, and wait until tomorrow to work on that history of the U.S.S. *Missouri* and naval bombardment.

The Badger went straight to his BOQ, took a long last swallow of his Johnny Walker black label, thought how excited Americans can get about things, combed his beard, and hit the sack. Just before he fell asleep with his beard in his navel, he thought about Janey and, startled, thought she might actually be a lot of fun back in England.

Ensign Max Siegel drove down the long hill towards the sea, which was catching up the morning light. He kept thinking of Mr Seguro's words, 'What'll they think up next …?' Well, what would they? Against his heel he could feel the bottles wrapped in the blanket. Never, he thought, had he been less happy to win a bet.

What'll they think up next? he thought. Don't know, don't care, don't intend to stick around to see, he thought, pointing the jeep back down the road which led across the island to Tanalolo. And Melora.

Ten: All good things must come to an end

THE spirit that filled the officers' club was an odd mixture. It was the relieved feeling that before long none of them there would ever see the others again, and the feeling permitted by this, that they hadn't been such bad fellows after all. The new officers' club, achieved by such sweat and tears, was as delightful a place as one could have chosen to observe the end of the war, and everyone had chosen it. Rigged in 'full dress' with dozens of Navy pennants and flags which streamed brilliantly from lines near the ceiling, and crowded to the last inch with celebrating officers, it was a picture of the greatest gaiety. The pennants and flags had been procured from the Fleet Supply officer by Ensign Max Siegel, who had been chosen by the acclamation of all hands to arrange the celebration and serve as master of ceremonies for any proceedings. On the bandstand in the corner the officers' club orchestra, a group of enlisted men, was filling the air with music, and Marine bartenders wearing red jackets above their khaki pants scampered back and forth keeping the drinks filled. Tonight even the usual price of five cents a drink had been abolished. Anticipating at least two more years of hostilities, the club had fore-sightedly laid in heavy stores. Now the abrupt end of the war had caught it with a monstrous over-supply of bourbon, rye, Scotch, and rum. To help equalize this situation, all drinks were on the house. By ten o'clock strong depletions were being made in the over-supply, but a great deal more remained to be made, and the celebration, which had begun four hours earlier, was none the less still on the shank of the evening.

'We have not yet,' said Ensign Siegel at one point, paraphrasing a famous naval quotation, 'begun to drink.'

But it was neither the Four Roses nor the end of the war that made Ensign Siegel, sitting at his table on the edge of the dance-floor, feel so remarkably free and light-headed. It was his guest for the occasion, and he had trouble even momentarily taking his awe-filled eyes off her where she sat across from him. A good many other officers were having the same trouble, and ensigns, jgs, lieutenants, lieutenant-commanders, and upper ranks kept hanging around the table like flies around honey. Melora was creating quite as much interest as the termination of hostilities. Siegel had never seen her so beautiful. The white-linen party dress set off her palomino skin and her long black hair in an effect the Hollywood gown-men so often strive for and so seldom achieve, probably because they have so much less to work with. The other women in the club, nurses and Red Cross girls, also were casting many looks, of a green hue, upon Melora. 'I wouldn't look bad either in a party dress like that,' the massive Red Cross girl,

Janey, muttered peevishly. 'Now, Turtledove,' her escort, Lieutenant-Commander O.S.B. 'The Badger' Badgett, said sweetly, 'I like you, however you are.' This attempt at soothing only made Janey more peevish. On Siegel's other side sat Mr Alba. He wore formal black trousers, white jacket, and dark red cummerbund, and looked as distinguished as an ambassador to the Court of St James.

With the swarms of officers crowding, sniffing, around the table, Ensign Siegel was reluctant to leave it. But he had his duties concerned with the celebration, so finally, picking up his portable wire recorder, he asked Melora and Mr Alba to excuse him briefly. Now he passed through the heavy throng soliciting the emotions of various officers on the conclusion of the greatest war history has ever known up to this point.

'Here, ladies and gentlemen' – Siegel spoke resonantly into the microphone as he reached a bevy of officers crowded into a corner red bankette – 'we have Lieutenant-Commander Arnold Gladney, chief of the radio section of the Public Relations Section. Commander, I want to thank you personally for everything you've done to make victory possible. You, that is, handled the transmission arrangements for radio correspondents. Commander, will you tell us succinctly how you feel on the successful conclusion of this most successful war?'

'Ladies and gentlemen ...' Lieutenant-Commander Gladney began as Ensign Siegel stuck the microphone in front of him.

'Thank you, Commander,' Siegel said, jerking the microphone away. 'Sitting alongside here we have Lieutenant-Commander Wayne Hereford, the chief of the photographic section. Commander, how can I describe your contribution to the final triumph? You supervised the legions of Navy photographers who kept the Navy so gloriously photographed, so stupendously undermanned. Commander, would you mind telling us in a word what's in you at this moment?'

'Ladies and gentlemen ...' Lieutenant-Commander Hereford began, 'I ...'

'Thank you, Commander,' Siegel said, yanking the mike back amid outbursts of laughter. As he moved on, suddenly a hand swooped out hawk-like and grabbed the microphone from him.

'Well, it's certainly good to get one of these back in my hands,'

Lieutenant (jg) Pendleton, who had had about fifteen rum sours, said affably. 'It makes me feel, well, so *natural* again. For the benefit of any sponsors who may be listening in, the first string is back! Ross Pendleton is available again! Starting salary, $80,000 ...'

'Thank you, Ross, old man,' Siegel said, wrenching the microphone out of Pendleton's hands. 'I can see Lieutenant Junior Grade Pendleton was "born to the mike", as we say in Radio City. However, there are a couple other officers,' Siegel said, moving on, and pausing to grab a whisky sour from a tray borne by a roving Marine bartender, 'who would like to get a word in ...'

Before continuing he stopped for a check-up. He was surprised as he came up to see Vice-Admiral D. D. Boatwright sitting at the table chatting away with Mr Alba.

'Yes, sir,' he heard the admiral say in respectful, emotional tones to Mr Alba, 'the United States Navy has had no better friend in the Pacific Ocean Area than you. When I think of your contributions to the United States Navy, ranging from your organizational help during the liberation to your generous donation of the very ground on which this lovely officers' club stands ...'

Siegel was astonished. Mr Alba had never mentioned a word to him about these rather intimate relations with the Navy. So Mr Alba and Admiral Boatwright were old buddies!

'It was little enough to do,' Mr Alba said. 'You know how I feel about the United States Navy, D. D. Isn't this an interesting occasion?' he said, to re-channel the subject.

'Indeed it is,' Admiral Boatwright said benignly, watching the junior brass disporting themselves. 'Well, I like to see spirit in a young naval officer ...'

The sound of crashing glass, prompted by an officer's rum-loosened elbow, came from near by.

'I see what you mean,' Mr Alba said. He had seemed a little bored at first, but now his face was beginning to take on a studious cast.

Ensign Siegel backed away. He was pleased at the comradeship between Mr Alba and Admiral Boatwright. Also, even with the war's end and the natural breaking down of rank barriers – the club's usual separation of flag and non-flag rank had been dissolved for the occasion – the presence of a three-star admiral was effectively keeping the junior-officer flies away from Melora. Siegel, moving off, even heard one or two expressions of irritation at this development. 'If that's all this fraternization means,' he heard one jg mutter, 'that an admiral can come over and take over the girls, then I say – Let's put the barriers back up!'

Happily Ensign Siegel resumed his wire recording.

'And now it's time we heard from the reason we're all here in the first place. I see one of the reasons standing right over here. A man,' Siegel said quietly into the mike as he approached from behind, 'at the mere breath of whose name the highest brass trembled and swore. Rip,' Siegel said loudly, 'we're asking the dignitaries present to say a few words.'

Gordon Ripwell, startled, came around to see Ensign Siegel holding the mike. His face lit up.

'Rip, do you mind if I turn the tables on the most aggressive question-asker in the Pacific and ask one or two of this famous correspondent?'

'Well, as you say, Max.'

'Rip,' Siegel said, 'are you satisfied personally with the way the war has been conducted?'

'In parts,' Ripwell said soberly. 'Certainly the enlisted men did a fine job. The enlisted men are ...'

'... the American people,' Siegel cut in.

'As correspondent for the Chicago *Gazette*,' Ripwell said, 'I represent ...'

'... two million readers,' Siegel said.

'And I regard myself ...' Ripwell said.

'... as the watchdog of their interests out here. This war is not any naval property!' Ensign Siegel suddenly boomed into the microphone. 'This war belongs to the American people! Or did until about five hours ago. Rip, now that the war belongs only to the ages, what do you intend the hell doing? I can hardly see a man of your experience back covering City Hall.'

Suddenly a forlorn expression filled the correspondent's face. 'There isn't any more war to cover, is there?' he said in realization of the stark fact.

'I'm sure they'll find a place for you somewhere, Rip,' Siegel said comfortingly.

'Also, there'll probably be some more wars in a couple of years or so,' Ripwell said, brightening. 'Some little wars, anyhow,' he said affectionately.

'For your sake, Rip,' Ensign Siegel said benevolently, moving on, 'we'll all pray for a nice little war.'

He made his way towards the bar. 'Over here,' he intoned into the microphone, 'I see the officer who has set the example for us all in evading work as the canny sub evades the hunter-killer destroyer. Concentrating whatever energies he has on his efforts, deriving from his interest in the diplomatic field and Australian women, to get to Sydney as United States Navy Public Relations liaison officer with His Majesty's Royal Navy. Lieutenant Morey Griffin!'

Ensign Siegel parked the machine on the floor beside Griffin, who said nothing, but sat hunched and staring aggressively dead ahead.

'Three more double whisky sours,' Griffin said to the Marine bartender.

The bartender took three empty glasses away and presently brought three more full ones.

'Listen, Morey,' Siegel said; 'don't you think that's overdoing it a little, even for the end of the war – for so early in the evening, I mean.'

Griffin said nothing, but drank off the first double whisky sour in one gulp.

'Listen, Morey,' Siegel said solicitously; 'maybe you better take it a little easy ...'

Griffin reached for the second glass and tossed it off.

'Morey ...' Siegel said.

Griffin grasped the third double whisky sour and drained it.

'My God!' Siegel said, alarmed. He put down the mike and placed his arm on Griffin's shoulder. 'What the hell's wrong with you, Morey! Just because the war ended without you getting that Sydney job – you ought to be damn glad you didn't ...'

Suddenly Griffin wheeled around, wild-eyed. 'You know what? Nash told me this afternoon that he had some good news for me. You know what it was? He said they'd finally approved that liaison job and were assigning me to Australia. I got it!' Griffin screamed. 'I got it! *Now!*'

Siegel was stupefied. He looked across at the teeming celebrating officers, then down at his stricken friend. He tried to think of words of comfort, but there seemed none to say.

'Give him three more double whisky sours,' he said to the Marine bartender, and picking up his wire recorder, made quietly away.

Siegel inched his way through the crowd of officers and out through the double doors.

'From here,' he said into the microphone, 'I can see two important bodies of water. One of salt – the Sea of the Pacific, far down below me. One of fresh – the swimming-pool alongside the terrace. To-night's three-quarters moon is reflected in the fresh water, and showers a path miles wide across the sea. The terrace is filled to the last flagstone, dancing is in progress, and the sounds you hear are of officers happy that the war is over. The happiest sounds are coming from the junior officers. However, junior and flag rank are frolicking jointly, heedless of rank. Such is the democracy that the end of a war evokes. Indeed, right here in front of me I see one of our important rear-admirals, Rear-Admiral Coffelt, who before coming to Tulura a month or so ago participated importantly in the Second Battle of the Philippine Sea. Admiral.'

Ensign Siegel, seeing a girl he wanted to dance with, moved up and took a seat at Admiral Coffelt's table.

'Admiral,' Siegel said, 'this is the combined networks of CBS, NBC, and MBS. We are reviewing the highlights of the late war for the American people. Since you played such a prominent role in one of the chief highlights, the Second Battle of the Philippine Sea, I wonder if you would mind giving us some of your memories of that decisive naval battle?'

The admiral wavered slightly in his chair. It made Siegel feel warmly affectionate towards him.

'This is all those networks, son?' the admiral gave a rum-sour whisper in Siegel's ear.

'Careful, sir,' Siegel said, clamping his hand over the mike, 'we're on the air. Now go right ahead, sir.'

Ensign Siegel took his hand off the mike and the admiral cleared his throat.

'The Second Battle of the Philippine Sea,' he began into the mike, 'has never been fully explained to the American people, and I am glad of this opportunity to set a few of the so-called facts straight. I have in mind in particular the part played in that great engagement by the particular group of ships which it was my good fortune to command. All credit is due to the ships' companies of these ships, of course, without whom I could not have done what I did. Now at zero seven hundred on …'

Taking the admiral's rather horny hand, Ensign Siegel placed it gently but firmly around the mike and got up and walked on to the dance-floor. He tapped a three-striper on the shoulder.

'Cutting in, Commander,' Siegel said with a broad, sweet smile.

Despite the end of the war, and the breaking down of rank barriers and all, the commander gave Ensign Siegel quite unfriendly look. However, he left the floor, and Ensign Siegel took Ensign Alice Thomas into his arms.

'Well, the war's over!' Siegel said suddenly as they danced the medium-slow fox-trot. He looked down at her. 'You look like it just started.'

'I'm sorry, Max,' she said unhappily.

'The war's over! That ought to mean something for you – I mean it ought to mean something for you and Garrett.'

'Well, maybe so, Max,' she said, and she was not happy. 'But, oh, I don't know. He's out there somewhere' – she vaguely indicated the Pacific down below them – 'and I'm – here. Sometimes I just don't know about anything. Sometimes it all seems like it never happened, just a mirage of some kind, just one of those things that happen during the war and are meant just for the war, and I haven't heard from him in two weeks!' she said suddenly.

It was quite a cloudburst, and Ensign Siegel felt a little overwhelmed.

'Well, it sometimes takes mail a while,' he said, shuffling his feet to the music, 'when a man's out on a ship.'

'You know that isn't true, Max,' she said promptly. 'You know they pick mail up every two or three days, even from destroyers at sea. I checked with the Fleet postal officer,' she said, 'and he told me that himself!'

'Well,' Ensign Siegel said lamely, feeling a little helpless, 'I'm sure if Garrett hasn't written it's for some reason.'

'So am I,' the nurse said promptly, pressing her lips together. She seemed terribly unhappy.

But, happy or unhappy, Ensign Alice Thomas was a pretty girl, and presently Ensign Siegel was cut in on by a lieutenant (jg). He went back to his wire recorder.

'... And so, American people, at zero seven thirty I gave orders to attack.'

Good Lord! Ensign Siegel thought, Admiral Coffelt had only progressed a half-hour in the Second Battle of the Philippine Sea.

'Admiral,' Ensign Siegel said gently, placing his hand on the microphone, 'we want to get a few of the other officers ...'

The admiral jerked the microphone out of Siegel's reach and reared back in his chair so hard he almost toppled over backward.

'... At that point,' he continued, 'I dispatched two of my destroyers off to starboard ...'

'Admiral,' Ensign Siegel said.

'... The purpose of this maneouvre,' the admiral continued, clutching the mike in an iron grip, 'was very shrewd ...'

'Admiral,' Ensign Siegel said, 'if you'll let me have it for just a few minutes, I'll come back with the machine and we'll continue with the Second Battle of the Philippine Sea clear to the end ...'

'... The purpose was to decoy off a Jap task unit which was ...'

Ensign Siegel leaned over until his mouth was very close to the admiral's ear.

'Admiral,' he said, 'I hate to trouble you, but ComFleets has requested me to bring this broadcasting machine, sir, over to him on the double quick!'

Instantly, though with reluctance, Admiral Coffelt released the microphone. Ensign Siegel picked up the wire recorder and disappeared in the noisy crowd. The noise was steadily increasing. Siegel went back inside the club and made his way with the machine to a small platform that had been set up near the bar. Lieutenant-Commander Nash was standing by the platform, as if waiting for something. He had a far-away look in his eyes.

'Commander!' Siegel greeted him warmly. 'Just been getting some of the boys wire-recorded. You'll probably want a copy to preserve in your memory book.'

'Splendid, Max!' the exec said. 'You always think of the right thing to liven up an event. A splendid idea!' The exec leaned over and whispered in Siegel's ear: 'Max ... you want to make the announcement now?'

'I was just getting ready to lead up to it, Commander,' Ensign Siegel said. 'I thought it would be better to wait until everybody was in a happy mood.'

'Very clever, Max.' The exec hesitated. 'Of course, Max,' he whispered, 'if you don't think we ought to do it ...'

'Nonsense, Commander!' Siegel said. 'I think everybody will be extremely interested.'

'I don't want to seem immodest,' the exec said shyly. 'I just thought perhaps a lot of people would like to know.'

'Of course they would, Commander!' Ensign Siegel said. 'And don't you trouble your little mind at all about being immodest. They won't have the faintest notion that it was your idea.'

'Max,' the exec said, 'you always handle these things so well. What I've always liked about you is your complete sense of tact.'

'Well, I learned it from you, Commander,' Ensign Siegel said gratefully. 'I certainly had to learn what tact was, almost as a matter of survival.'

'Max,' the exec said, almost overcome with emotion, 'I'm so proud to have had you in my command.'

'Commander, I tell you,' Siegel whispered, 'I think this would have more effect if you went over there on the other side of the club and I sort of summoned you up here. That way you'll look more reluctant.'

'Roger, Max,' the exec, grateful for this delicate handling, said. 'Whatever you say.'

The exec left the area of the platform and made his way across the packed room. Siegel plugged the wire recorder into a public-address mike that had been set up on the platform. He waited a couple of minutes. Then he stepped up on to the platform.

'Ladies and gentlemen,' he said.

Despite the volume of the p.a. system, Siegel's repetition of this salutation, with mounting force, had no effect. Matters were getting quite raucous in the club. Finally he roared into the microphone:

'Look alive, meatheads!'

There was a relative silence as the officers faced towards the platform.

'I wonder,' Ensign Siegel said loudly, his eyes searching intently around the room, 'if Lieutenant-Commander Clinton T. Nash is anywhere in the club, and if so, if I could persuade him to step up here?'

There was a silence, and then someone on the far side of the club shouted, 'Here! He's over here!'

'Commander Nash!' Siegel called out.

On a motion from Siegel the orchestra went into, first, ruffles and flourishes, then struck up, 'See the Conquering Hero Comes!' As the officers cleared a wide path for him, the executive officer came marching across the room. His swagger stick tucked smartly under his arm, his hairy legs which emerged from his pressed khaki shorts carried him in long, almost goosestep-like strides across the floor on the tides of the martial music, while a spotlight which shone across the floor from above the bar caught up reflections from his marble-bald head. He was borne on his way by the hoarse shouts of the officers calling out, 'Nash!' 'The Commander!', and 'Vive le exec!'

As he neared the platform, Ensign Siegel reached his hand far out to shake the exec's. Siegel gave a yank, and the exec landed solidly on the platform. Ensign Siegel dropped his arm around the exec's shoulder, causing him to cough twice. The officers surged forward against the platform.

'Ladies and gentlemen!' Ensign Siegel boomed out, 'I will dispense with unnecessary introductions here. What introductions are needed for the Architect of Public Relations Victory? For the Clausewitz of the typewriter and mimeograph machine? For the man – officer, that is – who has led us through the white water and mined seas, the torpedo-infested depths?'

'Bravo!' someone shouted.

'In a moment,' Siegel said, 'I am going to make a very special announcement which will come as a complete surprise to the executive officer and to many another here. But first I want to work into it. Commander,' Siegel said, raising his arm and dropping it heavily around the exec's shoulder, causing him to cough three times, 'you must realize that this observance of the end of the war is a pretty joyous occasion for most of us. If it isn't for you, we understand it.'

'Oh, no, Max,' the exec said into the microphone. 'I'm glad to have the war over, too.'

'Now, Commander, you old fox, you, we know you don't mean that for a moment.'

'Really, I'm not a bit put out by it, Max,' the exec said.

'Yes,' Ensign Siegel said in tones of sadness, raising his arm and dropping it heavily across the exec, who coughed four or five times, 'we can but imagine what emotions must be yours at this moment, Commander. What it must be like to have the years of one's leadership cease so abruptly, that is, for the war to be over two years before one expected.'

'Not at all, Max,' the exec said. 'I won't be unhappy at all to get back to Merrill Lynch.'

'However,' Ensign Siegel continued, 'all good things must come to an end. Commander, I wonder if you care to say a few benedictory words of your own?'

The executive officer cleared his throat. He came quite to attention, his hairy legs together.

'Well, Sailors, I feel quite auld lang syne tonight. Tonight,' the exec said, smiling, 'I'm in such a mellow mood I can't think of a thing to criticize any of you about. I shall always remember and treasure how we welded together a task force here that in its own field was as hard-hitting and fast-striking as the Fifth Fleet. Many's the time we were caught in a bight, but we always fought our way out. If the American people knows today that it has a Navy, it is due almost exclusively to what we've done here. And you know what I think? I think this is something we can all be really proud of the rest of our lives all down through each of us! Sailors! I want to tell the last one of you, in that ancient but thrilling Navy phrase which says so terribly much in such little space: "Well done!"'

A raucous cheer went up, many bravos were shouted, and glasses raised to cries of 'Vive le exec'. Ensign Siegel began to intone resonantly into the microphone:

'Now, ladies and gentlemen, we have that enormous surprise for which I have made the exec come up here. I'm sure no one here will contradict me when I say that if there was ever an officer who deserved something, it is the officer standing here by me. There is an award known as the Congressional Medal of Honour, but this award has the narrow limitation that it can be won only for valour in physical battle, so that certainly this officer never even had a chance for that one. There is the Navy Cross, except that that award has a similar restriction. There is the Silver Star – you also have to get shot at for that one. However, there is one award you can get, thank the Lord, without ever getting near the articulation of the artillery, or seeing the foamy wake left by a man-o'-war, turning hard about, guns blazing, to confront the enemy on the high seas. This award is much esteemed, certainly by those who possess it. Comrades-in-arms!' Ensign Siegel raised his arm and slammed it around the exec's shoulders, sending him into a paroxysm of coughing. 'I take enormous pleasure in announcing to him and to you all that our executive officer has been awarded the topmost non-combat award: the Legion of Merit!'

A cacophonous cheering broke out. The orchestra's enlisted-man drummer, helped along by a few sneaked rum sours – the bandsmen were the only enlisted men on Tulura to have drinking whisky under their belts tonight – began pounding on the big bass drum. A spasm of shouts filled the air. It was three or four minutes before Siegel could get order again, about the same length of time it took the exec to recover from his coughing fit. Siegel leaned the mike in front of the exec, who appeared to be choking both from coughing and emotion.

'Sailors!' the exec got out. 'What an emotional moment this is for all of us! Personally, I'm stunned. This is the biggest thing that ever happened to me. I never expected it. I only did my duty – as you all know! However, I accept this high award – but only on the condition that I'm accepting it as being given to all of you. You get the point? Each of you has just been awarded the Legion of Merit! Of course, you won't have the actual award in your possession – I'll have that – but you can consider it just as if you had been awarded it yourself. Any time you see me wearing it, you can say, "That's mine!" Under these conditions, Sailors, I accept my Legion of Merit!'

'Thank you, Commander!' Ensign Siegel said. He spoke loudly into the microphone. 'Now, men!'

Moving forward, the officers appreciatively seized the executive officer. To loud huzzahs of 'Bravo, Marblehead!' they began tossing him into the air. Where the exec's face could be glimpsed as he came back into the officers' arms, it appeared to be beaming at this spontaneous outburst of affection. But then, as he soared higher and higher and his hairy legs kicked out in all directions, a certain apprehension got mixed in with the beaming. 'Now, Sailors ...' The exec's voice was soon trying to rise over the shouts as he came down. But before he could get further, he was heaved ceilingwards again with a loud and choruseed, 'Bravo, Marblehead!'

After one final throw the officers set the exec back on his feet on the platform. He staggered for a moment, then straightened up.

'Well!' he said. 'That was quite a demonstration.'

'Not a bit more than you deserved, sir,' Ensign Siegel said. 'Commander, I know I express the sentiments of every officer in the section when I say: "There was never an executive officer quite like our executive officer." I don't know about the rest of you, but as for Ensign Siegel, I'm going to be pretty proud to tell my grandchildren how old grandpappy owns part of a Legion of Merit, and I just hope the hell they take my word for it and don't ask me to show it to them. Speaking of my grandchildren,' Ensign Siegel said, 'I have another announcement to make. I'll be right back. ...'

Jumping abruptly off the platform, Ensign Siegel ploughed his way through the throng of officers. His big body rammed its way across the floor with an air of such heedlessness, like a destroyer under way at thirty knots, that the officers fell back hurriedly on both sides to leave a swath for him. Then he was at the table and looking down at the girl in the white linen dress. He was breathing heavily. The girl smiled up softly at him.

'Melora,' Ensign Siegel said, and his voice was strangely unsteady. 'Will you step up here? And you, sir?' he said to Mr Alba.

Back over the wide swath Siegel escorted Melora and her father up to the edge of the platform. With them came Admiral Boatwright, trailing slightly behind Mr Alba like a naval convoy. Siegel stepped up on the platform and grasped the microphone.

'My friends,' he said, and his voice was shaking a little, 'most of you have met them already tonight, but I would like formally to present Mr Alba and his daughter Melora Alba – of Tulura.'

There was a slight rustling, brought about by something like small bows which many of the officers performed. Melora and her father smiled back graciously.

'Ladies and gentlemen,' Siegel began, 'I have an announcement to make ...'

His eyes wandered down to Melora, and he stopped.

'Ladies and gentlemen,' he began again, 'there is something I want all of you to know …'

He stopped, and swallowed. He grasped the microphone more tightly and made a fresh assault.

'Ladies and gentlemen, this is something that I want very much that all of you, as my friends, should know …' Siegel faltered. 'Ladies and gentlemen, nothing anywhere near like this has ever happened, you see, to me, and I am very anxious to tell all of you about this great thing …'

He stopped and swallowed a couple of times. The officers were quite amazed, never having seen Ensign Max Siegel at a loss for words.

'Ladies and gentlemen,' he tried again. 'I have this announcement to make about something that means just about everything in the world, to understate the facts of the case, to me …'

Ensign Siegel stopped. He stood there, bewildered.

Suddenly, from off to his port side, a loud, commanding clearing of the throat of the kind possible only to the throats of flag rank split the silence.

'Here, son,' a gruff voice said in tones of command, 'give me that microphone.'

Taking two smart paces forward and one up on to the platform, Vice-Admiral D. D. Boatwright decisively seized the microphone out of Ensign Siegel's hand.

'Officers of the Navy!' Admiral Boatwright's voice rose in firm, unwavering address. 'What the ensign is trying to say is this. Mr Alba here – one of the leading citizens of this or any other Pacific island – has consented to give to the ensign the hand in marriage of his beautiful and charming daughter, Miss Melora.'

There was one vast moment of silence – a silence of many emotions on the part of the officers, among them astonishment, incredulity, and, perhaps chief of all, certainly on the part of the male officers looking at the black-haired, palomino-skinned prize, enormous envy. There was one moment of silence in which Admiral Boatwright started to plunge with a matter of historical interest.

'This engagement,' the admiral began strongly, 'of a daughter of a prominent Tuluran citizen to an ensign of the United States Navy is a fitting climax to the long and warm-sided history of Tuluran–U.S. relations …'

The admiral, who was quite prepared to go on, got no further. Suddenly the officers' club was pierced by a mighty shout – akin only to the rebel yell – which rose in one chorus from the officers, and by the sound of the orchestra, apparently to get something generally Pacific, striking up 'Sweet Leilani'.

For several minutes a complete pandemonium seized the club. The rebel yells rose ever more deafeningly against the soft backdrop of 'Sweet Leilani'. Nothing, not even the end of the war, could have given such a charge to the evening as the announcement. In the storm-like din Melora and Ensign Siegel stood quietly, Melora smiling softly, Siegel smiling foolishly. A soft smile also played across Mr Alba's face, reflecting considerable interest in the strange and primitive tribal customs of these people.

Holding on to the microphone, Admiral Boatwright tried several times to get quiet. Finally he really had to pull rank to get it.

'Atten-shun!' he bellowed through the microphone in a voice that would have rattled a quarterdeck. The word shut off the orchestra and momentarily sobered and silenced the officers. Admiral Boatwright, pleased, smiled.

'There is another detail to add. Ensign Siegel, it seems, had a certain pre-naval experience in the investment business in New York City. My friend Mr Alba here is taking young Siegel into one of his enterprises, the First National Bank of Tulura, which also engages in the investment business. Ensign – Mr – and Mrs Siegel look forward to a happy life on Tulura, with certain interruptions, the future Mrs Siegel tells me, to visit the United States occasionally for such things as the autumnal season of plays in New York.'

Now a fresh outburst of shouts broke through the club. Then suddenly the officers surged forward. Queuing up, they began going happily through the receiving line, which was quickly formed, consisting of the betrothed, the father of the bride, and Admiral Boatwright, who, in naval loyalty, seemed to have assumed unto himself the position of family of the groom-ensign. At about midpoint Lieutenant-Commander Nash arrived at the line, beaming. With both hands he reached out and grabbed Siegel's and Mr Alba's.

'Well! Isn't it wonderful how we're all investment people together? And Max here never even told me he was in the game – the bad boy, heh, heh.' Before moving on, the exec leaned over and whispered to Mr Alba, 'I'd like to talk to you later on behalf of Merrill Lynch, Pierce, Fenner, and Beane.'

When the last officer had passed through the line the orchestra struck up some dance-music.

'Melora?' Ensign Siegel turned to his fiancée.

Taking her into his arms, he moved on to the dance-floor. The floor was soon crowded, but in respect for the newly engaged the other officers made sure to leave Max and Melora room, though not too much room. In any case Ensign Siegel was not aware that anyone else was even there. His mind, as he and Melora danced, went back over the last several days. He thought of that trip shortly after the break of dawn when he had driven the Badger's jeep back across the island, parked it, and walked up the long lane to the Albas' house rising up there in the forest. He had stood a moment by the terrace watching the morning light pour across the Pacific far below and across that beach where he and Melora had gone for a walk and she had said, no, she could never live in New York, never leave this island that was her island. Well, he thought, if she couldn't leave it, he couldn't leave it. He had started to go up and knock. Then he was standing a moment longer in the great silence, like no silence he had ever known, that held this place. He looked down at the sea, blue and glistening. Then his eyes travelled across the green forest. Then up the beach that separated the two. How white that beach was and how endless! He remembered what she had said down there, 'It's my island.' Now all at once he knew what she meant. In a joy that almost made him cry out, it came over him. He wanted also to stay here. He, too, wanted this island. He, too, wanted this kind of life. Wanted it for itself.

He walked up to the door and knocked. His knock sounded terribly loud against the silence of the early morning, but still he had to knock again before he heard someone coming. Then the door opened and Mr Alba was standing there in a handsome dressing-gown.

'Sir,' Ensign Siegel said, 'I want to marry your daughter.'

Mr Alba must have felt something quite considerable. He would have felt it, doubtless, if Siegel had broached the matter after a chess game. He must have felt it very considerably now, being awakened from bed at such an ungodly hour to see a United States Navy ensign standing at the door making such a suggestion. But whatever Mr Alba felt he kept to himself, as he seemed so inscrutably to keep almost everything to himself. His expression did not change, and for several moments he said nothing, but stood there in his dressing-gown looking at Siegel. Ensign Siegel would never forget what Mr Alba said then.

'Have you had coffee yet?'

'No, sir,' Ensign Siegel said.

'I thought not. Well, you'd better come in and have some coffee.'

They must have talked for half an hour. Ensign Siegel never remembered what they talked about except that it was not on what had brought him here.

'I hope,' Mr Alba had said when the coffee was before them, 'that I have reached a sufficiently civilized stage in life to where I do not discuss before coffee the question of my daughter's marriage. Shall we just have our coffee, Max?'

'Yes, sir,' Ensign Siegel said. 'That will be fine.'

He liked to think now that Mr Alba had made up his mind about him, made it up some time before. One thing he felt sure of was that Mr Alba was a man who did make up his mind, one way or the other, about anything. He didn't mention the subject again until, from one of the back rooms, Melora came in. Before she could add any vocal comment to the wonderment in her face at Siegel's being here at this hour, Mr Alba explained it himself with entire casualness.

'My dear,' he said. 'This young man wants to marry you.'

She just stood there for a moment.

'Well, my dear,' Mr Alba said.

'Oh, Papa!' she said. 'Oh, Max!'

It was not until he felt her cheek against his that Ensign Siegel knew she was crying.

'I will not,' Mr Alba said, 'have so much emotion in my house before breakfast. Let's have breakfast.'

'It's fun, isn't it, Max?' Melora was saying.

He looked down at her, holding her, his feet moving very little in the dancing. 'Oh, yes,' he said, 'it is. Let's go swimming tomorrow.'

'Let's do,' she said, smiling.

'I'll pick you up at noon,' he said.

'Fine,' she said. 'We'll go on our beach.'

'Yes, up by the rock,' he said, very happy.

He would be doing lots of swimming, he thought. Also ... Ensign Siegel smiled. He was thinking of how his fellow-officers probably had visions of him sacking out for the rest of his life on the beaches of Tulura, and how this picture was not entirely accurate. He thought of that quite serious talk Mr Alba had had with him a couple of days after that visit at dawn. It was in this talk that Mr Alba had offered him the bank job. Mr Alba had made it clear that it was a working job. Siegel smiled again, thinking how Mr Alba, without at all saying it that way, had got the point over that he didn't for a moment expect to have a beach-combing son-in-law.

The evening marched on. Mr Alba sat at the table where he and his daughter and Ensign Siegel and his self-appointed foster-father Admiral Boatwright, who had now virtually taken over command of the engagement, had set up a sort of court, judging by the pilgrimages made over to it. From time to time Mr Alba got up and wandered, with an air of curiosity, around the club or out on the terrace. When Siegel had asked Melora and Mr Alba to come to the club this evening, he had explained very carefully to Mr Alba that they would not have to stay long. Now, several times throughout the evening, thinking that he might have had enough of it, he had mentioned to Mr Alba that they could be getting along. At first Mr Alba had courteously said, presently. Now, however, as the officers' overt observances of the war's end increased with the hours and the inroads into the over-supply, he seemed definitely reluctant to leave and finally, when Siegel suggested again that they really could be getting along, he had said quite clearly, 'What's the hurry, Max?' By now Mr Alba was sitting back in his chair as if he fully intended to make a night of it. His face had taken on the rapt expression of an anthropologist watching the rites of some esoteric tribe.

The rites which Mr Alba witnessed were many. At various times among other things: (1) The Badger hoisted Janey, the Boston-Irish girl, on to the bar, where to the orchestra's accompaniment she gave out a loud rendition of 'Rule Britannia!' swishing her shovel hips in time to the stirring strains and at the word 'Britons', in the supernal line 'Britons never, never shall be slaves', reaching down to yank her paramour's beard. (2) Ensign Christopher Tyson III, who had perhaps the biggest serve of any tennis-player on Tulura, produced his tennis-racquet and was going around, amid great outbursts of laughter from a small corps of fellow-ensigns trailing him, suddenly slapping it with resounding playfulness against the startled rears of all dancing officers over the rank of ensign with a ringing 'Mind your rudder!' (3) The correspondent Jerry Wakeley was sitting on one end of the bar, his legs crossed under him like a yogi, chewing on a dead cigar and dipping a teacup at frequent intervals into a large dishpan which rested beside him. The club's over-supply was really staggering, and to do his part Wakeley had poured twenty-four bottles of Paul Jones into the dishpan and was working on the over-supply directly. His sipping from the teacup, which he held with considerable delicacy, his little finger sticking out, was interrupted only by recitations of Navy poetry, on which it developed Wakeley was quite an authority. 'Spanish ships of war at sea! We have sighted fifty-three …!' his voice droned from the bar's end. Many of the observances, as is customary on these occasions, centred around the swimming-pool. There (4) the plump Lieutenant-Commanders Gladney and Hereford were goaded into having a swimming race, Gladney being dubbed the *Yorktown* and Hereford the *Enterprise*. The race ended abruptly when it turned out the *Enterprise* couldn't swim and had to be pulled out. (5) Admiral Coffelt, who had retrieved the wire recorder and was sitting by the pool continuing his account of the Second Battle of the Philippine Sea, reached the battle's climax, 'And so, American people, I sunk the …' when at this point, in his excitement, he tumbled with a loud plop into the pool, from which he was eagerly fished out and solicitously dried off by three ensigns. (6) Lieutenant Griffin, taunted by Lieutenant (jg) Pendleton about his untimely assignment to Sydney – Pendleton kept going up to Griffin and singing in his ear, 'A rapid trip to Sydney is a very urgent need' – finally in fury hauled Pendleton up bodily and threw him with a great splash into the pool. This act seemed somehow completely to lift Griffin's depression and he returned to the bar greatly cheered.

Mr Alba was much fascinated. After a while, when there were lapses of as much as fifteen minutes without a rite of some kind, he became downright impatient.

'When are we going to have some more?' he kept asking his future son-in-law.

Presently, Ensign Siegel left Melora dancing with Ensign Tyson and Mr Alba talking with Lieutenant-Commander Nash and looking a little restless – as Siegel walked away Nash was saying to Mr Alba, 'Can you honestly say that you've had an expert go over your invest-ment portfolio recently?' – and wandered out on the terrace himself for a breath of air. Looking over at the swimming-pool, he became aware that it was occupied by a water-buffalo. This didn't surprise him in the least and he idly watched the huge beast, whose face in his natural habitat wore an expression of great contentment, cruising around the pool. But then Ensign Siegel's eyes came up from the pool and came to rest on the diving-board.

'Mr Seguro!'

The old Tuluran looked up.

'En-sine!' he cried out.

Siegel made his way happily over to the diving-board and out on it.

'Mr Seguro!' Siegel reached down his hand to pump vigorously that of his friend. 'Glad to see you!'

Mr Seguro pointed affectionately to the animal in the pool below. 'I'm just making sure he doesn't get in any trouble. He's got to be out ploughing the fields tomorrow. I rented him for the evening for big sum of money – five dollars – to five en-sines.'

'Listen,' Siegel said, 'you wait here and I'll be right back.'

Siegel made his way back up the diving-board. He returned presently and placed a tray of whisky sours on the diving-board between himself and Mr Seguro and sat down.

'This is one of our native beverages, Mr Seguro. Try it.'

Mr Seguro picked up one of the whisky sours and gulped it off. Immediately his face showed a displeased look. But courteously he drained another one. He set the glass disgustedly down.

'Tastes like lemonade,' he said. 'Is this what the children drink in Yew-nited States?'

'Well, we do have a more virile drink, called the martini,' Siegel apologized. 'The martini is really our national drink and is nice and strong,' he said patriotically. 'Unfortunately, gin – the chief in-gredient of the martini – is the one beverage which we do not have in supply at the officers' club. We have lots of everything else,' he added.

'Pretty strange officers' club not to have national drink,' Mr Seguro said disapprovingly. 'Here! Have a real drink.'

Mr Seguro reached over to the side of him away from Ensign Siegel and produced a jug. At the end of the diving-board Ensign Siegel and Mr Seguro sat taking turns from the palm toddy jug and watching the huge water-buffalo swimming around below.

'He looks pretty happy there,' Siegel observed.

'He's always happiest in the water. Why do you think they call him *water*-buffalo?' Mr Seguro said aggressively.

'Yes, I guess that's why,' Ensign Siegel said, sighing.

'You don't know much about water-buffaloes, do you?' Mr Seguro said, contemptuous of this gap in Siegel's education.

'No, I never saw one before I came to Tulura,' Siegel said.

Mr Seguro was baffled. 'What in the world do they use in Yewnited States to do all the work? The water-buffalo is a very important animal and we take good care of them and they know it. I wouldn't have thought of letting those five en-sines take my water-buffalo off without me,' Mr Seguro said, bristling. 'No, sir! You think for one second I let my water-buffalo go anywhere without ...'

Suddenly Mr Seguro leaped to his feet. The diving-board bounced, almost chucking Siegel into the water. He grabbed on to the board. Mr Seguro stood entirely surefooted on the bouncing board.

'Mr Alba!' Mr Seguro cried out in amazement.

Stepping lithely over the ensign Mr Seguro hurriedly made his way down the board. Siegel, finally getting to his feet, followed him up to Mr Alba, who stood looking down at the beast in the pool. He had the look of a man who by now would be fazed by none of the strange rites of these people.

'Well, Mr Seguro' – he turned to his fellow-Tuluran – 'I'm glad to see you're joining in the celebration of the end of the war – and that so is your water-buffalo.'

'Yes, sir.' Mr Seguro shuffled his feet. Finally he blurted it out:

'Mr Alba, what are you doing here? I didn't know you would come to a place like this,' he said, his respect for Mr Alba blended with reproach.

Mr Alba smiled softly. 'Well, I thought it would be all right this one time, Mr Seguro. You see, this young man here is marrying Melora.'

Mr Seguro's mouth dropped open. 'Him?' he said incredulously, and pointed a blunt finger at Siegel, which made the ensign feel quite self-conscious.

'Yes, Mr Seguro,' Mr Alba said, smiling softly. 'Him.'

Mr Seguro shook his head. 'Well, if Melora's going to marry a foreigner,' he said finally, 'I guess the en-sine is pretty good.'

Ensign Siegel immediately felt relieved.

'Well,' said Mr Alba, 'I didn't realize you two were such old friends.'

Mr Seguro switched suddenly to a full-blown pride. 'Why, it's because of me the en-sine is marrying Melora!'

For the first time since Siegel had known him, Mr Alba looked slightly startled.

'How is that, Mr Seguro?'

'Why,' Mr Seguro burst out, 'I introduced him to Melora! If it hadn't been for me, they never even would have known each other. No, sir! This whole marriage is all my doing!'

Ensign Siegel looked in astonishment at Mr Seguro. He remembered that time which seemed so long ago now when Mr Seguro had quite clearly refused to introduce him to Melora for fear of Mr Alba's anger. Siegel reflected that two months ago Mr Alba would certainly have reacted vividly to this intelligence of Mr Seguro's confessed role. He looked definitely surprised now.

'Well that's very interesting, Mr Seguro,' he said, a little coolly. 'I never quite realized before your romance-promoting side.'

'Oh, that's all right, Mr Alba,' Mr Seguro said frankly.

Out of the corner of his eye Mr Seguro had all the time been watching his water-buffalo.

'Excuse me now,' he said suddenly. 'He'll get sick! No! No! No!' he began shouting, which was one American word Mr Seguro knew, and hurried over to shoo away some U.S. naval officers who were feeding potato-chips to his water-buffalo.

After this drink Ensign Siegel figured he would do his duty by asking Mr Alba once more if he didn't really want to go. If Mr Alba said no this time – and Siegel was beginning to have the feeling he couldn't drag Mr Alba away – Siegel would himself be happy to stay all night.

The happy-in-love man wants to see everyone else happy; especially he doesn't want to see another unhappy-in-love. Sitting by Melora, Ensign Siegel caught sight of Ensign Alice Thomas dancing with a captain over by the terrace, and saw the unhappiness in her. To escape the sight of it, feeling a little guilty as he did it, he turned his eyes away.

In doing this his eyes described an arc of almost exactly 180°. They passed from Alice and the captain, across the teeming, jostling crowds of officers, by the packed bar, and finally reached the main club entrance at the opposite side of the room. At this point Ensign Siegel's idly roaming gaze came to a full halt, for the door of the club opened. An enlisted man stood there.

He was bronzed and hard-muscled and remarkably fit-looking, especially by comparison with the somewhat flabby-fleshed, bilious-looking officers who filled the club. He stood there on the club's threshold, erect and confident, his eyes quietly searching the room.

'Christ Almighty!' Ensign Siegel said.

He jammed his drink down and sprang up.

'Excuse me, honey,' he said to his startled fiancée.

Ensign Siegel flailed his way across the room and up to the enlisted man. For about five minutes he stood talking excitedly with him. Then, turning sharply, he started elbowing his way violently towards the terrace. He was smiling broadly. Then he saw her, just inside the terrace door, and came up to where she was dancing with the captain.

'Alice,' he interrupted.

Siegel leaned down and whispered something in the nurse's ear. She gave a muffled cry. Her head snapped around towards the door. Then she was tearing herself out of the four-striper's arms.

'Here!' Siegel stopped her. 'Take these.'

Siegel fished in his pocket, got out his jeep keys, and handed them to Ensign Thomas. She took them and started away.

'Here, here!' the captain called after her in a highly annoyed voice. 'Where are you going?'

Ensign Thomas paused a moment. Then a slow smile spread across her pretty face.

'To Yeoman Garrett, sir,' she said. And she was gone, her pretty hips flouncing her quite saucily across the officers' club.

Ensign Siegel had decided to make a night of it – or rather, Mr Alba had decided. This decision was fine with Ensign Siegel, who was dancing again with Melora. Now and then he thought about Garrett and Alice. He thought of Garrett standing there in the doorway of the club, like a Viking come to raid the very stronghold of rank and triumphantly carry off his woman. His ship, Garrett had explained, had just put in, as many ships were already beginning to do. Dancing Melora around, Siegel grinned a little foolishly. By now, he thought, and gave a deep and beneficent sigh, Garrett and Alice were probably on one of their beaches.

'All right, Buster. I'll have this dance.'

It was Lieutenant Griffin cutting in.

'You and Max will have to come visit me in Australia,' Siegel heard Griffin saying as they danced off. 'I expect to be there for the next several years. ...'

Siegel started towards the bar. The club was still crowded and noisy, though some of the higher ranks had cleared out, leaving somewhat more room for manoeuvre. Siegel walked slowly along the line of bankette tables, some of which were now empty. Nearing one, he saw Lieutenant-Commander Nash sitting all alone. He looked very glum and unhappy. Then Siegel noticed that the exec was not alone. Sitting in the middle of the table, like a centrepiece, was his sextant. The exec did not see Siegel, for he was staring at the instrument with an expression of final defeat.

The two officers stood on the ridge. Behind them, fifty yards away, rose the muted sound of music and occasionally a determined merry-making shout. Far below them stretched the vast Pacific, its edges touched with the first thin approach of dawn. In the great sky above them the brightest stars still shone.

'I can't say how much I appreciate your offering to do this,' Lieutenant-Commander Nash said.

'Not at all,' Ensign Siegel said. 'May I have it, please?'

Submissively the exec handed the instrument over.

'You see that cross-shaped constellation of four stars up there, Commander?' Siegel said, pointing.

'Yes, Max,' the exec said meekly.

'Well, that's the Southern Cross. Now, you see that brightest star in it?'

'Yes, Max,' the exec said humbly.

'Well, that's Alpha Crucis,' Ensign Siegel said. 'Now, you see the sea horizon out there?'

'Yes, Max.'

'Well, the object is to bring the star down to the sea horizon in the instrument. Now observe ...'

As Lieutenant-Commander Nash watched raptly, Ensign Siegel ceered through the sextant's telescope, moved the index arm, then plamped it and after a moment made a final adjustment with the tangent screw.

'Now look right through here,' Ensign Siegel said.

Lieutenant-Commander Nash took the sextant and for some time squinted through it. Finally he lowered the sextant. He stood a moment in complete awe. Then slowly his chest swelled in an air of utter achievement.

'So that's how it's done,' he said. Abruptly the exec gave a superior little laugh. 'Really it's very simple, isn't it, Siegel? – unlike Public Relations. Why, any meathead could be a sea-going officer.'